Cormyr in Peril

As the phantom neared the dais, Filfaeril saw that the rags he carried were black weathercloaks with bronze throatclasps. The war wizards had found her after all. The queen's fingertips began to ache, and she realized she was digging her nails into the arms of her throne.

The phantom dumped the clothes in a heap and ascended the dais. "There is no need to call for someone else." As he drew closer, the stench of blood and battle offal grew overwhelming. "I am never far from you. Ever."

The Cormyr Saga

Cormyr: A Novel

Ed Greenwood & Jeff Grubb

Beyond the High Road

Troy Denning

Death of the Dragon

Troy Denning & Ed Greenwood

BEYOND THE HIGH ROAD

Troy Denning

BEYOND THE HIGH ROAD

©1999 TSR, Inc.
©2004 Wizards of the Coast, Inc.

Distributed in the United States by Holtzbrinck Publishing. Distributed in Canada by Fenn Ltd.

Distributed to the hobby, toy, and comic trade in the United States and Canada by regional distributors.

Distributed worldwide by Wizards of the Coast, Inc. and regional distributors.

Printed in the U.S.A.

Cover art by Matt Stawicki
Map by Todd Alan Gamble
First Printing: December 1999
Library of Congress Catalog Card Number: 98-88707

9 8 7 6 5 4 3

US ISBN: 0-7869-1436-X
620-21436-001-EN

U.S., CANADA,	EUROPEAN HEADQUARTERS
ASIA, PACIFIC, & LATIN AMERICA	Wizards of the Coast, Belgium
Wizards of the Coast, Inc.	T Hofveld 6d
P.O. Box 707	1702 Groot-Bijgaarden
Renton, WA 98057-0707	Belgium
+1-800-324-6496	+322 467 3360

Visit our web site at **www.wizards.com**

For Mark Acres, an old friend and a true one.

Acknowledgements

I would like to thank my editor, Phil Athans, for his support and insight; Mary Kirchoff for making this happen; Ed Greenwood, Jeff Grubb, and Kate Novak for letting me play with their toys; Steven Schend and Julia Martin for their invaluable input; the rest of the FORGOTTEN REALMS group for their advice and reviews; and, most especially, Andria Hayday—just because.

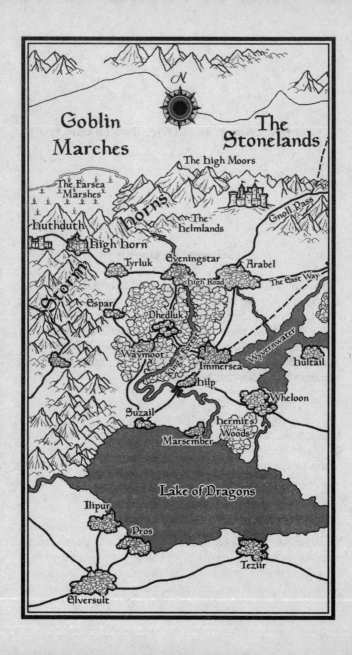

Prologue

ne man could not kill so many. It was not possible. The murderer's trail led down to a gnarled fir tree, where an entire company of Purple Dragons lay strewn across the landscape as still as stones. There were more than twenty of them, sprawled alongside their dead horses in every manner of impossible contortion. Arms and legs hooked away at unexpected angles, torsos lay doubled back against the spine, heads rested on shoulders staring in the wrong direction. Many had died with their shields still hanging from their saddles. A few had fallen even before they could draw their weapons.

Emperel Ruousk unsheathed his sword and eased his horse down the hill, keeping one eye on the surrounding terrain as he read his quarry's trail. There remained just one set of tracks, each print spaced nearly two yards apart. After a hundred miles, the murderer was still running—an incredible feat for any man, let alone one who had been roaring drunk when he fled.

The trail of the Purple Dragons paralleled the killer's at the regulation distance of one lance-length. The hoof prints ran in strict double file, with no stray marks to suggest the presence of outriders or point scouts. The commander had taken no precautions against ambush, no doubt thinking it a simple matter to capture a drunken killer. Emperel would not make the same mistake.

As he neared the site of the massacre, a murder of crows rose from among the bodies and took wing, scolding him raucously. He watched them go, then stopped to make certain the killer was not lying in ambush among the corpses. The area reeked of rotting flesh. Clouds of black flies hovered over the dead bodies, filling the air with an insane drone. The soldiers' breastplates were cratered and torn and streaked with sun-dried gore. Their basinets were either staved-in or split open. Some helmets were missing, along with the heads inside. Many shields had been smeared with the vilest sort of offal, completely obscuring the royal crest of the purple dragon, and several men had died with their own eyeballs in their mouths. One had been strangled with his own entrails.

Emperel began to feel nauseated. He had seen dozens of slaughters in the Stonelands, but never anything so sick and angry. He rode over to a headless corpse and dismounted, then kneeled to examine the stump of the neck. The wound was ragged and irregular and full of gristle strings, just like the stump of the tavern keeper's neck in Halfhap. According to witnesses, the murderer had simply grabbed the poor fellow beneath the jaw and torn off his head.

Emperel stood and circled through the dead bodies, taking care to keep his horse between himself and the gnarled fir at the heart of the massacre. With a twisted trunk large enough to hide ten murderers, the tree was a particularly huge and warped specimen of an otherwise regal species. Its bark was scaly and black, stained with runnels of crimson sap. Its needles were a sickly shade of yellow. The tangled boughs spiraled up to a cork-screwed crown nearly two hundred feet in the air, then withered off into a clawlike clump of barren sticks.

On the far side of the tree, Emperel discovered a large burrow leading down beneath the trunk. The soil heaped around the opening was lumpy and dark, with lengths of broken root jutting out at haphazard angles. A string of ancient glyphs spiraled up the trunk above the tunnel opening, the letters as sinuous as serpents. He did not recognize the language, but the shape of the characters struck him as both elegant and vaguely menacing.

Emperel studied the burrow for several minutes, then approached and tethered his horse to the tree. The hole itself was oval in shape and barely broad enough for a man to enter on his belly. There were several boot prints in the dirt outside, but the walls and floor of the tunnel had been dragged smooth by a passing body. Emperel lay down beside the entrance and peered into the darkness. The interior was as black as night. He could hear a muffled sound that might have been a man's snoring, and the musty air carried an undertone of rancid sweat.

Emperel scanned the massacre once again. Seeing nothing but flies and corpses, he withdrew a black weathercloak from his saddlebags and slipped it over his armor, closing the throat clasp to ready the cape's protective enchantments. As a confidential agent of King Azoun IV, he had access to all of the standard magic in the Royal Armory, and today he was glad for it. He clamped a pair of steel bracers on his wrists, slipped an amethyst ring onto his finger, traded his steel sword for a magic dagger, then dropped to his belly in front of the dank hole. The snoring became an erratic rumble, and the smell of sour sweat grew rife.

Emperel inhaled one last breath of fresh air, then crawled into the darkness, moving slowly and silently. The hole was musty, cramped, and lined with broken root stubs as thick as his wrist. Though there was little room to fight—or retreat—Emperel gave no thought to trying to outwait his quarry. Before beheading the tavern keeper, the murderer had been boasting about how he would ruin King Azoun, and such traitors received no respite from Emperel Ruousk. They received only justice, as quick and sure as an Agent of the Realm possessed of all the magic and might implied by that title could deal it out.

A few feet into the tunnel, the darkness grew so thick Emperel could no longer see the dagger in front of his nose. He paused and whispered, "King's sight."

The amethyst on his ring twinkled faintly, then Emperel began to perceive the passage walls in hues of blue and crimson. The warmth of his body made his flesh glow red, while the dagger in his hand shone silver with magic. A dozen feet ahead, the tunnel opened into a small, oblong chamber surrounded by dangling amber strands—the tips of shallow roots. Strangely, there was no sign of a taproot, an absence that did much to explain the fir's twisted form.

As Emperel neared the entrance to the little chamber, he saw the murderer lying on his back, glowing crimson against the violet pallor of a stone floor. If not for the crust of gore covering him from head to foot, Emperel would have sworn it was the wrong man. The man's eyes were closed in blissful sleep, his lips bowed in an angelic smile and his arms folded peacefully across his chest. He looked too emaciated to have slaughtered a whole company of dragoneers. His arms were as slender as spears, his shoulders gaunt and knobby, his cheeks hollow, his eyes sunken.

Suddenly, Emperel understood everything—where the man had found the strength to run so far, how he had slain an entire company of dragoneers, why he had defiled their bodies so wickedly. Sweat began to pour down Emperel's brow, and he considered returning to Halfhap for help—but what good would that do? The vampire had already shown that he could destroy superior numbers, and Emperel had the advantage now.

He continued forward to the end of the tunnel, the smell of his own perspiration overpowering the fetor of the musty lair. Though his stomach was queasy with fear, he reminded himself that safety was just a gesture away. All he need do was slip a hand into his weathercloak's escape pocket, and he would be standing beside his horse, outside in the brilliant sunlight where no vampire could follow. He crawled silently into the chamber and pulled his legs in after him.

As Emperel stood, something soft and wispy crackled in his ears. His heart skipped a beat, and he found himself biting his tongue, not quite sure whether he had let out a cry. He glanced down and found the murderer as motionless as before, hands folded across his haggard chest, mouth upturned in that angelic smile. Trying not to think of what dreams could make a vampire happy, Emperel raised a hand and felt a curtain of gossamer filament clinging to his face. It was stiff and sticky, like the web of a black widow spider.

Emperel experienced the sudden sensation of hundreds of little legs crawling down his tunic. Hoping the feeling was all in his mind, he stooped to get his head out of the web, then removed a gauntlet from his belt and slipped the steel glove onto his right hand. When presented palm outward, the glove became the holy symbol of his god, Torm the True, and it would keep any vampire at bay. Next, he drew his hand axe from its belt loop and, using the enchanted dagger, began to whittle the wooden butt into a sharp stake.

Though it seemed to Emperel that the sound of his breathing filled the chamber with a bellowslike rasp, the vampire continued to sleep. The silver-glowing dagger peeled the axe's seasoned handle away in shavings as thick as coins, and it was not long before Emperel had sharpened it to a point. He sheathed his dagger again, then kneeled beside the vampire and raised the stake. His arm was trembling.

"Torm, guide my hand," he whispered.

A bead of sweat dropped from his brow and landed on the vampire's shoulder. The monster's eyelids snapped open, its angry eyes shining white in Emperel's enchanted vision.

Emperel brought the stake down, ramming it deep into the vampire's ribcage. Blood, icy cold and as black as ink, seeped up around the shaft. An ear-piercing shriek filled the chamber, then something caught Emperel in the breastplate and sent him tumbling across the stone floor.

He passed through a curtain of gossamer filament and crashed into a dirt wall, his head spinning and chest aching. When he looked down, his mouth went dry. There was a fist-shaped depression in the center of his breastplate, and he had not even seen the murderer's hand move.

Emperel spun to his knees—he was too dizzy to stand—and struggled to gulp some air into his lungs. A few paces away, the vampire lay on its side, writhing in pain and slowly pulling the stake from its chest. Emperel's jaw fell. He had slain more than a dozen vampires, and not one had done such a thing. Had he missed the heart?

The vampire's white eyes swung toward the wall. Emperel raised a finger, pointed at its gaunt hands, and shouted, "King's bolts!"

Emperel's bracers grew as hot as embers and sent four golden bolts streaking across the crypt. The magic struck the vampire's hands with a brilliant golden flash, then sank into its flesh and spread up its arms in a pale saffron glow.

The vampire jerked the stake from its heart, then struggled to its feet and turned toward Emperel. Gouts of dark blood pumped from the hole in its chest, but it did not seem to care. It merely hefted the axe and stumbled forward.

Emperel jumped to his feet and stepped to meet the monster, drawing his magic dagger and boldly thrusting the palm of his steel gauntlet into its face.

"Back," he commanded, "in the name of Torm!"

The vampire slapped the offending arm down so forcefully that the steel gauntlet flew from Emperel's hand. "Do I *look* undead to you?"

Emperel's mouth went dry, and he brought his magic dagger up, driving the silver-shining blade into the thing's stomach and up toward the heart. The vampire—or whatever it was—closed its eyes and nearly collapsed, then reached down and clamped Emperel's hand.

"How . . . treacherous," it hissed.

Emperel tried to twist the blade, but found the thing's grasp too powerful to fight. Struggling against a rising tide of panic, he pulled away, then slammed an elbow into the side of its head.

The blow did not even rock the monster.

"By the Loyal Fury!" Emperel gasped. "What manner of devil are you?"

"The worst kind . . . an angry one."

The killer slammed Emperel into the wall, unleashing a cascade of pebbles and loose dirt, then pulled the dagger free. The silvery glow had all but faded from the enchanted blade, and as Emperel watched, the weapon grew cold and utterly black. The murderer tossed it aside and staggered forward, dark blood now pouring from two wounds.

Unable to believe what he was seeing, Emperel raised his ring finger and said, "King's light!"

The amethyst setting burst into light, filling the chamber with a blue-white glow. Caught by surprise, the murderer closed its eyes and turned away, momentarily blinded. Emperel, who had known what to expect, leaped forward, drawing his sword and slamming a foot into the back of his foe's knee. The murderer hit the floor rolling, tangling legs with Emperel and sweeping him off his feet.

Emperel landed hard, his head slamming against the stone floor. His vision narrowed and his ears began to ring, then his foe was on him, tearing at his throat and denting his helmet. He raised his arm to ward off the blows, and the murderer caught hold of his hand. His ring finger gave a sickening crack, then a terrible pain shot up his arm. Emperel cried out and brought his sword hand up, slamming the pommel into his attacker's head.

The killer went sprawling, ripping the weathercloak off Emperel's shoulders and pulling the magic ring off his finger—no, not *off*.

In the murderer's hand was something thin and bloody, with the white nub of a knucklebone protruding from the red stump. Emperel's ring was still attached, illuminating the killer's head in brilliant blue-white. Its face was mantislike and skeletal, with ovoid eyes as red as embers and an impossibly slender chin. Even in the light, the creature's complexion remained shadowy and dark—but not so dark Emperel failed to recognize something familiar in its arrow-shaped nose and upturned lip. He brought his sword around, placing the tip between himself and the man-thing.

"Do I . . . I know you!"

8

The murderer's eyes narrowed to red slits and it hissed, "Not for long."

Emperel heaved his aching body to its feet and advanced a single step, bringing his sword to a high guard. The killer smirked and retreated the same distance, closing one fist around the stolen ring. A sigh of satisfaction slipped from its lips, and the amethyst's light began to flow into its hand, filling the tiny chamber with eerie fingers of light.

Emperel felt a chill between his shoulder blades. The murderer was absorbing the ring's magic—just as it had absorbed the magic bolts from his bracers and drained the magic from his dagger. The chamber began to dim rapidly. Realizing he would soon be trapped in total darkness without his weathercloak or any other means of escape, Emperel glanced at the exit passage. The murderer stepped over to block the tunnel mouth.

Perfect. Emperel sprang forward to attack, allowing himself a confident smile as the last light faded from the ring. His sword had no magic at all, and when the blade hit home, the murderer groaned and fell into the darkness. Emperel spun on his heel, bringing his sword down in a vicious backhand slash. Sparks flew as his blade clanged off the stone floor. He pivoted away, blindly weaving his weapon in a defensive pattern. A gentle thud sounded beside him, so soft he barely heard it over the whisper of his flying blade. He spun toward the noise, bringing his sword around in a hissing arc. The blade bit into the corner of the tunnel entrance, sending a spray of dirt and pebbles clattering down onto the stone floor.

A low moan sounded deep within the tunnel, followed by the scrape of leather on dirt. Emperel flung himself into the passage, blindly whipping his sword to and fro. He struck nothing but dirt and roots.

A moment later, his horse screamed, and the murderer was gone.

1

hey sat swaying in unison, the four of them quietly watching each other as Princess Tanalasta's small carriage bounced across the High Heath toward Worg Pass. The shades were drawn tight against blowing dust, and the interior of the coach was dim, dry, and warm.

The Warden of the Eastern Marches sat at an angle across from Tanalasta, square and upright in his polished field armor, his steely eyes focused curiously on the wiry priest at her side. The priest, Harvestmaster Owden Foley of Monastery Huthduth, rested well back in the shadows, his slender head turned slightly to smirk at a portly mage whose moon-spangled silks touted him as one of Cormyr's more powerful war wizards. The mage, Merula the Marvelous, perched at the edge of his seat, bejeweled hands folded atop the silver pommel of his walking cane. He was staring at Tanalasta with a bushy-browed glare that could only be described as rather too intense. Tanalasta sat studying the Warden of the Eastern Marches, a gangly, horse-faced man who was still somehow handsome in his scarlet cape and purple sash of office. She was thinking that a princess could marry worse than Dauneth Marliir.

Tanalasta did not love Dauneth, of course, but she liked him, and princesses could rarely marry for love. Even if he was five years her junior, Dauneth was loyal, brave, and good-looking enough for a noble, and that should have been enough. A year ago it would have been, but now she needed more. With her thirty-sixth year approaching and all of Cormyr waiting for her to produce an heir, suddenly she had to have bells and butterflies. Suddenly, she had to be in love.

It was enough to make her want to abdicate.

Seeming to feel the pressure of her gaze, Dauneth looked away from Owden. "My apologies, Princess. These mountain roads are difficult to keep in good repair."

"A little bumping and jarring won't hurt me, Dauneth." Tanalasta narrowed her eyes ever so slightly, a face-hardening device she had spent many hours practicing in the reflection of a forest pond. "I'm hardly the porcelain doll you knew a year ago."

Dauneth's face reddened. "Of course not. I didn't mean—"

"You should have seen me at Huthduth," the princess continued, her voice now light and cheerful. "Clearing stones out of fields, leading plow oxen, harvesting squash, picking raspberries, hunting wild mushrooms . . ."

Tanalasta paused, thinking it better not to add "swimming naked in mountain lakes."

Merula the Marvelous raised an eyebrow, and she felt a sudden swell of anger. Could the wizard be reading her thoughts?

"You were hunting wild mushrooms, milady?" asked Dauneth. "In the forest?"

"Of course." Tanalasta returned her gaze to Dauneth, still struggling to decide how she would deal with the wizard's intrusion. "Where else does one hunt for mushrooms?"

"You really shouldn't have," Dauneth said. "The mountains around Huthduth are orc country. If a foraging mob had come across you. . . ."

"I wasn't aware that protecting me was your purview, Dauneth. Has the king told you something he has yet to share with me?"

Dauneth's eyes betrayed his surprise at the woman returning from Huthduth. "No, of course not. The king would hardly confide in me before his own daughter, but I do have a . . . a reason to be concerned with your safety."

Tanalasta said nothing, allowing Dauneth a chance to make himself sound less presumptuous by adding some comment about a noble's duty to safeguard a member of the royal family. When the Warden remained silent, she realized matters were worse than she had expected. With King Azoun turning sixty-three in two days and Tanalasta on the far side of thirty-five and still unmarried, people were starting to wonder if she would ever produce an heir. Certain individuals had even taken it on themselves to hurry things along—most notably the Royal Magician and State Pain-in-the-Princess's Arse, Vangerdahast. The crafty old wizard had no doubt arranged to celebrate the king's birthday at House Marliir for the purpose of advancing Dauneth's courtship.

That would have been fine with Tanalasta, who knew better than anyone that her time to produce an heir was fast running out. In the past year, the princess had grown more conscious than ever of her duty to Cormyr, and Dauneth had proven himself both a loyal noble and a worthy suitor in the Abraxus Affair fifteen months before. Nothing would have made her happier than to summon the good Warden to the altar and get started on the unpleasant business of producing an heir, and the princess had made up her mind to do exactly that when she received word of the celebration in Arabel.

Then the vision had come.

Tanalasta quickly chased from her thoughts all memory of the vision itself, instead picturing Merula the Marvelous trussed naked on a spit and roasting over a slow fire. If the wizard was spying on her thoughts, she wanted him to know what awaited if he dared report any particular one to the royal magician. Vangerdahast would hear of her vision soon enough, and Tanalasta needed to be the one to tell him.

Merula merely continued to glower. "Something wrong, milady?"

"I hope not."

Tanalasta drew back a window flap and turned to watch the High Heath glide by. It was a small plain of golden checkerboard fields divided into squares by rough stone walls and dotted with thatch-roofed huts. The simple folk who scratched their living from the place had come out to watch the royal procession trundle past, and it was not until the princess had waved at two dozen vacant-eyed children without receiving a response that she realized something was wrong.

She turned to the Harvestmaster beside her. "Owden, look out here and tell me what you think. Is there something wrong with those barley fields?"

The thin priest leaned in front of her and peered out the window. "There is, Princess. It's too early for such a color. There must be some sort of blight."

Tanalasta frowned. "Across the whole heath?"

"So it appears."

Tanalasta thrust her head out the window. "Stop the carriage!"

Merula scowled and reached for his own drape to countermand the order, but Tanalasta caught his arm.

"Do you really want to challenge the command of an Obarskyr, wizard?"

The wizard knitted his bushy eyebrows indignantly. "The royal magician's orders were clear. We are to stop for nothing until we have cleared the mountains."

"Then proceed on your own, by all means," Tanalasta retorted. "Vangerdahast does not command me. You may remind him of that, if he is listening."

The carriage rumbled to a stop, and a footman opened the door. Tanalasta held out her hand to Dauneth.

"Will you join me, Warden?"

Dauneth made no move to accept her hand. "Merula is right, milady. These mountains are no place—"

"No?" Tanalasta shrugged, then reached for the footman's hand. "If you are frightened. . . ."

"Not at all." Dauneth was out the door in an instant, jostling the footman aside and offering his hand to Tanalasta. "I was only thinking of your safety."

"Yes, you did say you have reason to concern yourself with me."

Tanalasta gave the Warden a vinegary smile, then allowed him to help her out of the coach, prompting a handful of peasants to gasp and bow so low their faces scraped ground. Outside, it was a warm mountain afternoon with a sky the color of sapphires and air as dry as sand, and the princess was disappointed to note they had already crossed most of the heath. The foot of Worg Pass lay only a hundred paces ahead, where the barley fields abruptly gave way to a stand of withering pine trees.

Tanalasta motioned the peasants to their feet, then turned to Harvestmaster Owden, who was climbing out of the carriage behind her. "Do you think your assistants could do anything to save these fields, Harvestmaster?"

Owden glanced toward a large, ox-drawn wagon following a few paces behind the princess's carriage. A dozen monks in green woolen robes sat crammed into the cargo bed among shovels, harrows, and other implements of Chauntea's faith. They were eyeing the blighted fields and muttering quietly among themselves, no doubt as concerned as Tanalasta by what they saw.

Owden motioned his assistants out of the wagon. "It will take a few hours, Princess."

"A few hours!" Merula hoisted his considerable bulk through the carriage door with surprising ease. "We can't have that! The royal magician—"

"—need not know," Tanalasta finished for him. "Unless he is spying upon us even as we speak—in which case you may inform him that the Crown Princess will spend the afternoon walking."

Tanalasta eyed the Purple Dragons guarding her carriage, one company mounted on their snorting chargers ahead of the procession and the other bringing up the rear, lances posted and steel helmets gleaming in the sun. At the end of the official column followed a long line of merchant carts taking advantage of Tanalasta's escorts to ensure a safe passage through the mountains. Sighing at the futility of trying to find a little privacy with her suitor, Tanalasta turned to Dauneth.

"Will you join me, Warden?"

Dauneth nodded somewhat uncomfortably. "Whatever the princess wishes."

Trying not to grind her teeth in frustration, Tanalasta took Dauneth's arm and led him past the long file of riders to the front of the column. Though her shoulders were draped in a silken cape of royal purple, underneath she wore a sensible traveling smock and a pair of well-worn walking boots, and it was not long before they reached the foot of Worg Pass. She sent the company captain ahead with two scouts and instructed the rest of the company to follow twenty paces behind, but she could not quite make her getaway before Merula the Marvelous came puffing up from behind.

"I trust . . . the princess will not object to . . . company," Merula panted.

"Of course not. Why should she?" asked Owden Foley, appearing from the other side of the horse column. The weatherworn priest winked a crinkled eye at the princess, then looped his hand through Merula's arm. "My friend, what an excellent idea to join them. We could all do with a nice, brisk walk. Nothing like a stroll to get the heart pumping and keep the fields in water, is there?"

Merula scowled and jerked his arm away. "I thought the princess asked you to attend to the peasants' fields."

"And so I am," Owden replied, digging a good-natured elbow into the wizard's well-padded ribs. "That's why one has monks, is it not?"

"I wouldn't know," grumbled Merula.

Owden merely grinned and continued to prattle on about the wholesome benefits of mountain sunlight and pine-fresh air. Tanalasta smiled and silently thanked the priest for coming to her rescue. With the Harvestmaster expounding about the benefits of mountain life, Merula would find it impossible to eavesdrop on her conversation—or her thoughts.

Tanalasta led the way up the road at a lively gait. The pass climbed steeply along the flank of a lightly forested mountain, and soon enough the sound of Merula's huffing breath faded from her hearing—though it was replaced by the somewhat lighter panting of the Warden of the Eastern Marches.

"If I may say so, Princess, you have changed much since . . ." Dauneth paused, no doubt as much to summon his tact as to catch his breath, then continued, "Since the last time I saw you."

16

Tanalasta eyed him levelly. "It's all right, Dauneth. You can say it."

"I beg your pardon?"

"You can say, 'since Aunadar Bleth made a fool of you,'" Tanalasta said lightly. She continued up the road. "The whole kingdom knows how he tried to marry me and steal the crown. Really, it's insulting to behave as if I'm the only one unaware of it."

Dauneth's face reddened. "You were under a terrible strain. With your father poisoned and—"

"I was a damned ninny. I nearly lost the kingdom, and it was nobody's fault but my own." Despite the steep climb, Tanalasta betrayed no sign of fatigue as she spoke. A year at Huthduth had conditioned her to harder work than hiking. "At least I learned that much from Vangerdahast. I swear, I don't know why he didn't tell Father to name Alusair crown princess."

Dauneth cocked an eyebrow. "Perhaps because he saw what you would make of the experience." The Warden grew thoughtful, then added, "Or, since we are speaking frankly, maybe it is because he knows your sister. Can you see Alusair as queen? No noble son would be safe. If she wasn't getting them killed in a war, she'd be entrapping them in her boudoir."

Tanalasta let her jaw drop. "Watch your tongue, sir!" Smiling, she cuffed Dauneth lightly on the back. "That's my baby sister you are maligning."

"So the crown princess wishes to acknowledge her own weaknesses and remain blind to those of everyone else?" Dauneth shook his head sagely. "This will never do. It runs contrary to the whole spirit of sovereign tradition. Perhaps I should have a talk with old Vangerdahast after all."

"That will hardly be necessary." Tanalasta lowered her voice and leaned closer. "All you need do is mention it in front of our companions. I've no doubt Vangey knows everything the moment Merula hears it."

"Really?" Dauneth glanced back at the pudgy wizard, who looked almost as weary of climbing as he did of Owden's nature lecture. "I didn't realize the royal magician was such a voyeur."

"That's just one thing you'd need to accustom yourself to, if . . ."

Tanalasta let the sentence hang, as reluctant to reveal her condition for giving her hand to Dauneth as she was to commit herself to giving it.

The Warden was too good a military man not to press for an advantage when he saw the opportunity. "If what, milady?"

Tanalasta stopped climbing and turned to face Dauneth, bringing the whole procession of guards and merchants to a clamorous halt. Only Merula and Owden continued to climb, the wizard more eager than ever to eavesdrop, and the priest just as determined to fill his ear with valuable nature lore.

Trying to ignore the fact that she was being watched by a thousand eyes, Tanalasta took Dauneth's hand and answered his question. "*If* we are to do what my father and Vangerdahast want us to, but first we must trust each other enough to speak honestly and openly."

Dauneth's face grew serious. "I am sure the princess will find me a very honest fellow."

"Of course. No one can doubt that after the Abraxus Affair, but that's really not what I meant."

Noticing that Merula's huffing was growing audible again, Tanalasta turned up the road and started to climb. They were almost at the summit now. At any moment, she expected to crest Worg Pass and see the bulky towers of High Horn in the distance.

Dauneth clambered to keep up. "So what did you mean, Princess?"

"Tanalasta, please. If you can't even call me by name—"

"I didn't want to take liberties." Dauneth's voice had grown defensive. "You haven't invited me to."

"I am inviting you to now."

"Very well. Then what did you mean, Tanalasta?"

Tanalasta rolled her eyes, wondering how she could say what she meant without making it seem a command, and without sounding like the same ninny who had nearly let Aunadar Bleth steal a kingdom from beneath her nose. The princess had little doubt that Dauneth, raised in the fine tradition of noble families everywhere, would find her wish to marry for love as laughable as Vangerdahast found it. On the other hand, it was she who wanted to speak honestly and openly, and she could hardly demand such a thing of Dauneth if she was unwilling herself. Tanalasta took a deep breath and began.

"First, Dauneth, there must be trust and respect."

Dauneth's lips tightened, and Tanalasta saw that she had gotten off to a bad start.

"Oh no, Dauneth! I have the utmost trust and respect for you. Everybody does." Tanalasta paused, choosing her next words carefully. "What I mean to say is . . . well, it must be mutual."

Dauneth frowned. "I do trust you, Prin—er, Tanalasta. Of course I respect you."

"If that were true, you would not be lying to me now."

"Milady! I would never lie—"

"Truly?" Tanalasta allowed her voice to grow sharp. "You still respect my judgment after the Abraxus Affair? You would trust the kingdom to the care of someone so easily manipulated?"

Dauneth started to reply automatically, then his eyes lit with sudden comprehension. "I see your point."

Tanalasta felt a hollow ache in her stomach, which she quickly recognized as the pang of wounded pride—and evidence that Dauneth was listening well. She forced a smile, but could not quite bring herself to take Dauneth's arm.

"Now you're being honest. Thank you."

"I wish I could say it was my pleasure, but it really isn't. This is truly what you want from me?"

"It's a start."

"A start." Dauneth sounded somewhat dazed. He plucked at the fabric of her woolen traveling frock. "If I am being honest, would you also like me to tell you that gray really isn't your color?"

Tanalasta swatted his hand away. "I said honest, not brash!" she chuckled. "After all, I am still a princess, and I expect to be courted."

2

analasta bustled down the Family Hall of House Marliir, one hand tugging at her gown's brandelle straps, the other holding her skirts off the floor. The corridor seemed a mile long, with an endless procession of white pillars supporting its corbeled arches and a hundred oaken doors lining its walls. On the way down from High Heath, she had stopped so often to restore blighted fields that the journey had taken an extra day, and she had arrived just that morning to discover that the ball gown she'd had sent up from Suzail was a size too large. There had been no chance to see to her father's birthday gift. She could only trust that Harvestmaster Foley had been able to arrange things on his own.

At last, Tanalasta came to a door with two Purple Dragon guards standing outside. They snapped to attention, clicking their feet and bringing their halberds to their shoulders. Tanalasta stopped and raised her arms over her head.

"Anything out of place, gentlemen?" she asked, executing a slow twirl. "Loose threads, anything showing that shouldn't?"

The guards glanced at each other nervously and said nothing.

"What's wrong?" Tanalasta looked down. The gown was an amethyst silk with a tapered bodice and a scooped neckline, and she could imagine something peeking out that a modest princess would prefer to keep hidden. "Tell me."

The youngest guard extended his arm, shifting his halberd to the stand ready position. "Nothing's wrong, Princess." The glimmer of a smile flashed across his lips. "You look . . . well, stunning. I'd be careful about showing up the queen."

Tanalasta's jaw went slack. "What?"

The older guard shifted his halberd to the stand ready, then stammered, "B-beg your pardon, princess. Lundan meant no offense. It's just that we haven't seen you in Suzail for quite some time, and a lot has, er, *changed*."

"Truly?" Tanalasta broke into a broad smile, then kissed both men on their cheeks. "Chauntea bless you!"

She pulled the ribbon from her brown hair, setting her long tresses free to cascade down her back, then nodded.

The dazed guards opened the drawing room door, and she entered the chamber to find Dauneth Marliir standing at the marble fireplace with her father and Vangerdahast. The three men were deep in conversation, each sipping a glass of spirits and chuckling quietly at some joke that Tanalasta hoped did not concern her tardiness. Surprisingly, Vangerdahast had made a special effort to dress for the occasion. He had combed his long beard into a snowy white mass, and his ample girth was cloaked in an indigo robe with yellow comets that actually seemed to streak across the silk. Dauneth wore a gold-trimmed doublet that was a perfect complement to

Tanalasta's amethyst gown—a coincidence she felt certain had not been left to chance. King Azoun wore a linen tunic and velvet cape in the Royal Purple, with Symylazarr, the royal Sword of Honor, hanging in its bejeweled scabbard at his side. With stony features and piercing brown eyes, her father looked as handsome as ever—even if the royal beard had a few more gray streaks than a year ago.

"By the Morninglord!" The gasp came not from the fireplace, but from the wall left of the door. "Can that be my Tanalasta?"

The princess turned to see her mother rising from an elegant chair with gold-leafed spindles. Despite the guard's warning, Tanalasta saw at once that she did not need to worry about upstaging the queen. Wearing a simple violet dress that only served to emphasize her exquisite carriage, Filfaeril was as stunning as ever. With ice-blue eyes, alabaster skin, and hair the color of honey, she always seemed to be the most beautiful woman in the room, even when she was not trying— and today she was trying.

The queen took Tanalasta by the shoulders and studied her. "The mountains agree with you, my dear. Dauneth said you had changed—but he didn't say how much!"

The princess feigned disappointment. "No? And I had so hoped to smite him with my dusty traveling clothes." Tanalasta hugged her mother, then whispered, "And speaking of the good warden—what is he doing here? I thought only the family was to gather in the drawing room."

"Vangerdahast's idea, I'm afraid." The queen's whisper was sympathetic, but she stepped back with a cocked brow. "Is that a problem?"

Tanalasta sighed. "Not really—but I had hoped to have a few words with you and the king. There's something I must tell—"

"Princess, you look absolutely bewitching!"

Tanalasta looked up to see Dauneth leading her father and Vangerdahast away from the fireplace. Giving up any hope of a private moment, she smiled and presented her hand.

"Thank you, Dauneth, but what did we say about my name?"

The warden blushed and kissed her hand. "Forgive me, Tanalasta."

The approving glances that shot between Vangerdahast and Azoun did not escape Tanalasta's notice.

She curtsied to her father and said, "I apologize for being tardy, but we made a rather alarming discovery on the way from Huthduth."

"Yes, yes, Dauneth has told me all about the blighted fields." Azoun took his daughter's hand, then gave her a gently reproachful smile. "A princess really shouldn't trouble herself with such things. That's why we have wizards, you know."

"Oh?" Tanalasta looked to Vangerdahast, who was eyeing her up and down, appraising her as a man might a horse. "The royal magician has determined the nature of the problem?"

"The royal magician has more important things to do than watch barley grow," Vangerdahast replied, "but Merula the Marvelous has assured me that this 'blight' is not serious—certainly no reason to keep the king waiting."

"Merula? What does that wand waver know about farming?" Despite her tone, Tanalasta was secretly relieved. Had the royal magician already discovered the nature of the problem, the value of her gift would have been less apparent. She smiled at her father. "If you want to know what's happening, you must ask Harvestmaster Foley—"

"As I certainly will," Azoun interrupted, "if you will be good enough to introduce us—*after* the party."

"Of course," Tanalasta said, secretly delighted. Even for her, it was not easy to arrange an introduction without first winning the consent of the royal magician, and the king's willingness to meet Owden Foley without Vangerdahast's approval bode well for her gift.

"I doubt the blight will overrun Cormyr during the celebration," she conceded. "I do apologize for keeping you waiting."

The king's smile broadened. "Are we running late? I really hadn't noticed—and even if I had, the wait was well worth it." He turned to Vangerdahast. "Don't you think so, old wizard?"

The royal magician regarded Tanalasta sourly, then said, "She *has* lost weight, though I don't find it healthy for a woman to be so bony—especially not at Tanalasta's age."

Filfaeril slapped the wizard's shoulder. "Vangerdahast! Tanalasta was hardly large when she left."

"There's no need to defend me, Mother," Tanalasta said. She forced a smile and patted the wizard lightly on his ample belly. "Vangey and I understand each other, don't we, Your Portliness?"

Vangerdahast's eyes widened. "I see you have gained in cheek what you have lost from other places. If you will excuse me, I have an important matter to attend to."

The wizard retreated across the room to sprawl on a burgundy settee, where he put his head back and closed his eyes. Filfaeril smiled approvingly, but the expression on Azoun's face was more pained.

"I wish you wouldn't antagonize him, Tanalasta. He is going to be your—"

"My Royal Magician—I know." Tanalasta took a deep breath, then launched into a prepared response. "While it would behoove us all to remember that it is the magician who serves the crown and not the reverse, there is no need to lecture me on Vangerdahast's virtues. My regard for him is as deep as your own—even if I no longer choose to quietly abide his slights."

The king raised his brow, but Tanalasta took heart from the surprised twinkle in her mother's eye and refused to back down. After the Abraxus Affair, she and Vangerdahast had spent a few months traveling together, and the ordeal had been enough to convince the princess she could no longer allow the royal magician to intimidate her. While he had helped her learn the ways of the world and forget her humiliation at the hands of Aunadar Bleth, he had also attempted to dampen her emerging interest in Chauntea and steer her down 'more appropriate' paths of inquiry. The trip had finally come to a bad end when the princess rebelled and declared her decision to enter the House of Huthduth. She could only imagine what Vangerdahast had told her parents about the decision, but she felt certain he had been less than candid about his own part in the events that caused it.

At last, the king laid a hand on Tanalasta's shoulder. "I see you have found some iron in those mountains," he said. "That is good, but if you wish to make a fist of it, you mustn't forget the velvet that covers it."

Tanalasta tipped her head, deciding it wiser not to put the king into a bad mood by protesting such a gentle rebuke. "I will bear your advice in mind, Father."

"Good." The king smiled, then led her toward the settee, where Vangerdahast still sat with his head back and eyes closed. "Now let's see if we can locate your sister and get this party underway."

The mage lifted his head. "We'll have to start without Alusair, I'm afraid."

"Start without her?" demanded Filfaeril. The queen narrowed her pale eyes. "Where is she?"

"I—er—I don't know, exactly." His face reddening, Vangerdahast hefted himself off the settee. "Still in the

Stonelands, perhaps. I have just contacted her, but all she said was 'not now, Old Snoop.'"

"Then go get her! We decided to have the king's party in Arabel so—" Filfaeril caught herself and glanced in Dauneth's direction, then began again, "When we decided to accept Raynaar Marliir's kind invitation to host the celebration, it was to make it easier for *both* our daughters to attend."

"So it was, Majesty," Vangerdahast said, inclining his head, "but I am afraid Alusair has removed her ring again."

Tanalasta saw Dauneth's eyes flick to the signet rings on the hand of each royal.

"I have a thirst, Dauneth." She took the warden's arm and directed him toward the door. "Would you fetch me a sherry?"

"You needn't send him away, Tanalasta." The king toyed briefly with his signet ring, then continued, "I think we can trust Dauneth with our little secret. Besides, the warden knows more about this situation than you do."

As if to prove the king correct, Dauneth turned to Tanalasta and said, "Emperel is missing."

"Missing?" Tanalasta asked, feeling slighted that the king had not seen fit to send word of this to her in Huthduth. Emperel was the confidential guardian of the "Sleeping Sword," a secret company of brave young lords put into magical hibernation as a precaution against an ancient prophecy forecasting Cormyr's destruction. That the king trusted Dauneth with this covert knowledge was a sign of his confidence in the man, and also of his faith that the good warden would one day be his son-in-law. "What happened?"

"That is what Alusair went to find out," said Azoun. He turned to Vangerdahast. "Should we be concerned about her?"

"Of course!" the wizard snapped. "The girl will never learn. You know how many times I have told her not to remove her ring. What if it was an important matter?"

"The matter *is* important," said Filfaeril. "This is Azoun's sixty-third birthday. Alusair's absence speaks volumes, and not only to us."

"Let us not overstate matters," said the king. "I'm sure she has a good reason for not being here."

Tanalasta bit her tongue, knowing it would only make her seem jealous to point out the double standard. It was perfectly fine for Alusair to vanish into the Stonelands and forgo his birthday celebration without so much as a word of apology, yet it would not do for the crown princess to speak sharply to Vangerdahast. It was no wonder Tanalasta felt more at home in Huthduth's austerity than in the luxury of her family's palace.

The king offered his arm to Filfaeril, then turned toward the great double doors leading into the ballroom. "Vangerdahast, you will have to enter alone," the king said, "and do keep trying to reach Alusair. I'm sure she would contact you if she needed help, but with Emperel missing. . . ."

Vangerdahast nodded. "I'll pass word when I reach her."

The royal magician flicked his hand toward the door, producing several loud raps. From the other side came the barked command of a guard and the muffled blare of trumpets, then the doors swung open. The king and queen stepped through to a thunderous roar of applause.

Dauneth stepped to Tanalasta's side and offered her his arm. "If I may."

"Of course."

Tanalasta looped her hand through the crook of his elbow and stepped into House Marliir's famous Rhodes Room. The huge ballroom was so packed with nobles that she could see nothing of its renowned treasures, save the gold-leafed capitals of its marble columns and the luminescent vault of its alabaster cupola. Her parents were about ten steps ahead, strolling down a plush purple runner that demarcated the Aisle of Courtesy, a small lane to be kept clear for the royals alone. They were simply nodding and waving as they passed the lesser nobles in the rear of the room, but their progress would slow to a crawl as they stopped to exchange pleasantries with the important nobles waiting in the front of the chamber near the Royal Rostrum.

Tanalasta forced a smile and followed, acutely conscious of the rising brows and appraising gazes that greeted her passage. She did not doubt that even the lowest baron present knew how Aunadar Bleth had tricked her into falling in love with him, then tried to seize the throne. Their applause was polite but subdued, a sure sign of the concern they felt over what would become of Cormyr when she took her father's place. The princess continued to smile and nod, calling upon memories of green mountain meadows to remain calm and composed. The first step to restoring her reputation was to appear confident in herself, and to do that she had to be relaxed inside.

As they progressed up the Aisle of Courtesy, the wool tabards and linen smocks of the lesser nobles gave way to embroidered capes and chiffon gowns. Brass closures and pewter brooches began to appear in strategic locations, often decorated with brilliant tigereyes or ghostly moon crystals. Dauneth greeted these men and women by name, and Tanalasta would say what a pleasure it was to make their acquaintance. They never failed to return her smile with somewhat dazed expressions, a sign the princess took to mean she was making a better impression than expected.

Tanalasta and Dauneth reached the high nobles at the front of the room, where the air smelled of sweet lavender oil and lilac water. The chamber seemed lit by the twinkle of sparkling rubies and gleaming sapphires, and the low murmur of self-important voices reverberated in the pit of her stomach. The men wore feathered caps and doublets of brilliant silk, while the women had gowned themselves in veritable yards of lace and gossamer. Unlike the lower nobles standing farther back, the lords and ladies gathered here knew the royal family well, and they did not hesitate to compliment the queen's appearance or congratulate Azoun on another year. Tanalasta thought of mountain brooks and pushed her smile wider, then entered the gauntlet.

She turned first to the families of five young nobles who had tried to assassinate her late in the Abraxus Affair, both to show she held no grudges and to prove she did not fear them. The dukes managed to stammer out their compliments, but the duchesses were so stunned they could hardly return her greeting. Tanalasta took her leave graciously, then breathed a sigh of relief and led Dauneth down the aisle to more comfortable territory. Her friends the Wyvernspurs were next, Cat looking resplendent in pearl-white, Giogi as flamboyant and affable as always in gold-trimmed velvet.

"By the Lady, Princess!" Giogi embraced Tanalasta warmly, then stood back to admire her with a frankly lascivious gaze. "What happened? You've become a real beauty!"

"Giogi!" Cat slapped her mate on the shoulder, then stepped to the edge of the purple carpet to wrap her strong arms around Tanalasta. "Forgive my husband, Princess, you know what a clod he can be."

"I will take Giogi's compliments over a Bleth's flattery any day," Tanalasta laughed. She motioned to Dauneth. "You remember the good warden, I am sure."

Cat's eyes twinkled as she took in Dauneth's gold-trimmed doublet, noting how it complimented Tanalasta's amethyst gown—and how close its indigo fabric came to the royal purple.

"As handsome as ever." Cat squeezed Tanalasta's hand, then leaned close to whisper, "You're a lucky woman, my dear."

Tanalasta raised a brow, but said nothing about the hastiness of her friend's assumption. "We'll talk later, Cat."

"I'm looking forward to it." Cat released her hand and curtsied. "I want to hear all about your adventures in Huthduth."

"Adventures?" Giogi asked, looking confused. "Isn't Huthduth a monastery?"

"It is." Cat elbowed him in the ribs. "Take your leave, Giogi."

Giogi bowed. "Until later, Princess."

Tanalasta acknowledged the bow with a friendly nod, then continued up the Aisle of Courtesy. They had now closed to within a few paces of the Royal Rostrum, where Tanalasta was delighted to see the tall, white-haired figure of Alaphondar Emmarask standing slightly apart from the crowd. As the Sage Most Learned of the Royal Court, Alaphondar was Tanalasta's instructor in law, philosophy, history, and almost everything else. The two had become far more than friends over three decades of study, though never in the way sometimes whispered in the royal halls. Hoping to have a few words with him about the blight that had delayed her journey from Huthduth, she pulled Dauneth gently forward— only to have a stumpy little woman step onto the Aisle of Courtesy and block her way.

"Princess Tanalasta, your beauty exceeds even the wildest claims of my son."

So shocked was Tanalasta that she required a moment to comprehend what she was seeing. The woman was draped in organdy and pearls, with sapphires dangling from her earlobes and rubies glittering on every available digit—even her thumbs. Her powdered hair was piled into a spiraling tower and held in place by eight diamond hairpins arranged in a moonlike crescent. Clearly, the woman was a dame of the realm, yet she behaved as though she knew no better than to block a royal's path.

A pair of bodyguards slipped past the princess and took positions to both sides of the woman, awaiting some sign of how to handle the situation. Tanalasta glanced at Dauneth, whose reddening face confirmed the duchess's identity, then decided not to have the woman removed. The warden disengaged himself politely and went to his dauntless mother's side.

"Your Highness, may I present my mother, Lady Merelda Marliir."

Tanalasta sensed a spreading circle of silence and knew that half the nobles of the realm were watching to see how she handled the delicate situation—and also to judge the progress of Dauneth's courtship. The princess did not gesture the duchess to rise, but neither did she insult the woman by signaling the guards to return her to her proper place.

"Lady Marliir, how kind of you to present yourself." As Tanalasta spoke, she glimpsed her parents at the base of the rostrum, watching in shock. "I have been looking for you. I wish to express my gratitude for hosting the king's birthday party."

Merelda flushed in delight. "Not at all. The pleasure is mine," she said, rising without invitation. If the woman heard the gasps that surrounded her, her fleshy smile did not betray it. "I am so happy to meet you, my dear. Dauneth has told me so much about you."

"Indeed?"

"Oh yes." Oblivious to the ice in Tanalasta's voice, Merelda glanced around to be certain her fellow noble-women were watching, then took her son's hand and stepped forward. "He speaks of you all the time, and only in the fondest terms, I assure you."

Dauneth's face turned as red as the rubies on his mother's fingers. "Mother, please." He clasped her hand tightly and tried unsuccessfully to draw her toward the edge of the carpet, where Raynaar Marliir stood looking on in helpless mortification. "Are you trying to disadvantage me with the princess?"

The question drew a round of good natured chuckles from everyone but Tanalasta, who was fast losing patience with Lady Marliir. Evidently, the woman believed she could bend Tanalasta to her will as easily as had the traitor Aunadar Bleth. The princess glanced in her parents' direction, silently signaling them to give her some help before she was forced to embarrass their hostess. The king started to turn toward the rostrum, which would trigger the trumpet blast calling the party to order, then glanced over Tanalasta's shoulder at Vangerdahast and suddenly stopped.

"I am so looking forward to—"

"Don't say it, please," Tanalasta warned. Her sharp tone was due as much to her ire at having her signal overridden by Vangerdahast as her impatience with Lady Marliir. "It would be embarrassing—"

"Embarrassing? My dear, Dauneth dances better than that." Merelda threw her head back and joined the other nobles in a round of laughter, then caught Tanalasta's hand between hers. "But if you don't approve of his footwork, you will have plenty of time to correct it—won't you?"

The silence grew as thick as smoke, and Tanalasta found it impossible to control her mounting anger. If the king insisted on allowing Vangerdahast to countermand his daughter's wishes, then it would be up to him to deal with the consequences. The princess jerked her hand from the woman's grasp, and put on her most guileless smile.

"I am sorry, Duchess Marliir. I cannot follow your meaning. Are you under the impression that Dauneth and I are betrothed?"

A quiet murmur filled the room, and Lady Marliir's smile stiffened into a cringe. Her jaw began to work fitfully, trying to string a series of disjointed syllables into some sort of explanation, but Tanalasta refused to give the woman a chance to push her further. She looked to the guards, but Dauneth was already pressing his mother into the grasp of her flabbergasted husband. Duke Marliir clamped onto his wife's elbow and turned toward the nearest exit.

As soon as King Azoun saw what was happening, he cast the briefest glance in his daughter's direction, so quick that only the most astute of observers would have noted the inherent reproach. Tanalasta returned the gesture with an innocent shrug. She had no wish to sour her father's mood, lest it affect how he received the birthday gift she had brought from Huthduth, but she had to stand up for herself. If that created a problem, it was Vangerdahast's doing and not hers.

Azoun pasted a stiff smile on his face, then disengaged himself from Filfaeril. "Lady Marliir, one moment if you please."

The Marliirs stopped and slowly turned, Raynaar's face flushed with embarrassment and his wife's white with mortification. Merelda curtsied deeply and did not rise.

"Y-yes, Majesty?"

The king came down the aisle and took her by the hands. "It has just occurred to me that I have done you a small injustice." He drew Merelda to her feet. "The royal protocol chamberlain should have invited you and Lord Marliir to walk the carpet with us."

The woman's eyes grew round with surprise, and another murmur, much louder than the last, filled the ballroom. "He should have?"

"Quite right," Azoun said. "A hostess should be honored—especially the hostess of such a grand and lovely ball. I do hope you will pardon the oversight. The protocol chamberlain really is a most dutiful fellow, and it would be a shame for him to spend the rest of the tenday in a dungeon."

The joke drew the appropriate response from everyone near enough to hear it. Lady Marliir blushed and glanced around to make certain everyone had seen her reputation restored, then Azoun kissed her hand and returned to Filfaeril's side. The crown princess smiled diplomatically and tried not to show her seething anger. The party had been spared an unseemly scandal, but at no small cost to Tanalasta's prestige. She could only hope her father would seize the opportunity to undo the damage when she presented her birthday gift.

Dauneth returned to Tanalasta's side and rather stiffly offered her his arm. Feeling as ill at ease as he did, she slipped a hand through his elbow and followed her parents onto the Royal Rostrum. The trumpets blared, calling the party to order, and the ballroom quieted as they ascended the stairs.

Tanalasta's anger gave way to thoughtfulness, and she began to wonder if someone had suggested to the poor woman that she push matters along. Of course, her suspicions fell instantly upon Vangerdahast. The old wizard had never been above helping destiny along—especially when Cormyr's fate depended on it.

They reached the top of the rostrum and found four purple-cushioned thrones, flanked by a pair of simpler chairs for Dauneth and Vangerdahast. Azoun and Filfaeril sat in the middle thrones, and Tanalasta sat in the one to her father's right. The royal magician dismissed the extra throne with a half-muttered word and a flick of his wrist, then pulled his chair to the queen's side and dropped onto it heavily. He did not look in Tanalasta's direction.

Once they were all seated, Dauneth formally welcomed the guests to his family's home, glossing over the scene of a few moments earlier with an apt joke about the hearing of would-be grandmothers. The announcement that Princess Alusair would not be in attendance was greeted with a murmur of profound disappointment, but the warden quickly recaptured the crowd's enthusiasm by drawing them into a rousing cycle of sixty-three hoorays—one for each of Azoun's years. So thunderous were the cheers that they soon had Vangerdahast casting nervous glances at the ballroom's alabaster cupola.

Once the cheers were finished, Dauneth asked the high nobles to clear a space in front of the rostrum, then brought on a company of singing acrobats. Within minutes, everyone in the room, from the lowliest lord to the king himself, was crying in laughter. Though Tanalasta could not forget Lady Marliir's behavior, she did find herself able to forgive it—especially given that someone in the royal party had most likely put her up to it. By the time the show ended, the spectators were so exhausted from laughing that many had sunk to the floor holding their ribs.

As the performers cartwheeled and back-flipped out of the chamber, Dauneth invited the high nobles to ascend the rostrum in turn and present their gifts to the king. After the mirth of the acrobats, it was a welcome chance for the audience to relax and refresh themselves, and a pleasant drone descended over the chamber as Azoun opened the artfully wrapped packages. For the most part, the gifts reflected the families that had given them. From the seafaring Dauntinghorns there was an intricately modeled cog of pure gold, with silken sails that furled or unfurled at the tug of a tiny chain. The Hawklins presented an archaic sword crafted in forgotten Netheril, too ancient and brittle to wield in combat, but a valuable addition to the king's collection in Suzail. Cat and Giogi Wyvernspur produced a huge white stag captured in their Hullack Forest, tame enough to eat from a man's hand, yet so proud it allowed only the king to approach it.

Azoun thanked each giver profusely, displaying the offering and expressing his appreciation so sincerely that no one in the crowd could doubt how deeply the present had touched him. Tanalasta quickly lapsed into a performance of look, exclaim, and applause that required only a small fraction of her attention—a routine shared by many high nobles as they circulated through the front of the room, conversing quietly and congratulating each other on the genius of their gifts. At the base of the rostrum, Merelda was the center of much attention, even from the aloof Huntsilvers and the ever-envious Illances.

Once the process seemed well underway, Dauneth returned to his seat and leaned over to speak quietly with Tanalasta. "I apologize for my mother's eagerness. As you can see, she was quite taken with the idea of our marriage."

Despite her anger, Tanalasta forced herself to smile and speak in a teasing voice. "Of course you have said nothing to encourage her."

Dauneth withdrew slightly, apparently sensing the pique behind her tone. "I would never presume!"

"No?" Tanalasta pushed her lip out in a parody of a pout. "What of those 'wild claims' about my beauty? Are you telling me you said no such thing?"

Dauneth looked confused. "Of course, I find you ravishingly beautiful, but in truth—"

"Say no more, Dauneth. There are some things a princess should not hear." Tanalasta laughed lightly, then laid a hand on his arm. She glimpsed Lady Marliir drawing Alaslyn Rowanmantle's attention to the gesture, but did not draw back. If she wanted Dauneth to relax, she had to seem relaxed herself. "Besides, I do not think your mother was the only one eager to push us along."

Dauneth glanced uneasily toward her parents and Vangerdahast, then said cautiously, "I am sure everyone wants to see you happily wed."

"Truly? I was under the impression that Vangerdahast just wants to see me wed—happily or not." Tanalasta gave another laugh. "Really, his schemes are so transparent."

Dauneth avoided looking in the wizard's direction. "I am sure he is only thinking of the kingdom's welfare."

"So he *is* the one!"

"The one what?" Dauneth asked.

"The one who convinced your mother to behave as she did." Continuing to hold Dauneth's arm, Tanalasta smiled in Merelda's direction. "I know Lady Marliir's reputation, Dauneth. She is hardly the kind to blunder in such a matter."

Dauneth looked as relieved as he did surprised, and Tanalasta knew that in his eagerness to vindicate his mother, he would take her bait. She waited quietly and continued to look in Merelda's direction, nodding pleasantly when Lady Marliir flashed a puzzled smile.

Finally, Dauneth said, "Now that you mention it, I did see her talking to the royal magician earlier this morning. He must have told her to behave as though we were betrothed."

"And what did he tell *you*?" Tanalasta's tone was casual.

Dauneth turned in his seat. "I beg your pardon?"

"I thought we were going to be honest with each other, good warden." Tanalasta removed her hand from his arm, then said, "I know Vangey too well to think he would execute only half a plan. When were you to ask me?"

Dauneth closed his eyes for a moment, then sighed. "During our dance. I was to whisper the question in your ear. But I knew nothing about my mother. That surprised me as much as it did you."

"Which does nothing to excuse your own behavior." Tanalasta cast a furious glance across the rostrum at Vangerdahast, who remained oblivious to her anger and watched in weary amusement as the king set a silver clockwork cat after a golden mouse. "Why, Dauneth?"

"Why what?"

"Why would you do this?" Tanalasta was struggling to hold back tears of rage. "I know you didn't do it for the throne—not after the loyalty you showed during the Abraxus Affair. So why did you betray me?"

"I . . ." Dauneth looked away.

Tanalasta noticed several nobles watching from the ballroom floor. She ignored them. "Tell me."

When Dauneth looked back to her, his face was stern. "I did not betray you. If anyone is a betrayer here, it is you."

Tanalasta raised her brow, shocked. "Me?"

"To your duty," Dauneth said. "If you do not produce an heir, the Abraxus Affair will be a mere game compared to what follows your father's passing."

"*My* reign will follow my father's passing," Tanalasta said.

"And without an heir of your own, your reign will be one of plots and intrigues, with every noble family maneuvering to claim the throne upon your death. Sooner or later, one of them will see an advantage in assassinating you, and Cormyr will have a usurper for a king—or a war to unseat him."

"And you think to prevent this travesty by getting a child on me? I think not. I will have a husband I can trust—or none at all."

The hurt showed in Dauneth's eyes. "I meant no offense, milady, nor do I say this for my own good, but you must take a husband, and soon. If you are angry with me, there are plenty to choose from." He pointed into the crowd below. "There is Amanthus Rowanmantle if you fancy someone handsome, or one of the Silversword boys if you like wit, and perhaps even Dier Emmarask if you prefer someone who shares your love of learning."

"Thank you for the suggestions," Tanalasta said, struck by the absurdity of Dauneth recommending his own rivals. "If I were to choose a husband I did not love, it would probably be you. Even if I cannot trust you, you are loyal to Cormyr, and that counts for much."

"Thank you, milady." A hopeful light returned to Dauneth's eyes. "Do you really have time to think of love? We must think of Cormyr."

"I *am* thinking of Cormyr." Tanalasta started to rebuke the warden for trying to argue her into marrying him, then realized there was no point. She did not love Dauneth, and she was not going to marry him. "I am always thinking of Cormyr."

"If that is true, you will—"

"Dauneth, please don't presume to tell me what is good for Cormyr."

The warden flushed and looked away, clearly aware that he had been doing just that. Tanalasta wanted to explain to him, to tell Dauneth of the vision she had experienced at Huthduth, but how could she expect him to understand something she could barely put into words? The revelation had been one of those slippery things that a sharp mind could twist into a thousand meanings, but in which a true heart perceived only one. How could she trust Dauneth to trust her feelings, when he had already proven that she could not trust him?

"I'm sorry, Dauneth, but it must be love. I really cannot abide less."

A look of exasperation came over the warden, then he nodded and said, "Very well, milady. I shall fall in love with you on the morrow."

Tanalasta's jaw dropped, then she caught the note of self-mockery in his voice. "I wish it were that easy, good warden," she laughed. "I truly do." After a moment, she stopped laughing and gently took his hand. "But I fear your feelings would go unrequited. You don't respect me in your heart, and after Vangerdahast's meddling, I can never trust you as a woman should her husband. Forgive my bluntness in this matter, but you deserve to know. Your loyalty to Cormyr demands it."

Dauneth's face fell, and he sagged away from Tanalasta in shock. The nobles below did not seem to notice. They gasped in awe as Azoun displayed a four-foot dragon carved from a single crystal of amethyst, then applauded Ayesunder Truesilver as he descended the rostrum beaming with pride at the king's superlative words of royal gratitude.

Seeing that there were no more nobles waiting to ascend the stairs, Dauneth gathered himself together, then went forward to express his admiration for the many treasures strewn across the rostrum. After swearing that it would take a whole caravan of war wizards to return the hoard safely to Suzail, he invited Alaphondar Emmarask to present his gift. The Sage Most Learned ascended the rostrum and presented the king with a massive leather-bound volume entitled, *The Dragon Rides: A Complete and Accurate Account of the Life of Azoun IV of Cormyr, Volume Sixty-Two*.

Filfaeril drew a raucous round of chuckles by remarking that she hoped it was not "completely complete," then Vangerdahast stood to present his gift, pulling a simple switch of willow from the billowing sleeve of his robe. The king accepted the stick with a somewhat puzzled look.

"We thank you, Magician," said Azoun. "What kind of wand is it?"

"None, Majesty. It is a plain switch." Vangerdahast looked directly at Tanalasta, then added, "I think you shall soon have need of it."

Much to Tanalasta's dismay, the wizard's wry response sent the room into convulsions of laughter. She could do little except pretend to enjoy the joke and fume inwardly. If Vangerdahast could not bend her to his will through tricks and traps, then he seemed determined to undermine her prestige with outright mockery. The princess could imagine the campaign continuing until her father died, and no matter that it would weaken her own crown when she ascended the throne. The old staff swinger believed that only he knew what was good for Cormyr. Usually, he did, and if that had been so this time, Tanalasta would have married Dauneth on the morn. But this time the royal magician was wrong; this time, the future of Cormyr was not a matter of the mind, but of the heart, and she was not sure that Vangerdahast even had a heart.

Once the mirth faded, Dauneth turned to the princess and cocked a querying eyebrow. Though he was careful to maintain an expression of practiced congeniality, the rest of his face was at odds with his broad grin. Hoping the audience could not read his disappointment as clearly as she, Tanalasta smiled and nodded.

Dauneth extended an arm. "Lords and ladies, I give you the Princess Tanalasta Obarskyr."

Tanalasta took a deep breath, then rose to a polite ovation and stepped to the front of the rostrum. "Thank you."

The princess needed to say this only once to silence the applause.

"As you know, I have been in retreat at Huthduth for the last year. While the royal magician seems to fear that I have been somehow corrupted by Chauntea's humble monks—" Tanalasta was interrupted by a round of nervous laughter as she waved at the switch lying across her father's knees, then continued, "Let me assure you nothing could be further from the truth. The mountains were a place of great peace and harmony for me, and my gift is to bring some of that bounty to King Azoun IV, and through him, to all of Cormyr."

Tanalasta waved toward the entrance of the ballroom, where Owden Foley stood beneath the Grand Arch with a silk-wrapped gift box the size of a peasant hut. As the crowd turned to look, the Harvestmaster took up a golden rope and began to haul the gift across the floor. At first, his progress was labored and slow, for he seemed able to drag the huge box only a few paces before stopping to rest. Several minor nobles volunteered their help, which he gladly accepted.

The lords began to haul on the cord, and the box flew toward them so fast that they fell to the floor in a heap. A puzzled silence descended over the chamber, until Owden returned to take the golden rope. Claiming that earls and counts were too clumsy for such dangerous work, Owden shooed them away to a chorus of laughter, then resumed his labored trek toward the rostrum. This time, however, the box seemed to have a will of its own, sometimes flying toward him so fast that he barely kept from being run over, other times refusing to budge no matter how he pulled, cursed, or kicked at it. By the time he reached the rostrum and climbed the stairs to present the cord to Tanalasta, the ballroom was shaking with laughter.

Tanalasta beamed, for she and Owden had worked out the act together, spending much of her last tenday in Huthduth choreographing every move. She thanked the Harvestmaster for his hard work, then presented the rope to her chuckling father.

"You have but to pull the cord, Sire."

"If I dare!" Azoun chuckled. He stood as though bracing himself for an onslaught, then jerked the cord.

The walls of the box fell instantly away, revealing twelve guilty-looking monks on a small pedalcart crowded with large earthenware kettles. As the audience erupted into guffaws, two of the priests leaped off the cart and placed a pair of pots on the lowest step of the rostrum, then spoke a quick prayer to Chauntea. By the time they had finished, two more monks were placing another pair of pots on the next step.

As this duo spoke their prayers, a pair of small trees sprouted from the first two kettles and began to grow before the eyes of the astonished crowd. Another team of priests ascended the rostrum and placed their pots on the third stair, and so it continued until a pair of pots had been placed on every step. The trees blossomed as they grew, drawing gasps of wonder and delight from everyone in the room save Vangerdahast, who regarded the whole display with an air of wary impatience.

The last blossoms had barely appeared before the limbs of the first trees began to grow heavy with fruit. Smiling in delight, the king descended three steps and plucked a pear from the branch, then bit into it with relish.

"The sweetest fruit I have ever tasted!" he announced. The king used his sleeve to wipe the juices from his beard, then climbed the stairs back to Tanalasta. "A most excellent gift, Princess. We thank you for this wondrous orchard of mountain fruit trees!"

Tanalasta smiled and curtsied. "You are very welcome, Majesty, but I fear the trees will fade as quickly as they grew. It is not the orchard I am giving you. It is the priests."

Azoun's smile grew confused. "The priests?" He looked from her to Harvestmaster Foley to the twelve monks waiting to collect the dying trees, then finally leaned close to Tanalasta's ear. "I don't understand, my dear.

Surely, you don't mean to say that you have brought me slaves?"

"Hardly." Buoyed by the success of Owden's entrance, Tanalasta spoke loud enough for the crowd to hear. "I have persuaded Harvestmaster Foley and his priests to return home with us to establish the Royal Temple of Chauntea."

Azoun's expression changed from one of confusion to one of shock, and Vangerdahast stepped to the king's side at once.

"The *Royal* Temple of Chauntea?" the old wizard gasped. "She can't be serious!"

"I am quite serious." Tanalasta ignored the ire in Vangerdahast's voice and spoke directly to the nobles below. "The Royal Temple is established to ensure the health of all lands in Cormyr. We shall start with those blighted fields right here in the north."

3

he music of the final allemande still rippling through his mind, Vangerdahast sat hunched in one of the Marliirs' overstuffed wing chairs, frowning peevishly at the cold ache in his old joints. The clatter outside had all but died as the last of the guests' carriages departed the courtyard below, and still Azoun insisted on pacing back and forth between him and the warmth of the crackling fire.

"See here, Majesty, you're going to have to quit that." Vangerdahast wagged a gnarled finger at his liege's feet. "An old man needs his fire."

Azoun stopped directly in front of the hearth and faced him. "What could she be thinking?"

"I wouldn't know," Vangerdahast said. "Perhaps His Highness forgets that he forbade me from reading her mind?"

"That doesn't mean you don't," said Filfaeril, rising from where she had been resting on the royal magician's bed.

Vangerdahast ignored the queen's remark and muttered a few arcane syllables, then made a series of quick gestures with his fingers. Azoun did not seem to notice as he floated away from the fireplace, then slipped around to stand beside the chair.

"I'm beginning to worry about what kind of queen Tanalasta is going to make," said Azoun. "First Bleth nearly tricks her into giving away the throne—"

"Tanalasta was not the only one fooled by Aunadar," said Filfaeril. Still dressed in the violet gown she had worn to the ball, she took a seat in the chair next to Vangerdahast. "As I recall, we were quite keen on the man ourselves. Had I not slipped him into the library at an opportune moment, nor had you invited him on the hunt that day, Tanalasta would never have given him a second look."

A pained look came to the king's eye. "Just because a man wants to know his daughter's suitors does not mean he is thrusting them on her."

"No more than we have been thrusting poor Dauneth on her." Filfaeril shot a glance at Vangerdahast, who pretended not to notice and continued to gaze into the fire. "It is no wonder his mother assumed more than she should have."

Azoun nodded. "Yes, I suppose that mess was my fault—but a father can encourage, can't he? I only want to see her happy."

"Happily married," Filfaeril said, "and pregnant with an heir."

Azoun shot his wife a rare frown. "Happy first."

"Regardless of the cost to Cormyr?" the queen asked.

Azoun thought for a moment, then said, "The price of the realm's good does not have to be Tanalasta's happiness. Perhaps it is time I realized her calling may not lie in being a ruler."

Vangerdahast was so surprised that he nearly choked on his own saliva. Of course, the same thought had been in the back of everyone's mind since Tanalasta's embarrassment in the Abraxus Affair, but this was the first time Azoun had voiced it aloud.

Filfaeril did not seem so shocked. She merely raised a brow, then spoke in an eerily neutral voice. "That would be a big decision."

"But not necessarily a hard one. Tanalasta is thirty-six years old. By the time you were her age, she was already fifteen, and Foril would have been . . ." Azoun did not finish, for neither he nor his queen liked to dwell on the loss of their young son. "Perhaps Tanalasta would be happier without the burden of producing an heir."

"Perhaps," Filfaeril allowed. "She is approaching the age when the choice may no longer be hers, and we must also think of the kingdom."

Vangerdahast's heart sank. Until now, the queen had always been Tanalasta's greatest supporter, maintaining that the princess would grow into her responsibilities when the time came. If even Filfaeril had lost faith in her eldest daughter, then what support could Tanalasta have left in the rest of the kingdom?

Azoun stepped over to the hearth and stared into the flames, blocking Vangerdahast's heat. "Tanalasta isn't the same. She may have been naive before that Bleth trouble, but she was hardly stupid. Now . . ." The king let the sentence trail, shaking his head in dismay. "Embarrassing Lady Marliir like that was bad enough."

"Majesty, we must recall that Tanalasta had some—ah—help in that," Vangerdahast said. "I seem to recall shaking my head as you turned to start up the rostrum."

Azoun regarded Vangerdahast with a look of puzzlement. "I thought you were at odds with the crown princess."

"I do not always agree with you either."

"Nor do the two of you seek every opportunity to vex each other," said Filfaeril. "So why are you defending her now?"

"Because fairness demands it," said Vangerdahast. "She was merely standing up for herself in an unfair circumstance."

"Unfair?" Filfaeril's eyes narrowed to ice-blue slits. "What game are you playing at now, old trickster? You were the one who said we should give destiny a push and ask the Marliirs to host the king's party."

Vangerdahast felt the heat rising to his face, but it was impossible to disguise the reaction with both royals watching him so closely. In a voice as casual as possible, he said, "I may have pushed rather too hard, milady."

" 'Rather too hard?' " Filfaeril demanded. "If you cast any spells on them—"

"Of course not!" Vangerdahast was truly indignant. "Would I use magic to manipulate the princess's emotions?"

"Only as a last resort," Azoun growled. "So tell us what you *did* do."

"It was but a little thing." Vangerdahast held up his hand, pressing together his thumb and forefinger to illustrate. "Merely a matter of a few words, really."

"Whispered into whose ear?" Filfaeril asked. "Lady Marliir's?"

"For one," Vangerdahast said. "But that really isn't important."

"No wonder Tanalasta has so little use for you!" The king shook his head in disbelief. "That doesn't excuse this royal temple nonsense. Half the nobles in the land will convert to Chauntea merely to win favor at court, and the other half will take up arms to defend their own faiths. How can she expect me to let this happen?"

"Because if you don't, her reputation will be ruined," Filfaeril said. She went over to stare into the flames, and now Vangerdahast was completely blocked off from the warmth of the fire. "Forgive me for saying so, Azoun, but I think we're the dense ones here. Our daughter knows exactly what she's doing."

Azoun furrowed his brow. "Let us assume that is so— but to what purpose?"

"To force our hand, of course," said Filfaeril. "Obviously, she does not wish to be queen."

Vangerdahast was up and standing between the royals in an instant. "Let us not leap to conclusions, milady! No one has heard Tanalasta say any such thing."

The queen whirled on him with a vehemence that, until that moment, had been reserved for poisoners and plotters. "What do you care, you old meddler? You've never wanted Tanalasta to be queen, not since the day she crawled onto Alaphondar's lap instead of yours."

Vangerdahast forced himself to stand fast in the face of her fury, and in that moment he saw the first hint of frailty he had observed in the queen's character in more than forty years of knowing her. It was not the princess who had reservations about ascending the throne, but Filfaeril herself who wanted Tanalasta to rebuff the crown. The queen simply could not bear the thought of the grief and sacrifice her bookish daughter would suffer in having to become something so much larger than she was by her own nature.

Had the old wizard known her feelings a year earlier, before leaving on his journey with Tanalasta, perhaps he could have honored her wishes. Filfaeril was the closest thing he had to a sister or a wife or a mistress, and he would not have hurt her for all the treasure in the Thousand Worlds, but it was too late now. Screwing on his most enigmatic glower, the wizard met the queen's furious gaze with an angry conviction he did not quite feel.

"What you say simply is not true, milady. If I have been hard on the princess, it is only because you and the king have been too soft on her."

Filfaeril's eyes flashed white. "What are you saying, Magician?"

"That you spoiled your daughter, Majesty—a sin pardonable enough, except that she happened to be the crown princess of Cormyr."

"How dare you!"

Filfaeril's hand flew up so quickly that it would surely have sent Vangerdahast sprawling, had Azoun not caught her wrist.

"Not yet, my dear." Azoun's eyes were as angry as those of his wife. "First, I'd like him to explain himself."

Breathing an inward sigh of relief, Vangerdahast turned to the king and inclined his head. Azoun, at least, would not strike unless he meant to kill.

"It is simple enough, Highness," he said. "Between childhood and adulthood is rebellion. You and the queen have been loving parents but not stern, and so your daughters had no one to rebel against. I am privileged to be that person for Tanalasta."

"So you have been deliberately provoking her?" Filfaeril demanded.

"Quite," Vangerdahast said, almost proudly. "I would say I've done rather well, wouldn't you?"

Again, Azoun's quick hand was all that kept the queen's fist from knocking the old wizard off his feet. Vangerdahast's heart broke a little as he realized that the fury in her eyes would not soon fade. Still, one sometimes had to pay a steep price for always being right.

"I want it stopped," said Azoun. "It isn't working anyway."

"I'm afraid it can't be stopped." Vangerdahast did not relish saying that to the king. "Now that it has been stirred, Tanalasta's fury will not simply fade away—not when it has been corked up inside her for twenty years. This thing will have to run its course now, and it's better that she is angry at me than at you. That way, we avoid the possibility of treason."

"Have you lost your mind?" Filfaeril screeched. "Treason? From Tanalasta?"

"That won't happen," Vangerdahast assured her. "As I said, matters are well under control. Tanalasta will develop into a splendid queen."

"Like bloody hell she will!" Azoun said. "I suppose the next thing you'll tell me is that I should let her have this Royal Temple of Chauntea?"

"Of course not. I didn't expect that." Vangerdahast was struggling to keep hold of his own patience. "But I'll have to be the one to deal with it. If you start trying to deny her at this stage—"

"I am the king!" Azoun roared. "I'll do what's best for Cormyr, and if that means telling the crown princess she can't have a royal temple to play with, then I will!"

"To 'play with?' " Vangerdahast rolled his eyes. "That's what I'm talking about. She's not a little girl, Majesty. She's a thirty-six year old princess who needs a suitable husband—and fast."

"I don't like this, Azoun." Filfaeril turned from the fireplace and started across the room, toward the door that led to their suite of rooms. "What does a wizard know about raising children? I understand my daughter. She doesn't want to be queen, and I say we don't make her. Alusair is a year younger anyway."

"Alusair?" Vangerdahast gasped, finally losing control of himself. "And who is going to make *her* be queen? She doesn't want it at all, and I couldn't even begin to address her problems."

"Vangerdahast's right about that, I'm afraid." Azoun was speaking to his wife's departing back. "If we don't want to make Tanalasta do it, it's hardly fair to make Alusair do it either."

"Then perhaps you will have to father another heir, my husband, one that Vangerdahast can mold into a proper monarch." Filfaeril's voice was as icy as her glare. "But I fear you will need a younger queen for that. One a decade the junior of your daughters, so you can be certain of the matter."

Filfaeril turned and pulled the door shut behind her.

Azoun sighed and sank into the chair she had vacated, then tossed his crown onto the floor and began to rub his forehead.

"Vangerdahast, please tell me that you have some idea what you're doing here."

"Of course, Sire. You may recall that I helped guide you through—"

The wizard was interrupted by nervous rapping at the door, then Alaphondar Emmarask poked his head into the chamber. His long white hair was more disheveled than usual, and the expression on his face was atypically frazzled.

"Pray excuse my interruption, Sire, but a rather spontaneous flood of high priests seems to be, well, *appearing* in the Marliir courtyard."

"No doubt offering to establish Royal Temples of their own," Azoun surmised.

The Sage Most Learned glanced at the floor. "I would say they are doing rather more than offering."

"And so it starts." The king exhaled heavily, then snatched his crown off the floor. "Is there anything else?"

"Yes, sire. Merula the Marvelous begs leave to consult with Vangerdahast regarding the hazard that will be caused by a subversion of the War Wizards in favor of a religious—"

"Tell Merula I will speak with him later," interrupted Vangerdahast, "and assure him the War Wizards' influence is not threatened."

Azoun glanced at Vangerdahast from the corner of his eye. "Quite sure of ourselves, aren't we?"

"Quite," the wizard replied, voicing more conviction than he felt.

The Sage Most Learned still did not leave.

"Something else?" Azoun asked.

"I'm afraid so, Majesty. Duke Marliir is demanding an audience," said Alaphondar. "He's angry about being asked to host a party so Princess Tanalasta could announce she would *not* be marrying his son."

"Of course. Show him in." Azoun sighed heavily, twirling the crown on his fingers, then looked up at Vangerdahast. "Lord Magician, by the time we finish today, I am sure you will have a plan for untangling this brilliant mess you've made."

"Of course, Sire." Vangerdahast took the crown, then placed it on Azoun's head at an angle just jaunty enough to make it appear the king had been celebrating his birthday a little too hard. "Whatever you command."

* * * * *

The stables smelled of straw and leather and predawn dew, and of the many other joys of honest labor that had remained so carefully hidden from Tanalasta throughout much of her life. She would miss the odor of toil when she returned to Suzail, but at least she would know where to find it again when the palace's bouquet of perfume and prevarication grew overwhelming. Tanalasta slipped the breast collar over the mule's neck, then buckled it into place and passed the reins to Harvestmaster Foley, sitting above her on the driver's bench. The rest of the priests were kneeling in the wagon cargo bed with their tools and gear, eager for the day's work to begin.

The crunch of approaching feet sounded from the stable yard outside. Tanalasta turned to see her parents advancing through the early morning gloom, Vangerdahast and the usual entourage of guards in tow. Though the sun would be up in less than half an hour, their eyelids remained heavy with sleep and their hair uncombed.

"The king and queen," Owden gasped, "and they don't look happy."

"I wouldn't read much into their appearance," Tanalasta said. "It's not the palace's custom to rise before the sun." Not so long ago, Tanalasta too would have regarded a predawn rising as an interruption of the choicest pillow time. "I'm sure Vangerdahast spent the night bending their ears about the royal temple."

A distressed look came to Owden's face, but Tanalasta gave him a reassuring smile and went outside to meet her parents.

"Your Majesties, I did not expect to see you up so early."

"No? Then you were hoping to sneak out under cover of darkness?"

The king made his query sound like a joke, but there was a bitter edge to the question, and Tanalasta could sense the schism between her parents and the royal magician. Though the trio was normally close-knit, Azoun and Vangey barely looked at each other, and her mother stood a little apart from both of them. Tanalasta curtsied, acknowledging the irritation in her father's tone.

"It is the custom of Chauntea's folk to start early." As Tanalasta spoke, the royal guards formed a small circle around the group, lest any of the Marliir stable boys scurrying through the gray morning pause to eavesdrop. "We have had disturbing news from Tyrluk. The blight has broken out in ten places around the village, and the crop was already half lost before the messenger left town."

Owden Foley stepped gingerly past a guard to come up beside Tanalasta. "At that rate, Majesty, every field between the High Road and the Storm Horns will be a total loss within the tenday."

"That is why we keep the royal granaries full." Azoun ignored the Harvestmaster and continued to focus on Tanalasta. "We have not seen the princess in over a year. I would really rather she didn't run off—"

"Within a tenday, you say?" Vangerdahast interrupted, stepping past Azoun toward Owden. "That is exceedingly fast, is it not?"

Owden nodded grimly. "The fastest I have ever seen. If we do not move quickly, the whole of Cormyr could lose its crop."

"Truly?" Vangerdahast ran his fingers through his long beard, then turned to the royal couple. "Majesties, we may have a situation here worthy of our closest attention."

Azoun frowned in confusion. "Just yesterday, you told me that Merula the Marvelous—"

"I fear Tanalasta may have been right about him," Vangerdahast said, again interrupting. "Unless you want a dragon blasted apart or a company of orcs put to sleep, Merula the Marvelous *is* a bit of a wand waver."

The king and queen exchanged perplexed glances, then Filfaeril asked, "I beg your pardon?"

"Merula wouldn't know a blight from a blotch," said Vangerdahast. "He assured me the disease would never escape the mountains, and the next day here it is in Tyrluk. When it comes to plants, we might be better to put our faith in the judgment of the good Harvestmaster."

Tanalasta wondered what trick Vangerdahast was working now, then frowned as the old pettifogger turned to address Owden.

"Harvestmaster Foley, what would you say is the origin of this blight?"

"It appeared first in the mountains, and it molds the roots just below the surface." Owden rubbed his chin thoughtfully, then said, "It may very well be some sort of cave fungus—carried by orcs, I imagine. The filthy creatures spend a lot of time crawling about in caverns, and a wandering band would explain why the disease seems to be jumping around."

"Excellent observation, Owden . . . if I may be so informal," said Vangerdahast.

"Of course, Lord Magician," said Owden.

"Vangerdahast, please, or Vangey if you prefer. We really don't stand on ceremony in private." The old wizard cast a sidelong glance at Tanalasta, then added, "As you may be aware, sometimes I am even referred to as 'that damned old staff-swinger.'"

"Really? I hadn't heard that," said Owden, lying beautifully. Tanalasta had spent her first tenday or so at Huthduth complaining about the wizard and doing very little else, and she considered it a tribute to the harvestmaster's patience that she had not been asked to leave. "The princess always referred to you in a rather fatherly fashion."

"How kind of you to say so."

Suspicious of Vangerdahast's polite tone, Tanalasta studied her parents for hints as to why the royal magician was trying to befriend Owden. Even in the rosy dawn light now spilling across the stable yard gate, their expressions betrayed nothing beyond the same confusion she felt.

Vangerdahast turned to the king. "Majesty, perhaps we should send word to High Horn to triple their orc patrols and see to it that the beasts are kept far clear of Cormyr. If I may borrow a few scouts from the Purple Dragons, I'll also have the War Wizards send out teams to seal the mouths of any caverns the orcs have been inhabiting."

"And you'll claim it was the War Wizards who stopped the blight," Tanalasta surmised. "I see what you're doing, you old thief."

Vangerdahast turned to her with an innocent expression. "I am trying to stop the blight," he said. "I thought that was what you wanted."

"Of course," said Tanalasta, "but if you think you can use Owden's knowledge to steal the credit from the Royal Temple—"

"Vangerdahast isn't stealing the credit from anybody," said Azoun. "There isn't going to be any Royal Temple."

"What?" Tanalasta whirled on her father so fast that several bodyguards glanced reflexively over their shoulders. "You let Vangerdahast talk you out of it without hearing me first? That's hardly fair."

"Actually, Vangerdahast never said a word against the Royal Temple," said the king. "Your mother and I had barely retired from the ball before high priests began to fill the Marliir's foyer, all insisting that the palace establish royal temples to their own gods and goddesses."

"Why shouldn't we?" Tanalasta asked evenly. Owden stood at her side looking serene. They had decided earlier that their best strategy in an argument would be for Owden to maintain an air of patient confidence. "As long as each church pays its own costs, what harm can it do to curry the favor of the gods?"

Filfaeril regarded Tanalasta as though she were mad. "Curry favor from the Prince of Lies? Or the Maiden of Pain?" The queen shook her head in disbelief. "Perhaps you should be Loviatar's first royal acolyte. You're certainly causing your parents enough anguish."

Tanalasta fell silent, not because she had failed to anticipate the argument, but because she was surprised to hear the queen voicing it instead of Vangerdahast. Before, her mother had always supported her against the wizard, and it shook her confidence to see the normal order of things reversed. She smiled at a gawking stable boy stumbling past with two buckets of warm goat's milk, then returned her attention to the queen.

"The term 'royal' implies the sponsorship of an Obarskyr, does it not?" Tanalasta did not put as much acid as she had planned into the question, for she could not quite bring herself to speak to the queen in such tones. "I have faith enough in our family to think that even Cyric's new Seraph of Lies could not arrange such a thing."

"And I share that faith," said Azoun. In contrast to Filfaeril, the king spoke in a patient, if firm, voice. "But other considerations take precedence. First, you know how the nobles make a vogue of anything we do."

"There are worse fads to start," Tanalasta said.

"Perhaps, but we must also think of the War Wizards. They will take it as a grave insult to their skill and loyalty if the crown suddenly finds it necessary to establish another corps of magic-users."

"And the crown princess should not need to be told of the War Wizards' importance to the realm," added the queen. The dawn had finally turned yellow, and in its golden light Filfaeril looked more like an angry celestial seraph than Tanalasta's mother. "Nor of the dangers of undermining their value by creating a divisive atmosphere. Already this morning, I have heard several wizards refer to your priests as 'spell-beggars' and 'mommy's boys.'"

Vangerdahast gave Owden an apologetic nod. "No offense, of course. I'll have a word with them about such epithets."

"Not necessary," said the harvestmaster, not quite managing to mask the indignity in his voice. "Their jealous—ah—resentment is understandable."

Vangerdahast only smiled at what everyone knew to be an intentional slip of the tongue, and Tanalasta began to fear that her mother's argument had merit. If Owden could not handle Vangerdahast on his best behavior, she shuddered to think of the enmity that would be unleashed when the old guttermouth gave himself free rein.

Tanalasta addressed herself to the queen. "If the crown must fear the consequences of the War Wizards' anger, then perhaps they are not as great an asset to the realm as we believe." She smiled in Vangerdahast's direction. "I am sure we may be confident of the royal magician's ability to keep them under control. Really, it would be a shame to let petty politics prevent us from doing what is best for the realm. Vangerdahast himself has pointed out that only the priests of Chauntea can deal with crises such as this."

Even on his best behavior, this was a bit too much for Vangerdahast. "That is not quite what I said, young lady. A small crop blight is hardly a crisis for a kingdom like Cormyr."

"Nor do we want to make it seem like one," said Azoun. "Creating a new organization to respond to it is bound to do just that. It could cause a general panic that would lead to hoarding, thievery, and profiteering. I'm sorry, Tanalasta. You'll have to announce that Chauntea called Owden and his priests back to Huthduth."

"But she hasn't," Tanalasta said. "The goddess wouldn't do such a thing."

"It's no reflection on Owden or Chauntea, or even on your decision to venerate the All Mother," said Filfaeril. "This simply isn't the time to establish a royal temple. You shouldn't have announced it without discussing it with us first, and I'm sure you know that. Trying to force this on us is unforgivable—as unforgivable as Vangey's attempt to embarrass you into taking a husband before it is too late."

"Too late?" Tanalasta fairly shrieked the words, for her mother had touched a tender chord. She turned to Vangerdahast. "So that's how it is. You would turn my own parents against me to get what you want."

Vangerdahast arched his bushy eyebrows, and something like sorrow seemed to flash in his dark eyes. "I am sorry, milady, but I have no idea what you mean."

"A marriage for a royal temple. Is that to be the agreement?" Tanalasta looked to her parents. "If a child is the only thing I am permitted to give the realm, then at least let me do that well. Trust me, it would be better to leave my field fallow than to plow it with a man I do not love."

Azoun paled and glanced around the stable yard, then, with a few quick nods, signaled the guards to clear it. Filfaeril's reaction was different. Though her eyes filled with tears, she flashed Tanalasta the same icy glare that had crushed razor-tongued duchesses and iron-willed army marshals.

"Your father's decision has nothing to do with anything Vangerdahast may have said." Filfaeril's voice cracked, but she stepped closer to her daughter and continued in an even harsher tone. "The king is thinking of Cormyr. It is time for you to stop being so selfish and do the same thing."

Vangerdahast's eyes grew wide. "Your Majesty, you mustn't."

A small wad of cotton appeared in the wizard's hand, but Filfaeril's hand was clamped on his wrist before he could speak his incantation.

"Vangerdahast!" Filfaeril's tone was threatening. "If you cast that silence spell, even Azoun will not have the power to keep your head on your shoulders."

The wad vanished into the wizard's sleeve. "Filfaeril, I beg you. You're making a mistake."

"Perhaps, but she has had twenty years to find a husband she likes." The queen turned back to Tanalasta. "Now she will settle for Dauneth Marliir."

Owden Foley stepped to the queen's side. "Your Majesty, if I may, there is something you should know."

"Owden, no!" Tanalasta grasped the harvestmaster's shoulder and shoved him toward a guard. "This man is dismissed."

"Not yet," said the king. He gestured to Owden. "Is there something we should know about Tanalasta's condition?"

" 'Condition,' father?" Tanalasta said. "If there were something I thought you should—"

"I was talking to Owden," said Azoun.

Tanalasta glared at the priest furiously. "You heard the king's command."

Owden swallowed hard, then looked back to Azoun. "Sire, I think you should know that your daughter thinks of nothing but Cormyr. In fact, when Lady Marliir's invitation arrived at Huthduth, she told me that she would be returning to Cormyr to wed a man she did not love."

"Then why isn't she?" demanded Filfaeril.

"I'm afraid that is my fault." Owden looked at his feet. "I advised her that she would be a better queen for Cormyr if she waited until she found a man she loved."

Tanalasta had to struggle to keep her surprise hidden, for she had not realized quite how effective a liar the harvestmaster could be. The truth was that Owden had wished her well and said that by all accounts Dauneth Marliir was a fine man. Then she had sneaked out for one last hike and experienced her vision, and there had been no need for Owden Foley to convince the princess of anything.

Filfaeril narrowed her eyes at the harvestmaster's explanation. "Under the circumstances, your advice could be considered treason."

"Or sound advice." Azoun cast a stern eye in the direction of both Filfaeril and Vangerdahast. "That is for Tanalasta to determine, and Tanalasta alone. What is not for her to decide is the fate of the royal temple. She will announce that Chauntea's priests have been called back to Huthduth."

Vangerdahast shook his head vehemently. "But Your Majesty . . ."

Azoun raised his hand. "And we will trust our war wizards to deal with the blight. Even if they take somewhat longer to stop it, the people of Cormyr will take comfort from their presence."

Tanalasta's thoughts began to spin. Filfaeril's harsh words had left her so hurt and disoriented that she found it impossible to concentrate, and she could not help feeling she must have done something terrible to make the queen so angry with her. Nor could she take comfort from Vangerdahast's unexpected support. She had seen his cobra's smile charm too many foes to fall prey to its poison herself.

Azoun nodded to Owden. "We thank you for coming all this way, Harvestmaster, but you may take your priests and return to Huthduth. Tanalasta will see to an explanation."

Owden's face showed his disappointment, but he bowed deeply to show his obedience, then turned and grasped Tanalasta's hands in farewell. As the harvestmaster said his good-byes, his words barely registered, for she suddenly felt her mother's gaze and looked over to see Filfaeril's pale eyes glaring at her. The ice in the queen's expression caused her to recoil involuntarily, and Tanalasta's earlier fury returned tenfold. No matter what her mother believed, the princess was doing the best thing for Cormyr, and allowing anyone to tell her otherwise would bring disaster down on the kingdom.

When Owden started toward the stable, Tanalasta caught him by the arms. "Harvestmaster Foley, the king is wrong. I am not going to explain your departure."

Azoun's face grew instantly stormy. "You are defying me?"

Tanalasta glanced toward her mother and noticed the queen's lower lip beginning to quiver, then nodded. "I must follow my convictions, Sire."

Owden's face grew as pale as the king's was red. "Princess Tanalasta, there is no need to argue—"

"But there is, Harvestmaster," said Tanalasta. "Cormyr has need of you and your priests—now, and in the future."

"I am king," Azoun said in that even voice he used when he was angered almost beyond control. "My convictions determine what Cormyr needs."

"And what happens when you are gone, father? Am I to have Vangerdahast rouse you from your rest to see what is best for the realm?" Tanalasta shook her head. "I must do what I believe to be right—now, because I am certain of it, and in the future, because I will have no other choice."

Vangerdahast sighed heavily and muttered something indiscernible, and Filfaeril's hand rose to her mouth. The anger vanished from her eyes, only to return a moment later when she looked in Vangerdahast's direction. Azoun merely stared at Tanalasta, his eyes growing steadily darker as he tried to bring his temper under control.

Finally, he said, "Perhaps I can spare you that burden, Princess. I have two daughters."

Tanalasta struggled to keep from staggering back. "I know that."

"Good," said the king. "Vangerdahast has been unable to contact Alusair. You will take your priests and ride into the Stonelands to find her. You will tell her that I have something important to say to her. She is to return to Arabel in all possible haste, and she is to guard her life as carefully as that of any crown heir."

With that, Azoun spun on his heel and marched back toward the manor house, leaving Vangerdahast and

Filfaeril standing gape-mouthed behind him. Tears began to trickle down the queen's face. She started to reach out for Tanalasta, then suddenly pulled her arms back and whirled on the royal magician.

"Damn you." Her voice was calm and even and all the more frightening. "Damn you for a lying child of Cyric!"

Vangerdahast's shoulders slumped, and he suddenly seemed as old as Cormyr itself. "I told you it was too late," he whispered. The rims of his baggy eyes grew red and wet, and he looked at his wrinkled old arms as though it took a conscious act of will not to grasp the queen's hands. "I'll go with her. I'll be there every step of the way."

"Should that comfort me?" The queen glanced again at Tanalasta, then turned and scurried after Azoun.

Tanalasta stood where she was, trying to puzzle out what had just happened, and felt Owden grasp her arm. She quickly shook him off. To her astonishment, she did not need his support.

She felt stronger than at any other time in her life.

65

4

There would be no turnips for LastRest this year.

A mat of ash-colored mold covered the field, filling the air with a smell of must and rot so foul that Tanalasta had to cover her mouth to keep from retching. Little mounds of gray marked where the stalks had pushed up through the earth, but nothing could be seen of the plants themselves. At the far edge of the field, a free farmer and his family were busy loading the contents of their hut into an ox-drawn cart.

"By the Sacred Harrow!" cursed Owden. "What an abomination!"

"It is a sad sight," agreed Tanalasta. She motioned the commander of her Purple Dragon escort to set a perimeter around the area, then urged her horse forward. "Strange we have seen no other sign of blight in the area."

"Strange indeed," said Owden, following her along the edge of the field. "Why would the orcs raid this grange, when it is so much closer to town than others we have passed?"

"Perhaps they had a taste for turnips," Vangerdahast said, riding up beside Tanalasta. "I doubt even orcs know why they raid one farm instead of another."

"I am not as interested in *why* as *whether*," said Tanalasta. She had noticed the orc track a mile earlier, in the bed of a rocky creek they had been crossing. Over Vangerdahast's rather feeble objections, the princess had led the company upstream, following a patchy trail of overturned stones and sandy hoof prints to within a few paces of the blighted field. Now that she saw the farmer's undamaged hut, however, she wondered if the place had been raided at all. She pointed at the little house. "It's not like orcs to spare such a defenseless target."

"Now you are troubled that they *didn't* raze some shack?" Vangerdahast looked to the heavens for patience. "Aren't you wasting enough of our time without fretting over such things? The king sent us north to find Alusair—"

"And you are certain these farmers can't help us?" Tanalasta stared at the old wizard evenly. "I know why the king sent us north, and it has less to do with finding Alusair than getting me out of Arabel. I doubt he would object to our taking the time to determine if these orcs are the ones spreading the blight."

"Very well," Vangerdahast sighed, giving up the argument far too easily, "but we won't be going after them."

Tanalasta studied the wizard thoughtfully. She had spent the last two days alternately trying to puzzle out his game and feeling oddly pleased with herself. She did not know whether her father had been serious about naming a new heir, but she now realized she did not care. As they had ridden out of Arabel, an unexpected sense of relief came over her, and she took the feeling to mean she had never wanted to rule Cormyr at all.

Later, as she grew accustomed to her new status, she began to experience vague sensations of loss and came to understand that what she felt was not relief, but pride. For the first time in her life, she had staked her whole future on her own conviction. The possibility that in the process she had thrown away a kingdom did not frighten her—it made her feel strong.

Once Tanalasta came to that realization, it grew easier to focus on Vangerdahast's strange behavior. Given his attitude toward her recently, she would have expected him to endorse her replacement as heir. Yet he seemed quite disturbed by the king's pronouncement, and since then he had been almost civil to her. She would have to be careful. Vangerdahast was definitely plotting something, and he was at his most dangerous when cordial.

After a time, Vangerdahast raised one of his bushy eyebrows and asked, "Well? Do we have a bargain, or must I slip you into a bag of holding for the rest of the trip?"

"That won't be necessary," Tanalasta replied. "I'm no orc-hunter. I only want to find out what they did to this grange."

As Tanalasta and her company rounded the corner of the field, the farmer sent his family into the hut, then turned to curtly salute his visitors. Despite his tattered tunic and mane of untrimmed hair, the princess felt certain he had once been a soldier—probably an ex-Purple Dragon who had accepted a tract of frontier land in lieu o' mustering out pay.

As she approached the man, Tanalasta slipped her signet ring into her pocket, then returned his salute somewhat awkwardly. As a princess, she normally ignored military protocol, but her company was traveling disguised as a Purple Dragon patrol. Like Vangerdahast and Owden, Tanalasta wore the black weathercloak of a war wizard, while the twelve priests behind her were dressed in the capes and chain mail of common dragoneers.

The farmer's eyes seemed to absorb all this in an instant, then he returned his gaze to Tanalasta. "Hag Gordon at your service, Lady Wizard. Didn't hear there was a new patrol assigned to Gnoll Pass."

"There isn't," Tanalasta replied. She could tell by Hag's tone that he had already deduced this was no ordinary company. "And you were with the . . . ?"

"The Hullack Venomeers." Hag's eyes shifted pointedly to the badgeless capes worn by Owden's priests, then he added, "Milady."

Tanalasta sensed that she was missing some subtlety of military decorum, but she could hardly reveal the true nature of her company. Even had she known Hag's loyalty to be beyond question, there was no need for him to know that the crown princess—or former crown princess—was riding about the realm protected only by a small escort of Purple Dragons. One simply did not reveal that sort of information casually.

Tanalasta gestured toward the far end of the man's field. "We were passing by when we noticed orc tracks in the creek."

"Orcs?" Hag's eyes widened. "There are no orcs this side of the pass."

"I know an orc track when I see one," Tanalasta insisted. "Even underwater. They love to wade. It makes it harder for the hounds to stay on their trail."

Hag raised his brow and studied her with a thoughtful air, and that was when Tanalasta realized her mistake. She turned to Owden and Vangerdahast.

"The orcs didn't cause this," she said, waving at the blighted field. "At least not the ones we've been following."

Owden frowned, looking from the princess to the ruined field. "It must be. The coincidence is—"

"Just a coincidence—or related in some way we don't understand," she said. "Even in a slow current, the tracks in the stream couldn't be more than a few hours old."

"And my turnips started molding a tenday ago," added Hag, clearly making the connection between Tanalasta's inquiries and the condition of his field. "What are you looking for?"

"As a former sergeant in the Hullack Venomeers, you should know better than to ask such questions," said Vangerdahast. While the rebuke failed to intimidate Hag, it did impress Tanalasta. It seemed impossible that even Vangerdahast could know the rank of every man who had served in the Purple Dragons. The wizard continued to glower at the man. "Had it been any of your concern, we would have explained the company's lack of insignia."

"And would you also have explained why your dragoneers carry maces where they should have swords? Whatever happened to my field, it's happening to others, and old Bolt-and-Blow must be scared to death."

Vangerdahast's face darkened to deep burgundy. "Bolt-and-Blow, Sergeant Gordon?"

"The royal magician," Hag explained.

Tanalasta had to bite her cheeks to keep from bursting into laughter, but Vangerdahast's complexion only continued to darken. If the sergeant realized how perilous it was to anger this particular war wizard, he showed no sign.

"Everyone knows how old Ringfingers clutches the reins of power." As he said this, Hag glanced at Vangerdahast's bejeweled hands, then stepped even closer. "He'd never muster a whole company of priests if this thing didn't scare him. If he's scared, so am I. So what happened to my field . . . sir?"

Vangey turned to Tanalasta, eyes bulging like red-veined eggshells, and said nothing. He didn't have to. One of her father's many misgivings about establishing a royal temple had been causing a needless panic, and now she could see why.

"I wouldn't read too much into the composition of the Badgeless Maces," said Tanalasta. Again, a glimmer of a frown flashed across the free farmer's face, and the princess could not help feeling that she was making some error of protocol that aroused the man's suspicions. "But as a former dragoneer, you are obliged to serve at the crown's recall. Must I invoke that obligation to secure your cooperation?"

Hag seemed no more intimidated by Tanalasta's threat than he had by Vangerdahast's blustering. "That duty is invoked by royal writ. If you can produce one, then I will gladly obey your command. Otherwise, I am entitled to as many answers as I give."

"Royal writ!" Vangerdahast spewed, reaching into his robe. "I'll writ you into a—!"

"The world has no need for more toads, Sir Wizard." Tanalasta motioned for Vangerdahast to hold his attack, then turned back to the stubborn farmer. "While I'm sure we can trust a former dragoneer to hold his tongue, can the same be said for his children?"

Tanalasta glanced toward the hut, where the man's family was peering through the cracked door. Hag's eyes lit with sudden comprehension, and he nodded gravely—exactly as the princess had hoped he would. She had not lived nearly four decades in the Palace of the Purple Dragon without developing at least some talent for making people feel special.

Hag gestured toward the nearest corner of his field. "Come with me," he said, "there's something you'll want to see."

"Of course." Tanalasta smiled and dismounted, thankful that at least some of her palace experience proved useful outside Suzail. She motioned to Owden and, somewhat reluctantly, Vangerdahast to follow. "Hag, since you have already deduced the true nature of our 'Purple Dragons,' would you care to have them do what they can to restore your field? I doubt they can save this year's harvest, but perhaps they can keep the blight from ruining the soil."

Hag's dismay showed in his face, and Tanalasta could tell that it had not even occurred to him that the field might be ruined forever.

"I'd be grateful for whatever they can do," he said. "It'll be hard enough doing city work this year without knowing I have to clear another field before spring."

Owden nodded to his priests. They dismounted and began to sort through the small assortment of tools piled in the farmer's cart, having left their own shovels and hoes back in Arabel. Despite the offer of help, Hag still did not seem inclined to volunteer any information. He led Tanalasta and her two companions to the corner of his field, then stopped and looked at them expectantly.

Tanalasta put her hands into the pockets of her weathercloak. "You must swear on your honor as a Purple Dragon to hold what I tell you in the strictest confidence." With a practiced motion, she slipped on two of the handful of magic rings that Vangerdahast had pressed on her before setting out from Arabel. "You may not tell even your wife."

"I swear," said Hag. "Not even my wife."

"Good. Clearly, you have realized by now that I am no war wizard, and that many of those traveling with me are not normal Purple Dragons."

Vangerdahast cleared his throat gruffly. "Milady, I hardly think this is wise—"

"But it *is* my decision, Lord Wizard." Tanalasta removed her hand from her pocket, displaying to Hag the hardened gold band of a Commander's Ring of the Purple Dragons. "I have no doubt that you also recognize this, and what it must mean for someone who wouldn't know a troop from a tulip to be wearing it."

"I know what it is, as you say," said Hag, "but I can't imagine why you'd be wearing one."

"Of course you can." Tanalasta motioned to the twelve priests already poking around at the edge of his field. "You've already guessed, and with little enough help from us. We're trying to stop this blight before it becomes a serious problem for Cormyr. To do that, we need to find the orcs who are spreading it."

Hag cocked an eyebrow and thought for a moment, then said, "I suppose it doesn't really matter who you are."

"Not if you value your tongue," Vangerdahast threatened.

The free farmer nodded reluctantly, then picked up a long stick. "You'll be wanting to see this." Talking as he worked, Hag began to scrape the mold away from the soft soil underneath. "He must have snuck up on us. The dogs didn't start barking until he was already in the field, and by the time I saw him, he was halfway across."

"Who?" asked Owden.

"Whoever left that." Hag pointed to a track he had uncovered. It was shaped like a man's bare foot, save that it was half-again too long, with the narrow line of a claw mark furrowing the ground in front of each toe.

"No orc made that track," Tanalasta said.

"He looked more like a beggar," said Hag. "A tall beggar, with a huge ragged cape and some sort of tattered hood. I was going to invite him to sleep in the goat shed, until he turned and I saw his eyes."

"His eyes?" Tanalasta asked.

"They were full of blood." Hag hesitated, then added, "And they . . . well . . . they had to be shining."

"Had to be?" Vangerdahast demanded. "Be specific, sergeant."

73

Hag's bearing grew a touch more proud and upright. "It was dark, Lord Wizard. He was really only a shadow, but I could see his eyes. They weren't bright, it's just that they were the only thing I could really see."

"Did he do anything threatening?" asked Tanalasta.

Hag flushed. "Not really . . . but he frightened me all the same. I set my dogs on him. They chased him over to the corner by where you came in, and that was the last I saw of them alive."

"How were they killed?" Vangerdahast asked.

"I couldn't say. In the morning, my son found them sleeping on the stream bank. They wouldn't wake up."

"You sent your son to look for them?" Owden asked.

"To call them," Hag said, bristling at the note of disapproval in the harvestmaster's voice. "My wife and I were busy in the field."

"The blight?" Tanalasta asked.

"A diagonal stripe right where he walked. We pulled every turnip within two paces of his footsteps, but the whole crop had wilted by evening." Hag gestured at the field. "You know the rest."

Owden and Vangerdahast exchanged worried looks, then the harvestmaster said, "It appears I was wrong about the orcs. I'm sorry."

Vangerdahast laid a hand on the harvestmaster's shoulder. "I wouldn't be too hard on myself. It was only a working theory, and a good one at that." He turned to Hag. "What else can you tell us about this vagabond?"

Hag shrugged. "Nothing. He came and went in the night, then everything just died."

"Came from where?" Vangerdahast demanded, scanning the rocky farmyard around them. "Went to whence?"

"It'll do no good to search for a trail now. There was a good wind two days ago," said Hag. "Besides, I looked after

Jarl found the dogs dead. The vagabond—or whatever he was—didn't leave any more tracks."

Tanalasta studied the surrounding area. The grange was located just a few hundred paces north of the tiny hamlet of LastRest, near where The Mountain Ride ascended the foothills of the Storm Horn Mountains into Gnoll Pass. The vegetation was alternately scrub willow and thin copses of beech, with plenty of boulders and stones to hint at the difficulty of clearing a pasture. It would have been hard for anyone to approach the field through so much brush without leaving some sign of his passage.

"I'm no scout, but I know how to look for a trail," said Hag, correctly interpreting Tanalasta's scrutiny of the area. "There were no broken twigs, no overturned stones—at least not that amounted to a trail."

Vangerdahast used his hand to trace a path from the far corner of the field to where they were standing, then turned to continue the line. He was pointing between two massive peaks just to the left of Gnoll Pass.

"The Stonelands," Tanalasta observed.

Vangerdahast nodded. "Well, I suppose that's no surprise. Nothing good has ever come from the Stonelands."

Owden turned to Hag. "Perhaps we can learn something about this stranger from the death of your dogs. Would you mind if I had a look at them?"

"If you want to dig them up." Hag pointed toward a mound on the far side of his goat shed.

Vangerdahast frowned and looked to Tanalasta. "I'm sure there is no need to remind you of our mission. We hardly have time to tarry here all afternoon while the good harvestmaster digs up those poor creatures."

"Of course not," Tanalasta said, starting for her horse, and motioning for the others to follow. "You and I will cross the Storm Horns with all due haste. The harvestmaster and his priests will stay here to learn what they can from Hag's field, then set off after this vagabond."

Now Vangerdahast really scowled. "It's hardly necessary to send them back. Either one of us can report—"

"Those are my orders," Tanalasta said. "And if you care to argue them, I can simply release the Badgeless Maces from the king's service. Of course, then I would also have to confiscate their cloaks, leaving them to ride about the realm asking questions and chasing vagabonds without any disguise whatsoever."

"You wouldn't!"

"You think not?" Tanalasta reached her horse and took the reins from the young priest who had been holding it, then swung into the saddle. "Try me."

Vangerdahast did his best to warp his wrinkled face into a mask of outrage. "The king himself shall hear of this."

"I have no doubt. I suspect he might even be expecting it." Trying hard to suppress a smile, Tanalasta turned to Hag. "You have the thanks of the realm, and I hope the priests are able to save your field."

Hag bowed low. "And you have my thanks for trying. Rest assured that I shall keep your secrets—all of them."

"That is well for you," growled Vangerdahast, hoisting himself into his saddle. "You may be certain that I will be listening."

Hag bowed again, and this time his face had finally grown pale with intimidation. Tanalasta said her farewells to Owden, promising to meet him in Arabel within the space of two tendays, then signaled the real Purple Dragons to close the perimeter and resume their marching order.

As they rode down the creek toward the ford where Tanalasta had first noticed the orc tracks, Vangerdahast splashed up beside the princess and said, "You should know I'm serious about contacting your father. You can't keep flouting his wishes and expect him to forgive you."

"I'm more concerned about these orcs running around loose than my father's forgiveness." Tanalasta gestured at the stream bed. "Have you sent word to Castle Crag about them?"

"I . . . uh . . . certainly."

"Really, Vangerdahast?"

Vangerdahast's cheeks reddened above his beard. "I'm confident Lord Commander Tallsword has already sent a patrol to track them down."

"I'm sure he has." Tanalasta smiled to herself, then asked, "Tell me, when did you hear about that field?"

Vangerdahast looked confused. "Milady?"

"Hag Gordon's former rank," Tanalasta said. "How could you have known it, if Bren Tallsword hadn't already told you about the blighted field? I only hope the good sergeant wasn't part of the deception. I'd hate to think Harvestmaster Foley will be running around smashing in vagabond heads for no good reason."

Vangerdahast sighed wearily. "Unfortunately, I fear the harvestmaster will find plenty of reason. Bren Tallsword told me about the Gordon field three days ago, but today was the first I had heard about the vagabond—and yes, I have already contacted the Lord Commander and told him to watch for the man." The old wizard smiled, then added, "I have also asked him to do his best to keep your priest friends out of the king's sight."

"It's not father's sight that I'm worried about," said Tanalasta. "He has ears in as many places as you do."

Vangerdahast regarded her doubtfully. "A princess shouldn't exaggerate."

"What makes you think I am?" Tanalasta laughed. She fell silent for a time, quietly appreciating the kind of moment that she had not experienced with Vangerdahast since before her twentieth birthday, then said, "It won't work, you know."

"Princess?" Vangerdahast's wrinkled brow rose in a parody of innocence. "I'm sure I have no idea what you mean."

"I'm sure you do, but you won't trick me into changing my mind. I'm old enough to know what I believe in and what I don't."

"Truly?" The expression that came to Vangerdahast's face was one of genuine envy. "How nice that must be."

* * * * *

Azoun eyed the plate of liver-smeared wafers in Filfaeril's hand and his mouth instantly filled with a taste that could only be described as minted cow dung. He and the queen were attending their fifth reception in as many days, this one at the overdone mansion of the powerful Misrim merchant family, and he had grown so weary of the local delicacy that he could not even look at it without his gorge rising.

Pretending to listen earnestly to young Count Bhela's suggestion that the crown establish a system of cobble-paved merchant roads across the realm, Azoun caught his wife's eye and turned his head ever so slightly, signaling her to be rid of the ghastly stuff.

Filfaeril grinned viciously and glided to his side without stumbling or tripping or finding some other excuse to let even one of the awful canapés slide off the tray. She managed to interrupt young Bhela's diatribe with a flash of pearly teeth, accomplishing with a single smile what the king had been attempting in vain for the last half-hour, then pushed the platter forward. The smell of minted grease filled Azoun's nose, and he suddenly felt so ill that it took an act of will to keep his wineglass in his hand.

"Liverpaste, my dear?" Filfaeril asked. "It's quail."

"Love one!" Azoun took a wafer and bit into it, then chewed three quick times and swallowed quickly in a futile attempt to keep his tongue from registering the taste. "Excellent. Won't you have one, Count Bhela?"

Bhela's eyes grew as round as coins. "Off *your* plate, Majesty?"

Azoun nodded enthusiastically. "I know your family well enough to trust you won't slip me any poison."

Bhela eyed the wafers with unconcealed longing and nearly reached for one, then caught himself and shook his head. "It wouldn't be right, Sire. I'm only a count."

"Please, I insist."

Bhela's expression grew nervous, and he glanced around the room at all the other nobles who had been glaring at him for the last quarter hour.

"I beg you, Majesty. The superior lords will consider me haughty," he said. "In fact, you really should allow me to take my leave. They'll think I have been monopolizing your time."

"Yes, yes, of course. How mindless of me." Azoun dismissed him with a hearty clap on the shoulder, then sighed wearily. "Do send me a study on that idea of yours, Count. Imagine, cobbling an entire highway!"

"Within a tenday, Your Majesty."

Beaming with pride, Bhela bowed deeply to both the king and queen, then turned and strutted off to bask in the glow of his lengthy audience with the king. Filfaeril took another minted liverpaste off the plate and offered it to Azoun. He accepted the wafer with a smile, but held it between two fingers and allowed himself a generous swig of wine, trying to wash the lingering taste of the last one from his mouth.

"Eat up, my dear," urged Filfaeril. "You wouldn't want our hosts to think you fear poison."

Azoun lowered his glass, then concentrated on maintaining a pleasant smile as he spoke to his wife. "Show some mercy. I'll never get through this without your help."

"I am helping. If we are to repair the damage done by Tanalasta, we must be accessible to our nobles." Filfaeril looked across the chamber toward a boorish man in yellow stockings and crossed garters. "Isn't that Earl Hiloar? He has a wonderful plan for clear-cutting the Dragon Wood. I'll fetch him."

Azoun stuffed the minted liverpaste into his mouth whole, then caught Filfaeril by the elbow and said, "Not yet." Somehow, he managed to mumble the words without spewing wafer over her damask gown. He chewed half a dozen times and gagged the canapé down. "Tanalasta gave me no choice."

"You always have a choice. You're the king."

Azoun allowed himself a quick scowl. "You know better. And why are you angry with me, anyway? From the way you were inciting her, I thought you wanted a new heir."

"I want what is best for Tanalasta," Filfaeril countered. "Instead, you allowed Vangey to manipulate her into defying you."

"You helped."

"Not knowingly." Without taking her eyes off Azoun, the queen held out her free hand. A waiter scurried forward and placed a glass of wine in it, which she sipped until he had retreated out of earshot. "Vangey used me. Had I known how much she had changed, I would never have . . . I just didn't know how much she had changed."

"After the Abraxus Affair, I should think you would consider that a good thing," said Azoun. "*She* certainly does. So do I, and so does Vangerdahast."

"It will make her a stronger queen, yes," said Filfaeril, "but will it make her happy?"

A pang of sorrow shot through Azoun's breast, and he had to look away. He loved Tanalasta like any father loves a daughter, but the truth of the matter was that he could not concern himself with her happiness. The good of the realm demanded that he think only of making her a strong ruler. That was a steep price indeed to demand of any parent.

After a moment, he said, "Tanalasta was my favorite, you know. Always so eager to learn. You had only to tell her a thing once, and a year later she would repeat it back to you word for word. And so sweet. How her guileless smile would light the room. . . ."

"I remember." The queen's voice remained cold. "I fear what we loved best in her is what Vangey destroyed."

Azoun grew stoic. "The royal magician did what is best for the realm." He forced himself to meet Filfaeril's gaze, then said, "We were wrong to shelter the crown princess from the harsher side of royal life. Even had Aunadar Bleth never set foot in Suzail, Tanalasta's innocence would have served her poorly on the throne."

Filfaeril lowered her voice to an angry hiss. "And now that Vangerdahast has stolen her innocence, you do not like the result? *Now* you deny her the throne?"

"She has not lost the throne yet," said Azoun. "Tanalasta may still make a fine queen someday—provided she finds a man she can abide as a husband and stops being so headstrong about this business with Chauntea."

Filfaeril's pale eyes grew as hard as ice. "You and Vangey are the ones who made her. If you do not like what she has become, then it is your fault and not hers." The queen finished her wine in a gulp, then held the empty glass out for a servant. "Besides, how can you be sure she isn't right? The blight is spreading, you know."

"Yes, I know," said Azoun, "and Tanalasta is defying me in that, as well. There are reports from the Immerflow to the Starwater of Purple Dragons using Chauntea's magic to save blighted fields."

"Good." Filfaeril gave her glass to a waiter and waved him away, then thrust another liverpaste under Azoun's chin. "Enjoy."

Azoun had no choice but to accept the loathsome thing. As he began to nibble at it, the queen flashed a smile to Raynaar Marliir, signaling him to come forward. The king groaned inwardly, though he knew there was no avoiding this moment. He had heard that Marliir had put together an odd coalition of nobles, War Wizards, and high priests who wished to discuss "the destiny of the realm." Though he suspected they were less interested in discussing destiny than dictating it—specifically that of the crown princess— he would have to listen politely. The loyalty of the Marliir family was his strongest bulwark against Arabel's disagreeable habit of rebelling at the kingdom's most trying moments.

Azoun ran his tongue over his teeth to cleanse them of liverpaste, then smiled as broadly as he could. "Duke Marliir, how good to see you again. I trust Lady Marliir is feeling better."

"Sadly no," Raynaar answered curtly. "She is still bedridden with ague, or else she would certainly be in attendance today."

They had exchanged similar greetings on each of the previous four days. After Tanalasta's rejection of Dauneth, Merelda Marliir had fallen ghastly ill and asked the royal party to depart her home for the sake of its own health. Knowing he might well have to return to crush a revolt if he left so soon after the stir Tanalasta had caused, Azoun had seized on the northern blight as an excuse to remain another tenday, imposing on his Lord Governor, Myrmeen Lhal, to house the royal party in the city palace. He had then invited all the local notables to an extravagant state dinner. They had responded with a chain of increasingly exotic liverpaste receptions that would, he was quite certain, be the end of him. Of course, Lady Marliir had been too ill to attend any of the events, and Azoun was quite certain she would continue to be ill until a day or two after he left.

Azoun allowed Marliir's response to hang in the air long enough for everyone present to be certain he knew the truth, then said, "Tell her that I certainly hope she feels better soon."

Marliir cocked an eyebrow at the lack of a "please," then turned to gesture at his odd gathering of supporters. "I am sure Your Majesty knows these good people: Lady Kraliqh, Merula the Marvelous, and Daramos the High, of the Lady's House here in Arabel."

"Of course."

Azoun smiled at each in turn: the grave-looking Lady Kraliqh, the rotund Merula, and the zealot-eyed Daramos. Of the three, he knew the most about Daramos Lauthyr. The man was a fanatic, almost as dedicated to the glory of his goddess Tymora as he was to establishing a central church in Arabel, with himself as its divinely-ordained patriarch.

Azoun took the platter from his wife's hand, then held it out to Marliir's odd coalition. "Liverpaste, anyone? They're quail."

The offer seemed to disarm the four. They exchanged a flurry of startled frowns, then Duke Marliir snatched a wafer off the plate, and the other three followed suit. Unfortunately, there was one left. Azoun pushed it toward Filfaeril.

"Canapé, my dear?"

She smiled at him adoringly, then took the plate from his hand and passed him the wafer. "No, you can have it, my dear. I'll go and fetch more."

Azoun accepted the wafer and tried not to make a sour face as he bit into it. "Lovely, aren't they?"

"Quite," said Duke Marliir. "Your Majesty, there is something of great import we must discuss."

"Really?" Azoun swallowed, then asked, "What can that be? If you are worried about this blight, I assure you the War Wizards have the matter well in hand."

"The blight is only a part of it," said Lady Kraliqh. According to Azoun's spies, her dealings with Duke Marliir were seldom limited to matters of business. "We are concerned more with the future of the crown."

"The future of the crown?" Azoun feigned a surprised look, but took note of the lady's no-nonsense tone. She would not be put off easily with platitudes or vague promises, and he decided not to try. "You are speaking of Tanalasta, then."

"We are concerned about her refusal to take a husband," said Marliir. "Matters between her and Dauneth seemed to be progressing nicely. There must be some reason she chose to dismiss him so out of hand. It was embarrassing, really."

"I am the cause of that confusion, Lord Marliir," said Azoun. "I am so fond of Dauneth myself that others may have misinterpreted my affection when I asked him to escort Tanalasta to the party. I apologize for any embarrassment it caused, and I want everyone in Arabel to know I hold him in the highest regard. In fact, I was thinking of naming him Lord High Warden of the North." Azoun turned to Duke Marliir. "Do you think he would have time for the extra duties?"

Marliir's jaw dropped. "Of—of course."

"Good." Azoun could see by the man's astonished expression that he had won back the loyalty of the entire Marliir clan. "Have him stop by the Arabellan Palace tomorrow, and we shall discuss the arrangements."

"That is very nice for Dauneth," said Lady Kraliqh, "but it still does not address our concerns about the future of the crown. After all, I know that when a woman reaches a certain age, it grows difficult for her to bear children."

"Truly? Then you must look very young for your age—and Tanalasta is even younger than you appear. I doubt there is any need to worry about her ability to provide an heir when she has not even tried yet . . . or if she has, she has not seen fit to tell her father about it!"

Azoun winked as he said this last, drawing a raucous chuckle from everyone but Lady Kraliqh. He looked away, trying to catch the eye of some other notable before his growing irritation with the woman got the best of him.

"If that is all you are worried about," the king continued, "I believe I see—"

"There is another matter, Majesty," interrupted Merula. The wizard did not wait for an acknowledgement before continuing. "This unfortunate business of the Royal Temple. Perhaps the princess has not given thought to the question of where the loyalties of her royal priests might lie. A servant with two masters cannot help having divided loyalties."

"And yet the realm might benefit immensely by courting the blessing of the gods," said Daramos. "Tymora has always shown great favor to Cormyr. Had she not taken refuge here during the Time of Troubles, surely the realm would have suffered more than it did."

"No one can argue that her presence proved a blessing," agreed Azoun, "but I hardly think that calls for a royal temple."

The veins in Daramos's eyes grew as wide as string, and before Azoun could finish what he had been about to say, the high priest burst into a fit of righteous indignation.

"After the kindness Tymora showed your kingdom, you would insult her by establishing a royal temple to Chauntea instead?" Daramos backed away, his face trembling and turning crimson with a zealot's rage. "Do not anger the Lady, little king! Fortune has two faces, and only one is pretty."

The threat silenced the reception almost instantly, and a trio of bodyguards stepped forward to flank the high priest.

"This is what I was talking about, Majesty," said Merula. As the wizard spoke, he was returning a small glass rod to the sleeve pocket inside his cloak. Apparently, he had feared for a moment that Daramos was actually deranged enough to attack the king. "Priests cannot be trusted. They must beg their spells from their gods, and so they always serve at the pleasure of those fickle masters."

"We thank you for your opinion, Merula." Silently, Azoun cursed Daramos's outburst, and wondered just how obsessed the man was. Because of the goddess Tymora's stay during the Time of Troubles, the Lady's House had almost as much power in Arabel as did his own governing lord, and it simply would not do to have Daramos Lauthyr angry—not unless Azoun wanted to crush another Arabellan revolt. He waved the guards back, then said, "The Lord High Priest's point is well taken. Though the princess and I have had little time to discuss the matter, there will be no royal temple in Cormyr—to Chauntea or anyone else."

The redness began to drain from Daramos's face, but the man looked far from calm. "Of course you are right about the other gods, Majesty, but Tymora has blessed the Obarskyrs for more than a thousand years."

"Which is why I would never dishonor her by establishing a royal temple," said Azoun.

Daramos looked confused. "Dishonor her?"

"Tymora took refuge here in Arabel during the Time of Troubles, but the capital of Cormyr is Suzail," Azoun said. "I cannot help but think it would offend her to establish a greater temple in the South. I was under the impression that she wished your own temple to be the center of her faith."

Daramos's eyes lit in alarm. "I see what you mean, Majesty."

Azoun shrugged sadly, then turned to Merula. "I am afraid you are right, Merula. Cormyr will have to do without a royal temple after all."

A wry smile came to the wizard's lips, and he said, "Then I guess you have only the War Wizards to rely upon for your magic."

"It would appear so," Azoun replied. "It is a good thing for the realm that they have proven themselves so many times through the ages. I would hate to think what might become of Cormyr without them."

"It would be a travesty, undoubtedly," said Lady Kraliqh. "Which brings us back to the question of Tanalasta. There will be no Royal Temple while you reign, Majesty, but what of when you are gone—may that be a hundred years from now?"

Azoun forced a smile and turned to the duchess. "Lady Kraliqh, you are so bad at guessing ages that I am beginning to think your eyes have grown weak," he joked, trying to guess what it would take to placate her. "Even with the many blessings of Daramos's goddess, I doubt I will see another twenty years."

"Which is all the more reason to answer my question now." As Lady Kraliqh spoke, she stepped aside to make room in the conversation circle for Filfaeril, who was returning with a fresh platter of minted liverpaste. "Of late, Tanalasta has proven herself to be a most intelligent and strong-willed princess. I doubt very much that even you could bend her to your will from the grave. What do you intend to do about that?"

"Yes, Azoun," said Filfaeril, offering the canapé platter to Marliir and the others. "What will you do then?"

Troy Denning

Azoun glanced around the little group and saw that despite the concessions he had made already, he would find no help from them. Tanalasta had returned from Huthduth stronger and full of her own ideas, and that scared them far more than the possibility of someone like Aunadar Bleth ruling from the shadow of her skirts. It scared him, too.

"While I am king, I'll rule the way I think best—and that includes choosing a fit heir," he said, waving off the canapés. "Once I have chosen, it will be up to Cormyr to live with her queen."

Filfaeril smiled, then thrust the platter into the Lady Kraliqh's astonished hands. "Will you have someone take these away?" she said. "The king hates minted liverpaste."

5

searing wind full of grit and ash howled south out of the Stonelands, rolling up the northern face of the Storm Horns in throat-scorching clouds as thick as fog. Through the haze came the distant clang of sword-on-sword and voices cursing in guttural Orcish and civilized Common. Tanalasta could sometimes glimpse small gray figures scurrying about hacking and slashing at one another. She recognized the stooped postures of orcs pressing the attack and the more upright forms of men defending an egg-shaped ring of blocky shapes that could only be wagons.

The orcs had caught the caravan at the edge of the plain, where the Stonebolt Trail descended out of the mountains to start across the empty barrens toward Shadowdale. The location was a favorite place for such raids, as it was where the hot wind sweeping south out of the distant Anauroch Desert crashed into the Storm Horn

Mountains and dropped its load of airborne sand. The result was a mile-wide band of boulder-strewn sandlands that slowed wagon travel to a crawl.

"A largely band of swiners," observed Vangerdahast.

"Aye," agreed Ryban Winter. A rugged-faced man of about Tanalasta's age, Ryban was the lionar of her Purple Dragon bodyguard. He spit a mouthful of grit onto the ground, then added, "Though this stonemurk makes it hard to be certain."

"There are at least two hundred of them," Vangerdahast said. He pointed at the ring of wagons, the presence of which was the only visible indication of the Stonebolt Trail's existence. "That is no small caravan. The orcs wouldn't have attacked unless they outnumbered the guards."

"Then the caravan must need help." Tanalasta turned to the royal magician and added, "Are we going to do something? Or is this just another of your ruses, Vangerdahast?"

"What could I hope to gain by something like this?" Vangerdahast cast her a menacing glance, then turned to Ryban. "Take the princess and go around. I'll scare the swiners off and join you in an hour."

"Scare them off?" Tanalasta asked. "And let them attack some other caravan? I think not. We'll destroy that orc band now—before it gets to be an army."

Vangerdahast scowled. "That is easier for a princess to say than a wizard to do. Even I can't kill that many orcs without getting the caravaneers, too."

"*You* don't have to," said Tanalasta. "We have twenty-five Purple Dragons with us. Lionar Ryban will stay here on the mountain with twenty men while we ride around behind the orcs and drive them up the hill away from the caravan."

Ryban looked doubtful. "Two hundred against twenty? In this murk?"

"The murk will be to your advantage. The orcs won't know how many of you there are," Tanalasta said. "You need only slow them long enough for Vangey to come up from behind, then you'll want to ride fast and furious anyway. I really don't see you sticking around to fire more than a volley or two of arrows."

Ryban raised his brow and turned to Vangerdahast.

"No," said the wizard. "Too much can go wrong. We can't take the risk—not with the princess here."

A cry arose from the battlefield, and Tanalasta glimpsed a dozen orc silhouettes pushing a caravan dray onto its side. A trio of men jumped out from behind the toppled wagon and laid into their foes with sword and spell, then the scene vanished into the stonemurk.

"Would Alusair settle for just scaring them off?" Tanalasta asked.

"You are not Alusair."

"And I am no longer the crown princess," Tanalasta said, prompting a startled look from Ryban. "We could talk all day about what I am not, but that will not stop those orcs." She turned to the lionar and held out her arm. "Give me a sword."

Vangerdahast caught hold of her wrist. "The king did not say he had made a final decision. I'm sure he is eager to reconsider, if you'll only accommodate some of his views."

"Would those accommodations include relinquishing the Royal Temple?"

Vangerdahast nodded. "Of course, but the king has made it clear you must choose a husband of your own liking."

"How very kind of the king, but I think we can take his decision as final. Unless he is willing to accommodate my views, I won't be assuming the crown." Tanalasta turned to Ryban, wondering if she were speaking too quickly. Her vision had foretold specifically only the consequences of marrying badly, but she felt now that it concerned her ability to stand behind all of her decisions. "You may give me that sword, lionar. Alusair is the one who will be needing special protection now."

Ryban glanced at Vangerdahast.

"Why are you looking at him, Ryban?" Tanalasta demanded. "I am the royal here. You answer to me—as does Vangerdahast, when it suits him to recall it."

Ryban clenched his jaw at the rebuke, but drew his sword from its scabbard. "As you command."

He laid the blade across his forearm and offered the hilt to her. Tanalasta leaned across the space between their horses and took the heavy weapon from his hand, then traced a quick guarding pattern in the air. The balance was not quite as refined as the epees she used in the palace's gymnasium, but it was a well-made officer's blade that would serve her nicely.

When Ryban raised his brow, the princess laughed and said, "Don't look so surprised, lionar. I may not be Alusair, but I am an Obarskyr. I've been fencing since I could stand."

Ryban's astonishment changed to concern. "This will be a little different, milady. Have you ever fought orcs before?"

"Not unless you count Aunadar Bleth." Tanalasta chuckled at the lionar's uncomfortable expression, then said, "Perhaps you care to offer a few suggestions."

"That would be a waste of time," growled Vangerdahast. He guided his horse around so that he was facing Tanalasta, then plucked the sword from her hand and returned it to Ryban. "She won't be needing this."

Tanalasta fixed him with her most commanding glare. "Then the king has changed his mind about the royal temple?"

"I doubt that very much, but if you insist on doing this, I won't have you risking the lives of good men with this nonsense about swinging a sword yourself." The wizard angled a gnarled finger down across the hillside, to where a high outcropping of granite overlooked the west side of the battlefield, and said, "You will wait down there with five of Ryban's best men. If an orc comes within a hundred paces of you, the dragoneers will take you—by force, if necessary—and flee westward at a full gallop. Do you understand?"

Tanalasta bristled at Vangerdahast's tone, but one glimpse of the relief in Ryban's eyes confirmed that the lionar shared the wizard's concerns. Silently, she thanked the goddess for sparing her what she felt certain would have been more adventure than she really wanted. Though Tanalasta was determined to play the reckless princess and force Vangerdahast's hand, she was also smart enough to realize that ten-to-one odds might be a bit ambitious for her first battle—even with the royal magician along to even things out.

Putting on a defiant air, Tanalasta turned to the lionar. "Is that your recommendation as well, Lionar?"

"It is," he said. "No offense to your fencing skill, Princess, but swiners don't play by the rules. Your presence would be a burden on us all."

Tanalasta let her shoulders slump. "Very well." Her disappointment was not entirely feigned, for she had often envied the marvelous combat tales her younger sister brought home from each journey into the Stonelands. "You may send two men to accompany me. If I am not to take part in the fighting, you will have greater need of the extra swords than I."

Vangerdahast scowled at this reduction of guards, but reluctantly held his tongue and nodded toward her saddlebags. "You have the rod and bracers I gave you?" he asked. "And the rings as well?"

Tanalasta put her hand into her cloak pocket and found the rings in their special pouches, then slipped them on.

"Don't worry. I'll take every precaution." She waved her fingers to display the rings. "I wouldn't want anyone to trouble themselves about me. In fact, I can even recall that spell you taught me to keep bears at bay."

Vangerdahast looked surprised. "And it is prepared to use?"

"If I must." Tanalasta ran her hands through the necessary gestures. "You see? Our time together wasn't altogether wasted."

"Life never ceases to be a wonder—even at my age." Vangerdahast shook his head in amazement. "Perhaps we'll make a war wizard of you yet, if you remain determined not to be queen."

With that, the royal magician turned his horse away and galloped off to circle around behind the battle. Ryban quickly sent three Purple Dragons along to offer hand-to-hand support, then assigned a pair of riders to escort Tanalasta.

Tanalasta and her companions dismounted and led their horses across the slope on foot. The foothills were as barren as the sandlands below, save that the ground here was as jagged and rocky as the heart of the Stonelands, and any orc who happened to glance up at a clear moment would see a trio of riders crossing the hillside. Proceeding on foot hardly guaranteed that this would not happen, but at least they would be harder to notice with a lower profile. The princess did not worry at all about the clatter their horses made on the rocky ground. Even she could barely hear it above all the clanging and shouting below.

As Tanalasta approached her assigned station, the stonemurk grew steadily thinner, and she realized Vangerdahast had not chosen her post solely to keep her out of harm's way. While the outcropping dropped away in a sheer cliff on its three downhill sides, it was also close enough to the fighting to offer a good view of the battle. She guessed there were close to two hundred and fifty stoop-backed figures trying to clamber over an irregular oval of toppled and burning wagons. Inside this defensive barrier stood no more than fifty caravan guards, hacking at their attackers with swords, axes, and the occasional lightning bolt or flame tongue, struggling to defend a small knot of women, children, and cursing merchants huddled together in the center of the circle.

Several women and most of the merchants were clutching wooden spears, ready to charge any swiners that broke through the guards' perimeter. Judging by the number of bodies both human and orc that lay scattered across the tiny circle, they had been called upon several times already. The princess saw no signs of dray beasts. The creatures had either been cut free or dragged away by the orcs.

The trio tethered their horses out of sight behind the rim of the cliff. Tanalasta opened her saddlebags, slipped her bracers onto her wrists, and grabbed her little black baton, then led the way forward on hands and knees. Though she had never had occasion to use either the bracers or the baton before, she had practiced with them a few times and knew how to use their magic. She considered it a testament to the danger of the Stonelands that before leaving Arabel, Vangerdahast had made a point of requisitioning so much magic for her from the armory of the Purple Dragons. When he had dropped her off in Huthduth, he had given her nothing more than a magic dagger—no doubt because he had expected her to contact him within a tenday and demand to be instantly teleported home. Only the determination to prove him wrong had given her the strength to abide that first month of boredom, before she had discovered the joy of hard, honest work.

The princess reached the rim of the cliff to find a stream of orcs pouring between two toppled wagons, stampeding over the fallen bodies of four burly caravan guards. A quavering battle yell rose from the women and merchants huddled together in the center of the circle, and they edged forward to meet their foes.

Tanalasta fingered her signet ring, then pictured the royal magician's face inside her mind. "Vangerdahast?"

He came into view, a faint gray silhouette two hundred paces beyond the caravan, rising from behind a sandy ridge, swinging a wooden staff over his head and flinging a ball of fire into the air. The sphere arced over the wagons and crashed down in the heart of the orcs' charge, licking out around their crooked legs and curling skyward in a flash of scarlet. The swiners disintegrated into columns of sooty black smoke and writhing heaps of ash, and on the wind came the anguished squeals of the dying.

A trio of blackened swiners stumbled from the conflagration haloed in fumes and flame. A swarm of women and merchants were on them instantly, thrusting and jabbing with their spears until the orcs collapsed in burning heaps.

Yes? Vangerdahast's voice came to Tanalasta inside her head. *I'm rather busy now, if it isn't important.*

The wizard leveled his staff, and half a dozen forks of lightning struck down a mob of orcs trying to overturn a heavy wagon. On the opposite side of the circle, Tanalasta noticed another throng about to overpower a trio of weary caravan guards.

Trouble on the right—er, your left. Tanalasta spoke the words within her head. *About half way down. I can see everything from up here.*

Of course. Did you think I only meant to rob you of the fun?

Vangerdahast thrust his staff into its saddle holster, then pulled something from the sleeve pocket of his robe and flicked his fingers in the indicated direction. A yellowish mist appeared over the orc throng and settled groundward. Any warrior touched by the haze let the weapon slip from his grasp and collapsed in an unmoving heap. For the sake of the caravan guards, Tanalasta hoped the cloud had been sleep magic and not a death spell.

The support riders finally appeared behind Vangerdahast, their bodies pressed tight to the necks of their galloping mounts as the beasts struggled in vain to keep pace with the royal magician's peerless stallion. The men carried swords in their hands and wore bucklers fastened to their arms, but it seemed to Tanalasta that by the time they caught the wizard, their poor horses would be too exhausted to carry the fight.

As Vangerdahast closed to within a hundred paces of the battle, he drew his staff from its holster again. He tucked the back end under his arm and began to swing the tip back and forth, casting crackling bolts of lightning down one side of the wagon circle and sizzling meteors along the other. Orcs dropped by the dozens, and soon the ones at his end of the circle began to fall back in confusion. The weary caravan guards paused long enough to glance in his direction and raise their swords in thanks, then rushed to help their hard-pressed companions closer to Tanalasta's end of the fight.

It did not take the angry orcs long to determine the source of their trouble. As Vangerdahast closed to within seventy paces of the wagons, a large swiner on the right began squealing commands and shoving his fellows toward the charging wizard. Ignoring the constant stream of death flying at them from the end of Vangerdahast's staff, more than fifty orc warriors streamed forward to place themselves between the royal magician and the caravan.

Vangerdahast veered off to attack from another angle.

Wrong way! Tanalasta warned. *The leader's on the other side. If you can—*

I know ... what to do! Vangerdahast's retort was labored. *I was winning ... battles for Cormyr ... before your father was king!*

97

The royal magician reined his horse around, angling across the plain toward the opposite side of the caravan. A boisterous cheer rose from the orcs who had gathered to stop him, but Vangerdahast quickly demonstrated their error by lobbing a fireball into their midst. The wizard's support riders cut the corner and finally caught up to their ward, taking positions to the rear and on both flanks.

The orc leader glared in Vangerdahast's direction, then pushed more of its fellows forward and scurried off at an angle. When the wizard did not adjust his course, Tanalasta realized that either his view was blocked or he was having trouble separating the leader from the orcs around it.

A pie slice to the right, Tanalasta ordered.

A pie slice? Despite his mocking tone, the wizard reined his horse hard to the right.

I said a slice, not a whole quarter! Tanalasta corrected. The size of Vangerdahast's belly should have given her a clearer idea as to what he considered a slice. *The orc you want is larger than the rest, with a blocky head and pointed muzzle.*

Got him!

A bolt of lightning crackled from the tip of Vangerdahast's staff, blasting apart a simple warrior whom the leader happened to shove forward at that moment. The commander hurled himself to the ground and disappeared into the swirl around him. The wizard loosed another spell from his staff, engulfing the entire area in a huge fireball.

Vangerdahast and his companions reached the wall of swords and tusks the leader had been shoving forward to stop them. The wizard paid the swiners no attention at all, simply urging his mount onward as orcish steel shattered against his horse's breast. His companions, lacking his magic shielding, had to rely upon more conventional defenses, pushing through the wall in a flurry of slashing blades and flashing hooves.

Once they were past, Vangerdahast wheeled around long enough to spray the orc wall with a stream of flame, then worked his way toward the wagons at a walk, scattering orcs before him with bolt and flame—and sometimes with a mere wave of the staff. The wizard's escorts had nothing to do but sit on their horses and look mean. Their foes did not dare approach close enough to engage.

The caravan guards were just starting to drag a wagon aside to let Vangerdahast into the circle when Tanalasta noticed the orc commander crouching behind a small boulder, wetting the tips of several long spears in an earthenware vessel. A handful of orc warriors were peering over the top of the boulder, nervously watching Vangerdahast and holding the spears their leader had already dipped.

Vangey, the leader's still alive, Tanalasta warned. *Behind you about twenty paces, a little to the left.*

The wizard stopped his horse and gestured for the merchants to close their perimeter. *Small slice or a large one?*

About an eighth of the pie, Tanalasta replied. *Behind that boulder where they're bunching up. Be careful. They've got spears, and they're dipping the tips in something.*

Vangerdahast's only reply was a chuckle. He returned his war staff to its saddle holster, then took the shield from one of his support riders and passed his hand over it. Tanalasta could not see what he was sprinkling on it, but she did see his lips moving as he uttered the incantation.

The orcs began to regain their wits, forming a broad semi-circle around Vangerdahast and his three companions. Vangerdahast paid them no attention, continuing to pass his hand over the buckler and mouth arcane syllables. This seemed to distress his foes far more than his death-flinging staff, a fact Tanalasta suspected the wizard of intentionally playing up. While he undoubtedly knew many spells that took this long to cast, he was far too cunning to use one in the middle of a combat. A nervous squalling began to arise from the ranks of the orcs. Twice, a handful of brave warriors attempted to initiate a general charge, only to stop dead in their tracks the moment the royal magician looked in their direction.

At last, Vangerdahast pressed his hand to the face of the shield and fell silent. *I take it Ryban and his company are ready?*

Tanalasta glanced up the slope, where she could barely see the silhouettes of Ryban and his Purple Dragons. They were spread across the crest of the hill with their horsebows in hand and their quivers hanging from their saddle horns. To a man, they were craning their necks toward the plain, peering through the stonemurk to track what little they could of the battle's progress.

They're ready, Tanalasta said. *You might even say eager.*

Vangerdahast nodded, then began to swing the shield back and forth, as though he were a water diviner seeking the best place to dig a well. Each time the shield swung past, the orcs in the semi-circle would mewl in alarm and cower on the ground. Then, once it had drifted past, they would leap to their feet and make a great show of shouting and waving their swords at the wizard.

Unfortunately, the rest of the tribe was experiencing no such reluctance. Axe-wielding warriors were slowly returning to the sections of perimeter Vangerdahast had cleared earlier, while the orcs at Tanalasta's end of the caravan seemed to be hurling themselves at the wagons more ferociously than ever. Already, Tanalasta could see exhausted guards kneeling in wagon beds or bracing themselves against the wheels, using both hands to swing swords that even she could have wielded with one hand.

Tanalasta was about to urge Vangerdahast to get on with the attack when she glimpsed a large bird streaking out of the western sky. The creature was a mere blur in the stonemurk, and the princess could tell little about it, save that it appeared far larger than any eagle she had ever seen and flew faster than a falcon on the hunt. It descended in a steep dive, then suddenly circled away from the battle and vanished behind a sandy ridge.

"What was that thing?" Tanalasta asked.

"What thing?" asked one of her guards.

"Didn't you see it?" She pointed in the direction the bird had vanished. "It was a huge bird, twice the size of an eagle—and fast. Very fast."

"Probably just a vulture, Princess," said the second guard. "They're drawn to the smell of battle."

"This was larger than any vulture," Tanalasta retorted. "And vultures aren't that fast."

The guards exchanged knowing glances, then the first said, "The stonemurk has a way of playing tricks on your eyes, milady. It's nothing to worry about."

Though it angered her to be condescended to, especially when neither guard had seen what she was talking about, the princess saw no use in arguing. Whatever the thing was, it had apparently wanted no part of the battle. Tanalasta swallowed her irritation and returned her attention to Vangerdahast, who finally seemed to be tiring of theatrics. As the wizard swung his ensorcelled shield past the orc commander's hiding place, he slowed, then swung the buckler back toward the boulder and stopped.

The orcs around the leader began to trill nervously. The leader sat up to peer over the top of the boulder. Vangerdahast set his heels to the flanks of his mount, and the big stallion sprang to a gallop so quickly the wizard was halfway to the boulder before his escorts urged their own mounts after him.

The orc commander rose and began to gesture wildly at Vangerdahast. The spearmen rushed out from behind the boulder and arrayed themselves before their leader, jamming the butts of their weapons into the ground and angling the tips toward the wizard's charging horse.

In the name of the king! Vangerdahast started to haul back on the reins, then seemed to change his mind and dropped his shield, pressing himself close to the neck of his mount. *You said spears, not pikes!*

Before Tanalasta could reply, one of her guards cursed, "By the iron glove!"

"Is he trying to impale himself?" demanded the other.

Tanalasta cringed and started to look away—then recalled how the orcs' brittle swords had snapped against the horse's chest earlier.

"He'll be fine," she said, expecting the wizard to barrel straight through the barricade of poisoned tips.

Instead, the magnificent stallion leaped skyward, then continued to gallop through the air as though its hooves were on solid ground. As the horse passed over the astonished orcs, Vangerdahast pulled something from his pocket and sprinkled it on his foes. The terrified swiners dropped their pikes and leaped to their feet, brushing at their scalps and screeching in fear.

They did not die until Vangerdahast's support riders arrived to cut them down in a tempest of whirling horses and slashing steel. So furious was the attack that Tanalasta did not realize until an instant later that only two escorts were involved in the assault. The third lay back at the wagon circle, his chest opened by a gaping wound visible even from the princess's perch. The man's horse was a few feet from the body, stumbling around in fear and tossing its head.

Tanalasta had no time to ask her companions if they had seen what happened. Vangerdahast's mount dropped down behind the orc leader, prompting the huge swiner to turn and sprint across the sandy ground so fast it took even the royal magician's powerful horse a full second to catch up. By then, Vangerdahast had once again drawn his staff from its saddle holster and lowered it like a lance.

Tanalasta expected to see some spell blast the orc's skull into a spray of blood and bone, but Vangerdahast simply aimed his lance at the back of his quarry's head and allowed the momentum of his charge to drive it home. The leader sailed half a dozen paces before finally crashing to the ground in a limp heap. The royal magician reined his horse to a stop and wheeled around to face the caravan.

The orcs began to scatter, wailing and screeching as though their demonic lord had risen from the pits of the Abyss. A couple of well-placed fireballs helped the panic along, then the swiners on Vangerdahast's side of the battle broke and fled en masse. The wizard threw up a pair of fire curtains to force them toward Ryban's hiding place on the mountain, then started around the caravan to rout the warriors on the opposite side of the caravan.

A black streak shot from beneath a burning dray wagon, then seemed to explode into a crescent-shaped phantom of darkness. Before Tanalasta registered that this was the same huge bird she had seen earlier, the shadow sprang into the air and struck one of Vangerdahast's escorts full in the flank. The rider's torso simply fell off, leaving the man's terrified horse to gallop off with his seat still in the saddle and his boots still jammed into the stirrups.

The phantom was on the second escort even as the man turned to see what had become of his companion. The dragoneer vanished beneath the thing's black wings, still struggling to bring his sword around. His horse emerged an instant later, saddle gone and blood pouring from three long gashes in its flank.

"Helm guard us!" gasped one of Tanalasta's guards. "What is that thing?"

"You called it a vulture," Tanalasta remarked bitterly.

When Vangerdahast continued forward, oblivious to what had just happened behind him, she pictured his face in her mind.

Vangerdahast, behind you! It's some sort of demon, or . . .

Tanalasta did not finish, for even as she sent the warning, the phantom was spinning to look in her direction. The thing seemed a grotesque fusion of woman and wasp, with a powerful torso, impossibly small waist, and long sticklike limbs folded into inhuman shapes. Its hair was as smoky and black as its eyes were white and blazing, and the princess could just make out the crescent of a yellow-fanged smile.

Tanalasta, stay still.

The princess glanced back to Vangerdahast and saw the wizard struggling to wheel his galloping horse around. He leveled his staff at the phantom and unleashed a brilliant bolt of emerald light, but the creature was already launching itself into the air. The streak blasted to ground where the thing had been half an instant before, hurling the mangled remains of the second rider in every direction.

The phantom's wings pounded the air, catapulting it over the caravan toward Tanalasta's hiding place. Already, the princess could see a pair of naked female breasts and ten ebony talons curling from the ends of the thing's slender fingers. A small flaming orb sizzled up from Vangerdahast's direction to strike the creature full in the flank. It veered slightly, then lowered its dark wings and streaked away, leaving the wizard's sphere to explode into a roiling ball of flame. As the thing drew closer, the princess could make out the narrow blade of a nose and a long haggish chin smeared with red gore.

An unaccustomed fury rose up inside Tanalasta, and suddenly she could think of little more than slaying her foe. She jumped to her feet and thrust a hand into her cloak pocket, in her excitement fumbling for the steel Peacemaker's rod Vangerdahast had given her. To her amazement, she felt no fear at all, only a thrilling blood-lust that filled her with a strange euphoria and muddled her thoughts. Could this be the battle rapture Alusair was always talking about?

One of Tanalasta's guards grabbed her collar and pushed her toward the horses. "Run!"

The dragoneer's shove brought Tanalasta back to her senses, and she was seized by a queasy terror as she recalled how easily the phantom had slain Vangerda-hast's escorts. She stumbled back two steps, then stopped when her guards drew their swords and stepped forward to meet the phantom at the edge of the cliff.

"Don't be fools—retreat!" Tanalasta yelled. She released the steel rod and pulled her hand from her pocket, then began to fidget with one of the rings Vangerdahast had given her in Arabel. "Now!"

The guards did not obey. They merely roared their battle cries and raised their swords, and it was too late. The phantom swooped over the rim of the outcropping, impaling one man on a long talon and batting the other off the cliff and continuing toward Tanalasta at lightning speed.

She pointed her ring at the ground, commanding, "Dragon's wall!"

Tanalasta felt a sharp pain in her finger, then a shim-mering wall of force sprang up between her and the phantom. A muffled whump reverberated across the outcropping, and the creature was hanging in the air before her, its night black wings spread across the hori-zon on the other side of the magic barrier.

The phantom gave an ear-piercing scream, and its white eyes turned human and ladylike. The darkness drained from its face, revealing the visage of a handsome noblewoman about the same age as Queen Filfaeril. Tanalasta staggered away from the inexplicable apparition, so shocked and terrified that she forgot to run.

Vangerdahast's voice came to her. *Tanalasta?*

The phantom pulled its head free of the magic wall and turned toward the wizard. Tanalasta's heart sank as she realized the implications. The creature could hear their thought-talk.

Answer me!

The phantom pulled a wing free of the barrier, and Tanalasta's sense of danger came flooding back.

Quiet, you old fool! The princess turned toward the horses.

Then suddenly Vangerdahast was there before her, sitting on his stallion between her and her own horse, swaying and blinking with teleport afterdaze. Tanalasta glanced back and saw the phantom springing over the top of her magic wall, its face once again a mask of gore-dripping darkness. Tanalasta spun around, stretching an arm in its direction and slapping the opposite hand down on her wrist bracer.

"King's bolts!"

A searing pain shot through her hand, and four bolts of golden magic streaked toward the phantom's chest.

The creature's wing curled around in a blur of darkness, and the bolts erupted against it in a series of dazzling yellow flashes. The appendage turned briefly translucent, revealing a fanlike network of finger-thick bones, then began to darken again.

Vangerdahast's staff tapped Tanalasta's shoulder. "You have proven your point, Princess," he said. "Now why don't you leave your old fool to have his fun with this nasty wench?"

Too tired to trade banter, Tanalasta merely nodded and sprinted to her horse, pulling herself into the saddle as the wizard's first spell cracked across the outcropping behind her. She leaned down to free the reins of the dead guards' mounts, then glimpsed the phantom hurling toward Vangerdahast in a blazing ball of white fury. He turned his staff horizontal and raised it in front of him. A hedge of silver-tipped thorn bushes sprang up to intercept his shrieking attacker.

Tanalasta started to turn her mount toward the rest of the company, but saw a horde of orcs streaming up the mountain and realized she would never reach them alive. Praying to the goddess that Ryban could see what was happening on the outcropping, she turned in the opposite direction and urged her mount to flee.

The terrified beast sprang up the rocky slope as though it were a mountain goat, and the last thing Tanalasta heard behind her was Vangerdahast's astonished curse:

"What gutterspawning succubus hatched you?"

6

he royal wizard was frightened, of course—only a fool wouldn't have been—but he was also mad with fury. His heart was hammering in his chest, pounding like it had not pounded in seventy years. Every beat urged him to battle, to pelt the phantom with bolt and blaze, to attack and keep attacking until he reduced the thing to a scorch mark on the cliff top.

Never before had Vangerdahst experienced such a combat rage, and he did not understand where it came from now. Vangerdahast had warned Azoun a dozen times that battles were won not through anger, but through cold, emotionless calculation, and now here the wizard was himself, fighting as hard to control his own emotions as to defeat the enemy. It was unnerving, really. The remnants of his last harmless lightning bolt were still tracing crooks of transparency across the phantom's leathery wing, and the wizard caught himself lowering his staff to cast the same useless spell again. Damned unnerving.

Vangerdahast threw his staff down and slipped a hand into the sleeve of his robe. In the second he needed to find the tiny pocket where he stored his spider web, the phantom peered over its furled wing and sprang. Vangerdahast's mount bolted, nearly catapulting him from the saddle. The phantom banked, herding the terrified horse toward the rim of the cliff. The wizard pulled his hand from his sleeve, flicking a ball of web in the dark thing's direction, then yelling his incantation.

At the first sound of Vangerdahast's voice, the phantom furled its wings and dropped to the ground. As it fell, a huge tangle of sticky fibers blossomed around it, completely engulfing the creature in an amorphous mass of white filaments.

Vangerdahast's horse drew up short at the edge of the outcropping, pitching him forward out of the saddle. Cursing his mount for a witless coward, the wizard made a desperate grab for the beast's mane as he tumbled over its head, then found himself plummeting toward a sandy dune a hundred feet below.

Vangerdahast experienced a fierce nettling as his weathercloak's magic triggered itself, then the cape's lapels spread outward to create a sort of crude sail. He fluttered to the ground not far from the guard who had been batted off the outcropping earlier. The poor fellow had landed headfirst in the sand, burying himself to the shoulders, then snapping his neck as he fell onto his back. A bloody crease angling across his breastplate marked where the phantom's powerful wing had struck.

Vangerdahast spun away and pulled a wing feather from inside his robe. Still consumed by his strange fury, he uttered a quick spell and extended his arms, then sprang into the air, telling himself that he had a good reason for returning to the battle before checking on Tanalasta. He needed to know where the phantom had come from. He needed to know why it had aided a petty tribe of orcs. He needed to kill the thing before it shredded his magical web. He needed *that* most of all.

The wizard rose swiftly, flying close to the outcropping so his foe would not see him. As he ascended, he heard clanging swords and whinnying horses farther up the mountainside. For some reason he could not fathom, Ryban had engaged the orcs instead of fleeing them as planned. Cursing the man for an over-brave dunce, Vangerdahast touched the throat clasp of his weathercloak. When the brass began to tingle beneath his fingers, he pictured Ryban's face.

Unless you are defending Tanalasta already, disengage and go to her!

Can't find the princess, and wouldn't run if we could, came Ryban's reply. *See you in Everwatch!*

The throat clasp became cold and dead beneath Vangerdahast's fingertips, and he grew faintly aware of feeling both mournful and perplexed. It was not like the lionar to neglect his duty, nor to think he could reach Everwatch by disregarding an order. Everwatch was the celestial palace of Helm the Watcher, and only the most faithful guardians could expect to spend eternity there.

Vangerdahast circled around to come up on the opposite side of the outcropping from where he had plunged off, then stepped onto the cliff top. He found his magic web dissolving into a gummy morass of translucent gray silk, beneath which lay the form of a shapely female spine flanked by the bases of two leathery white wings. Little more could be seen of the figure. It seemed to be curled into a ball, with its neck and shoulders hunched forward, its legs drawn up in front of it, and its wings wrapped securely around its body.

Vangerdahast crept forward, fighting to regain control of his emotions before he attacked. The butt of his war staff was sticking out from beneath the gummy mess. The phantom did not seem to be struggling, but the web was dissolving far too quickly, shriveling down around the creature like some sort of cocoon. He summoned to mind the incantation of a spell as deadly as it was quick and stopped five paces away.

The white wings twitched, then a breathy voice rasped, "Well done, wizard. Not many capture a ghazneth and live to tell of it. What is it you wish?"

"Ghazneth?"

"Is that your wish?" the phantom asked. "To know what I am?"

The web continued to contract around the ghazneth— or whatever the monster was.

Vangerdahast aimed his finger at the phantom's back. "Among other things, yes."

"What other things?" The ghazneth's voice was beginning to sound vaguely human—feminine, actually, with an oddly archaic Cormyrean accent. "You receive only one wish, you know."

"I am not the one with a death finger aimed at my back," Vangerdahast replied. "Nor do I want any wish of mine granted by the likes of you. I will ask and you will answer. If you are honest, perhaps I will send you back to the hell you came from, rather than allow your rotting corpse to pollute this land."

The ghazneth's wings flexed ever so slightly—just enough for Vangerdahast to notice that the thing was not as trapped as it would have him believe—then it said, "A wish for no wish. An odd thing to desire, but granted."

"I asked for nothing," Vangerdahast snarled, all too aware of how the phantom was trying to twist his words around. The trick angered the wizard so greatly he nearly unleashed his death spell. "I owe you nothing."

"Not true."

The web had contracted now to a mere glove around the ghazneth's body. Vangerdahast stepped forward to retrieve his war staff, then quickly stepped back when he noticed the black beginning to creep along the edges of the creature's wings.

"You owe me more than you know, Vangerdahast," the ghazneth continued, "and you are going to pay—you and Cormyr."

"Vangerdahast? You honor me too much, ghazneth. I'm just a simple war wizard."

"Be careful of the lies you tell," said the ghazneth. "Or you'll end up like me."

"As unnecessary as that advice is, I'll certainly keep it in mind," Vangerdahast said, more determined than ever to deny his name. The thing was beginning to sound like a demon, and it was never a good idea to admit one's name to a demon. "Where did you say you knew Vangerdahast from? I'll be glad to inform him of his debt."

"I may speak of the matter with Vangerdahast and no other." The ghazneth's body began to glisten with a glossy sheen, all that remained of Vangerdahast's dissolving web spell. "But you may tell him this much: if he doesn't pay, Cormyr will."

"How?" When the creature did not respond at once, Vangerdahast snarled, "Answer! My patience is wearing as thin as my web."

"What a pity—then it is gone!" The phantom rolled toward Vangerdahast, raising one wing to shield itself and another to push against the ground.

The wizard leaped back, placing himself well out of wing's reach. He had time to glimpse the sour, thin-nosed visage of an older woman, then the ghazneth's eyes turned from blue to white and its face vanished into a veil of darkness. He pointed his finger at its chest and spat out the command word that unleashed his deadly spell. The ghazneth's upper wing started to furl down to protect itself, but Vangerdahast had barely spoken before a white circle blossomed in the creature's torso.

The phantom screeched and clutched at its chest, its long talons scratching deep furrows into its naked breast. The flesh beneath its hand grew pale and soft and began to ooze up between its fingers like hot wax.

The wizard shrugged. "So you were right. I *am* Vangerdahast."

He should have known better.

The ghazneth's hand dropped from its chest, revealing a jagged void where the breastbone had erupted from the inside out. Through the hole showed a tangled snarl of veins and a lump of oozing fungus shaped vaguely like a heart. Vangerdahast stumbled back, surprised to feel a rising panic. He could not recall the last time he had experienced such a thing—certainly long before Azoun took his crown.

The ghazneth ambled forward on its waspish legs. Vangerdahast forced himself to think. So the thing's heart had moldered away. That didn't mean it was indestructible. It was either undead or demonic, and he had ways to deal with both. All he had to do was guess which and sneak another spell or two past those magic-absorbing wings without letting the thing slit him from groin to gullet first.

The ghazneth scuttled two steps to the side, placing itself between Vangerdahast and the battle still raging between the orcs and Ryban's Purple Dragons. The wizard wondered whether the time had come to make use of what many war wizards considered the weathercloak's most useful device: the escape pocket. He reached for the secret fold in the cloak's lining, then realized fleeing was not an option. Tanalasta was still somewhere nearby, and the creature would be too likely to notice her if it took to the air again.

The ghazneth stretched its wings, cutting off every avenue of escape, save those that involved flying or leaping off the cliff. Vangerdahast's panic became determination, and he found the peacemaker's rod sheathed inside his weathercloak. A common tool available to every lionar in the Purple Dragons, the little club was hardly as powerful as many of the slender wands still tucked into their pockets inside his cloak, but it did have the advantage of swiftness.

The ghazneth started forward, keeping a careful eye on the wizard's hand. Vangerdahast allowed it to herd him back toward the cliff edge, praying the thing did not realize he could fly. There was no reason it should. The creature had been imprisoned inside the web spell when he tumbled over the cliff, and it had been facing the wrong direction when he returned.

Vangerdahast reached the rim of the cliff and stopped. The ghazneth gathered itself to spring, and he pulled the black peacemaker's rod from inside his cloak. "Last chance to surrender. Otherwise, there won't be enough left of you to make a good pair of boots."

He leveled the steel club at the ghazneth, and predictably enough, the phantom brought its dark wing around to absorb the coming fireball.

Vangerdahast flung himself backward off the outcropping and was instantly flying again. He performed a quick reverse roll and came soaring up straight along the cliff face, returning to the same place he had just been. The ghazneth appeared in the same instant, hurling itself over the edge with wings stretched wide.

Vangerdahast smashed the peacemaker's rod into its mangled chest, then cried, "Go east!"

The ghazneth shot skyward as though launched from a catapult, then banked eastward and streaked off screeching in confusion and rage.

Vangerdahast chuckled lightly, and stepped back onto the outcropping. It would take the creature a good half hour to recover from the rod's repulsion magic. That would be plenty of time for him to reunite with Tanalasta and be long gone. He returned the peacemaker's rod to his pocket, then reached for his signet ring.

* * * * *

Crouching behind the last dune before the barren expanse of the Stonelands proper, Tanalasta watched the phantom streak eastward over her head, then slipped her signet ring into a secure pocket in her weathercloak. The last thing she needed was to have Vangerdahast contact her now. The creature had already proven it could hear their ring-talk, and whatever the old wizard had done to the thing, she did not want it venting its anger on her.

The phantom faded to a dot and disappeared entirely, and only then did Tanalasta return to her horse. She started back across the dunes toward the outcropping, taking care to stay in the troughs as much as possible. The first two times she was forced to crest a dune, she saw Vangerdahast searching for her from the cliff top, peering up the mountainside or scrutinizing the caravan as it struggled to put itself back together. The third time, she noticed the wizard's stallion hiding in the trough below, pressed against the shady side of a boulder and trembling in terror. She guided her own horse over toward it, speaking to the frightened beast in a soft and reassuring voice. The horse regarded her warily, its eyes large and suspicious.

Tanalasta halted a dozen paces from the big stallion. "There now, Cadimus." She kept her hands on the horn of her own saddle, realizing she would only spook him by trying to rush matters along. "Don't you recognize me? I'm Vangerdahast's friend."

The horse pricked his ears forward at the mention of his master's name. Tanalasta raised her hand slowly and pointed toward the outcropping.

"Vangerdahast," she said. "You know Vangerdahast, don't you? Vangerdahast is well. Why don't we go see him? Vangerdahast is right over there."

The horse peered around the boulder in the indicated direction. When he did not see the outcropping, which remained hidden behind a low sand dune, he stepped cautiously forward. Tanalasta leaned forward to grab his dangling reins, but he snorted a warning and jerked his head away.

"All right, Cadimus." Tanalasta pulled her hand back. "Follow me on your own. We'll go see Vangerdahast."

She turned her own mount up the trough and started forward, moving slowly so as not to alarm the skittish beast. Whatever had happened up on the outcropping must have been terrifying indeed. Cadimus was a powerful stallion bred for fighting spirit. His brother, Damask Dragon, was her father's favorite war-horse.

At length, they drew near enough to the outcropping that the summit began to show over the crest of the dune. Cadimus grew more skittish than ever, pausing to snort and scrape the ground with his hoof. At first, Tanalasta tried to reassure him with soft words, but the more she talked, the more determined the stallion became to convince her to turn around.

Finally, she decided to try a different strategy and looked away, then rode on without saying anything. It was a risky strategy, and not only because she was reluctant to leave the poor beast wandering the Stonelands alone. Vangerdahast was a portly man. Even if her own horse was strong enough to carry them both, Tanalasta did not look forward to sharing her saddle with the wizard for the next tenday or two.

The princess rode almost fifty paces before Cadimus finally came trotting up beside her, snorting angrily and trying to shoulder her mount around. Tanalasta put up with the stallion's bullying just long enough to grab his reins and jerk his head around.

"Some war-horse you are!"

Cadimus snorted in disgust, but lowered his ears and stopped pushing against her mare. Tanalasta sighed in relief and led him another dozen paces up the trough, then reluctantly turned to cross the dune crest.

Already in the shadow of the outcropping, they had to start up the mountainside if they wanted to reach the top. Cadimus nickered in protest and pulled against his reins, but Tanalasta angled away from the outcropping and managed to persuade him to keep climbing.

As they started down the other side of the dune, a loud swooshing noise sounded behind them. Cadimus let out a terrified whinny and bolted, nearly jerking Tanalasta from the saddle. She caught herself on her saddle horn, then dropped to the ground and spun around, one hand pointed toward the sound and the other already slapping at her magic bracers.

"Don't you dare!" snapped Vangerdahast, landing atop the dune in a small sandstorm. "I've had quite enough abuse today."

Tanalasta lowered her arm, only slightly surprised by the sight of the flying wizard. "Perhaps you could give me some warning next time?" She looked down the trough after Cadimus's fleeing form. "Look what you've done."

"I've no time to waste on warnings!" The wizard pointed at the bare finger where her signet ring should have been. "Besides, how was I to warn you? I've been trying to ring-speak to you for fifteen minutes!"

"I thought you would." Tanalasta pulled herself back into the saddle. "That's why I took it off."

Vangerdahast's cheeks darkened to the color of rubies. "What?"

"I was afraid of drawing the phantom's attention." Reluctantly, Tanalasta offered her hand to help the wizard into the saddle behind her. "It can hear our ring-talk."

"Don't be ridiculous." Vangerdahast frowned, then raised his brow and absentmindedly waved her off. "On the other hand . . ."

Not bothering to finish the sentence, he stuck two fingers into his mouth and whistled for his horse.

"On the other hand what?" Tanalasta demanded.

"Come along." Vangey spread his arms, then leaped into the air and flew over Tanalasta's head. "We don't have much time."

Tanalasta did not need to ask the cause for the wizard's hurry. If he had been trying to ring-speak with her, the phantom would know they had become separated and might well return in the hope of finding her alone. She galloped after the wizard and was quickly joined by Cadimus, who seemed to have regained his proud spirit with the sight of his master.

Tanalasta caught up to the flying wizard and positioned herself beneath him. "Vangey, why are we running from that thing?" She had to crane her neck back to call up to him. "Why didn't you just kill it when you had the chance?"

When Vangerdahast glanced down, he actually looked embarrassed. "It took me somewhat by surprise," he admitted. "And to tell you the truth, I really don't know what in the Nine Hells a ghazneth is."

"Ghazneth?"

They reached the base of the hill, and Vangerdahast had to fly up out of speaking range. They angled up the slope westward until the slope grew rocky enough to conceal hoof prints from casual detection, then cut eastward away from the orcs still milling about on the battlefield on the Stonebolt Trail. Tanalasta glimpsed the area just long enough to see that Ryban had stayed to engage the swiners. She saw a dozen Purple Dragons lying among the dead, and small bands of orcs were already squabbling over the carcasses of at least twice that many horses. Her stomach grew hollow and queasy, and she prayed the lionar had not stayed to fight because he thought she was in danger—though of course that was the only reasonable explanation.

Once they had ascended high enough that the plain below vanished into the stonemurk, Vangerdahast led the way around the shoulder of the mountain. He guided them into the shelter of a rocky gully, then left Tanalasta to tether the horses and keep watch while he surveyed possible escape routes. When he returned, he pointed up the mountain about three quarters of a mile, to where a large, spirelike rock sat on the crest of a ridge.

"If the ghazneth finds us, use your cloak's escape pocket to go up there, then slip around the other side and start riding." He glowered at her from one eye. "You haven't used it yet, have you?"

Tanalasta shook her head.

"And you *do* remember how?"

"I'm inexperienced, not daft." Tanalasta motioned toward the secret pocket inside her weathercloak. "These cloaks aren't that hard to use. Why all this bother anyway? Just kill the damned thing and be done with it."

Again, Vangerdahast flushed. "I'm afraid it's not that easy."

Tanalasta raised her brow. "I thought you could kill anything."

"I didn't want to be hasty," said Vangerdahast, neatly dodging the question. He pulled a handful of spell components from his pocket and began to lay them out on a boulder, using his work as an excuse to avoid Tanalasta's gaze. "It knew my name."

"Of course it knew your name." As she spoke, Tanalasta continued to keep watch. "It was listening to our ring-talk."

Vangerdahast said something else, but Tanalasta did not really hear it. A terrible thought had occurred to her, and she was trying desperately to think of a reason it could not be true. When she failed, the princess grasped Vangerdahast's elbow.

"Vangey, what if that's the reason Alusair removed her signet?"

Vangerdahast looked confused and said nothing, and the princess realized he had been paying no more attention to her than she had to him. She pulled her signet from her pocket and displayed it in her open palm.

"Vangerdahast, I took this off so it wouldn't draw the ghazneth to me," she said. "What if Alusair did the same thing?"

Vangerdahast frowned. "Why should she do that? The ghazneth is *here*." The wizard's eyes lit in comprehension, then he said, "No!"

"We don't know anything's wrong," said Tanalasta, trying to calm him. "Alusair's silence could mean she's being cautious. After all, she has no way of knowing where the thing is."

Looking more concerned than ever, Vangerdahast turned to face Tanalasta. "I wasn't worried about Alusair, thank you very much." The wizard's face was paling before Tanalasta's eyes. "I told you. The ghazneth said I owed it something. If I don't pay, Cormyr will."

"You *talked* to this thing?" Tanalasta found herself looking at the wizard's wrinkled face instead of keeping watch.

"It's not as though we had tea," Vangerdahast growled. "The thing was bound in a magic web."

"And you let it out?"

"I didn't let it do anything. It dissolved my web, or absorbed it, or something. I really don't know." The wizard went over to Cadimus and removed a spellbook from the stallion's saddlebags. "When we get back to Arabel, maybe the Sage Most Learned can tell me what exactly a ghazneth is. I can't teleport us back until tomorrow, but if we can last the night—"

"Back?" Tanalasta echoed. "To Arabel?"

Vangerdahast opened his spellbook and absently began to flip through the pages. "Of course. You can't think I intend to keep you out here."

"And you can't think I would return until we've found Alusair!"

Vangerdahast slammed his spellbook shut. "Enough, Princess! Your games have already cost the lives of too many good men."

"*My* games, Vangerdahast?"

"*Your* games," the wizard insisted. "Were you not the one who insisted that we destroy the orc tribe 'like Alusair would?' "

"Yes, but that doesn't mean—"

"And now we have lost Ryban's entire company."

"How can you call that my fault?" Tanalasta was genuinely hurt. "They were supposed to loose a few arrows and flee!"

"That does not change what happened," Vangerdahast insisted. "You have been playing with men's lives, and I will have no more of it."

Tanalasta narrowed her eyes. "I'm sorry for the loss of Ryban and his men, Vangerdahast, but I am not *playing* at anything. If you and the king are, tell me now."

"The king is quite serious, I assure you. He will not have an order of spell-beggars placed in such a position of influence."

121

"He won't, Vangerdahast?" Tanalasta demanded. "Or *you* won't?"

"Our thoughts are the same on this matter," insisted Vangerdahast. "But that has nothing to do with your imminent return to Arabel. It's treason for you to blackmail the crown by placing yourself—and others—in this kind of danger."

"It's only blackmail if the king is bluffing," Tanalasta said. "And if he is, the treason lies on your head, not mine. I have done nothing but take him at his word."

"The king does not bluff his own daughter."

"Then our duty is clear," said Tanalasta. "The king sent us to find the crown princess, and this ghazneth creature only makes it that much more urgent for us to do so."

Vangerdahast exhaled loudly, clearly frustrated by the dilemma in which he found himself. Tanalasta turned back to her duties as a watchman, scanning the stonemurk for the first dark hint of wings on the horizon.

"Princess, be reasonable," said Vangerdahast. "While everything you say is true, even you must admit your father hardly had something like this in mind when he sent you—"

"I can't know what the king had in mind," Tanalasta said. "What I do know is that I am here, and that the king himself charged me with finding Alusair."

Silently, the princess added that she needed to complete her mission precisely because the king had not expected the mission to be dangerous. Allowing the phantom to force her back to Arabel would only confirm his belief that she needed to be protected. But if she actually located Alusair and discovered what was happening in the Stonelands, perhaps he would begin to have confidence in the decisions she would one day make as queen.

After a moment, Vangerdahast sighed. "Very well. If you must pretend not to understand what this trip is really about, I shall explain it to you."

Tanalasta held up her hand. "That won't be necessary, Vangerdahast. What *you* don't seem to understand is that I do know what this is about. The war wizards are afraid the royal priests will take their place, you're afraid you'll soon have a high harvestmaster competing for the monarch's ear, and the king is afraid of making you both angry."

"Our reservations are hardly of such a petty nature," Vangerdahast replied. "I am concerned about the jealousy of the other religions, while the question of divided loyalties is entirely insurmountable—"

"Yes, yes. I know the arguments, and I know you're only thinking of the realm. You think of nothing else." Tanalasta paused, then added in an acid voice, "I would never question your loyalty, only your belief that no one else can possibly know what is good for Cormyr."

Vangerdahast actually flinched. "Milady! That is unfair."

"It is also true. Maybe you *are* the only one who knows what is good for Cormyr. Even I must admit that you're usually right about everything else." Tanalasta paused to gather her courage, then continued, "What you don't seem to understand is me. If I can't be queen in my own way, then I will not be queen at all."

Vangerdahast regarded the princess as though meeting her for the first time. "By the Weave! You would refuse the throne on account of a handful of priests?"

"I would refuse it on many accounts," said Tanalasta. "Which is why it falls to me to find Alusair. I seem to be the only one who takes this situation seriously."

Vangerdahast turned and gazed into the stonemurk.

Tanalasta left him to his thoughts, content to believe she had won the argument. They remained that way, each plotting the next maneuver in their battle of wills, until a blurry black **V** appeared to the east. The thing was so tiny that had the princess not been looking for it in that very section of sky, she would not have seen it at all.

The distant shape grew larger at an alarming pace, and soon Tanalasta could see the thing's leathery wings rising and falling as it streaked through the stonemurk. It came parallel to their hiding place on the mountain and continued past without turning, and the princess hoped for their sake the caravan drivers and any survivors from Ryban's company were long gone.

Once it had disappeared around the shoulder of the mountain, Vangerdahast turned in the approximate direction of the outcropping and stacked three stones on the rim of the little gully. "It will be coming from there."

"Coming?" Tanalasta asked.

"If you're right about it hearing our ring-talk," the wizard explained. He plucked a wand from inside his weathercloak, then added, "Strictly speaking, I will be using a sending, though I doubt it makes any difference. If the thing can hear one form of telepathy, I suspect it will hear another."

Tanalasta frowned. "What are you talking about?"

"Finding Alusair, of course," said the wizard. "You did say that was what you wanted to do."

"I meant by looking for her, not inviting the ghazneth to come after us."

"And where, exactly, do you intend to look?" Vangerdahast asked.

"You don't know?" Tanalasta asked, disbelieving. "You haven't even tried to locate her?"

"What's the use? When she doesn't want to be found, she takes off her signet and puts on her Hider." The wizard was referring to the magic ring of privacy Alusair had prevailed upon Azoun to have made. By slipping it on, she could prevent even Vangerdahast's magic from locating her. "Even if she isn't wearing the Hider, Alusair moves quickly. There's no use trying to locate her until you're in a position to start the chase."

"And until you've had time enough to talk her sister out of her inconvenient ideas," Tanalasta added dryly.

Vangerdahast shrugged. "Perhaps. It still leaves us with the same dilemma: where to look."

"Since she was looking for Emperel, sooner or later she would check the Cavern of the Sleeping Sword," said Tanalasta. The cavern was the secret resting place of the Lords Who Sleep, the company of slumbering warriors whom Emperel was charged with safeguarding. "I thought we could start there."

"And lead the ghazneth there?" Vangerdahast countered. "That doesn't strike me as very wise. We *are* trying to keep the company's location secret from our enemies, you know."

Tanalasta narrowed her eyes at his condescension. "So where would you start?"

"Why not by asking Alusair herself?" Vangey replied.

"Because Alusair isn't wearing her signet," Tanalasta said, exasperated. "And because we have grounds to believe she has a good reason not to be."

"True, but that reason is over there looking for us." Vangerdahast pointed toward the unseen outcropping. "This is probably the only chance we'll have to contact Alusair without putting her life in danger. Besides, we can test your theory about the ghazneth eavesdropping on our mind talk."

The wizard did not point out that if Tanalasta was right, they would have to move quickly to avoid a fight with the ghazneth. Judging by Vangerdahast's preparations, though, he did not really intend to avoid the fight.

"Before I agree, tell me what you're planning." Tanalasta gestured at the hodgepodge of knickknacks arrayed on the boulder. There was a clove of garlic, a sprig of rosemary, a vial of holy water, and several other strange items. "What's all that for?"

"Just a small experiment." Vangerdahast gave her one of those innocent smiles that had been making Tanalasta nervous since she grew old enough to speak, then he picked up a dove's feather. "Without knowing exactly what a ghazneth is, it's hard to guess what it despises, but I bet this will work. I haven't met a demon yet who likes feather of the dove."

"You're going to banish it?"

"If you're right about this mind-speak business, yes." Vangerdahast picked up a rock, then began to trace a pentagram on top of the boulder. "I'll send it straight back to the hell it came from—wherever that is."

"And if you don't?"

Vangerdahast waved a gnarled finger toward ridge, gesturing at the spirelike stone he had pointed out earlier. "That's what escape plans are for. Are you going to help me or not?"

Tanalasta nodded. "I just hope you're doing this for more than your pride." After lecturing the wizard earlier about their duty, she could hardly decline to aid him now. "What do you want me to do?"

Vangerdahast outlined her part in his plan, then turned to continue his preparations while she untethered the horses. By the time she returned with the beasts, the wizard had completed his protective pattern and was ready to proceed. He climbed onto the boulder and stepped into the center of the star, the strange assortment of spell components grasped securely in one hand.

"You can watch from the ridge," he said. "If this works, you'll see a portal open and suck the ghazneth back to its home hell."

"And if the ghazneth doesn't go?" Tanalasta asked.

"Then I'll join you on the ridge—and don't waste any time getting us out of there." He nodded to her, then turned to face the three stones he piled on the edge of the gully. "I'm ready."

Tanalasta turned toward the ridge and pictured Alusair's ash-blonde hair and dark-eyed visage in her mind, then touched the throat clasp of her weathercloak. The metal tingled under her fingers, and her sister's head suddenly cocked to one side.

Vangey is with me on Stonebolt Trail, at the edge of the Storm Horns. Phantom after us. Need to find you.

Tanalasta? Alusair's weathered face betrayed her irritation. *Orc's Pool—Vangey knows it. And no more magic, or you'll never make it!*

Alusair's visage faded with that. Tanalasta shook her head clear, then glanced back at Vangerdahast. "You know some place called Orc's Pool?"

"I've been there many times." The wizard continued to study the sky above the stones he had piled on the gully edge. "Now off with you."

Tanalasta did not reach for the escape pocket. "She said no more magic."

"What?" Vangerdahast glanced down aghast. "How does she expect us to find Orc's Pool?"

Tanalasta had a sinking feeling. "I was more concerned about our plan. She said no more magic or we'd never make it."

It was difficult to say whether Vangerdahast's expression was more puzzled or irritated, but it was definitely not alarmed. "It's too late to change plans now." He glanced back toward the outcropping, then made a shooing motion. "Off with you. Here it comes already."

Tanalasta's gaze rose involuntarily, and she glimpsed a dark figure streaking over the mountain's shoulder. She spun in her saddle, looking toward the spire on the next ridge and thrusting her hand into the weathercloak's escape pocket. Her arm went numb, then there was a sharp crack, and a door-sized rectangle of blackness hissed into existence in front of her.

Cadimus whinnied in alarm and tried to shy back, threatening to pull his reins free of the princess's grasp.

"Not now, you coward!" Tanalasta jerked the stallion forward and urged her own mount through the doorway.

The world went black, and the princess experienced a strange, timeless sense of falling she thought would last forever. She grew queasy and weak, and a sudden chill bit at her fingers and nose. Her ears filled with a hushed roaring, at once overpowering as a waterfall and as soft as a whisper, and her stomach reverberated as though to the roll of a thousand drums. Then, in less than the instant it had taken her to blink, she was back in the light, her head spinning and the wind whistling around her ears.

Cadimus nickered behind her, sounding as confused as he was alarmed, and Tanalasta recalled with a rush where she was and what she was doing. She kicked her own mount's flanks urgently, and the poor horse stumbled forward blindly, as dazed and reeling as her rider. The princess let the mare continue on until she felt the ground sloping away beneath them, then dismounted and tethered both glassy-eyed horses to a scraggly hackberry bush.

By the time Tanalasta returned to the ridge, her head had stopped spinning. She lay down beneath the tall spire of granite and peered over the crest. Across the way, the ghazneth was already swooping down the gully toward Vangerdahast.

As the phantom neared him, it suddenly veered and pulled up. For one awful instant, she thought it was coming for her, then it wheeled on a huge black wing and extended its talons to attack the wizard from behind. Vangerdahast whirled, wand in hand, but the ghazneth was already on him. Tanalasta knew the wizard's spell would never go off before the creature's talons tore him gullet to groin. She was on her feet before she knew what she was doing, one hand disappearing into her weathercloak's escape pocket and the other reaching for her peacemaker's rod.

Fortunately for both the princess and the royal magician, Tanalasta remained where she was. Like the message-sending throat clasp, her weathercloak's escape pocket could only be used once a day. She dropped back to the ground, then watched in amazement as the ghazneth ricocheted away from the wizard's protective star and slammed into the mountainside.

Vangerdahast's shoulders slumped with relief, then his voice began to echo off the rocky slopes as he bellowed his incantation and tossed his strange assortment of knick-knacks into the air. The ghazneth circled the boulder where he stood, hurling itself at him time and again, only to bounce away and crash into the mountain with stone-splitting force. A shimmering spiral of light appeared in the air behind the creature and began to shadow its move-ments like some strange tail it did not know it had.

When the ghazneth finally grew tired of slamming into the mountainside, it alighted in the gully next to Vanger-dahast. It seemed to say something, then squatted down and wrapped its arms around the boulder. The stone began to tremble, and Tanalasta could tell by the sudden tension in the wizard's shoulders that he had not antici-pated the possibility of having his perch ripped out of the very ground.

Vangerdahast's echoing voice rumbled off the moun-tains more urgently, and he stooped down to fling his knickknacks directly onto the shoulders of his attacker. The tornado at the ghazneth's back grew larger and faster, sucking the thing's leathery wings backward toward the whirlpool's spiraling depths. The creature glanced nervously over its shoulder, then a small eye appeared in the heart of the tornado. From Vangerdahast's description, Tanalasta expected to see some sort of flaming hell or blood-drenched wasteland, but the small circle resembled nothing quite so much as the Stonelands themselves.

The ghazneth let out a great roar and gave a tremendous twist. A sharp crack reverberated off the mountainside, then the boulder rose out of the ground and Vangerdahast's legs went out from under him.

Tanalasta was on her feet again, yelling for the wizard to use his escape pocket, though she knew he would never hear her over the rumble of the cracking stone. As Vangerdahast tumbled from the boulder, he reached out with the dove's feather and struck the creature on the head.

A terrible shriek reverberated across the slope. The ghazneth vanished into the whirlpool, dragging Vangerdahast's boulder along with it. The wizard landed facedown in the gully and lay there trembling, then the spell whooshed in on itself and there was silence.

Tanalasta let out a joyful whoop, then saw a familiar shape in the sky and dropped to her belly. Vangerdahast raised his head, and she rose to her knees to point behind him. The wizard stood and turned to face the shoulder of the mountain, where the ghazneth was already streaking down out of the stonemurk.

Vangerdahast stood there looking for what seemed an eternity, but in fact may have been less than a second. Tanalasta started to rise and yell, but she did not even make it to a crouch before the wizard turned and was suddenly beside her, swaying and blinking with teleport daze and blindly reaching out to catch hold of her sleeve.

"Get us out of here!"

7

hey were lost in a sea of brown. The sun was hiding behind an overcast of dirty-pearl clouds, and a stiff northerly wind had draped the horizon behind a curtain of tannish stonemurk. The plain was paved in jagged slabs of red-brown basalt, set unevenly into a bed of yellow-brown sand, and the few scraggly salt bushes hardy enough to grow in such a wasteland were a sickly shade of hazel. Even Tanalasta's riding breeches and Vangerdahast's glorious beard had turned olive-brown beneath a thick coating of Stonelands dust.

As uncomfortable as the stonemurk made travel, the princess was glad for its foglike veil. After Vangerdahast's futile attempt to banish the ghazneth, anything that helped conceal them was a great comfort to her. They had glimpsed the thing twice since fleeing the Storm Horns. The first time had been two evenings ago, when its dark form streaked across the horizon between them and the mountains. The second time had been only a few hours ago, when it had appeared in the far north, circling like a hawk searching for its next meal.

The banishment's failure seemed to have sapped Vangerdahast's confidence. He would spend long hours deep in silent thought, then suddenly subject Tanalasta to a lengthy hypothesis about why he had failed to exile the ghazneth to its home plane. Having read—some said memorized—every volume in the palace library, the princess was able to debunk most of his theories with a little careful consideration. So far, the only notion to stand the test of her scrutiny was that the banishment had not failed at all, that the ghazneth *had* been sucked back to its home plane. Unfortunately, that plane happened to be Toril.

Vangerdahast dismissed the possibility as a contradiction of itself, simply proclaiming that a demon could not be from Toril, and something from Toril could not be a demon. Tanalasta considered the argument pure semantics. To her mind, anything that looked, acted, and killed like a demon *was* a demon. Moreover, when she pointed out that the thing had been affected by two spells that affected only demons—the protective star and the banishment itself—Vangerdahast had been unable to refute her argument. Maybe the creature wasn't a demon by war wizard definitions, but it was close enough for a princess.

Tanalasta wished she had not let Vangerdahast trick her into parting ways with Owden Foley. She had read in the *Imaskari Book of War* (Alaphondar's translation, of course) that priests were better suited to dealing with demons than wizards. Priests tended not to let their pride get them killed as often.

For the second time in a quarter hour, Tanalasta found her vision obscured by brown grime. She wiped the gobs from her eyes, then opened her waterskin and washed the grit from her teeth. Either they had drifted off their westerly course or the wind had shifted, and if she remembered one thing from Gaspaeril Gofar's little *Treatise on the Flora of the Barren Wastes*, it was that the wind seldom shifted in the Stonelands.

Tanalasta glanced over at the lodestone dangling from the wrist of Vangerdahast's rein hand. They were still traveling at a right angle to the tiny rod, which meant they should have been facing west. So why was a northerly wind blowing in their faces? And if it was not northerly, why was it still full of Anauroch sand? When the wind shifted, the stonemurk vanished. Gaspaeril's treatise had been clear about that.

Tanalasta reined her horse to a stop. "Something's wrong."

Vangerdahast continued forward, lost in thought and oblivious to the princess's absence. She waited until Cadimus had carried the wizard several paces, then shook her head at the inattentiveness of her 'protector.'

"Vangerdahast!"

The wizard's back straightened and his gaze snapped to the side. When he did not see the princess in her customary place, he cursed foully and looked skyward, reaching for a wand.

"Vangerdahast, no magic!" Tanalasta yelled.

Since escaping the ghazneth, they had taken Alusair's advice and avoided magic like the plague. They had banished their rings, bracers, and weathercloaks to their saddlebags and buried their peacemaker's rods, enchanted daggers, and everything else that radiated a constant aura of magic. So far, they had every reason to be happy with the results.

When the wizard still did not see her, Tanalasta waved her hand in the air. "I'm right here."

Vangerdahast reined his mount around, his rheumy eyes betraying his relief. "What is it?" He continued to scan the horizon. "Did you see something?"

"It's what I haven't seen that concerns me," Tanalasta said. "Shouldn't we have reached Crimson Creek by now?"

Vangerdahast finally pulled his hand from his weather-cloak. "Apparently not, since we haven't. Have patience. The Stonelands are a big place."

"If you consider four thousand square miles big, then yes, they are," said Tanalasta, "but that's not the point. You said we would reach Crimson Creek in a day. We're now going on two."

"How am I to know how long it takes?" Vangerdahast shrugged. "I've never *ridden* there, you know."

"I suppose not," Tanalasta sighed. As busy as he was, the wizard was hardly likely to waste his time riding when he could teleport. "How far is it from the Stonebolt Trail?"

The wizard only shook his head. "It hardly matters, does it?" He waved his hand at the rocky plain around them and added, "It's not like we can miss it."

"We can if we never cross it." Tanalasta pointed at the lodestone hanging from Vangerdahast's wrist. "You're sure that thing's accurate?"

Vangerdahast extended his arm at an angle. The lodestone swung briefly from side-to-side, then pivoted back to its original position—perpendicular to the wind. "You see? It always returns to north."

"Then how come we're riding into a northerly wind?" Tanalasta asked.

Vangerdahast's answer was as quick as it was certain. "It is not a northerly wind, it's a westerly one."

"Full of Anauroch sand?" Tanalasta asked.

The wizard frowned and fell silent for a moment, then pointed at the ground. "The sand comes from the Stonelands themselves."

"Not according to Gaspaeril Gofar." Tanalasta extended her hand. "Let me see the map. Unless Crimson Creek is more than forty miles from the trail, we've gone too far."

Vangerdahast made no move to do as she asked. "I would say that the creek is just about forty miles from the Stonebolt Trail."

Tanalasta continued to hold her hand out. "You *do* have a map, don't you?"

"Of course." Vangerdahast tapped a saddlebag. "A magic one."

"Wonderful," said Tanalasta. "I suppose we should be thankful. This is teaching us a valuable lesson."

"Us?" Vangerdahast frowned. "What do you mean, 'us?'"

"We can't even open a map without magic. You don't think that's a little over-reliant?" Tanalasta asked. "What if we needed that map to win a battle?"

"If this were a battle, *we* would not be here," said Vangerdahast stiffly. "And if you are trying to intimate that your spell-beggars would do better, do recall that they also speak their incantations one syllable at a time."

"Vangey, that's not what I mean at all." Tanalasta reached across to touch the wizard's arm. "I'm only trying to say that magic has its own vulnerabilities, like anything else."

"My magic is powerful enough to see us both to safety in Arabel." Vangerdahast jerked his arm away. "Which is exactly what we should do, now that we have established that Alusair is safe."

"We have established that she's alive, not safe." Tanalasta's tone grew sharp. "Nor do we know what she has discovered about Emperel's disappearance or the ghazneth, which I suspect to be related. Most importantly, we have not yet informed Alusair that she is the new crown princess. You may stop talking to me about your teleport spell and start riding."

Tanalasta urged her horse past Vangerdahast's, then turned perpendicular to the wind and began to trot in what she hoped was a westerly direction. The wizard started after her.

"If you insist on this foolishness, will you at least ride in the right direction?"

"This *is* the right direction." Tanalasta recalled a pamphlet on sea navigation one of the Dauntinghorn ancestors had written a hundred years before, then stopped and turned to the wizard. "If I can prove it, will you stop badgering me about teleporting back to Arabel?"

Vangerdahast's bushy brow furrowed. He studied her without answering, and Tanalasta began to fear he had thought of the same thing she had.

When the wizard finally spoke, it grew clear he had not even considered the possibility that she might be right. "And when you can't prove it, you will return to Arabel in all due haste and let me see to this matter properly."

"Agreed."

Vangerdahast could not quite keep from smirking. "Very well, then. Prove away."

Tanalasta smiled and patted the wizard's cheek. "I have a feeling we're going to be a lot better friends after this."

She dismounted and transferred her belongings to one side of her saddlebags. After the compartment was empty, she refilled it with fist-sized stones and walked to the front of her horse.

"Lead on, Vangerdahast. We'll set our course by your lodestone for a few minutes."

Vangerdahast eyed her saddlebags as though she meant to stone him to death, but nodded and lifted his rein hand to let the lodestone beneath it dangle free. He started forward at a right angle to the tiny rod, being careful not to stray off course. Tanalasta followed on foot, leading her horse and pausing every ten steps to stack one of the rocks from her saddlebag atop a larger stone along Vangerdahast's trail.

The royal magician kept looking back, watching first with scorn, then with puzzlement, bewilderment, and—

finally—chagrin. By the time the saddlebag ran out of stones, his cheeks were crimson with embarrassment. He shook his head in disgust, then pulled the lodestone from his wrist.

"We've been riding in circles!" The wizard raised his arm to throw the tiny rod away.

"Wait—it's not the lodestone!" Tanalasta turned to look back along their course and saw that the stones traced a gentle, but distinct curve. "Cecil Dauntinghorn noticed a similar effect about a hundred years ago, when he found himself sailing around a tiny island in the Sea of Fallen Stars. As it turned out, his lodestone was pointing at a strange cliff of black rock. It started to point north again after he was far enough away."

Vangerdahast eyed the stone-strewn plain sourly. "Don't I look the fool. I hope you're proud of yourself."

"Not really." Tanalasta began to redistribute the load in her saddlebags. "Well, maybe just a little bit, but I wasn't trying to make you feel foolish. I just want you to trust my judgment."

Vangerdahast cocked an eyebrow. "I'd trust it more if you would let me teleport us—"

"Vangey—"

The wizard raised his hand. "Not to Arabel, to Orc's Pool. I've no doubt Alusair is fuming at our tardiness already, and now it'll take us twice as long to find it—if we ever do."

"Alusair can wait a few hours longer. I suspect she'd be even angrier with us if we led the ghazneth into the middle of her company." Tanalasta fastened her saddlebags, then wiped another gob of brown grime from her eyes. "Besides, I doubt we lost much time. I'd have noticed if we had veered into the wind earlier."

The princess mounted and turned perpendicular to the wind, now confident that she was heading westward. They rode for another three hours, and twice they noticed small bands of stoop-shouldered silhouettes skulking through the stonemurk. Both times they swerved away and rode briefly in the opposite direction, then resumed their westward travels. At last, the yellowish sky began to grow brown and dim, and Tanalasta was about to suggest that they make camp for the night when the wind suddenly filled with the overpowering scent of old death.

The princess pulled up short, and the odor vanished as quickly as it had come.

"Did you smell that, Vangerdahast?" She felt certain that her face had gone pale.

"Something like rancid blood?" He pointed into the wind. "From somewhere up there?"

Tanalasta nodded.

"No, I didn't smell anything."

The wizard turned Cadimus into the wind and urged him forward, leaving Tanalasta to puzzle over his rash behavior. She followed a few paces behind, wishing she had some way other than magic to defend herself. The odor returned again, this time stronger, then began to vanish and return at increasingly frequent intervals. Vangerdahast kept altering his course until the stench grew more or less constant. The princess began to notice mats of green moss and rich grass growing between the stones. Finally, a curtain of white steam appeared ahead, silhouetting a column of scraggly smoke trees arrayed along a chain of low, rocky hummocks.

Vangerdahast stopped beneath a wispy bough and peered down at the base of the hummocks. Tanalasta joined him, nearly gagging on the smell of brimstone and iron as she approached, then found herself looking down into a steepsided ravine of raw red ground. Through the bottom of the gulch ran a steaming brook of blood-colored water, gurgling northward over a bed of jagged, rust-stained boulders.

"Crimson Creek?" she asked.

Vangerdahast nodded. "Right where you said it would be." He turned upstream and started to ride along the rim of the gulch. "Come along. We'll make camp at Orc's Pool."

"You know where we are?"

Vangerdahast shook his head. "Never seen this place before."

"I think we'd better make camp here." Tanalasta glanced at the dimming heavens, then added, "It'll soon be too dark to ride."

"We have time." Vangerdahast continued to ride. When Tanalasta made no move to follow, he stopped and looked back over his shoulder. "Perhaps you'd like to bet? Double or nothing?"

"Double what?" Tanalasta studied the steaming creek and shook her head. For the water to be that hot, the source had to be nearby. "No deal, Old Snoop. I see your game."

"Do you now?" Vangerdahast smiled, then urged his horse forward. "I guess you're just too smart for me, Tanalasta, too smart by far."

The pool turned out to be even nearer than the princess expected. She followed Vangerdahast along the ravine for a quarter mile, then the steam began to thin, and the creek suddenly grew as colorless as air. They spent several minutes staring into the ravine in puzzlement, then finally dismounted and started to lead their horses down the embankment. As they descended, a scarlet ribbon appeared in the steam opposite them, curling down between the nebulous bulges of two rocky hummocks on the far shore.

Tanalasta pointed toward the ribbon. "I assume Orc's Pool is rather bloody looking?"

"That would be correct. Are you certain those spell-beggars in Huthduth didn't make a diviner out of you?"

Tanalasta frowned, trying to decide whether the wizard was mocking her or trying to compliment her. "It's just common sense."

"I've heard that's all priestly divination is," the wizard replied. "Now, real magic—"

"Would do us no good, under the circumstances," said Tanalasta. "And I would like you to stop referring to my friends as 'spell-beggars.'"

Vangerdahast tipped his head. "As you command, Princess."

They reached the ravine bottom and crossed a mat of mossy grass to the water's edge, then tested its temperature with their fingers before mounting and riding across. On the far side, they followed the scarlet brook up a small, gently-sloping vale. Though no vegetation grew within two paces of the creek, a luxuriant growth of grass covered the walls of the valley, and the stench changed from brimstone-and-iron to just iron. Once Tanalasta grew accustomed to the odor and no longer associated it with blood, she actually found the smell tolerable.

At length, they reached the end of the valley, where the brook spilled over a rocky headwall from a steaming basin above. When no sentries emerged to greet or challenge them, they tethered their horses to a wild mulberry tree and crept the rest of the way on foot, mindful of the possibility that an orc tribe—or something worse—had forced Alusair to abandon the rendezvous. They found nothing but a small pool of blood-colored water, ringed on all sides by a boulder-strewn collar of green grass and low cliffs of rusty red basalt.

"This is Orc's Pool?" Tanalasta asked.

"Of course. How many red pools do you think there are in the Stonelands?"

Tanalasta frowned. "Now that you mention it, Gaspaeril Gofar's treatise mentioned over sixty bodies of iron-tinted water."

"This is the one," Vangerdahast said. "I recognize it."

The wizard clambered over the headwall and led the way toward a ring of boulders on the southern shore of the pool. As they crossed the meadow, Tanalasta noticed a single square yard of freshly-turned ground. Leaving Vangerdahast to continue on his own, she stopped to examine it. The stones had been carefully removed from the dirt and piled along the edges, and there was a small dimple in the center where the soil had been wetted by a cupful of water.

From up ahead, Vangerdahast called, "They're here—at least someone is."

Tanalasta went to join the wizard at the circle of stones. As she approached, she smelled a familiar haylike odor and saw the broom of a horse's tail swing out from behind a boulder.

"Alusair?" she called.

"I don't think so," answered Vangerdahast.

Tanalasta stepped around the boulder to find a hidden, well-used camp large enough to accommodate a company of twenty people. At the present time, there was only a tethered horse and Vangerdahast, seated on the saddle that had been taken from the beast's back. A pair of dusty boots sat on the ground next to him, and he was going through the pockets of a tunic and breeches that had been left beside a neatly folded traveling cape.

"Vangerdahast, what do you think you're doing?" Tanalasta demanded.

"Trying to find out who this belongs to," the wizard replied, "and whether or not he's one of Alusair's boys."

"He is."

The voice came from behind Tanalasta, so close that it made her scream and leap into the air. She came down facing the speaker, clutching a sharp stone she had been carrying in lieu of her magic dagger. The man was naked and wet, with shoulder-length hair and skin still flushed from the heat of the pool, and he didn't look half-bad. In fact, he looked more than half-good, with dark hair and darker eyes, chiseled features, and a proud chin with just a hint of a cleft. He had shoulders as broad as a door, arms the size of Tanalasta's thighs, not even a hint of a belly, and . . . she blushed, for it was not every day that a princess saw such sights.

"Your Highness, forgive me!" The man sounded mortified. Still holding his sword and scabbard, he lowered his hands and covered himself. "I wasn't expecting you with the stonemurk today, and I was availing myself of the water when I heard someone approaching."

When Tanalasta did not reply, the man tried to slip past. "I do beg your forgiveness, Princess, but we've lost a few men on this journey, and I had to be cautious."

It finally dawned on Tanalasta that she was staring. "On my honor!" The princess let the stone drop from her hand and turned away, her face burning as though she were the one who had just climbed from the pool's steaming waters. "P-please, think no more of it."

Out of the corner of her eye, Tanalasta saw Vangerdahast smile.

"Well then, maybe this trip was worth it after all," said the wizard. He passed the man his clothes. "And who might you be, son?"

"My name is Rowen," the man said. Tanalasta heard the snap of pant legs being flapped open. "Rowen Cormaeril."

Tanalasta felt the blood rush from her cheeks even more quickly than it had rushed into them. She turned, slowly, to find the man now standing in tunic and breeches.

"Of . . . of relation to Gaspar Cormaeril?" she asked.

Rowen nodded. "Gaspar was my cousin, and as great a traitor to our family as he was to the realm."

Tanalasta's heart fell. Along with Aunadar Bleth, Gaspar Cormaeril had been one of the ringleaders in the Abraxus Affair. As punishment for his prominent role, her father had seized the lands of the entire Cormaeril family.

When Tanalasta could not find the words to express her dismay, Rowen bowed deeply and did not rise. "I apologize for vexing you with my presence, Majesty. Had it been possible, I'm certain the Princess Alusair would have sent someone else."

"I doubt it," growled Vangerdahast. The wizard looked to Tanalasta and shook his head. "She couldn't have been happy to hear from you. This is her way of showing it."

"Must you always think the worst of people, Lord Magician?" Tanalasta went over to Rowen. "I'm sure she sent Sir Rowen because she knew him to be the best man for the job."

The princess presented her hand to Rowen, who was so startled that he looked up and did not take it. She smiled and nodded, holding it in place. Somewhat reluctantly, he took her hand by the fingers and brushed his lips to the back.

"Only Rowen, Majesty," he said. "My title was taken with the family lands."

"Just Rowen, then." Tanalasta noticed Vangerdahast rolling his eyes and shot him a frown, then gestured for Rowen to rise. "Tell me, Rowen, is that your Faith Planting I noticed at the edge of the meadow?"

Rowen's eyes grew as round as coins. "Yes, Majesty, it is—but I'm surprised you know that. I didn't think anyone but Children of Chauntea would recognize it."

Tanalasta smiled. "They wouldn't—and please, don't call me Majesty. Tanalasta will do."

Vangerdahast hoisted himself to his feet. "By the Blue Dragon!" he cursed. "Alusair sends us a groundsplitter!"

8

he cabbage had already started to go, the big
leaves curling and turning brown along the
edges, the immature heads wilting open. A tall
beggar in a ragged cape was striding across the
field diagonally, paying no heed to the angry free farmer
hurling insults and dirt clods in his direction. In the dusky
light, the intruder was a mere silhouette half again as tall
as a man, with a lurching gait and beady red eyes just
bright enough to be seen beneath his billowing hood.

"That's the signal," Azoun whispered. "He has them."

"Well done, Sire," said Dauneth Marliir. "It will be good
to be done with these rabble."

"They're hardly rabble, Lord Warden." Azoun eased his
horse into the shadows beneath a young ash. "They're
trying to help."

"Yes, but help whom?" Dauneth followed him into the
shadows. "I am sure it has occurred to His Majesty that

144

they might be spreading this alarm purposely, to win support for their royal temple. And I must say it's working. As matters stand now, the blight could spoil half the fields in the realm and the peasants would still hold these seed-flingers as heroes."

A dozen riders burst from the woods on the other side of the field and started across at a full gallop, yelling promises of restitution as they passed. The beggar, now only a few paces from the ambush site, paid his pursuers no attention and continued forward at the same even stride.

"If the blight takes half the fields in the realm, perhaps they would be heroes," said Azoun. "It would certainly mean *we* have not been seeing to our duties, Lord Warden. Besides, Owden and his priests are not the only ones who have seen the blight-spreader."

"Indeed—the peasants see the fellow everywhere," said Dauneth. "In Bospir, they burned another tinker at the stake this morning—and he wasn't even tall. This one just happened to be wearing a black cloak when a free farmer saw him doing his business by the side of the road."

Azoun winced. That was the seventh lynching he had heard of in the last three days, and the rate seemed to be increasing. Perhaps he should have listened to Dauneth two days ago and sent a squad of war wizards to track down the "Badgeless Maces" then, but he had not wanted to embarrass Tanalasta by returning her friends to Arabel in shackles. Moreover, he had regarded Dauneth's motives as somewhat suspect, fearing the young lord had made the suggestion out of anger at Tanalasta.

Of course, Azoun should have known better. The High Warden was too loyal to let his personal feelings interfere with duty. The priests had indeed created the panic Dauneth feared, and now innocent people were being killed. The king was almost relieved to find his own judgment in this matter less sound than that of the High Warden; it suggested that Dauneth was not holding a grudge, and the throne had need of a loyal warden in Arabel. Once they brought Owden Foley and the "Badgeless Maces" under control, perhaps Azoun could even declare the damage wrought by Tanalasta undone.

The red-eyed beggar lurched past Azoun's hiding place and disappeared into the trees at the rear of the small clearing, the Badgeless Maces close behind. A row of Purple Dragons emerged from the trees to meet the company of priests. The dragoneers wore their visors raised and held their lances posted on their stirrup rests, but their grim expressions left no doubt that they were present on a serious matter. The Badgeless Maces hauled back on their reins, barely managing to bring their mounts to a stop before the dragoneers.

As confused as they were, the priests remained determined to capture their quarry. A handful tried to ease through the Purple Dragons only to find their way blocked by a lowered lance. Several more wheeled around to circle the line, only to find another row of dragoneers emerging from the trees to block their way. Even then, it did not seem to occur to the priests that this was anything more than a chance meeting.

"What are you doing?" Owden gestured into the woods where the tall beggar had disappeared. "After that man! He's a danger to the land!"

"Hardly." Merula the Marvelous stepped out of the wood, his eyes still glowing red and the hood of his black cloak now pulled down on his collar. "I am not the one riding about the north, scaring witless peasants half-to-death with tales of dark phantoms and impending famine."

Owden's shoulders slumped, then he lowered his mace and fixed his gaze on the portly wizard. "Merula the Massive? Explain yourself! You're interfering with a royal commission charged with a matter of the highest urgency."

"Really?" Azoun urged his horse out of his hiding place behind the priests, bringing with him Dauneth Marliir and the final rank of Purple Dragons. "Strange, I do not recall commissioning a company of 'Badgeless Maces' into the Purple Dragons."

The entire band of priests wheeled at once, their faces paling at the sight of Azoun's battle-crowned helm.

"Majesty!"

Owden swung out of his saddle, then knelt on the ground and bowed his head. His priests followed half a step behind, moving so quickly that several overcautious dragoneers lowered their lances.

Azoun motioned the lances up again, then continued to look at Owden and his priests. "In fact, I don't recall commissioning any company of priests at all, nor charging them with . . ." He looked to Dauneth. "What was the phrase, Lord Warden?"

"I believe it was 'A matter of the highest urgency,' Sire."

"Ah yes." Azoun repeated the phrase as though trying to refresh his memory, then shook his head. "No, I'm quite certain I never said such a thing."

Owden dared to raise his head. "Forgive my presumption, Majesty, but we, ah, assumed the title."

"*Assumed,* Harvestmaster Owden?" asked Merula. He stepped to Owden's side, then glanced in Dauneth's direction. "That would make you an imposter, you know. It would make you all impostors."

The king bit his tongue, trying desperately to hide a sudden surge of anger. Merula was doing his best to place Owden in the untenable position of confessing to the impersonation of a royal agent, or admitting that Tanalasta had defied the king's order. Apparently, the wizard remained concerned about the War Wizards' future after Tanalasta took the throne—this despite Azoun's personal guarantee that their position would be secure no matter who succeeded him.

"Perhaps it was Princess Tanalasta who commissioned you, Harvestmaster?" Merula continued to look at Dauneth.

Azoun forced himself to keep an impassive face and stay silent. The matter fell under the purview of the Lord High Warden, and any interference from the king would be taken either as a sign of favor to the priests, or as a lack of confidence in the crown princess's obedience to duty.

"I am sorry to say that Princess Tanalasta did not commission us." Owden addressed himself directly to Azoun. "You see, Sire, it was something of an emergency. We happened across a free farmer who had seen the blight-bearer—"

"This tall beggar you have been asking about," said Azoun, happy for any pretext to take control of the conversation. "You know, of course, that your inquiries have created a panic."

"I apologize, Majesty," Owden said, plucking at his purple cape, "but that is the reason for our disguises. We had hoped the inquiries of a company of Purple Dragons would seem less conspicuous."

"And well they might have, if you had acted like a company of soldiers," said Azoun. "In pausing to repair every blighted field you happened across, you persuaded everyone you met that I am so concerned about the situation that I have begun commissioning whole companies of priests."

"It may come to that yet, Majesty," said Owden.

"I'm sure you hope it will," said Dauneth, "but I won't have you causing a panic in these lands simply to promote yourselves. The peasants are already burning each others' fields at the first sign of a wilt, and seven men have been murdered for the crime of matching your beggar's description."

Owden's face fell at the news, but he kept his gaze fixed on Azoun. "I am sorry to have caused this trouble, Majesty, but it changes nothing. We must find this blight-carrier and stop him from wandering about. Until we do that, we must keep restoring the fields he infects and prevent the disease from spreading on its own."

"I am sure he'll be found soon," said Azoun. "Every company of Purple Dragons north of the High Road is watching for him. Nor do I think there is much chance of the blight spreading on its own—not with the peasants burning their fields at the first sign of a brown leaf."

"That will help certainly, but we are much practiced in these matters," said Owden. "You must let us continue our search—if not as Purple Dragons, then as humble clerics."

"I'm afraid that won't be possible," said Dauneth.

Owden finally directed his attention to the High Warden. "You're arresting us?"

"The Lord High Warden has no choice," said Merula, smirking. "Impersonating a royal agent is a high crime, punishable by death."

"By death?" This from one of Owden's priests, a young red-haired woman no more than twenty. "We were only trying to help!"

Merula gave the woman a crocodile's smile. "I'm sorry, but unless Princess Tanalasta commissioned you—"

"She didn't," said Owden. He shot the woman a warning scowl, then rose and stepped toward Dauneth. "Do with us what you must, Lord Warden, but I pray you, do not let this dark beggar wander these lands long. The blight may seem a little enough thing now, but that is only because we have contained it."

Moving slowly so as not to alarm the guards, the harvestmaster pulled his mace from its carrying loop and presented the handle to Dauneth.

Azoun shot Merula a look that left no doubt about how the wizard's mistrust had been received. Merula looked the other way and pretended not to notice, more secure than he should be in Vangerdahast's ability to shield him from royal displeasure. The man's smugness was a better argument than any Tanalasta had made for taking the war wizards down a notch.

Dauneth kept his hands on his saddle horn, making no move to accept Owden's mace. "Actually, Merula may have overstated matters." The High Warden cast a querying glance at Azoun, who smiled inwardly but kept a stern outer face and nodded curtly. "As I recall, those robes were issued to you on command of the royal magician for the purpose of escorting Princess Tanalasta into the Stonelands."

"And while that may fall short of a royal commission, it does excuse you for wearing them," said Azoun. Though he approved of Dauneth's quick thinking, he could not let the Badgeless Maces off the hook entirely. He had worked too hard to bring the tumult of the past few days under control. "What you must answer for is disobeying my wishes and returning to chase this beggar instead of going with her into the Stonelands."

Owden returned his mace to its carrying ring, relief flooding his face. "Of course, Majesty. That is really very easy to explain. In fact, I've come to think it was what Vangerdahast intended all along."

"Truly? Now that *will* take some explaining." Azoun raised his hand, commanding the harvestmaster to remain silent until he finished. "The queen will certainly wish a careful accounting of exactly what was said and done, in all the particulars—down to the minutest detail, I am sure. You and your priests are invited to return with us to Arabel, where you will be my guests until such a time as I am satisfied that you have prepared a record to the queen's liking."

Owden's eyes dulled as he comprehended the king's meaning. He bowed stiffly, then said, "As you command, Sire."

"Good. On the journey back, perhaps you would be kind enough to tell Merula and me what you have learned about this beggar and his blight." Azoun glanced darkly in Merula's direction, then said, "I'm sure the war wizards can handle the matter—once they have the vaguest idea what's going on."

The dig seemed to delight Owden as much as it irritated Merula. "It would be a pleasure, Sire. Merula and I do enjoy talking while we travel."

"Oh, immensely," growled the wizard.

Azoun smiled at Merula's glower. "Excellent," he said, feeling that he finally had matters once again under control. "Dauneth, what say we camp tonight? It's too late to start home, and we don't want to put that poor free farmer out of his hut."

"A fine idea, Sire," said the High Warden, motioning to his lionars to set things in motion.

Azoun looked up at the darkening sky and saw the first star appear in the east. "It's been too long since I've done this." He began to finger his signet ring, then pictured Vangerdahast's bearded face. "Too long indeed."

* * * * *

Vangerdahast was standing on the grassy collar on the outlet side of Orc's Pool, giving Cadimus and Tanalasta's mare a few minutes grazing time when he heard Azoun's voice.

I'll be sleeping under the stars tonight, old friend.

Vangerdahast looked down and sighed wearily. Though the wizard's own signet ring was in Cadimus's saddle bags with most of his other magic, that did not prevent Azoun from contacting him. Mindful of the fact that he needed to be available to the royal family even when he had removed his ring to work in the laboratory or take a bath, the royal magician had taken the precaution of fashioning the family rings so that they could contact him whether or not he was wearing his. This wasn't the first time he had had reason to regret his foresight—a late evening with a particularly frolicsome water nymph leaped immediately to mind—but it was the first time he had ever had reason to let it frighten him.

"And I won't be sleeping at all, thanks to you," Vangerdahast replied, speaking aloud. "What news?"

Matters are well in hand here. You can bring Tanalasta back any time.

"I'm afraid I can't." Vangerdahast began to root through Tanalasta's saddle bags, pulling out her bracers, rings, and weathercloak. "Tanalasta won a bet. We're at Orc's Pool."

A bet?

"Don't ask," the wizard said. "And it gets worse."

She won't give up on the temple?

"Worse."

What could be worse than that?

"A Cormaeril," Vangerdahast explained. "A Chauntea-worshiping Cormaeril ranger named Rowen. She seemed quite taken with him."

I thought you had a plan! Azoun complained. *What kind of plan is that?*

"Don't panic. Maybe he'll turn out to have a nasty temper or hate royals or something." Vangerdahast closed Tanalasta's saddlebags and started around the pool toward the camp. "But we have bigger problems than that, at the moment. Ask Alaphondar to find out everything he can about a creature called a ghazneth. It's a phantom or demon or something whose wings protect it from magic. I can't seem to kill it."

You what?

"It's been harassing us—and Alusair, too." As Vangerdahast approached the camp, he heard a soft splashing in
the water. "It may have something to do with Emperel's
disappearance, but I don't know. We haven't been able to
catch up with Alusair."

*This shouldn't be taking so long. What's going on up
there?*

"It seems the ghazneth is attracted to magic," Vangerdahast said, "which is why Alusair took off her ring when
I tried to contact her from House Marliir. I'm afraid we
won't be able to talk like this for a while, old friend."

Wait. Azoun sounded worried. *I'll send Merula and
some Purple Dragons—and Owden is here.*

"That would only make it harder to talk Tanalasta out
of this mess," Vangerdahast said. "If things get dangerous
again—"

Again?

"Have no fear, Sire, she handled herself quite well."
Vangerdahast stopped outside the boulders and lowered
his voice. "As I was saying, I can always teleport us back to
Arabel."

Vangerdahast, I hope you know what you're doing.

"Of course!" Vangerdahast was genuinely hurt. "We
can't give up now . . . unless you fancy turning your royal
parade ground into a vegetable plot."

Azoun's only reply was a groan. The wizard smiled to
himself, then stepped into the boulder circle to find Rowen
sitting at water's edge, staring out into the steam toward
a shapely white blur that could only be Princess Tanalasta
floating on the surface of the dark pool. Jaw set, Vangerdahast strode through camp and planted a boot square in
the ranger's back, shoving him headlong into the steaming water.

Rowen vanished under the surface for a moment, then
emerged three paces to the left with a raised sword.

153

When he saw Vangerdahast standing in the moonlight, he lowered his weapon. "It was you?"

"It was," Vangerdahast growled. "And you may consider yourself lucky to escape with a dunking. Spying on a royal princess's bath could be deemed a crime against the crown."

Rowen's jaw fell. "I wasn't spying!"

"No? Just peeping?"

"Vangerdahast!" Tanalasta swam over and stood, crossing her arms in front of her breasts. "You owe Rowen an apology. I asked him to keep watch while I bathed."

"I doubt you asked him to watch *you*," growled Vangerdahast, though he suspected the possibility had at least occurred to Tanalasta. The wizard glowered in Rowen's direction. "Had you been *guarding* the princess instead of leering at her, you would have heard me coming."

"I was watching the horizon," Rowen protested. Though Tanalasta was still covering herself with her arms, he took care to avert his eyes as he spoke. "Milady, you must believe me. Why I didn't hear him—"

"Pay him no heed, Rowen," said Tanalasta, still covering herself with her arms. "Old Snoop is famous for skulking about the palace halls. One does not dare hold a personal conversation without first examining every garderobe and alcove within twenty paces."

Though twenty paces was actually something of an underestimate, Vangerdahast feigned hurt. "Even were that true, Princess, I was not skulking this time." He stepped to the edge of the water and opened Tanalasta's weathercloak. "I was speaking with your father."

Rowen's face grew as pale as the moonlight, then he glanced across the circle of boulders. "The king is with you?"

"Hardly." Vangerdahast motioned the ranger out of the water, then averted his own eyes so Tanalasta could slip into the cloak. "Will you hurry? We may not have much time."

"Time?" Rowen climbed out of the pool, being very careful not to look back. "Why not?"

"The king is in Arabel," Tanalasta explained, slipping into the weathercloak. "They were far-speaking."

Rowen spun on Vangerdahast. "Magic? Alusair warned you!"

"It was the king she didn't warn, young man," Vangerdahast bristled. "Now, be a good lad and fetch the horses."

"Of course." Rowen's expression changed from anger to chagrin. "You're right, we don't have much time."

The ranger sheathed his sword, then snatched up his saddle and rushed off in the direction of the horses. Tanalasta started to follow, but Vangerdahast caught her by the arm.

"Aren't you forgetting something, Princess?" He pointed toward her neatly folded tunic and trousers. "You really shouldn't tempt poor Rowen. It's unfair to vaunt a prize he has no chance of winning."

"Who says he doesn't?" The princess snatched up her clothes and stepped behind a boulder.

Vangerdahast groaned inwardly. He pulled a gold coin from his pocket and tossed it into the air, then spoke an incantation as it started to fall. The coin stopped at about eye level.

"Vangerdahast, have you lost your mind?" Tanalasta peered out from behind her rock. "That's what attracts it!"

"So I've been told."

Vangerdahast plucked the coin out of the air and began to rub it between his palms. A faint green aura appeared around the coin, barely brighter than the moonlight illuminating it against his palm.

"Now, watch and learn, my dear, watch and learn." Vangerdahast waited until Rowen returned with the horses, then asked, "Which way will we be traveling, young man?"

When Rowen pointed into the hills, Vangerdahast turned and flicked the coin in the opposite direction. It whistled down the gulch and sailed out over the flatlands, vanishing from sight like a shooting star.

"A false trail?" Rowen asked.

Vangerdahast nodded. "It should buy us an hour or two."

"You may be underestimating the ghazneth's speed."

Rowen crouched behind a boulder, then pointed toward the mouth of the gully, where the distant silhouette of a moonlit ghazneth was wheeling out over the plain.

"How long will your coin stay in the air?" Tanalasta asked.

"About as long as it takes the ghazneth to catch it," Vangerdahast continued to stare out over the empty plain, astonished at how quickly the dark creature had faded from sight. "How long that will be, who can say?"

"But sooner than we'd like," concluded Tanalasta.

The princess stepped from behind her boulder, now fully clothed, both bracers clasped on one arm and the weather-cloak thrown unclasped over her shoulders. The bracers would not radiate magic until she transferred one to her bare wrist, but closing the cloak's clasp would automatically activate several magics sure to draw the ghazneth's attention. Vangerdahast pulled his own weathercloak over his shoulders, leaving it unclasped, then they mounted and quietly left Orc's Pool behind.

9

he slope lay blanketed in shadow as thick as ink. Vangerdahast rode in silence, keeping a careful watch on the dark sky behind them, cringing inwardly at the constant clatter of horse hooves on shifting stone. He expected to see the ghazneth come streaking out of the mists above Orc's Pool at any moment, but his greatest fear was that he would not see it at all, that it would swoop in from some unwatched corner of the sky and disembowel them all before he could cast a single spell. His fingers kept tracing patterns of protection. Only the knowledge that the magic would draw the phantom like a signal fire kept him from uttering the incantations to activate the enchantments.

Finally, the companions crested the top of the hummock and began to traverse a barren, moonlit clearing lacking so much as a boulder to hide behind. They did not have even the stonemurk to conceal them, for the rolling hill lands made the wind too erratic and scattered to sustain its load of sand and loess. The trio urged their mounts across the clearing at a trot.

Vangerdahast finally began to relax when they reached the other side of the hillock and descended into the sheltering shadows of the adjacent gulch, but not so Rowen. The ranger continued to push hard, leading them up a sandy creek at a near gallop for several long minutes, then abruptly dismounting to double back along a dangerous slope of blond bedrock. When they reached the summit, they mounted again and trotted across another exposed summit, then repeated the process three more times before Rowen finally dropped into a winding gulch and stayed there.

The ranger scanned the sky one last time, then waved Vangerdahast and Tanalasta up beside him. "We'll follow this gully up onto Gnoll Flats," Rowen said, "then turn south toward the Storm Horns. The stonemurk could be pretty bad up there, but it'll die down for a while about dawn. We'll be looking for a pair of mountains Alusair has been calling the Mule Ears."

"We'll know them when we see them, I take it," Vangerdahast said. He did not bother asking Rowen's reason for detailing the route. With the ghazneth on their trail, being separated was one of the more pleasant reasons it was wise for everyone to know the way. "Is that where we'll meet Alusair?"

Rowen shifted in his saddle and was a little too careful to keep his eye on the trail. "Actually, no. That's where she was three days ago, when she received Tanalasta's sending."

"And where is she now?" Vangerdahast was all too confident he would not like the answer.

Rowen shrugged. "We'll have to see." He turned to Tanalasta. "You can follow a trail, can't you?"

"I can," said Tanalasta.

Rowen nodded as though he had expected no less and drew a somewhat surprised smile from Tanalasta. Not seeming to notice the effect he had on her, he continued to address the princess, ignoring Vangerdahast entirely.

"Alusair was somewhat, er, *reluctant* to suspend her search," the ranger explained. "We'll return to the last camp and track her from there."

"Then she hasn't found Emperel." Vangerdahast leaned on his saddle horn and stretched over to infuse himself into the conversation. "So what has she been doing up here?"

"Following him, obviously," said Tanalasta. "Will you let the man speak, Vangey?"

Vangerdahast shot a scowl at the princess, but she did not seem to notice. Her gaze was fixed too sternly on the ranger.

"Continue, Rowen."

"As you command, Princess."

"She asked you to call her Tanalasta," grumbled Vangerdahast. The cad was winning her favor far too quickly with that respectful act of his. "And why not? You've already seen the crown jewels."

"Vangerdahast!" Tanalasta gave him a withering scowl, then looked back to Rowen. "Must I call on Rowen to remind you who is the royal here?"

Rowen's eyes grew bright and white in the moonlight. He glanced between the princess and Vangerdahast, allowing his sword hand to drift uneasily toward his sword pommel. The wizard started to utter a dark warning, then caught himself and thought better of it. The more he picked on the boy, the more determined Tanalasta would be to like him.

Vangerdahast looked away, preparing himself for a distasteful task. "I hope the princess will forgive me. I was only trying to put the boy at ease."

"His name is Rowen," said Tanalasta.

"Please, if the Royal Magician wants to call me a boy, I won't be offended," said Rowen. "To tell you the truth, it's been so many years since I've been called that I find it funny."

"Then I am happy to make you laugh, Rowen," said Tanalasta. "From henceforth, the Royal Magician may address us as 'boy' and 'girl,' and we will call him 'grandfather.' "

"I am sure the royal court will find your decision most amusing," Vangerdahast replied, finding himself grinding his teeth. As trustworthy as Rowen might be, Vangerdahast could not have the princess falling in love with a Cormaeril. After the Abraxus Affair, that would be tantamount to bedding a Sembian. "If we are done making young Cormaeril laugh, perhaps he could tell us about Emperel?"

Rowen looked to Tanalasta, and when she nodded, began. "There really isn't much to tell. We picked up his trail a few miles east of Halfhap and followed him across the Stonebolt Trail toward Shouk's Ambush, then he suddenly found someone else's trail and followed it south to a tomb in the foothills."

"A tomb?" Vangerdahast asked.

"How old?" Tanalasta asked. "What type?"

"It was very old, Milady," said Rowen. "As for the type—I'm no expert on such things. It was set beneath the roots of a great twisted oak, black of bark and so filled with rot that it's a wonder the thing was still standing. There were old glyphs carved into the trunk such as I have never seen."

"Glyphs?" Tanalasta asked, growing excited. "Were they Elvish?"

Rowen shrugged. "I wouldn't know. They were very sinuous and graceful."

Tanalasta said, "They sound Elvish."

"As does the tomb," Vangerdahast agreed.

"You're thinking Tree of the Body . . ."

"But twisted and black?"

Rowen's head pivoted back and forth between his escorts, not quite keeping pace with the exchange.

"Twisted and black," said Tanalasta. "Yes, that is interesting."

"No elf would sprout such a thing, and if it's rotting . . ."

"There *are* evil elves."

"True, but drow grow mushrooms, not trees," Vangerdahast said. "And they live underground."

"I'm talking about wood elves, not drow. Don't you recall the Year of Distant Thunder?"

Rowen turned to Tanalasta and said, "If I may—"

"The Bleth family, of course," said Vangerdahast, cutting the cad off, "but Mondar was in the wrong there."

"They could have told him that *before* they killed his whole family," Tanalasta said. "It was a massacre—an elven massacre."

"Excuse me!" Rowen said, raising his voice loud enough to be heard. "But I am sorry to disappoint you. The elves have nothing to do with this tomb."

Vangerdahast and Tanalasta both frowned, then asked together, "You're sure?"

"We found some garish old rings, a silver hair comb," said Rowen, "and a lady's stiletto hidden in the handle of a brass fan."

Tanalasta raised her brow. "That's certainly not elven."

"Nor were the vambraces in the next tomb," said Rowen.

"The *next* tomb?" Vangerdahast gasped. "There were two?"

Rowen shook his head. "Three . . . so far, all opened. Emperel followed whoever he was tracking to each of them. We think that's where he ran into the ghazneth."

Vangerdahast and Tanalasta fell silent, trying in their

own ways to make sense of what the ranger was telling them. The tombs Rowen described did not belong to the Sleeping Sword. Vangerdahast visited that cavern periodically to inspect its condition and renew the stasis spell that kept the young lords in suspended animation, and he knew for a fact there was not a tree within two miles of it.

"These tombs," Tanalasta said. "Were they all similar?"

"Some seemed older than others," said Rowen. "Or at least the trees were larger, and they had the same glyphs carved into the trunks. But the things we found in each one were different. In the last one, it was a war wizards' throat clasp."

The ranger gestured to the unfastened clasps at the throats of his two companions.

Vangerdahast raised his brow. "I don't suppose you have that clasp with you?"

"Sorry. Princess Alusair said—"

"I can imagine what she said," Vangerdahast replied.

"Quiet!" Tanalasta hissed.

The princess guided her horse over in front of her companions, forcing them to a stop. Vangerdahast's eyes went instantly to the sky and his hand to his throat clasp. If the ghazneth had found them anyway . . .

Tanalasta's shadowy hand reached out to catch him by the arm. "Orcs," she whispered.

Vangerdahast almost sighed in relief, then realized it would be impossible to scatter the orcs without using magic and alerting the ghazneth to their location. He scanned the gully slopes, already plotting a devastating sequence of fire spells. If Tanalasta could see the swiners, then the swiners could see her. Orc eyes were so sensitive they could see a creature's body heat in the dark.

When Vangerdahast detected no sign of the creatures, he asked, "Where?"

"I don't know," Tanalasta replied. "I smell them."

"Smell them?" Vangerdahast hissed. "If they were close enough to smell, we'd be dead by now."

"If we were relying on *your* nose, yes," whispered Rowen, "but Tanalasta has taken a bath. She can smell something other than herself."

The ranger dismounted and scraped a fistful of dirt from the gully floor, letting it pour from his hand. Once he had determined that the breeze was blowing across the gully, he led Vangerdahast and Tanalasta over to the windward side of the ravine and motioned for them to dismount. The trio spent the next half hour stumbling along in the shadows without seeing any sign of the orcs. Vangerdahast was about to insist that they mount again when a distant clatter began to echo up the gulch behind them. They paused to listen until the orcs had passed, then returned to their saddles and continued up the gully.

The companions remained silent for another half hour, until they reached the head of the gulch and ascended onto the moonlit expanse of the Gnoll Flats. Despite Rowen's earlier warning, the stonemurk was not bad—at least not compared to the plains closer to the Stonebolt Trail—and Vangerdahast could barely see the dark wall of the Storm Horns in the far distance. Try as he might, he could find no peaks that reminded him of mule ears.

They stayed close to the edge of the flats, ready to duck down the nearest ravine at the first sign of orcs or the ghazneth. After the sheltering confines of the gully, the empty expanses made Vangerdahast feel exposed and cranky, and only the thought of crossing the barrens in full daylight prevented him from suggesting they make camp in the shelter of one of the many ravines they were passing.

If the lack of cover made Tanalasta or Rowen nervous, they did not show it. The pair rode side-by-side for the rest of the night, their legs almost touching. Despite his weariness and petulant mood, Vangerdahast found he did not have the heart to intrude on the moment—not even for the good of the realm. Clearly, the ranger respected the princess for her knowledge and talent, and she seemed to return that respect with genuine fondness. Outside of Alaphondar and her own family, Tanalasta had experienced little enough of either in the palace. If she had found it in the Stonelands with Rowen Cormaeril, then the royal magician could put Cormyr's interests aside for a few hours. Despite the trouble she was causing him, Vangerdahast loved the princess like a daughter, and he wanted to see her as happy as it was possible for a queen to be.

Vangerdahast could never let them marry, of course. Allowing the child of a Cormaeril to ascend to the throne would insult the families who had stayed loyal during the Abraxus Affair, and invite mischief from those who had wavered, but marriage was not the only trail to carnal happiness. If their fondness continued to grow, perhaps he could talk to Tanalasta about working out a discreet arrangement. He had certainly done the same thing often enough for Azoun, and it might provide just the leverage he needed to disabuse her of this royal temple nonsense.

The eastern horizon was beginning to brighten with predawn light when Vangerdahast heard the pair murmuring quietly. He slumped forward and allowed his chin to drop onto his chest, then urged his horse slowly forward until he was close enough to hear their conversation. His eavesdropping spells were far more effective and convenient, but with the ghazneth flying about, he had no choice except to resort to conventional methods.

" . . . led you to worship the Mother?" Tanalasta was asking. "Chauntea is hardly a popular goddess among the nobility."

"Until Gaspar dishonored us, we Cormaerils were less a

family of politics than of land," Rowen explained. "Chauntea saw fit to bless our farms with her bounty, and we venerated her in return."

"I see," said Tanalasta. "You still worship her, though you have lost your lands?"

"I do." Rowen looked away, then added, "After I have redeemed my name in Princess Alusair's service, it is my hope that the king will someday grant me a small holding."

Tanalasta reached across to grasp the ranger's hand. "Have faith, Rowen. Chauntea rewards those who serve her."

"Aye, those who serve the Mother flourish in her bounty."

The exchange sent a shudder down Vangerdahast's spine. He urged his horse forward between theirs, forcing the princess to withdraw her hand.

"What is it?" the wizard asked, feigning a yawn. He saw now that Rowen would be more dangerous as a lover than as a husband. "Is something wrong?"

Tanalasta scowled. "Nothing a little consideration couldn't cure."

Vangerdahast blinked groggily. "Am I interrupting something?" There was just enough of an edge in his voice to hint that it had better not be so, and he looked from the princess to Rowen. "Have you been sizing up the crown jewels again?"

"Vangerdahast!" Tanalasta raised her hand as though she might slap the wizard, then shook her head in frustration. "You are the only one here who has been behaving poorly—and I'm quite sure you know it!"

Vangerdahast continued to glare at Rowen. "Well?"

The ranger's face darkened. "It would be a crime for me to respond as you deserve, Lord Magician, but you must know you are assailing my honor. I have only pure thoughts for the princess."

"Good." Vangerdahast glanced at Tanalasta just long enough to wince at the fury in her eyes, then looked back to Rowen. "Because you know how unfortunate it would be if she were to become, ah, *attached* to you."

Rowen looked confused. "Attached? To me?"

"Pay him no mind," said Tanalasta. "Vangerdahast has a notoriously tawdry mind."

Rowen's posture grew tense. "I see. Well, there is no danger of *that*. Roosters do not pursue swans."

"No, they don't," agreed Vangerdahast. "They keep their distance, lest people start mistaking the swan for a hen."

"I am not a poultry bird." Tanalasta raised her chin and slapped the reins against her weary horse's neck, goading it into a trot. "I will thank you both to—"

Her sentence was cut short by the pained shriek of a horse.

Fearing Tanalasta's mount had broken a leg, Vangerdahast sank his heels into Cadimus's flanks and shot after the princess. As he approached, she wheeled around and sprang past in the opposite direction, leaning out of her saddle to grab for something on the ground. A cacophony of snarling and snorting arose from the rim of the plain, and it finally dawned on the wizard that the horse's cry had been caused by something more serious than a broken leg.

Vangerdahast spun Cadimus toward the sound and saw a wall of orc silhouettes clambering over the rim of the plain. The swiners were no more than a hundred paces distant, with thick snouts and pointy ears outlined in black against the purple horizon. Closer by, a dozen hunch-shouldered shapes were rising from a line of shallow camouflage pits not far behind Rowen, who lay struggling to drag himself free of his thrashing horse. The poor beast had four crooked spears lodged in its rib cage, and every time it tried to roll to its knees, its breath would wheeze out around the shafts.

Tanalasta brought her mount to a stop beside the fallen

horse and stretched down toward Rowen. He reached up to grasp her hand, then his horse screeched again as its abdomen was pierced by a rough-hewn spear. Another shaft hissed through the air above the princess's back, and two more clattered into the stones around the hooves of her horse. The ranger looked back toward the camouflage pits, then quickly pulled his arm away—the first twelve orcs were only ten paces away.

"There's no time, Princess. Go!"

"And leave you here? What kind of lady would that make me?" Tanalasta swung out of the saddle and glanced back at Vangerdahast. "Do something!"

The command was hardly necessary. Vangerdahast was already holding one of his favorite wands. As soon as Tanalasta stooped down to shove Rowen's fallen horse off him, he shouted his command word and whipped the tip at the closest orc. The brute cried out in shock and went tumbling across the ground backward, limbs flailing and head cracking against the rocky ground. The wizard repeated the gesture three more times before the princess rocked the horse high enough for Rowen to pull out of his stirrup. The ranger dragged himself free and stood, blocking Vangerdahast's angle to the remaining orcs.

"By the Purple Dragon!" Vangerdahast moved forward to get a better angle, then sent another orc flying. The rest of the horde was fast coming in from the side, and they would soon be within spear-throwing range. "Tanalasta, get that fool out of the way!"

"Watch your manners, Vangerdahast." Tanalasta swung back into her saddle, then reached for her throat clasp. "See to your horse Rowen, then it's time for us to leave."

Vangerdahast stopped on the other side of Rowen's horse and cleared the area with three quick shakes of his wand, then jammed it back into its sleeve and reached into his cloak. It seemed to take forever to find the component he needed, perhaps because his eyes were already scanning the brightening sky for the ghazneth's dark wings.

Rowen brought his sword down across the back of his horse's neck, then grabbed the princess's outstretched hand and swung into the saddle behind her. He slashed at something on the other side of Tanalasta's horse, and an orc squealed in pain. Tanalasta slapped her bracer and blasted another with four golden bolts of magic. Then, finally, she wheeled her mount around and shoved her hand into the weathercloak's escape pocket. There was a nearly inaudible pop, and Vangerdahast found himself staring across Rowen's dead horse at three stunned orcs.

The wizard dropped his reins and gestured with his free hand, blasting two of them apart with magic bolts, then finally found a small bar of iron. He pointed this at the third trembling orc and rattled off a quick spell, then commanded, "Move nothing."

The orc's arms dropped to its sides, and Vangerdahast spun in his saddle to find the largest part of the horde only thirty paces away. He fished a small vial from his cloak pocket and quickly unstoppered it, then pointed his hand at a spot about fifteen paces away. The wizard started a long incantation and began to pour a stream of white grains from the small flask. As the granules fell, they flashed into smoke, and a tiny flame flickered to life where he was pointing.

By the time he finished, the orcs had begun to hurl their spears in his direction. The range was still too great for the crooked weapons to have any accuracy, but Vangerdahast did not feel like taking chances. He circled around Rowen's dead horse and waited for the leading swiners to reach the line of tiny flames he had created on the ground, then spoke his command word.

A searing curtain of flame sprang to life, rising more

than twenty feet into the air and stretching three hundred paces in each direction. The air filled instantly with the wail of dying orcs, and the stench of charred flesh grew overwhelming. Scarecrows of flame separated from the fiery wall and stumbled around blindly for a few minutes, then collapsed to the ground to burn themselves out.

Vangerdahast watched long enough to be certain none of his foes made it through the flame wall in one piece, then turned to the orc he had ordered to stand still. The swiner was standing in the same place, staring at his feet with wide, red-tinged eyes. The wizard rode up beside the trembling warrior, kicked the fellow's spear out of his grasp, and scanned the heavens one last time. The sun had already crested the horizon, and now a brilliant golden light was spreading westward across the sky. The winds were, as Rowen had promised last night, remarkably still, and there was no stonemurk to obscure visibility in any direction.

Vangerdahast studied the heavens until he felt certain the ghazneth had not yet come, then dismounted and rubbed a small square of silk over his prisoner's grimy armor. The orc snorted in its guttural language, begging his tormentor to stop toying with it and be done with it. The wizard only smiled and whispered a soft incantation. He stuffed the ruined silk into the creature's mouth and mounted his horse again, then rode a short distance off and called, "Flee!"

The orc stumbled a single step forward and caught itself. After a brief glance in Vangerdahast's direction, it turned and scuttled away without even taking the time to pick up its spear. The wizard turned south toward the Storm Horns and saw his companions waving to him from the crest of a small ridge nearly a mile distant. Behind them, the rocky barrens and scattered brush of Gnoll Flats gave way to a torturous labyrinth of dun-colored spires and twisting canyons that slowly rose toward the barren slopes of two high, slender peaks that could only be the Mule Ears.

Vangerdahast clasped his weathercloak and thrust his hand into his escape pocket. A black door hissed into existence before him, and he quickly urged Cadimus forward. He would not be able to use the pocket for the rest of the day, but he had plenty of other ways to leave an area quickly. Besides, Tanalasta had already used hers, and he had no intention of going anywhere without her—especially not with Rowen riding the same horse.

An instant later, Vangerdahast found himself sitting beside his companions, struggling to acclimate to his new location. No matter how many times he teleported, even over such a short distance, he still suffered from that first moment of bewilderment. Tanalasta's hand grasped his shoulder and quickly undid his weathercloak's throat clasp.

"Are you all right, Vangey?" she asked, still holding his arm. "You're a royal pain in the arse, but I'd hate to lose you to an orc."

"I'm fine." Vangerdahast blinked the last of his confusion away. They were much closer to the labyrinth than he had realized, with the mouth of a large, baked-mud canyon just a few hundred paces ahead. "Let's hurry. I slapped an orc with some decoy magic, but with this light, it won't take the ghazneth long to discover its mistake."

When Vangerdahast started forward, Rowen leaned over to grab his reins. "This is the way to the Mule Ears." He pointed toward a much smaller canyon a half mile to the east. "Nothing lies that way but trouble and dead ends."

"Then stop wasting our time telling me about it," the wizard grumbled. "And why don't you ride with me. Cadimus is . . ."

Vangerdahast did not bother to finish, for Tanalasta

170

had already turned and started toward the distant canyon at a stiff canter. He spurred his stallion after her, idly wondering if there was not some way to convince them that Chauntea would frown on burdening a poor mare with two riders.

10

By the time they ducked into the small canyon, the sun had risen a full span above the horizon. The terrain in the gorge was even more barren than that of the stony plain, consisting of little more than eroded dirt walls and a lonely scrub bush every ten or twelve paces. They stopped about thirty paces in to let their weary mounts drink from a muddy spring, and Vangerdahast crept back to the canyon mouth to watch for the ghazneth. It was not long before he saw a dark pair of wings swoop in from the west, then circle through smoke rising from his wall of flame and fly off in the direction his decoy had fled.

Vangerdahast waited until he was certain the thing was gone, then rushed up the canyon at his best waddle. "Time to go. We have about five minutes before our dark friend discovers my trick."

Rowen passed Cadimus's reins to the wizard and turned back toward Tanalasta's mount.

"Ahem—as much as I'm sure you enjoy sharing a saddle with the princess, young man, Cadimus is twice the mount she's riding." Vangerdahast mounted and offered the ranger his hand. "We'll all be faster if you ride with me."

"A good point."

Rowen turned and reached for the wizard's hand, but Tanalasta was already swinging out of her own saddle.

"It will be even faster if we switch horses." The princess reached up and patted Vangerdahast's ample belly. "Rowen and I together can't be much more than you alone. You take my mare, and let poor Cadimus carry us."

"A fine idea," the wizard replied, "but you know how temperamental—"

"Cadimus is more of a coward, actually," said Tanalasta. "I had no trouble controlling him back at the Stonebolt Trail—or have you forgotten who returned him to you?"

"Very well," Vangerdahast grumbled. "I can't have you arguing the matter until the ghazneth finds us."

They switched horses and started up the canyon again. Vangerdahast tried at first to keep a careful watch on the northern sky, but quickly realized the futility of that as they twisted and turned through the labyrinth. He could not imagine how Rowen could know where they were going. The ranger kept turning down narrow side canyons, which would double back in the direction from which they had just come, then double back again and angle off in some new direction that was impossible to guess. For a while, Vangerdahast thought the ranger was following his own tracks or a system of cairns, but when he dared to take his eyes off the sky, he saw no sign of either.

After nearly two hours of riding, the canyon opened up into a broad, flat-bottomed basin ringed by more than a dozen cramped gorges. The trio paused without dismounting and allowed their horses to drink from another pool of muddy water. Vangerdahast found the sun in the sky and was finally able to determine his bearings, for all the good it would do him.

"Rowen, how do you know which way to go?" he asked. "I can't even keep track of my directions."

"You mean there's one trick the Royal Magician doesn't know?" Tanalasta joked. "I'm not so sure we should tell."

"There are a lot of tricks I don't know," said Vangerdahast, "and you are teaching me more all the time."

"This one is not so difficult." Rowen passed Vangerdahast a small flat stick with notches carved at various angles along both edges and explained, "It's a map stick. You keep track of your turns—"

"By the notches on each side," Vangerdahast said, examining the stick. "And the angle confirms that you're on count."

"Very good," laughed Tanalasta. "We'll make a forest-keeper out of you yet."

Vangerdahast eyed her sourly, then passed the stick back to Rowen. "When you have magic, you don't need sticks."

"Except when you can't use magic," Tanalasta replied.

The princess pointed toward the western side of the basin, where a tiny speck of darkness could be seen arcing above the rim. Vangerdahast glanced back along their trail, noting the deep round depressions where their mounts' hooves had broken through the crust of dried mud.

"Tanalasta," the royal magician said, "I know I promised not to bring this up again—"

"Then don't," the princess interrupted sternly. "I'm not returning to Arabel until I have spoken with Alusair."

"Hear me out. This thing is dangerous. Let's gather a few more wizards and dragoneers, then come back."

"And when the king hears what is happening here and orders you to leave me in Arabel, you will defy him and bring me back?"

"I suppose not, but it was an idea." The wizard motioned toward the broken ground behind them. "After the ghazneth finds our trail, it won't take the thing long to find us."

"Longer than you think," said Rowen. "These badlands stretch for a hundred miles along the base of the mountains, and the canyons are deep. It isn't easy to see into them even from the rims—much less high in the sky."

"I hope you're right, Rowen," said Tanalasta, "but Edwin Narlok theorizes in his treatise *Falcon Fun* that the eyesight of birds of prey is far more acute than our own."

Rowen looked slightly embarrassed. "I haven't read that book, but the idea makes sense. Otherwise, it would be pretty difficult to hunt from on high."

"Of course, the ghazneth is not a bird of prey—"

"But it's wiser not to take chances." Vangerdahast took a linen glove from his pocket and folded it into his palm, where he could reach it instantly. "Remind me not to wager with you anymore, Princess."

Tanalasta narrowed her eyes. "If you even think of—"

"A bet is a bet," said Vangerdahast. "This is for the ghazneth. When it finds us, blast the thing with everything you have. You need to buy me a little time."

Tanalasta continued to eye the glove, but nodded. "As you wish."

She consulted Rowen's map stick, then led the way around the basin into a cool, shadow-filled canyon suffused with the smell of damp earth. The gorge was as deep as a well and so narrow that Vangerdahast sometimes found his knees brushing both sides at once. Even at its broadest, two horses could not have stood side by side, and it twisted and turned like a snake. The wizard could not recall a worse place to be ambushed, and he kept a constant watch on the crooked slot of sky above.

He saw the ghazneth twice over the next four hours. The first was when he glimpsed a tiny **V** streaking across the narrow strip of sky ahead of them. It was no larger than his fingernail, and visible for such a short time it could have been a large vulture instead. The second time, the wizard had no such doubts. It appeared over the canyon behind them, large enough now that its wings and body formed a distinct cross, slowly circling and peering down into the labyrinth.

Convinced the phantom had finally found their trail, Vangerdahast suggested again that it might be wise to teleport back to Arabel. Tanalasta's only reply was to ask him to leave the extra horse, and so they pressed on in silence for the rest of the afternoon. With the sun hidden most of the time behind one canyon rim or the other, it was difficult to mark the passing time, but Vangerdahast was convinced it had to be near evening when the gorge suddenly felt less murky. The walls did not seem to rise quite so high above their heads, and the musty air grew warmer and more arid.

"We'll leave the badlands soon," said Rowen, "It's only a short ride then to where I last saw Alusair."

"One of the opened tombs?" Tanalasta did not wait for the ranger to answer. "That will be interesting."

Vangerdahast was about to quote the old aphorism about cats and curiosity when a soft thud sounded next to him. He looked down and saw a two-inch crater in the dried mud, a gleam of gold barely visible in the bottom. The wizard frowned, trying to imagine how a golden coin had come to fall into the canyon—then looked skyward and shouted the alarm.

"Watch your—"

A squarish shape came tumbling down into the canyon and struck him in the chest. The breath huffed out of Vangerdahast's lungs and his feet flew out of the stirrups. He found himself flat on his back, gasping for air and groaning in agony. The canyon was filled with screaming voices and flashing magic and dancing hooves, and it finally came to him that he was lying on the ground with the battle already raging.

Vangerdahast pushed himself to a sitting position and found a legless, headless torso sprawled across his legs. He shoved the thing away in horror, then recognized the filthy armor as that of the orc he had used as a decoy. In his grogginess, he failed to see any humor in having it returned to him.

A horse hoof came down on Vangerdahast's ankle. A sobering bolt of pain shot up his leg, and he grabbed a hock and shoved the beast off his throbbing foot. Tanalasta's voice rang out, trolling the incantation of her one spell, and a flash of golden magic brightened the canyon. Vangerdahast shook his head clear and saw Rowen's boots dart past on the other side of the horse, and it occurred to the wizard he had better do something before the ghazneth killed them all. He opened his hand to discover that the glove he had been holding was gone.

"Vangerdahast!" cried Tanalasta. "I can't stall any longer!"

Vangerdahast glanced over and saw Cadimus turned sideways in the canyon, the princess sitting astride his back, pointing up the canyon wall and slapping ineffectually at her wrists. She had already used the bracers to discharge one set of magic bolts and the single combat spell she knew to fire another, and it would be some time before she could attack again. The bracers needed only a few moments to recharge their magic, but in the middle of a battle, a few moments could be a lifetime. The wizard followed the angle of Tanalasta's arm and finally saw the ghazneth.

Too large by far to fly into the narrow gorge, the thing was climbing down the canyon wall, descending headfirst with its huge wings gathered up alongside its body. It was already halfway down, its white eyes glaring at the canyon floor, where Rowen stood ready to meet it with nothing more than a sword and rust-coated dagger.

This was going to be easier than Vangerdahast thought. He fetched a wad of sticky spider web from his cloak pocket and flicked it in the phantom's direction, at the same time uttering his incantation. The ghazneth's head swiveled toward the sound of his voice, then the thing pushed off the canyon wall and dropped, its long-taloned hands already drawing back to rip Rowen open from shoulder to hip. A circle of web blossomed on the wall behind it, burbling out to engulf the phantom up to one knee and bring its dive to an unexpected halt.

Vangerdahast sighed in relief, then rolled to his feet and found his glove lying beneath his mount. He plucked it from under the beast's dancing hooves and shook the dust off, then blew into the collar and whispered his incantation. The fingers wiggled once, then it drifted from his hand and began to float in the air before him. The wizard pulled a vial full of dried fireflies from his pocket and placed one of the tiny insects in the palm of the floating glove.

As Vangerdahast worked, the ghazneth spewed a string of unspeakable curses and beat its wings against the cliff-side, trying to knock itself free of the entangling web. When that did not work, it twisted around and curled up toward its feet, drawing its arm back to slash at the web. The filament parted with a low pop, and the phantom came plummeting down the cliff backward. Rowen was on it as soon as it landed, beating aside its arms with two powerful sword strokes, then hurling himself forward to plant his orange dagger deep into its collar.

An unearthly shriek filled the canyon. The ghazneth rolled, slamming its wing into the ranger and launching him up the canyon to crash into Cadimus. Tanalasta and Rowen fell with the beast in a tangled screeching heap, and the phantom rolled to its feet. Though the hole Vangerda-hast had blasted in its chest a few days earlier was completely healed, the rusty dagger remained planted firmly in its collar, with gouts of dark blood pumping out around the blade.

Tanalasta's voice rang through the gorge. "King's bolts!"

Four golden streaks shot past in front of Vangerdahast, but the ghazneth was ducking behind its wing even as the bolts struck. The leathery appendage grew white and translucent, revealing the fanlike network of delicate bones within.

Vangerdahast made a fist and gestured toward the creature, and his floating glove closed around the firefly in its palm and shot in the direction indicated. Still hiding behind its wing, the ghazneth gathered itself to spring. The wizard guided his glove over its wing, then turned his hand palm down and made a slapping motion. The glove flipped over and slapped the firefly against the phantom's head.

"Light!" Vangerdahast commanded.

A brilliant globe of magic light engulfed the ghazneth's head. The creature cried out and jumped back, shaking its head madly. The light moved with it.

Vangerdahast lowered his hand and closed his fingers as though grasping a knife handle. The glove disappeared behind the phantom's wing, and a snarl of surprise rolled up the canyon. The wizard moved his hand up and down. The glove rose and fell with the motion, grasping Rowen's rusty knife and spattering the canyon walls with streams of dark blood.

The ghazneth shrieked and lowered its wing, fully revealing the brilliant aura that engulfed its head. Its arms and wings flailed about wildly, but its efforts to catch the floating glove were all in vain. It could see nothing inside the golden ball but blinding yellow light. Vangerdahast whipped his hand around, and the rusty dagger circled and came up beneath the phantom's ribcage. The ghazneth clutched at the black-bleeding wound and fled down the canyon, careening off the walls and wailing in rage.

Vangerdahast started after it, but the creature was as fast as a lion. Before his third step, the wizard realized he would never keep up and turned to find Tanalasta now on her own mare, pulling Rowen onto the horse behind her. Though the fellow had suffered no obvious wounds, he seemed to be reeling from his collision. Cadimus was standing behind her, looking wide-eyed and dazed, but little worse for wear. Vangerdahast rushed up the canyon and grabbed the stallion's reins, then swung into his saddle.

"Go!" Though one of Vangerdahast's light spells normally lasted close to a day, he suspected the ghazneth would not need nearly that much time to absorb the enchantment's magic and return more angry than ever. "I didn't kill it, you know!"

"Yes, but at least we wounded it." Tanalasta set her heels to the mare's flanks, and the horse sprang up the canyon at a gallop. "That's an improvement."

Vangerdahast started after her, at the same time motioning the glove back to his side. Fearful of losing Rowen's dagger, he plucked the bloodied weapon from the magical hand. To his astonishment, it was a simple blade of cold-forged iron. Demons hated cold-forged iron, but the ghazneth wasn't a demon—it couldn't be. He cleaned the blade on his saddle blanket and stuck it in his belt, then snatched his linen glove out of the air and returned it to his pocket.

They galloped around two sharp corners, then Tanalasta cried out and reined her horse up short. Expecting to find a band of orcs blocking the way—it was inconceivable that even the ghazneth had negated his light spell *that* fast—

Vangerdahast reached into his cloak for a chunk of brim-stone, then eased up beside the princess. Twenty paces ahead, the canyon was blocked by a huge steel gate.

"By the nine doors to hell! What's that doing here?"

Rowen peered over Tanalasta's shoulder, then pinched his eyes shut and tried to shake his head clear.

"Are you sure this is the way?" Tanalasta asked.

"It's the way," Rowen replied. "It must be an illusion. We ran into one before, just before we opened the second tomb."

"An illusion?" Vangerdahast waved his hand at the door and uttered a long string of mystic syllables. "Begone!"

The door vanished at once, revealing a dark, squat figure with large crimson eyes and a huge nose veined from too much drink. A tarnished crown sat tangled into his wild halo of long, spiky hair, and the gaping hollow in his unkempt beard could be identified as a mouth only because of its four yellow fangs and wagging red tongue.

"What? No knock?" the stranger croaked. He flung his arms to the sky in some strange gesture Vangerdahast did not understand. "You just vanish my door?"

The strange little man was as naked as the day he was born, with glistening skin the color of obsidian and a pot belly the size of a soup kettle. There were broken yellow talons at the ends of his fingers, a pair of tall wings folded behind his shoulders, and an unspeakable collection of parasites crawling through his sparse body hair.

"Another . . ." Vangerdahast was so astonished he could hardly gasp the question. "*Another* ghazneth?"

"Of course!" Tanalasta sounded more excited than fright-ened. "They've opened *three* tombs."

"Three . . . that we know of," Vangerdahast said.

The ghazneth flexed its wings. When the appendages hit the canyon walls, it cursed vilely and started forward at a walk.

"Enough is enough!" Vangerdahast dropped his reins and reached over to grab his companions by the wrists. "Hold on."

Rowen's eyes grew large. "Not me!"

The ranger jerked his arm free, then snatched the dagger from Vangerdahast's belt and slipped off the mare. The ghazneth closed to within ten paces.

Tanalasta twisted around in the saddle. "Rowen—"

"My duty is here," he said, backing away from the horse.

Tanalasta glanced at the ghazneth. Its long tongue snaked out between its fangs, and it gathered itself to spring. Vangerdahast leaned across Cadimus's back and reached for the ranger.

"Give me your hand," the wizard commanded. "Now!"

Rowen backed away. The ghazneth cackled madly and sprang into the air. Vangerdahast pulled his hand back and pictured the stables of the palace in Arabel. Tanalasta cried out, then ducked and twisted away, tearing her arm from his grasp as he spoke his incantation. The world went black and something heavy and hard slammed into Vangerdahast from above, then suddenly he was falling.

It seemed to take forever to reach the ground. The weight vanished from his back. He grew disoriented and queasy and lost all sense of time. This fall seemed to be taking forever, and he thought maybe this was what a quick death felt like—no pain, no fear, just a sudden, endless darkness—save that he could still feel something foul and hot touching his neck, and something bristly rubbing against his cheek.

The light returned the same instant it had vanished. Vangerdahast glimpsed Cadimus's brown flank slipping past his nose, then crashed headlong into the brown soft earth. The weight of the world came crashing down on top of him, and he found himself buried beneath a heap of cackling, rancid-smelling black leather.

For a long instant, the wizard lay there with his head spinning, trying to sort out where he was and what the terrible stench in his nostrils might be. He heard voices crying out in astonishment—men, and a few women, too—and he grew aware of a terrible crushing pain in the center of his back.

Vangerdahast reached out and dug his fingers into the soft ground, then slowly dragged himself forward. Now he heard the sound of clanking armor. Certain voices began to seem familiar to him. The wizard pulled himself forward and suddenly he was free of the terrible weight. He rose to his knees and saw the hem of a woman's gown and no fewer than fifty horse legs separating him from the white, daub-and-wattle walls of a well-kept stable, then it all came flooding back to him.

Vangerdahast craned his neck and found himself looking up at a fully armored company of Purple Dragons. With them were several familiar figures: a tall, gray-bearded man in dusty riding clothes and a golden field crown, a bushy-browed wizard with a plump face, a honey-haired beauty with eyes as blue as ice, a wiry priest with a thin, weather-beaten face. Azoun, Merula, Filfaeril, Owden—all staring at him with confused looks of horror on their faces.

Something fluttered next to Vangerdahast, and he looked over to see the tip of a leathery black wing beating the air.

"No!" He clambered to his feet, at once raising a hand to wave off his friends and whirling around to face the ghazneth. "Defend your—"

A black hand swept down to catch Vangerdahast in the side of the head, launching him end-over-end across the stable. He crashed down a dozen paces in front of Cadimus and tumbled onto his stomach, ears ringing and blood pouring from his opened scalp. His vision narrowed. He shook his head clear and thrust his hand into his cloak.

A dozen dragoneers managed to spur their mounts out to intercept the ghazneth. The dark creature streaked through them like an eagle through a field of gophers, then slapped the sword from Azoun's hand and settled into the saddle facing the horrified king.

"Usurper!"

The ghazneth snatched the crown from Azoun's head, then sank its filthy claws through his armor and hurled him from the saddle like a child's rag doll. Vangerdahast felt a sudden wave of nausea, and the darkness began to close around him. He gritted his teeth and grabbed his favorite wand, willing the darkness to stay away.

A flurry of Purple Dragons whirled on the ghazneth, hacking and slashing. It beat them off with a few strokes of its dark wings, then the war wizards cut loose with bolt and flame. The ghazneth furled its wings and roared with laughter as the spells languished against its defenses, then leaped over a wall of guards to land atop Filfaeril. The barrage of war spells ceased as suddenly as it had started. The queen shrieked in terror, and the creature hid her behind its wings.

Vangerdahast's vision continued to narrow. He pulled the wand from his cloak.

"No need to be frightened, my dear," said the ghazneth. A mad cackle sounded from the other side of the leathery curtain. "I wouldn't harm my queen—would I?"

The creature sprang into the air, Filfaeril clasped securely in its claws. Vangerdahast's vision narrowed to a keyhole. He whipped his wand toward the queen's flailing figure and shouted his command word as the keyhole closed.

11

he glyphs ringed the sycamore in an elegant spiral, as sinuous as a snake and as clearly defined as the day they were engraved. Though Tanalasta could not identify the era of the carving, she had studied enough elven literature to recognize the style as an archaic one. The letters flowed gracefully one to another, with long sweeping stems and cross arms that undulated so gently they appeared almost straight. While the language was definitely High Wealdan, the inscription itself seemed archaic and stilted, even by the standards of the Early Age of Orthorion.

This childe of men, lette his bodie nourishe this tree.
The tree of this bodie, lette it growe as it nourishe.
The spirit of this tree, to them lette it return as it grewe.

Tanalasta stopped reading after the first stanza and stepped back. Aside from its peculiar spellings and the reference to men, the inscription was the standard epitaph for a Tree of the Body, a sort of memorial created by the ancient elves of the Forest Kingdom. When an esteemed elf died, his fellows sometimes inscribed the epitaph in the trunk of a small sapling and buried the body beneath the tree's roots. The princess did not understand all the details of the commemoration, but she had read a treatise suggesting only elves who had been a special blessing to their communities were honored in this way. In any event, she had visited several of these memorials during her short-lived travels with Vangerdahast and never failed to be impressed by the majesty of the trees bearing such inscriptions.

The sycamore before her was a marked contrast to those ancient monuments. The tree was a warped and gnarled thing with a split trunk and a lopsided crown of crooked branches straying off into the sky at peculiar angles. Its yellow leaves looked like withered little hands dangling down to grasp at anything unlucky enough to pass beneath its boughs, and the bark changed from smooth and white on the branches to a mottled, scaly gray at eye level. The greatest difference of all lay at the base of the trunk, where a recently dug hole wormed down into the musty depths beneath the roots.

Tanalasta returned to the inscription and read the next stanza.

Thus the havoc bearers sleepe, the sleepe of no reste.
Thus the sorrow bringers sow, the seeds of their ruine.
Thus the deathe makers kille, the sons of their sons.

Tanalasta's stomach began to feel hollow and uneasy. Curses were rare things in elven literature, even in the

relatively angry era of King Orthorion's early reign. Of
course, the Royal Library did not contain works predating
Orthorion—apparently, early Cormyreans had lacked
either the time or interest to learn High Wealdan—but
the princess found it difficult to believe that such curses
had been any more common to pre-Orthorion poetry.
Aside from a single famous massacre and a few lesser inci-
dents, elves in the Age of Iliphar had been standoffish but
peaceful.

Tanalasta followed the inscription around the tree and
read the last stanza, which consisted of only a single line
of summoning:

*Here come ye, Mad Kang Boldovar, and lie among these
rootes.*

Tanalasta thought instantly of the crowned ghazneth
that had disappeared with Vangerdahast, then stumbled
back from the tree, hand pressed to her mouth, heart hammering in her chest. Boldovar the Mad was one of her own
ancestors, a king of Cormyr more than eleven centuries
before. According to the histories, he had slain a long succession of palace courtesans before being dragged off the
battlements of Faerlthann's Keep with one of his victims.
The unfortunate woman had died on the spot, less because
of the fall than the horrible wounds inflicted by the insane
Boldovar.

Less commonly known was that the king had lin-
gered on for several days while Baerauble Etharr,
the first Royal Magician of Cormyr, was summoned
from abroad. Fortunately for the people of the realm,
however, Boldovar "wandered off" alone before the
royal wizard could return. When a badly bloated body
dressed in the king's purple was found floating in the
Immerflow a tenday later, Baerauble announced his

liege's death and ordered the corpse burnt at once.
Until now, there had never been reason to believe the
wizard's hasty order due to anything but the sensibil-
ities of his nose, but Tanalasta could not help thinking
Baerauble had used the incident to solve a terrible
dilemma he must have been facing. As the Royal
Magician sworn to protect the crown of Cormyr at all
costs, he could hardly have condoned the overthrow
even of a mad king—but neither could he have
believed that Boldovar's reign benefited the realm.
Perhaps he substituted another body for Boldovar's
and spirited the mad king off to live out his days
someplace where he could do no harm.

Rowen came around the tree behind Tanalasta. "Is
something wrong, milady? You look . . . uneasy."

"I'm frightened, actually—frightened and puzzled."
Tanalasta did not take her eyes from the tree as she
spoke. "Were the glyphs on all the other trees the same as
these?"

Rowen answered without studying the characters.
"They looked the same."

"Yes, but were they *exactly* the same?" Tanalasta pointed
at the three characters that stood for *Mad Kang Boldovar*.
"Especially here?"

"I think so, Princess," Rowen said, sounding slightly
embarrassed. "To be honest, I can't even see the difference
between the glyphs you're pointing at and the ones next to
them. I'm sorry."

"Don't be." Tanalasta turned to him. "I should have
realized how difficult it would be to learn High Wealdan
without the Royal Library at your disposal."

"Or even with it," said Rowen. "I fear I've never been a
student of the old tongues."

Tanalasta smiled at the ranger's candor. "High Wealdan isn't really a tongue. It's closer to music. Listen."

The princess went around to the front of the tree and ran her finger along the initial glyph. A melodic rasp instantly filled the air, intoning the epitaph's first line in a haunting female voice as anguished as it was menacing. Of course, Tanalasta understood the words no better than Rowen, for no human ear could comprehend the full timbre of an elven weald poem.

Rowen's eyes grew wide. "I've never heard anything like it!"

"Nor have I." Tanalasta shuddered at the pain of the music. "That was an elven spirit-voice, if you can believe it."

She led the ranger around the tree, translating each glyph aloud both for his benefit and to assure herself that she was reading it correctly. By the time she finished, Rowen's face had grown as pale as alabaster.

"An *elf* made them?" the ranger asked, clearly referring to the ghazneths. "Why?"

"We won't know that until we discover who that elf was," said Tanalasta. "First, we need to be *sure* the ghazneths are related to these trees. That's why I want to know if this glyph looked the same on the other trees."

Rowen shrugged. "I just can't say. If I'd known what to look for . . ."

"How could you have?" asked Tanalasta. "I'm sure I can figure it out from Alusâir's notes."

"Notes?"

Tanalasta sighed. "I suppose Alusair isn't really the note-taking kind, is she?"

"She was trying to catch Emperel."

"I'm sure she was in a hurry." Tanalasta started around the tree toward the musty hole. "Alusair always is. Did she at least look inside the tombs?"

"That's where we found this." Rowen pulled the iron dagger from his belt and handed it to Tanalasta. "In the second tomb."

Tanalasta stopped beside the hole and examined the weapon, noting its stone-scraped cutting edge and the hammer marks on the face of its blade.

"Cold-forged iron," she said. "I'm astonished this survived. It was made in Suzail over thirteen hundred years ago."

"How can you tell?" Rowen frowned at the blade. "I didn't see any markings."

"That's how I know. Suzail built its first steel works in the year seventy-five, the Year of the Clinging Death. Before that, people smelted their own iron in ground ovens and beat the weapon into shape on a communal anvil." Tanalasta returned the knife to the ranger. "While this is a good piece of handiwork, no merchant bound for Cormyr would burden himself with iron when he knew the market wanted steel."

"I see." Rowen shook his head in amazement, then asked, "Is there anything you *don't* know?"

"Of course," Tanalasta said lightly. "To listen to Vangerdahast, he could fill volumes with the things I don't know."

Rowen chuckled lightly, then glanced back toward where the royal magician had disappeared. Tanalasta followed his gaze. The ghazneth could be seen circling over the labyrinth of canyons, its head still engulfed in a glowing gold orb. Though Vangerdahast had cast the spell less than thirty minutes earlier, the magical glow was already beginning to fade. Determined to finish her investigations quickly, the princess removed the Purple Dragon commander's ring from her cloak pocket and slipped it onto her finger.

"Keep watch," she ordered, stooping down at the rim of the hole.

Rowen caught her by the arm. "Where are you going?"

Though the gesture would have seemed condescending coming from anyone else, from Rowen it seemed merely an expression of concern. Tanalasta patted his hand.

"I need to look inside myself," she said gently. "We both know I'll see what others have missed."

Rowen gritted his teeth, but nodded. "It would be best to make it fast, Princess."

Tanalasta glanced in the direction of the ghazneth. "I won't be slow." The princess activated her ring's light magic and started into the hole, then glanced back and smiled. "And didn't I tell you to call me Tanalasta?"

Rowen stooped down to give her a stubborn smile. "As you command, Princess."

Tanalasta kicked a clump of dirt at him, then turned and started forward. The musty smell grew stronger and more rancid as she crawled, and her skin began to prickle with the wispy breath of evil. When she reached the end of the passage ten paces later, she had goosebumps the size of rose thorns, and her jaws ached from the strain of holding back her gorge. Ahead of her lay a body-shaped hollow, surrounded on all sides by a fine-meshed net of broken black roots. The tree had no taproot, at least that she could see. The tiny chamber was empty, save for a simple floor of flat stones littered with scraps of rotten cloth and an odd assortment of tarnished buckles, buttons, and clasps.

Tanalasta pulled herself into the foul-smelling chamber and nearly cried out when something soft and diaphanous clung to her cheek. She quickly brushed it off and found a transparent web of gossamer filaments stuck to her fingers. It took her a moment to recognize the stuff as raw silk, and she began to notice it everywhere—tangled among the roots above her head, hanging down around her to form the walls of the tomb, and clinging to the debris scattered across the floor.

The princess's first impulse was to leave, as the filmy stuff reminded her of nothing quite so much as the web of a black widow spider, but she clenched her jaw and forced herself to begin scraping the filament away from the walls. To her surprise, the silk came away in thick gobs, and she actually found herself digging a small tunnel that did not end for nearly ten paces—about the distance it would be to the sycamore's dripline.

Tanalasta suppressed the urge to shudder, realizing that the tree—or the corpse beneath it—had so corrupted the ground that the normal process of soil replacement had been halted. She returned to the center of the tree and examined a handful of buttons. The gold plating was so tarnished that she could barely make out the shape of a dragon rampant, its wings spread and its tail curled over its back. Any doubts she had about the ghazneth's identity vanished at once. It was the emblem of King Boldovar. Fearful of being tainted by the palpable evil she sensed in the place, the princess tossed the buttons aside and crawled out of the tomb.

Rowen was waiting at the mouth of the hole, holding the mare's reins and staring back toward the canyon lands. He did not even let her leave the hole before he asked, "How long before Vangerdahast returns?"

Tanalasta looked up to find an uneasy expression on his face. "We may be on our own until tomorrow. I doubt Vangerdahast had two teleport spells ready, and even he might need time to prepare another."

Rowen's uneasy expression changed to one of true distress. "We'd better hurry."

He reached down, and Tanalasta gave him her hand. Instead of helping her out of the hole, however, he slipped the commander's ring off her finger.

"Untie the saddle packs." He turned back to the mare. "We'll use the ring as a decoy."

"Don't you think that trick's getting old?" Tanalasta asked, climbing from the hole. "It barely worked last time."

"It's a new trick to this one."

Rowen was using both hands to tie the ring into the mare's mane, so he simply nodded northward. The first ghazneth was still circling over the maze of canyons, the golden halo around its head now faded to the point that she could make out the outline of a haggish head, but that was not the cause of his concern. A second dark speck was coming out of the north, growing larger even as she watched. The princess scrambled to the mare's flank and began to undo the saddle packs.

"Tie a loose knot," she said. "I know a decoy is our best escape, but this horse has been good to me. I'd like to give her a chance."

"Done." Rowen stepped back, leaving the glowing commander's ring fastened to the mare's mane by a loose but complicated knot. "Without a load to carry, I give her a better chance than us of getting home."

"That only seems fair," said Tanalasta.

The princess pulled the saddle packs free, then raised her hand high and slapped the mare hard on the flank. The beast bolted south, heading for the deep canyon that separated the two Mule Ear peaks. Tanalasta quickly pulled her bracers off and slipped them into the saddlebags, then unclasped her weathercloak and checked herself for any other magic that might give them away.

Once she felt satisfied she was radiating no magic, she asked, "Which way?"

Rowen nodded southwest past the face of the Mule Ears. "Go ahead. You'll see the hoof prints in about twenty paces. I'll cover our trail."

Though she did not like being separated from the ranger with the ghazneth so near, the princess saw the wisdom of his plan and set off at a steady run. As Rowen had promised, she soon came to a narrow trail of hoof prints left by Alusair's company. She pulled her cloak from her shoulders and began to sweep the dusty ground as she ran, cursing Alusair's sloppiness and doing what she could to help the ranger obliterate the tracks.

The hoof prints all but vanished twenty paces later, and Tanalasta realized that her sister had intentionally left an obvious trail to help Rowen determine the direction she had gone, but was now taking precautions. The princess continued to sweep away any tracks she noticed, but now the prints were few and far between. She shifted her own tactics, trying to stay on rocks or hard ground whenever possible and avoiding any bushes that might snap or snag as she dashed past.

The tiny speck grew steadily larger, becoming first a barely distinguishable **V**, then a tiny cross. Tanalasta found a series of four hoof prints turning slightly southward. She swept them away and adjusted her own course and found herself climbing a small ridge. The princess glanced back. Seeing Rowen less than fifty paces behind her, she decided to risk crossing the crest and dashed up the slope at her best sprint.

By the time Tanalasta neared the top, the approaching ghazneth appeared nearly as large as her thumb. She dropped to her hands and scrambled the rest of the way on all fours, taking care to step only on stones, and to keep the sparse brush between her and the approaching phantom. She crossed the summit itself on her belly, then ducked behind a bush and turned to watch the phantom.

Rowen was still ten paces from the hilltop when the thing grew large enough that she could make out the shape of its wings. She hissed a quiet warning to the ranger, then motioned him down. He fell to his belly and rolled beneath a bush, covering himself with his mottled cloak and growing almost invisible, even to Tanalasta.

They waited, exhausted and huffing, as the ghazneth flew past less than half a mile from the crest of the ridge.

It started to swerve toward the withered sycamore, then veered off over the canyons toward its golden-haloed fellow.

Tanalasta rose from her hiding place and motioned the ranger over the ridge. "Now, Rowen—and hurry!"

Rowen rolled from beneath his bush and swept his cloak across the ground quickly, then scrambled over the ridge beside Tanalasta. "You are quite . . . a runner," he gasped. "I didn't . . . know if I could catch up."

"Fear will do that to you." Tanalasta turned to angle down the ridge in the direction of Alusair's trail. "You'd have no trouble keeping up if you were as terrified as I am."

Rowen came up beside her. "If I'm not frightened, it's only because I have nothing to lose. You . . . you'll be queen some day. Why did you pull away from Vangerdahast?"

"The king commanded me to find Alusair," she said. "There is something he wanted me to tell her."

"No," said Rowen. "That is an excuse, not a reason. Even if you and Vangerdahast were not so open about your disputes, the air between you is as taut as a plow lead."

They reached the bottom of the ridge and dropped into a broad trough, with the craggy face of the Storm Horns soaring up on the south and the ridge rising more gently to the north. Rowen used his cape to sweep away four hoof prints leading directly up the furrow. Tanalasta glanced over her shoulder and found the sky mercifully free of ghazneths—at least for the moment.

"You're trying to coerce him . . . into something," huffed Rowen. "What?"

Tanalasta flashed a scowl in his direction—then stumbled on a rock and nearly fell. "Even if you were . . . right," she said, now starting to gasp herself. "It is not for you to question a royal princess."

"It is now, Princess." Rowen emphasized her title. "When you did not go with Vangerdahast, you made it my duty to ask."

"Very well." The princess was finding it more difficult to maintain the pace, though Rowen only seemed to be growing stronger. "I know you're familiar with how Aunadar Bleth embarrassed me. If I am to . . . rule well, I must win the respect of my subjects back. I won't do that by teleporting to safety every time there is the slightest danger."

"No." Rowen stopped running.

Tanalasta halted two paces later and turned around to face him. "What are you doing, Rowen?"

"You do not earn people's respect by lying to them," said the ranger. "That is how you lose it."

Tanalasta glanced at the sky behind him and saw two dark specks weaving back and forth through the air. "We have no time for this."

"You do not need to win my respect, Princess," said Rowen. "You have already done that with your bravery and your intelligence. Now, please show me that you respect me."

Tanalasta rolled her eyes. "*Then* can we go?"

Rowen nodded.

"Very well." Her gaze dropped, and she found it impossible to raise it again. "If you must know, I stayed because of you."

"Me?"

Tanalasta nodded. "You are certainly aware of the royal magician's concerns that I may be growing too old to provide an heir for the realm."

"Those concerns are shared by many," said Rowen. "But I hardly see—"

"Do you want to hear this or not?" Tanalasta snapped. She waved a hand toward the two ghazneths. "We don't have much time."

Rowen swallowed. "Please."

"My father's birthday celebration was a thinly disguised effort to prod me into marrying Dauneth Marliir. Everyone knows this." Tanalasta paused to grind her teeth, then continued, "What they don't know is that when the invitation arrived at Huthduth, I told the High Harvestmaster I would be returning to Cormyr to wed him."

"And what did the High Harvestmaster say to change your mind?"

"That he wished me well and knew Dauneth to be a good man." Tanalasta's reply was sharp. "My doubts arose later, when I was out alone, taking my leave of the mountains."

Rowen nodded and said nothing, as though he did not see anything alarming in the crown princess wandering orc-infested mountains alone.

Tanalasta continued, "When I reached the headwaters of the Orcen River, the air filled with the sound of songbirds and the light turned the color of gold. A magnificent gray stallion came out of the forest bearing an old crone with eyes of pearl and armor of silver lace, and when I called to her, the woman guided her mount down to the water across from me. She would not speak, but when the horse drank, an inky darkness passed from its nostrils into the stream. The grass along the shore withered before my eyes. On the hillside above me, the pine trees browned and lost their needles."

"And this was not a dream?" Rowen asked.

"I was as awake as we are now," Tanalasta replied. "A single tear ran down the crone's cheek, and she shook her head at me."

"And you think—"

"I did not think at all," Tanalasta said, cutting him off. "I was so frightened that I fled without regard for how far I ran or what direction. Before I knew it, I was lost and the day was nearly gone. After a time, I came to a copse of willow and choke-cherry so thick I could barely pass. I would have turned back, save that I heard a woman giggling and thought she might tell me how to return to the monastery."

Rowen's expression grew apprehensive. "And?"

"I fought my way through the thicket to the shores of a small pond, where the young woman I had heard was watering her mount from the pool. The beast was as white and luminous as a diamond, but even then I did not realize what it was until I called out to ask the way to the monastery, and the creature raised its head."

"It was a unicorn." It was not a question.

"The golden horn, the cloven hooves, everything," Tanalasta confirmed. "Instead of answering me, the woman leaped laughing onto the unicorn's back and vanished into the forest. Flowers and shrubs rose to blossom in its hoof prints."

Rowen stood without speaking for a long time, then finally asked, "And when it was gone, you found you had been at the monastery all along?"

"Almost," Tanalasta said, surprised. "I was at my favorite lake. How did you know?"

"Had you still been lost, it would not have been much of a vision." Rowen's expression changed from apprehensive to dazed. "And you think I am this unicorn?"

Tanalasta shrugged. "You're the best candidate so far—and I doubt it was a coincidence that I found your Faith Planting at Orc's Pool."

Rowen shook his head. "But my family . . ."

"Now who is being dishonest?" Tanalasta asked. In the sky behind Rowen, one of the ghazneths peeled off and started south after her mare. "You know as well as I do that the vision wasn't about politics. It was about love."

Rowen paled visibly and seemed too stunned to speak.

Tanalasta took his hand and turned to continue their flight. *"Now* can we go?"

* * * * *

Filfaeril sat alone in the apse of a silent throne room, staring down a long ambulatory bounded by double-stacked arches and tall columns of fluted marble. Though the chamber smelled of mildew and rot, it had been immaculately adorned in broad, vertical bands of brown and gold. The pattern was a simple one favored by Cormyrean royalty more than a thousand years earlier, when the kingdom had barely extended past the Starwater, and Arabel had been little more than a cluster of crossroad inns. The queen could not imagine any family of Arabellan nobles building such an archaic reception hall—nor, having gone to the expense of building it, allowing the place to grow as dank and musty-smelling as this one. It just did not make sense.

Then again, nothing made sense since Vangerdahast's return. She did not understand why he had brought the phantom with him, or why the lurid creature had abducted her only to abandon her here and wander off. Was the thing that confident of its prison, or had it simply forgotten her—and what was it, anyway?

As important as the answers to these questions were, they were not the ones to which Filfaeril's mind kept returning. More than anything, she wanted to know what had happened to Azoun and Tanalasta—and to Vangerdahast. And *those* answers she would not find in this throne room.

The queen forced herself to remain seated for a while longer, using the time to study her environs and look for any hint of her captor's presence. In the event of an abduction, Vangerdahast's instructions were quite clear. First, do as little as possible and wait for the war wizards to show up. Second, avoid giving a captor any excuse to harm her. Third, fight or flee only if death looked imminent. Vangerdahast had told her many times that once the war wizards were alerted to a royal's danger, a rescue company would arrive within minutes. But Filfaeril had been sitting on the throne for hours, and she had seen even less of the rescue company than of her captor. Clearly, something had gone wrong with the royal magician's plan.

Filfaeril stood and descended the dais. She paused to see if the phantom would show itself. When it did not, she walked down the ambulatory to the bronze grillwork gates at the end. Her captor had not bothered to shut them, so she stepped through . . . and found herself looking up the ambulatory toward the dais, as though she had merely turned around.

Filfaeril spun on her heel and found the gates hanging ajar between the same two pillars, looking out on the same gloomy foyer and huge oaken doors as before. She pushed the gate open and walked through. Again, she found herself looking up the ambulatory toward the two wooden thrones on the dais. Frowning, the queen pulled the gate closed, then opened it and stepped through—to the same result.

The queen slammed the bronze gate behind her, then started up the ambulatory. She had suspected all along that the phantom had not simply flown off and forgotten about her, but leaving the gate open was a hint of the creature's true cruelty. As every good torturer knew, the secret to breaking a victim's will lay in controlling her mind. Leaving the gate ajar had been a deliberate attempt to rob Filfaeril of hope. It had worked better than she cared to admit.

On her way back to the dais, she took the time to step through each of the arches along the ambulatory, but the result was always the same. She found herself standing on the opposite side of the room, facing the same arch through which she had come.

Finally, the queen resigned herself to the fact that her prison was as secure as any dungeon cell and returned to her throne. She sat down as deliberately and calmly as she could. After taking a moment to compose herself, Filfaeril pictured the royal magician's bushy-bearded face and rubbed her signet ring.

Her mind remained as quiet as the throne room, and a dozen possible reasons for Vangerdahast's silence leaped into her thoughts. She wished they had not. Had he been able to, the wizard would have answered. That he had not meant one of two things: either he was incapacitated, or the strange prison prevented him from hearing her.

A fanfare of trumpets echoed through the throne room, and the phantom appeared inside the gate. He was as gruesome as before, with his folded wings, tarnished crown, and red-tinged eyes glaring in Filfaeril's direction. In his hands he held a limp mass of gray rags that might have been a body or a wad of clothing, and from his talons dangled long strings of gore.

"Milady." He bowed deeply, then started up the ambulatory toward Filfaeril. "If I have let you grow lonely, you must forgive me. The traitors have kept me busy."

As the phantom neared the dais, Filfaeril saw that the rags he carried were black weathercloaks with bronze throat clasps. The war wizards had found her after all. The queen's fingertips began to ache, and she realized she was digging her nails into the arms of her throne.

The phantom dumped the clothes in a heap and ascended the dais. "There is no need to call for someone else." As he drew closer, the stench of blood and battle offal grew overwhelming. "I am never far from you. Ever."

He stopped beside Filfaeril's throne, then reached down and lifted her hand. She gave an involuntary shiver and shrank away.

"Come now." He clasped her signet ring and gently worked it off her finger, leaving her whole hand smeared with warm gore. "Do you really believe I would hurt you?"

Filfaeril could only look at him and wonder if she had gone mad.

The phantom closed the ring in his palm, then his eyes rolled back and his wings spread a quarter of the way open. He gave a low groan. Finding herself at eye level with his naked loins, Filfaeril turned away in disgust—but instantly thought better of it and reached for her hair. In a swift and practiced motion, she slipped her fingers between the tines of her silver comb and thumbed a tiny catch, then pulled a razor sharp fist-rake from its sheath. The queen twisted in her seat, driving the weapon's needlelike tines into her captor's abdomen and hissing the command word that activated the weapon's death magic.

The phantom snarled in pain, then opened his hand and let the signet ring clink to the floor. He did not fall.

Filfaeril yelled her command word again, pushing against the thing with all her might. The throne beneath her gave an ominous creak and collapsed, and she found herself sitting on the floor atop the moldering green remains of a rotten bench. On the stone before her lay a drab band of tin bearing the royal dragon of Cormyr. The queen was too confused to tell what had happened to the throne, but she knew when the magic had been drained from her signet.

The phantom plucked Filfaeril's comb from his abdomen and stood staring at it in confusion. Behind him, the majestic throne room had grown as dark and murky as a cellar, and the queen could barely make out the blocky shapes of several tall cask racks silhouetted against a distant rectangle of filmy light.

"Look what you've done to our thrones!" The phantom gestured at the splintered remains of the moldering bench, then fixed his red-rimmed eyes on Filfaeril. "When did you grow so fat? You're as big as a sow!"

And Filfaeril suddenly felt as large as a war-horse. Her breathing grew labored and slow, her body became ungainly and sluggish, and her stomach began to rumble and growl. A terrible feeling of despair and lethargy came over her, and she looked down to discover a mountainous lump of flesh in place of her once-svelte body. She cried out in shock, then tried to back away from the phantom and found she could not move her own weight.

"Who are you?" The queen was surprised to hear her demand pour out in a barely-coherent wail. "What are you doing to me?"

The creature kneeled beside her and ran his gore-caked fingers through her long tresses. She would have knocked the hand away, save that when she tried, her arm was too heavy to lift. Behind the phantom, the dank room once again became a majestic throne room.

"Why do you make me do these things?" the phantom demanded. He wrapped his hand into her hair, then jerked her head back. "Do you think this is the way I want to treat my queen?"

"Your *queen?*" Filfaeril took a deep breath and forced herself to look into the phantom's mad eyes. "I am nothing to you but a hostage—a hostage that you would be wise to treat well. When the king finds us—"

Something huge and hard slammed into the side of Filfaeril's face and sent her corpulent body tumbling across the dais. She did not stop rolling until she slammed into the plinth of a marble pillar.

"I am king!" The phantom sprang to her side, then grasped her chin and tilted her head back. "And you are my queen."

Filfaeril shook her head. "I am wife to Azoun."

As she spoke, the throne room grew murky again. The ghostly outlines of cask racks appeared along the ambulatory, and she began to see that her only hope of salvation lay in clinging to her true identity.

"I am Filfaeril, queen to King Azoun IV."

The cask racks grew more substantial.

"You are queen to no king but me!" The phantom slapped her again, and her vision went momentarily black. "You are wife to King Boldovar. To *me*."

Filfaeril began to tremble, and the murkiness vanished from the throne room at once. As adolescents, she and her sisters had delighted in keeping each other up nights by telling grisly tales of how King Boldovar had murdered his mistresses.

"B-boldovar the Mad?"

"Boldovar the King—husband to Queen Filfaeril!" The phantom pressed Filfaeril's comb-dagger to her fleshy breast, then ordered, "Say it."

"K-king Boldovar, h-husband . . ." Filfaeril stopped, realizing that to indulge the phantom was to lose herself in his madness—perhaps forever. She shook her head, then raised her chin. "I'd rather die."

Almost instantly, her body became slender and beautiful again, and she found herself lying on the floor of a dank wine cellar. Boldovar scowled and looked around in confusion, then shrugged and returned his attention to Filfaeril.

"As you command, milady."

The phantom scraped the sharp tines along the queen's flesh, opening four shallow cuts along the top curve of her breast. She closed her eyes, surprised that death's black fog had not risen up to carry her off already. Once Vanger-dahast's enchantment was activated, even the weapon's scratch was supposed to kill instantly and surely. She commended her soul to Lady Sune, then opened her eye-lids to find Boldovar's ghastly eyes still gazing into her own.

"What is this? Did I drink up all your magic?" He tossed the comb aside, then flashed her a needle-fanged smile. "Perhaps you wish to recant?"

12

he royal wizard woke bound and naked, covered by a single blood-stained linen, surrounded by enemies of the realm. To the right stood Owden Foley, a clammy cold cloth in one hand and a brass basin in the other. Alaphondar Emmarask and Merula the Marvelous watched from the foot of the bed, eyes beady and observant, alert as always for any sign that the royal magician knew their thoughts. He did of course, but he could not let them see it. They would kill him on the spot.

To the wizard's left stood Azoun IV, his arm hanging in a sling and his shoulder wrapped in a bloody bandage. Good. Vangerdahast had done some damage after all, even if he did not recall when or how . . . or why.

Vangerdahast's head ached from the bridge of his nose to the nape of his neck. His thoughts came slowly and for only short periods. His scalp felt crusty and swollen and strangely taut, with long stripes of hot pain crossing it from right to left. His body ached with fever. He was hungry enough to eat a cat, though of course he knew better than to ask for one. He refused to give his captors the pleasure of seeing him beg.

Owden, of course, was the torturer. The priest's implements lay on the table beside the bed, arrayed in neat rows of knives and needles and coarse loops of thread. Knowing they had only left the instruments in the open to frighten him, Vangerdahast looked away. Had his hands not been bound to the bed frame, he would have grabbed one of those knives and shown the traitors the error of their ways. Then again, had his hands been untied, he would not have needed a knife. He was, after all, a wizard.

If only he could remember his spells.

While most spells required gestures and special components and the uttering of mystic syllables, some required only an incantation. They would be ready for that. The enemies of the realm were as cunning as they were pervasive. If Vangerdahast wanted to escape and save the crown, he needed to be as clever as they were. He raised his head and glared at Merula.

"Help me, and I will forgive you this treason," he said. "Use your magic against them, and I will pardon you when the crown is mine!"

Merula's face paled, and he looked to Owden.

Owden looked to Azoun. "Forgive him, Majesty. It is the wound madness. You yourself raved on and on about how the Ladies Rowanmantle and Hawklin were jealous of the sons of your other—"

"Yes, yes!" Azoun's hand shot up to silence the priest. "I am quite familiar with the insane thoughts caused by the creature's wounds."

"Insane thoughts? The insanity is this." Vangerdahast strained to raise his left arm. "Unbind me, and I grant you safe passage to exile in a foreign land."

Azoun scowled at Owden. "I hope this madness can be cleared up soon." He looked back to Vangerdahast and grasped his arm, then said, "Old friend, I know your thoughts are muddled, but you must try to answer me. What happened to my daughter? Is the princess safe?"

Somewhere deep down beneath the madness, Vangerdahast felt a guilty pang. "Tanalasta?"

Azoun nodded. "Yes. Princess Tanalasta. She didn't return with you."

The battle in the canyon came flooding back to Vangerdahast—and with it a surge of anger.

"She defied me!" Vangerdahast's temples pounded with hot anguish. "The brazen harlot!"

"Harlot?" Azoun repeated. "Then she's with this Cormaeril fellow?"

"Spoiled now!" Vangerdahast spat. "He's spoiled her now."

"But is she safe?"

Vangerdahast tried to sit up and managed only to lift his head off the pillow before the restraints jerked him back down. He began to toss his head back and forth, trying in vain to shake loose the memory of some spell that would set him free. Azoun laid a palm on Vangerdahast's brow and pressed down to hold the wizard's head still.

"Don't smother me!" Vangerdahast cried. "How can I tell if you smother me?"

Azoun eased up. "I'm not going to smother anyone."

Vangerdahast laid very still and regarded the king suspiciously. "How do I know?"

"Vangerdahast, I would never hurt you."

"Tell me you don't want me out of the way."

Azoun shook his head. "I don't. You're my most trusted advisor. My best friend. Please, try to remember. Tell me about Tanalasta."

"Undo this." Vangerdahast jerked against the binding on his left hand. "Just this one—then I'll tell you."

Azoun cast a querying glance at Owden.

The priest shook his head. "He wouldn't tell you anyway, and it's too dangerous. He could wipe us all out with one spell."

"Don't listen to the groundsplitter!" Vangerdahast's head began to throb with the effort of finding some spell to help him escape. "He's afraid of my power."

"And rightly so," said Owden.

Vangerdahast turned to glare at the priest. Owden's hand came out of his pocket sprinkling yellow dust, but Vangerdahast was too quick for the priest and managed to shut his eyes.

"Do you know where you are, Vangerdahast?" asked Owden. "Do you remember what happened to your head?"

Vangerdahast did not open his eyes. "My head hurts. You did something to it."

"Not me," said Owden. "It was the thing that came back with you."

"You!" Vangerdahast insisted.

"It slapped you in the head, then went after Azoun—"

"No!"

At last, the incantation of a blinding spell popped into Vangerdahast's head. It would not free him, and it would only affect one person—but if he chose the right person, perhaps he could cause enough confusion to get at one of Owden's torture knives on the table beside him.

Vangerdahast turned his head toward Azoun and began to repeat the incantation, then smelled something strident and saw Owden sprinkle some glittering droplets into his face. He squeaked out one more syllable, then the room went dark, and he was seized by a sudden sensation of falling.

Sometime much later, Vangerdahast woke bound and naked, covered by a single fresh linen, surrounded by the haggard-looking enemies of the realm. To the right stood Owden Foley, a clammy cold cloth in one hand and a brass basin in the other. Alaphondar Emmarask and Merula the Marvelous watched from the foot of the bed, eyes beady and observant, alert as always for any sign that the royal magician knew their thoughts. He did of course, but he could not let them see it, or they would kill him on the spot.

To the wizard's left stood Azoun IV, arm hanging in a sling and his shoulder wrapped in a fresh bandage.

Vangerdahast did not recall how he had come to be the prisoner of the realm's enemies. He did not recall anything, save for a faint odor that faded from his memory even as he tried to hold onto it. The only thing that looked vaguely familiar were the log joists and rough hewn planks above his head—the ceiling of his prison, or the floor of the chamber above. It depended on one's perspective, really, and it seemed to him that there ought to be an escape in that, if he could just recall the right spell.

"Vangerdahast?" asked the rat-faced priest. "Do you know where you are?"

Vangerdahast knew exactly where he was—in a prisoner's tower—but he would not give his captors the pleasure of hearing him admit it. He felt a hand on his shoulder and looked over to see the king grasping his shoulder.

"Old friend, do you remember me?"

"Of course." Vangerdahast decided to stall for time and hope he could recall the spell he needed. "How could I forget the usur—er, the king?"

Azoun relaxed visibly. "Thank the All Mother!" he gasped. "Do you remember my daughter? Can you tell me what happened to Tanalasta?"

The battle in the canyon returned to him in a flood, the first ghazneth knocking him from his horse with the dismembered body of an orc, the steel gate suddenly appearing with the second ghazneth behind it naked and wild-eyed, reaching for Tanalasta and the ranger, the ranger leaping from his grasp, that harlot of a princess flinging herself after him . . .

"It's . . . it's all so fuzzy." Vangerdahast shook his head, then tried to sit up. When his bindings prevented it, he lifted his left arm and looked to the king. "Do you think I could—"

"Of course."

Azoun started to pull his dagger to cut the bindings, but Owden leaned across the bed to restrain him.

"Not yet, Majesty."

"Not yet?" Vangerdahast yelled. He whirled on the priest and screamed, "Release me! Release me now, or I swear you will rue this day when the crown is mine!"

A weary groan escaped Azoun's lips, and Vangerdahast saw at once that he was losing all hope of tricking his captors into releasing him. He turned to the king.

"It seems to be coming back." He closed his eyes in concentration, though what he was concentrating on was recalling some spell that he could cast without his hands. "Perhaps if you let me have just one hand so I could tug on my beard. Yes, that's it. Tugging on my beard always helps."

Azoun merely shook his head and glared at Owden. "How much longer?"

The priest could only shrug. "I'm sure His Majesty cannot recall, but his own convalescence was difficult as well, and his wounds were not nearly as grievous as those of the royal magician."

Vangerdahast blinked several times, then turned his head toward Owden. "Wait. I'm feeling much better now."

"That's good," said Owden. "Can you remember what became of the princess?"

Vangerdahast nodded, and the incantation of his dimension door spell returned to him in a flash. It was a quick and simple alteration no more than half a dozen syllables long. Confident that he would soon be looking at the planks from the other side, he fixed his gaze on the ceiling and started his incantation—then smelled something familiar and strident as Owden Foley's hand flashed into sight and flung a stream of glittering drops into his eyes.

Vangerdahast had the sudden sensation of falling, and the chamber went dark, and he woke later to find himself bound and naked, covered by a single linen, surrounded by enemies of the realm. Owden Foley stood to his right, a clammy cold cloth in one hand and a brass basin in the other. Alaphondar Emmarask and Merula the Marvelous watched from the foot of the bed, the one with eyes sunken and bloodshot from reading too much, the other dressed in a dusty robe, looking rather spectral and hollow-cheeked for a man of such robust proportions. To the wizard's left stood Azoun IV in badly dented field armor, a new steel patch covering a jagged hole high on his breastplate.

"Azoun?" gasped Vangerdahast. "Have you been fighting?"

"Thank the gods!" The king clasped Vangerdahast's shoulder. "You're back among us."

Vangerdahast glanced at the hand on his shoulder. "That's awfully presumptuous, don't you think?" The wizard lifted an arm to brush away the offending appendage, but found his wrist tied to the bed frame by a stout cord. He glared at the rope in disbelief, then demanded, "What's the meaning of this? Remove it at once!"

Owden Foley leaned over the wizard and grasped his other arm. "Perhaps later," he said. "Do you know where you are?"

Vangerdahast scowled. "Of course! I'm in my room in ... We're in the palace at . . ." He stared up at the familiar-looking joists and planks above his head, but for the life of him could not remember what city they were in. He pondered this for a moment, then reached the only possible conclusion. "You've kidnapped me!"

Azoun spewed an unspeakable curse on the goddess Chauntea, then started around the bed to leave. Owden raised a finger.

"One minute, Sire."

The king glared at the priest. "Just one. I still have a wife to save, even if my daughter is beyond hope."

Vangerdahast raised his head. "The queen?"

Owden nodded eagerly. "Yes, you remember the queen."

"Filfaeril?"

"Queen Filfaeril," Owden confirmed. "Do you remember what happened to her?"

"Of course!" Vangerdahast remembered everything: the battle in the canyon, Tanalasta flinging herself after Rowen, being attacked in the stable yard, trying to knock Filfaeril out of the ghazneth's grasp. "Is the queen well?"

"That is impossible to say," said Azoun. "The last time we saw her, she was definitely alive."

Vangerdahast's heart sank. "The *last* time you saw her?"

"I am afraid the ghazneth has her," said Owden. "The king has seen her once, as he was closing in on the creature's lair and it was forced to move her."

"By Thauglor's scales!" Vangerdahast started to rise, only to find himself still tied into bed. He stared at the silken bindings in confusion for a moment, then said, "Get these things off of me! We've got work to do."

"*Your* work can wait a little longer," said Owden. "You will not be fully cured until you have faced the demon within."

"The demon within?" Vangerdahast demanded.

"Each of us carries our own demon inside," Owden explained. "Most of us keep it imprisoned in the deepest, darkest part of our souls where it can do no harm. But when we undergo a terrible trauma such as you and the king suffered, these demons can escape."

Vangerdahast turned to Azoun. "What nonsense is this?"

"Vangerdahast, maybe you'd better listen."

"To a groundsplitter?" the wizard huffed. "Has Tanalasta finally gotten to you?"

A pained expression came to the king's face, and he looked away without speaking.

"I'm afraid that would be impossible," said Alaphondar, speaking for the first time. "We haven't been able to convince you to tell us what became of the princess."

Vangerdahast scowled. "What do you mean, 'convince'? She's with Rowen Cormaeril. They pulled away from me when I teleported back here." He looked from Alaphondar to Azoun to Merula. "Is somebody going to tell me what's happening here?"

"Of course," said Owden. "Your inner demon escaped, and you need to recapture it."

"Recapture it?"

"Before it consumes you entirely," confirmed the priest. "You must look deep within yourself and face it, here before these witnesses. You must tell us what the demon wants, then you will have the strength to control it."

Vangerdahast grew instantly suspicious. They were trying to extract a confession from him, but why? After all he had done for the realm, could Azoun actually be frightened of him? Or jealous of his power? The wizard turned to berate the king for his pettiness—and realized that was exactly what Owden wanted. Rebuking the king would only feed Azoun's suspicion and breed resentment, while confessing to a secret envy of the royal birthright—as far-fetched as that might be—would make it all but impossible for Azoun to trust him completely again. In either case, Owden would be standing by, ready to replace Vangerda-hast's counsel with his own—and to replace the war wizards with his Royal Temple of Chauntea.

Vangerdahast whirled on the priest. "You dirt-grubbing worm! You fork-tongued, scaly-bellied, lying snake. Do you really think you can meddle in royal affairs? I'll see you growing mushrooms in the dungeon cesspits before I name my demons in front of you!"

Vangerdahast summoned to mind a spell he could cast with voice alone and began to utter his incantation. Owden reached for something, but the king raised his hand and waved him off.

"I'd say Vangerdahast is back to normal."

Vangerdahast finished his spell, and in the next second was lying on his bed in the form of a small mink. He rolled to all four feet and dashed out from beneath the sheet, darting between Alaphondar and Merula into a nearby corner. There he stopped and changed back to his normal form, then turned to face his nervous-looking companions.

"Are you going to stand there and stare, or hand me a robe?" he demanded. "We've got work to do."

Owden started around the bed. "You can't do this," he said. "You're not ready."

"Harvestmaster Foley, if you mention my inner demon one more time, I swear you'll spend the rest of your life dodging thrushes in the palace gardens."

Owden stopped at the foot of the bed and looked to Azoun.

The king only smiled and shrugged. "What can I say? Vangerdahast has always had a bit of the demon in him." He looked to Merula, then added, "You heard the royal magician. Find the man his robe."

As Merula scrambled to obey, Vangerdahast bowed to the king and said, "Thank you, Sire. It's good to see that someone around here has returned to his senses."

The wizard smoothed his beard, then ran a hand through what remained of his hair and noticed the slashes across the top of his head. He ran his fingers along the scars, noting that they had already sealed themselves.

"By Thauglor!" he cursed. "How long did you let me sleep?"

Azoun looked uncomfortable. "You've been . . . *asleep* for five days."

"And you couldn't wake me?" Vangerdahast whirled on Owden. "Aren't you priests good for anything?"

Owden's expression turned stormy, but before the priest could say anything, Azoun took Vangerdahast by the elbow and guided him toward a table and chairs.

"We'd better sit down and have a talk, old friend," he said. "We've got some planning to do, and there are a lot of things we both don't know."

13

he swarm hung low in the northern sky, a whirling flock of dark specks almost invisible against the looming wall of Anauroch's golden sand dunes, spiraling down toward the jagged vestige of a lonely keep tower.

Alusair's trail ran toward the ruin as straight as an arrow.

Tanalasta did not have the courage to voice her thoughts, but there was little need. After four days of dodging gnolls and ghazneths in the dusty vastness that separated the Stonelands from the Goblin Marches, she and Rowen had developed an uncanny instinct for what the other was thinking. The ranger removed the saddlebags from his shoulder and opened the flap, then passed the princess her weather-cloak and bracers.

"I wouldn't worry," said Rowen. "If Alusair thought she was in more trouble than she could handle, she'd put on her signet and call Vangerdahast."

"And how many times have you seen her do that?" It was a rhetorical question, and Tanalasta did not wait for an answer. "Besides, what good would Vangerdahast be? With so many ghazneths, his magic would be useless."

Rowen regarded the distant specks for a moment. "I still think there is good reason to hope. If the matter were decided, why would they still be in the sky?"

He closed the saddlebags again and picked up his makeshift pike, which Tanalasta had fashioned by binding the iron dagger to the end of a sturdy elm branch. Though the weapon was more cumbersome to carry and use than a knife, it would also allow Rowen to strike with more power—and perhaps help keep him out of his foe's reach. The princess draped the weathercloak over her shoulders, then followed the ranger's lead and crouched down behind a waist-high clump of silvery smokebush. It would be a long crawl to the ruined keep, but the dusty plain was as level as a lake and cover was scant.

They moved in short bursts, running from bush to bush in a low crouch or crawling across open areas on hands and knees. They were careful to keep one eye fixed on the distant swarm of ghazneths and the other on the underbrush, since the plain's deadly assortment of snakes, arachnids, and chilopods all liked to hide in the relative safety of the spindly thorn bushes. Several times, Tanalasta found herself backing away from the widespread mandibles of a charging centipede or the upraised stinger of an angry scorpion, and once Rowen had to catch the fangs of a striking wyv snake on the butt of his pike.

As they drew nearer to the keep, they began to notice individual specks swooping down into the ruins or rising up from behind the bailey wall to rejoin the main swarm. Tanalasta's stomach grew hollow with dread, and she chafed at the delay of their stealthy approach. She and Alusair were not the closest of sisters, but they were sisters, and she kept having gruesome visions of ghazneths quarreling over Alusair's lifeless body.

Rowen seemed to sense Tanalasta's growing disquiet. He ran faster and for longer periods, paying less attention to concealment as they went. The princess appreciated his concern, but she also knew they would be no help at all if the ghazneths saw them coming. Already, she could see the distinctive shape of the creatures' outstretched wings, and it would not be long before they drew close enough for the things to spy them rushing through the brush. Tanalasta was about to remark on her concerns when the ranger suddenly stood up straight.

"Rowen, what are you doing?" Thinking he might have been bitten by a lance snake or—even worse—a tiger centipede, she circled to his side and took his arm. "What is it?"

He did not move. "Those aren't ghazneths."

Tanalasta peered at the spiraling swarm, but it was still too distant for her to identify individual shapes. She tried again to pull him down. "You can't be sure."

"Can't I?" He pointed toward the western edge of the spiral. "Watch their wingtips as they turn."

Tanalasta did so, and she noticed a ragged, rounded fringe—almost like tiny fingers—silhouetted against the looming sand dunes. "Feathers?"

"So it would seem," Rowen replied.

Tanalasta's heart sank. "They're vultures."

"We don't know what it means." He squeezed her arm. "Perhaps one of Alusair's horses died."

"That's too many vultures for one horse," Tanalasta replied.

The princess started forward at a near run, struggling to hold her imagination in check. Tanalasta kept telling herself that Alusair had outwitted a dozen creatures as terrible as any ghazneth, that she was an experienced leader with a full company of warriors, a pair of clerics, and plenty of magic at her disposal. But those assurances rang hollow in the face of so many swarming vultures. There had to be a lot of carrion—and the most obvious source of that carrion was a patrol of Cormyrean knights.

As they drew nearer, Tanalasta saw that the keep was one of those strange, lopsided towers described in Artur Shurtmin's tome, *The Golden Age of Goblins*. Constructed of slab sandstone and dark mortar, the spire had a conspicuous bulge near the top of one side and leaned noticeably in that direction, as though being dragged down by a great weight. Its girth was ringed by cockeyed bands of tiny windows, suggesting the presence of at least eight interior floors in a height of only forty feet.

The outer walls were streaked by long stains of scarlet and orange. Common myth held the stripes to be proof that the builders had used the blood of captives in their mortar, but Artur—whose love of the subject was perhaps too great for an impartial assessment of the evidence—maintained the streaks were merely evidence that ancient goblins often employed vertical stripes to make short things seem tall. Though Tanalasta had her doubts about both beliefs, the truth of the matter would never be known. The Goblin Kingdom had vanished long before history began, and it was known today only by the ruins it had left scattered across the wild lands between Anauroch and the Storm Horns.

Tanalasta tried to take some comfort from the presence of the goblin tower. Typically, such places were merely the entrance to decaying tunnel warrens now occupied by all manner of sinister creatures. Perhaps the vultures were feasting upon a tribe of kobolds or barbarian goblins that had been foolish enough to attack as Alusair's company passed through.

Tanalasta and Rowen were still a hundred paces from the bailey when they began to smell hints of death—the fetor of rotting meat, acrid whiffs of charred flesh, the musty odor of newly-opened earth. Knowing from Artur's tome that the goblins of the golden age always aligned their gates with the setting sun, Tanalasta guided them toward the west side of the bailey. The crowns of several large buckeye trees grew visible, protruding just far enough above the wall to reveal the starlike shape of their drought-yellowed leaves. The sickly odors grew heavier and more constant. As they drew closer, the princess heard the flapping and hissing of squabbling vultures, and also a sound she could not identify, an erratic rasping punctuated at odd intervals by muffled clattering and sharp snapping sounds.

Tanalasta stopped beside the gate and peered around the corner. She had been wrong about the number of buckeye trees. There was only one, with a twisted silver trunk as thick as a giant's waist and a tangled umbrella of yellowed boughs that covered the entire bailey. In the shadows beneath the tree's limbs, two dozen starving horses stood fastened to a tether line, so devitalized and weary they could hardly move to flick the vultures off. Several beasts already lay motionless beneath a cloud of droning flies and thrashing black feathers, while a tangle of scorched armor and charred bone lay piled against the base of the keep, directly beneath a tiny third-story window. Nearby, a dozen hissing birds played tug-of-war with the bones of a Cormyrean knight. Beside the corpse rested a primitive sword, its cold-forged blade covered with a layer of dusty red rust. Scattered across the bailey were dozens of huge dirt piles, each resting next to the dark cavity of a recently excavated hole.

A muffled clatter sounded from the far side of the bailey, and Tanalasta's attention was caught by the motion of several small stones rolling down a dirt pile. She saw something black and vaguely arrow-shaped dancing atop the mound. In the shadowy light beneath the buckeye, she took the shape for a vulture—until a cloud of dirt came flying over the pile and momentarily obscured it.

Tanalasta felt Rowen's hand close around her arm, then she finally recognized the dark shape as the top of a folded wing. She pulled back and turned to face the ranger.

"We'll have to lure it away," she whispered.

Rowen shook his head. "I'll take it from behind. With a little luck, it'll never hear me coming."

"And I'll be kept safely out of the way," said Tanalasta, voicing the unspoken reason for his suggestion. She shook her head. "If I thought it would work, maybe, but those things are too quick and too tough. Even if you could take it by surprise—and that's a big if—you'd never kill it with a single stroke. We have to do this together."

Rowen peered around the corner again, then returned with a clenched jaw. "Forgive me for saying so, Princess, but we must consider the possibility that you are the only remaining heir. It would be treason to risk your life."

"They're alive," said Tanalasta. "And so is Alusair."

"You can't know that," he said. "They've been burning their own, which means they've had disease, and—"

"And they have two clerics, a war wizard, and a whole saddlebag full of magic potions."

"No potions," said Rowen. "The wizard died the first time we met the ghazneth, and even if the clerics are still alive, they have certainly run out of water by now. You saw the condition of the horses; a human would not last half as long."

"There is water in the bottom of the warren—that's what the keeps were built to protect." Tanalasta hoped Artur Shurtmin had based this observation more solidly on fact than his fanciful explanation for the goblins' love of crimson streaks. "Even if Alusair is dead, we may assume by the ghazneth's digging that part of the company survives. Do you really think I would abandon them to the creature—whether or not they were alive?"

"I suppose not." Rowen thrust the pike toward her. "Take this, and I'll see if I can get Fogger's sword."

Tanalasta refused to accept the weapon. "I'm not strong enough to do much good with a pike, and I don't want to take the chance that the ghazneth would notice the missing sword. It would ruin my plan."

Rowen raised his brow. "Plan?"

"The Queen Feints." Tanalasta smiled confidently. "Boreas Kaspes used it to win the King's Challenge in 978 DR."

Rowen looked doubtful until Tanalasta explained her plan, then gave a grudging nod and admitted that it could work. He offered a few refinements and showed her how to roll over her shoulder so she would not be hurt when she hurled herself to the ground, then the princess kept watch while he used his heel to kick a shallow trench across the near side of the gateway. Once that was done, he clasped her shoulder and pulled her back behind the wall.

"Remember, this isn't chess," he whispered. "If the ghazneth does something unexpected, you won't have time to think about your next move."

Tanalasta nodded. "I'll just do it."

The princess started to step into the gateway, then thought better of it and pulled the ranger close and kissed him on the lips long and hard. She did not stop until long after he had gotten over his surprise, and even then she continued until her mind began to wander to matters other than the ghazneth.

Tanalasta drew back far enough to look into Rowen's dark eyes, then gasped, "For luck!"

"Indeed, I'm very lucky."

The ranger wrapped her in his arms and swung her deftly around to press her back against the bailey wall. The sandstone slabs felt jagged and hard against her spine, which was all the excuse Tanalasta needed to crush her body against his, and within moments the princess was filled with a joyous, god-sent hunger it would have been a sin to deny. She ran her hands along his torso and felt his running along hers, and she ached for him to touch her in all her sacred places—and that was when she knew she had definitely picked the wrong time for their first kiss.

Through a force of will, Tanalasta managed to slip her hands between their torsos and press against Rowen's chest. The ranger did not seem to realize she was trying to push him away—perhaps because she was not trying very hard. He slipped one hand around to caress the small of her back—actually it was a little lower—and brought the other up to touch the softness of her breast, and the princess's knees nearly buckled. She let herself go limp for the space of one very long breath, then summoned her resolve and broke off the kiss.

"Wait . . ."

When she pushed against his chest this time, a horrified look came to Rowen's face. He stumbled back, his cheeks as crimson as blood.

"Milady, forgive me! I thought . . ." The ranger directed his gaze to the ground, apparently unable to finish while he was looking at Tanalasta. "I thought you wanted me to."

"I did—I *do*." Tanalasta smiled and took his hand, but was careful to keep him at arm's length. "But I think I'd better keep a clear head, don't you?"

Rowen nodded, his expression changing from mortification to relief to anxiety. "We'd both better—it's just that I've never felt anything . . . well, a kiss has never been quite like that."

"What did you expect when you kissed a princess?" Tanalasta chuckled, then glimpsed the fleeting expression of guilt that flashed through Rowen's eyes. "Or have you done that before?"

Rowen looked away and started to answer, but Tanalasta quickly raised her hand to silence him. "Never mind."

"But—"

"I don't want to hear it." Tanalasta shook her head emphatically. "It might make me change my mind about rescuing the little trollop."

"But—"

"Rowen, that was a command!"

Tanalasta slipped around the corner and stepped through the gate, holding her bracers in her hands. On the far side of the bailey, the ghazneth's wing was still visible, protruding up from behind the dirt pile it had excavated. A cold chill crept down the princess's spine, and she found herself wishing that Rowen hadn't been so quick to see the wisdom of her plan. He was still taking the greatest risk by far, but Tanalasta was inexperienced at being bait and could not help fearing she would make some terrible error that would get them both killed. She checked to make sure her weathercloak remained secure on her shoulders, then angled toward the iron sword, counting the steps she had taken since coming through the gate.

When the count reached ten, Tanalasta slipped her bracers onto her wrists, then pictured her sister's face and closed the clasp. The metal tingled beneath her fingers. Alusair's image grew haggard and wan-looking. She had dark circles beneath her eyes and sunken cheeks, and she seemed to be lying on her back in a very dark place. When she showed no sign of feeling her sister's mind-touch, Tanalasta experienced a moment of panic and very nearly cried out in grief.

As the princess struggled with her alarm, the ghazneth's shadowy head appeared above the dirt pile. It turned toward the gate and stared directly at her, its beady eyes gleaming red in the murkiness beneath the tree. Tanalasta allowed her very real terror to voice itself in a scream, signaling to Rowen that she had been seen.

The vultures responded by launching themselves up through the buckeye's gnarled umbrella, and the ghazneth scrambled over its dirt pile, springing after Tanalasta with a bone-chilling hiss. She spun on her heel and sprinted for the gate.

Inside Tanalasta's mind, Alusair's gaze suddenly shifted and grew a little less glassy.

Outside keep with Rowen, Tanalasta sent. Though she had rehearsed the message a dozen times after describing her plan to Rowen, the princess found it astonishingly difficult to keep her thoughts straight with a ghazneth swooping after her. *Iron sword twenty paces outside portcullis on left. In this together!*

Alusair's image blinked twice. *Tanalasta?*

Tanalasta could not respond. The weathercloak's magic allowed her to send only one short message to the recipient, and the recipient to respond with only a few equally short words. By the time she reached the gate, her ears were filled with the throbbing of the ghazneth's wings beating the air. She spied the little trench Rowen had kicked into the dirt and hurled herself over the threshold, tucking her shoulder as he had taught her. A loud, sick crackle erupted behind her. Tanalasta rolled to her feet, howling in triumph.

It was a short-lived victory yell.

Rowen stood in the gateway, the butt of his pike braced in the kick-trench, his rear elbow locked over the long shaft and his forward arm braced against his hip to provide support. The ghazneth had impaled itself at the other end of the weapon as planned, but it was hardly the limp, lifeless heap Tanalasta had expected. The phantom was dragging itself down the shaft in a mad attempt to jerk the pike from its ambusher's grasp.

Though this ghazneth was as naked as the other two the princess had seen, it was much more powerful-looking, with a broad chest, hulking shoulders, and a blocky male face. It had three goatlike horns at its scalp, a jutting brow, and a flat, porcine nose from which it spewed clouds of foul-smelling black fog every time it exhaled. So long were the thing's arms that though it was only half-way down the pike, Rowen had to lean away when it swung at him to avoid being gouged by its curled black talons.

Tanalasta raised one hand toward the creature's chest. "Rowen, get down!"

"What?" Rowen ducked a massive claw, then tried to swing the pike back and forth in an effort to widen the ooze-pouring wound in the creature's chest. "I'm all that stands between you—"

"Do it!" Tanalasta commanded. Not waiting to see if he would obey, she slapped her bracers. "King's bolts!"

A fiery tingling shot up her arm, then Rowen hurled himself to the ground just as four golden bolts shot from Tanalasta's fingertips.

The ghazneth was as quick to furl its wings as its fellows, but the pike running through its breast prevented the leathery appendages from drawing completely closed. Tanalasta's magic bolts shot through the tiny gap, catching the creature square in the sternum and launching it backward through the gate.

The ghazneth slammed down on its back and rolled once, snapping the pike off at both ends. Behind it, Tanalasta glimpsed half a dozen figures staggering out of the goblin keep. Then the creature was on its feet again, gathering itself to spring.

"What now?" Rowen gasped, struggling in vain to recover even half as fast as their foe.

Tanalasta reached down for him. "My hand!"

This time, Rowen did not need to be told twice. He grabbed hold even as the princess was pushing her other hand into the weathercloak's escape pocket. There was that instant of dark timelessness, then they were inside the bailey, next to the picked-over skeleton Tanalasta had noticed from the gate, surrounded by the haggard, staggering, filthy-smelling survivors of Alusair's company. She and Rowen were staring at the jagged shaft of the broken pike protruding from between the ghazneth's broken wings.

"The sword!" Tanalasta urged, pointing at the ground.

Rowen cursed, and she looked down to discover that the iron sword was gone.

The ghazneth spun on them, spreading its wings wide to sweep its attackers off their feet as it turned. Alusair dropped out of the buckeye's tangled umbrella, bringing the iron sword down toward the phantom's skull. Her foot brushed one of its wings on the way down, and that was all the warning the thing needed. It slipped its head to one side, and the rust-coated blade slid down the side of its skull, slashing off an ear and biting deep into its collarbone.

The ghazneth roared in pain and used its good arm to slap Alusair off its back, then spun to finish her off. Tanalasta summoned her magic bolt spell to mind, but Rowen was already clutching the tip of their broken lance and hurling himself at the beast's back.

The ranger struck at a full sprint, driving the dagger through a leathery wing and pinning it to the ghazneth's back. The phantom roared and spun to face him, and then Alusair was behind it with the iron sword again, shredding its wings and hacking deep, oozing slashes into its legs. The ghazneth spun again, but this time it merely swatted the armored princess aside and hobbled through the gate as fast as a lightning bolt.

Tanalasta rushed to her sister's side. Alusair lay sprawled on the face of a dirt mound, both eyes closed and breathing in quick, faint rasps.

Tanalasta kneeled and cradled her sister's head in her lap. "Alusair! Can you hear me? Are you hurt?"

"Of course I'm hurt! You ever been hit by one of those things?" Alusair opened one brown eye and glared at Tanalasta. "And what in the Nine Hells are you doing here? This is no place for a crown princess!"

Seeing that her little sister would be fine, Tanalasta smiled and said, "No, Alusair, it's not."

14

he Royal Excursionary Company emerged from the timeless murk with a crackle like lightning, then sat swaying in their saddles, stomachs rolling and heads spinning with teleport after-daze. Slowly, darkness gave way to dun-colored light, and the warped sycamore appeared on the barren hillside ahead. A hot wind began to stipple them with brown moorlands dust, and the silence gave way to clattering and snorting, and stoop-shouldered silhouettes started to come into focus all around.

Something sharp struck Vangerdahast's ribs and bounced off his magic shield without causing harm, then the horses began to scream.

"Swiners!" Vangerdahast yelled, finally coming out of his afterdaze. "Ambush!"

A streak of swooping darkness came down from his right and caught him by the arm, jerking him from the saddle and lifting him high off the ground. He glimpsed his excursionary company below, fifty mighty war wizards backed by two hundred Purple Dragons, mingled in with a horde of shrieking, startled swiners. Vangerdahast cursed. Though they had foreseen the reception committee, no one had expected to teleport into the very heart of an orc tribe.

Vangerdahast drew a small lead ball from his sleeve pocket and rolled it between his thumb and forefinger, uttering a swift incantation. His body grew silvery and heavy. The ghazneth cried out in surprise and plunged toward the ground, its wings hammering the air in a futile attempt to keep the wizard aloft. Vangerdahast twisted around to clutch hold of its arm, though not because he feared being dropped and crashing into the ground. Like everyone else in the company, he had been magically shielded against any form of blow or cut before leaving Arabel. He was grabbing the phantom because of the mad bloodlust that had come over him the moment he glimpsed the thing—the same bloodlust he had experienced the first time he saw it. He wanted to drag it down to the ground and draw his iron dagger and slash the wicked creature into black ribbons.

As Vangerdahast expected when he looked up, he found himself staring into the haggish visage of the first ghazneth he had encountered. The thing was snarling down at him with flared nostrils and bare yellow fangs, its red-tinged eyes bulging with strain and hatred. Vangerdahast glimpsed the edge of the battle less than twenty feet below and pulled his black, cold-forged dagger from its belt sheath, and the phantom finally seemed to realize the hopelessness of its struggle. Hissing angrily, it opened its talons and let the wizard drop free.

In his mad battle fury, Vangerdahast could think of nothing but finishing the thing. He continued to hold onto its wrist—then yelled in agony as the full burden of his magical weight shifted to his own arm and jerked the shoulder out of its socket. His hand opened of its own accord, then he slammed to the ground and went tumbling backward across the rocks.

Even as he rolled, Vangerdahast heard the throb of a dozen bowstrings and glimpsed a flurry of dark shafts streak past above his head. The ghazneth shrieked, and the wizard knew at least one of the iron-tipped shafts had found its mark. On the next revolution, he jammed his feet into the ground and managed to bring his somersaulting to a stop, then tried to rise and found his body too heavy to lift.

Vangerdahast canceled the heaviness spell with a thought, then staggered to his feet still clutching his iron dagger. The ghazneth was already a hundred feet away, climbing back into the sky and banking north-ward, the shafts of half a dozen arrows dangling from its breast.

A pair of spear points slammed into Vangerdahast's back, knocking him off his feet and driving him back to the ground. Though the spears could not penetrate his magic armor, the fall did cause his separated shoulder to erupt in pain. He cursed loudly, then dropped his dagger and thrust his good hand into his weathercloak, feeling for his thickest war wand.

Seeing that their first attack had not pierced the wizard's woolen cloak, the orcs jammed their spear tips into his back again. A fresh wave of agony shot through Vangerdahast's shoulder.

"Stupid swiners!" He rolled onto his back, slamming his heel into the first warrior's knee and sweeping it off its feet. "Any kobold can see spears won't work!"

Vangerdahast leveled his wand and a thread of golden light lanced out to pierce the orc's chest. The creature dropped its spear, reached for its heart, and erupted into a crimson spray. The wizard turned away from the gory shower, then felt a pair of talons raking at his knees. He looked back to find the second swiner clawing its way up his legs, tusks gnashing and beady eyes burning with blood-hunger.

Vangerdahast raised his brow at the uncharacteristic display of courage, then leveled his wand at the orc's forehead. The rabid creature did not even cringe as the golden thread of light lanced out to blast its skull apart. The wizard pushed the headless corpse from his lap and leaped to his feet. A swiner scrambled past, its crooked spear braced for the attack. Vangerdahast leveled his wand, then was surprised to hear himself shouting in glee as its magic reduced the warrior to flying pieces.

A loud rumble sounded behind him. He turned toward the sound and found himself looking into the heart of the battle, where a web of flashing thunderbolts and glimmering death rays was littering the ground with smoking swiner corpses. The orcs, of course, could cause little harm against the might of magic. Their stone spear points shattered against the impenetrable armor of the Purple Dragons, their soft swords bent against the enchanted wool of the war wizards' weathercloaks, and their claws snapped against the magic-shielded flanks of the snorting warhorses. The Royal Excursionary Company countered with good Cormyrean steel and well-chosen spells, and orcs fell by the dozen. One dragoneer lopped the heads off three foes in a row, only to be outdone an instant later when a fireball reduced half a dozen swiners to charred bits of bone.

Finding the battle well in hand, Vangerdahast turned to look for the ghazneth. After a lengthy search, he found it circling high overhead, a mere speck well beyond arrow range. The battle clamor faded as quickly as it started, and the phantom continued to circle. Reluctantly, Vangerdahast tore his eyes away from the dark speck and began to wade through the carnage.

"Down magic!" he commanded, trying to find one of the company clerics to fix his separated shoulder. "Odd troops, iron. Even troops, steel!"

The Royal Excursionary Company scrambled to obey, the war wizards canceling their protective spells, the dragoneers wiping their blades clean before exchanging them for weapons of the appropriate metal. Vangerdahast waited on the exchange with ill-concealed impatience. The wizard had been drilling them in his special maneuvers for the last two days—the length of time required for the smiths of Arabel to forge a full complement of iron arms for every man in the company—and he was still not satisfied with their performance. The ghazneths were vicious, quick creatures who would repay any fumbling with swift death, and the wizard had no idea how many of them there were—or how they would respond to the presence of the Royal Excursionary Company.

There had been no sign of phantoms yesterday, when he and his war wizards had scouted the canyon where Vangerdahast had last seen Tanalasta, but it seemed clear that at least one ghazneth had watched them select the sycamore tree as the Royal Excursionary Company's assembly point. Vangerdahast doubted the thing had intended for them to teleport in on top of the swiners—no sensible commander would have risked the confusion of an enemy suddenly appearing within his ranks—but it had made known its feelings about the force's presence. Finding the royal princesses was not going to be easy, even with two hundred and fifty of Cormyr's mightiest warriors to help him.

Vangerdahast neared the front of the company, where a small cluster of men in mottled camouflage armor had dismounted and spread out through the carnage. They were dragging wounded swiners around by the tusks, growling and snarling in passable Orcish and threatening all manner of gruesome torture unless someone told them where to find "two humans riding one meal." The terrified orcs pointed in every which direction, a sure sign they had no idea what had become of Rowen and Tanalasta.

"Scouts! You're wasting your time." Vangerdahast waved his good arm around the perimeter of the battlefield. "Find me a trail—and be quick about it!"

The Royal Scouts were quick to obey, pausing only long enough to put the captured orcs out of their misery before scattering in all directions. Owden Foley appeared, leading Vangerdahast's horse and scowling at the rangers' efficiency.

"This isn't good," he said, dismounting. "This needless killing will only bring harm to us."

"These are not the lands of Chauntea," growled the wizard. Having agreed to bring the priest along only at Azoun's insistence, he was none too happy at being lectured on his men's treatment of orcs. "These lands belong to Gruumsch and Maglibuyet, and they have a thirst for blood. Besides, killing them is the kindest thing. A wounded orc can look forward to one of two things: a slow death by starvation, or, if he's lucky, being made a slave to his own tribe. Swiners don't care for their wounded."

"Then you are lucky we are not orcs." Owden passed the reins in his hand to an assistant and took hold of the wizard's limp arm. "But it was not the orcs I was thinking of. Did you not feel that lunatic bloodlust?"

Vangerdahast looked at the priest. "You felt it too?"

"Of course—I still do." Owden lifted one foot and braced it against Vangerdahast's ribs, then began hauling on the wizard's arm. "It was caused by this ghazneth—just as the last one caused your insanity."

Vangerdahast screamed until his arm popped into its socket, then dropped to his knees and tried not to groan.

"Battle-lust can make men foolish," said Owden. "What do you suppose will happen when the ghazneths are ready for us?"

"I suppose you know the answer," Vangerdahast growled. He struggled to his feet and tried to raise his arm. He could not lift it more than a few inches, and the effort made him hiss with pain. "I imagine you have a solution?"

"Chauntea does." Owden laid a healing hand on the wizard's aching shoulder. "Here, the goddess will help you with that."

Vangerdahast jerked his arm away. "I don't need her help." The wizard fished a healing potion from inside his own cloak and downed it, then said, "And the Royal Excursionary Company does not need her protection."

Owden pointed at the empty vial in Vangerdahast's hand. "That elixir was blessed by a god. There is no difference between drinking it and accepting the All Mother's help."

"The difference is that the Royal Treasury paid good gold for this." Vangerdahast could already feel the potion's fiery magic driving the ache from his strained shoulder. He used his injured arm to hurl the empty vial into a rock. "And that is all Tempus expects of us in return."

Owden shook his head. "I am not your adversary, Vangerdahast."

"Then why did you persuade the king to send you along?"

"Because you may need my help." Owden's eyes betrayed the anger he was struggling to contain. "I'm not trying to take your place. I'm only thinking of Tanalasta."

"You are *not* thinking of Tanalasta." Vangerdahast snatched Cadimus's reins from Owden's assistant, then swung into his saddle. "If you were thinking of Tanalasta, you would be back in Huthduth by now."

The wizard jerked Cadimus around toward the warped sycamore tree, leaving the priest to glare at his back. Despite the harsh words, Vangerdahast knew the harvestmaster to be a good and capable man—and that was the heart of the problem. Having cured both the king and the royal magician of insanity, Owden had risen high in the opinions of many influential people—including the Royal Sage Alaphondar Emmarask, many of the nobles who had at first opposed creating a Royal Temple, and most importantly Azoun himself. Not only had the king insisted on sending Owden along to help find his daughters, he had asked the rest of the harvestmaster's priests to help him and Merula rescue the queen.

Given Azoun's inherent decency, the king would certainly feel obliged to express his gratitude to the monks, perhaps by establishing Tanalasta's Royal Temple—and that Vangerdahast simply could not allow. As trustworthy and capable as Owden might be, there could be no guarantee that his successor would prove as valuable to the realm, or that Chauntea would not use him to impose her own will on the kingdom. It had been more than thirteen hundred years since the ancient elves had charged Baerauble Etharr with serving the first Cormyrean king as advisor and Royal Wizard. Since then, it had been the sole duty of every Royal Magician to protect both the king and his realm by steering them down the safest path. Vangerdahast was not about to let that tradition end under his watch—not when it had proven the wisest and most effective guarantee of the realm's safety for thirteen-and-a-half centuries.

When Vangerdahast reached the gnarled sycamore tree, he found old Alaphondar exactly where he had expected: stumbling absentmindedly around the trunk, squinting at the glyphs and painstakingly copying them into his journal. So absorbed was the Royal Sage Most Learned that he did not notice the wizard's presence until Cadimus nuzzled his neck—then he hurled his pencil and journal into the air, letting out such a shriek that half the company started up the hill to see what was wrong.

Vangerdahast signaled the riders to stop, then asked, "Well, old friend? Was it worth the trip?"

Alaphondar pushed his spectacles up his nose, then lifted his chin to regard the royal magician. "It's curious, Vangerdahast—really quite strange."

If the sage was irritated at being startled, his voice did not betray it. He simply retrieved his journal and pencil off the ground, then turned back to the tree and continued to work.

"These glyphs are First Kingate," he said. "In fact, they are quite possibly Post Thaugloraneous."

Vangerdahast had no idea what the sage was talking about. "First Kingate?" he echoed. "As in, from Faerlthann's time?"

"That would be Faerlthannish, would it not?" Alaphondar peered over his spectacles, regarding Vangerdahast as though the royal magician were the under-educated scion of a minor family. "I mean First Kingate, as in Iliphar of the Elves."

"The Lord of Scepters?" Vangerdahast gasped. "The first king of the elves?"

Alaphondar nodded wearily. "*That* would be First Kingate," he said. "Approximately fourteen and a half centuries ago—a hundred years before Faerlthann was crowned. More than fifty years before the Obarskyrs settled in the wilderness, in fact."

Vangerdahast glanced at the barren moors around them, trying to envision some unimaginably ancient time when they were covered with lush forest and home to a lost kingdom of elves.

"But the glyphs aren't the interesting part," said Alaphondar.

"They aren't?"

The sage shook his head, then said, "This tree isn't that old. In fact, it's three hundred years too young."

Vangerdahast knew better than to doubt the sage. "And you know this because . . ."

"Because of this."

Alaphondar turned and ran his hand over the glyphs. Instantly, the raspy voice of an anguished elven maid filled the air, and the sound of nervous horses and astonished men rose behind Vangerdahast.

Alaphondar translated the song:

This childe of men, lette his bodie nourishe this tree.
The tree of this bodie, lette it growe as it nourishe.
The spirit of this tree, to them lette it return as it grewe.

Thus the havoc bearers sleepe, the sleepe of no reste.
Thus the sorrow bringers sow, the seeds of their ruine.
Thus the deathe makers kille, the sons of their sons.

Here come ye, Mad Kang Boldovar, and lie among these rootes.

When the song was finished, Vangerdahast gasped, "Boldovar?"

Alaphondar nodded excitedly. "You see?" The sage ran his finger along a set of curls that looked identical to every other set of curls. "He died three hundred years after these serpentine beaks passed out of vogue."

"I'll have to trust your judgment, old friend," said Vangerdahast. He knew how to make the glyphs sing, but he could

not read them—much less identify the era in which they had
been inscribed. "What does it mean?"

"Mean?" Alaphondar looked confused. "Why, I couldn't
begin to tell you."

"But we can conclude that the elf who inscribed these
glyphs was over three hundred years old," Vangerdahast
prodded. Out of the corner of his eye, he noticed the Royal
Scouts returning from their search for Tanalasta's trail.
Their lionar was riding up the hill to report.

"Oh yes," Alaphondar prodded, "and more importantly,
that she had been living away from her people for at least
that long. Do you have any idea what that kind of loneli-
ness would do to an elf?"

Vangerdahast eyed the glyphs, recalling their bitter
words and the anguished tone of the song. "Yes. I'm afraid
I do."

Alaphondar started down the hill toward the hole that
led beneath the roots. "Perhaps I'll learn more in the
burial chamber."

"I'm afraid there won't be time for that." Vangerdahast
turned to face the scouts' lionar, who was reining his
horse to a stop in front of the wizard. "We'll be leaving
directly."

Alaphondar stopped in his tracks. "Leave?" he gasped,
spinning around. "We can't leave yet. It will take at least
a day to sketch the site properly, and another day just to
start the preliminary excavations."

"We don't have a day." Vangerdahast looked into the sky
and found no sign of the ghazneth. "We may not have even
an hour."

"But—"

"This is a military expedition, Alaphondar," Vangerda-
hast interrupted, motioning the scouts' lionar forward.
"Our goal is to find the princesses and return them to
Arabel—quickly."

The exhilaration vanished from Alaphondar's eyes. "Of course—how could I forget?" He started toward his horse, then had another thought and turned back to Vangerdahast. "Maybe you could go ahead . . ."

"You've seen two ghazneths now," Vangerdahast said. "Do you really want to face one of them alone—or even with a dozen dragoneers at your back?"

Alaphondar grimaced, then turned toward his horse. "Forget I asked."

Vangerdahast faced the lionar. "Did you find their trail?"

The scout nodded, then pointed into the valley between the Mule Ear peaks. "We found a few old hoof prints. They're heading south into the mountains."

"That's welcome news indeed," Vangerdahast said, sighing in relief. "Maybe Tanalasta has finally come to her senses and decided the time has come to return to Cormyr."

15

he air reeked of rank meat and mildewed earth, and in the cramped staleness of the tomb, Tanalasta felt feverish and dizzy. She had a queasy stomach, fogged vision, and goosebumps rising along her spine, and on the floor ahead lay something she did not really want to see. It was armored in tarnished plate and sprawled on its back, a sullied sword and battered shield lying on the stones to either side of it. An opulent growth of white mold had sprouted from the troughs of several clawlike rents across the breastplate, and the crown of the thing's great helm had been staved in. The face and limbs were lost beneath a thick blanket of the same white mold sprouting from the splits in the armor, and only the crumpled, striking-hawk crest over its heart identified the corpse as that of Emperel Ruousk, Guardian of the Sleeping Sword.

Holding the smoky torch before her, Tanalasta slipped out of the entrance passage into the tomb itself. Like the last one she had visited, this grave was surrounded by a fine-meshed net of black roots, many of which had been cut away during the battle that killed Emperel. Tangled among the roots, she could see the same web of gossamer filaments she had noticed in the first tomb. The floor was littered with tatters of rotted leather, buttons, buckles, and the mineralized soles of a large pair of boots.

Tanalasta pocketed a handful of the detritus to examine later, then removed the rope from her waist and stepped over to Emperel's body. Her queasy stomach revolted at the horrid fetor of the decaying corpse, and she barely managed to spin away before her belly emptied itself. When the retching ended, her temples were throbbing and her knees were trembling. The princess chided herself for being so qualmish; decay was as much a part of the life circle as growth, and it was an affront to the All Mother to treat it with aversion.

Tanalasta took a deep breath and returned to the body. Despite her determination, she felt weak and light-headed and feared she would pass out if she touched the moldy thing. She briefly considered retreating and leaving Emperel lie, but it would have been an insult to the memory of a brave knight to bury him in a place of such evil. The princess jammed the butt of her torch into a crevice between two floor stones and picked up the warrior's sword. She slid the flat of the blade under his back and, with a weary grunt, rolled him up on his side, then held him there with one arm while she fed the rope under his back.

By the time the princess finished, her joints were aching and she was out of breath. She trudged around the body and slipped the sword under the opposite side and felt something block it. She noticed the dark line of a satchel strap hidden beneath the white mold. Tanalasta used the sword tip to scrape the mold away, then took hold of the slimy strap and pulled the satchel from under Emperel's body.

It was a small courier's pouch, with a waterproof wax finish and a weather flap. Though the satchel was not closed tight, the flap was at least folded over the opening, and Tanalasta could think of only one reason Emperel would have been carrying an open pouch when he died.

"May the Great Mother bless you, Emperel Ruousk."

The princess laid the slime-smeared satchel aside, then used the sword to roll Emperel's body onto its side and pull the rope the rest of the way under his back. She tugged the line up under his arms, then tied a secure bowline knot and gave the rope three quick tugs. The line went taut, swinging Emperel around and dragging him toward the exit. When he came to the dirt wall below the passage, his head caught on the wall and tipped back, causing a muffled crack someplace in his neck.

Without thinking, Tanalasta reached behind his head and tipped it forward, sticking her hand into a fibrous mass of putrefying scalp and mold-coated hair. She fought back the urge to retch long enough to guide the body into the passage, then immediately grabbed a fistful of dirt and scoured the slime from her hand. Affront to the goddess or not, the princess simply felt too weak to abide having the stuff on her flesh.

Once her hand was relatively clean, Tanalasta returned to the pouch and opened the weather flap. Inside, she found a piece of charcoal, a pencil, a small leather-bound journal, some magic rings similar to her own—save for a striking-hawk signet, all standard issue for an officer of the Purple Dragons—and several small rolls of folded silk in relatively good condition. In the light of the flickering torch, Tanalasta unfurled the first of the silk rolls. It was about a foot wide, with two rough-cut edges that suggested it had been taken from a much larger bolt of cloth. The princess rolled it back up, then unfurled another.

This one had been rubbed with charcoal along the center, recording the smooth, erratically-fissured pattern of the bark of a white alder tree—and, in negative image, the familiar serpentine characters of ancient elven glyphs. The rubbing was rather fuzzy and difficult to read, but Tanalasta could make out the characters well enough to realize they were almost identical to the ones she had read in the moorlands several days ago. There was the peculiar epitaph enjoining a dead person's body to nourish the tree, and the tree to yield that spirit back, *"to them lette it return as it grewe."* Then there was the curse, condemning the *"havoc bearers"* to *"kille the sons of their sons."* Only the last line, the summoning, was different:

Here come ye, Faithless Suzara, and lie among these rootes.

In her shock, Tanalasta cried out and let the silk slip from her fingers. Like King Boldovar, Suzara was an ancestor of hers—in fact, one of her very oldest ancestors. She had been married to Ondeth Obarskyr when he came to the wilderness and built his cabin in what would one day become the kingdom of Cormyr. In fact, the city of Suzail was named for her. It was always possible that the summons referred to some other Suzara, but Tanalasta found that unlikely. Suzara had never been a very popular name in Cormyr, carrying as it did a certain connotation of frailty and selfishness. After it had finally dawned on Suzara that she would never persuade her stubborn husband to return to the comforts of Impiltur, she had taken their youngest child and left without him.

Without bothering to reroll the silk, Tanalasta pulled another spool from the satchel and unfurled it. This one was the duplicate of the invocation she had read just a few minutes before entering the tomb, on the buckeye tree above her head. It summoned a famous traitor, Melineth Turcasson, who had betrayed his King Duar—his trusting son-in-law—by selling the city of Suzail to a pirate band for five hundred sacks of gold.

The princess opened the rest of the silks in a flurry, but found only the name of Lady Merendil, a naive fool who had thought to use an apprentice royal magician to lure the first Prince Azoun to an early grave. This name actually gave Tanalasta cause for relief; all the other traitors had been her ancestors.

Tanalasta pulled Emperel's journal from the satchel. It was written right to left in High Halfling to foil uninvited readers, but the princess needed only a minute to recognize the trick and another minute to recall the basics of the ancient language. The first part of the journal was filled with unimportant entries detailing a two-day trip up the Moonsea Ride in preparation for investigating a series of reports claiming that the orcs were massing in the Stonelands. Matters grew more interesting once he entered the walled town of Halfhap, where a tenth of the local garrison had vanished while out searching for a murderer.

Apparently, a stranger had appeared in Halfhap one night raving drunk, boasting to anyone who would listen about how he was going to avenge his family's unjust treatment at the king's hands. When a tavern keeper had dared suggest that he take his business elsewhere, the stranger had used his bare hands to tear the man's head from his shoulders, then went outside and vanished.

The local commander had sent a company of dragoneers after the murderer, but they had failed to return, and it was shortly afterward that Emperel had stopped at the garrison and learned of the strange events. After a few inquiries, Emperel had set out after the killer, tracking him to a giant, twisted fir tree where Halfhap's missing company lay slain to a man. He had tracked the killer into a strange tomb beneath the tree and fought him there. During the battle, he had recognized the man as Gaspar Cormaeril, one of Aunadar Bleth's collaborators who died during the Abraxus Affair, somehow returned to life. There was a note in the margin noting that later, after making a few inquiries when he returned to Halfhap for a new horse, he had decided the fellow was most likely Gaspar's lookalike cousin, Xanthon.

Tanalasta stopped reading for a moment. Xanthon was familiar to her as one of Rowen's more "adventurous" cousins, who—along with Thaerilon, Boront, Cheldrin, Flaram, and Horontar—journeyed the Heartlands in search of wealth and excitement. From what she recalled, they were generally less successful in their pursuit of the former than the latter, often finding it necessary to ask King Azoun to convince some foreign mayor or monarch that executing them was not worth the trouble it might cause between the two countries. Azoun had always been happy to oblige, at least until Gaspar had taken part in the Abraxus Affair, since the Cormaerils never failed to repay the crown's expenses in quadruple. Now that the family was no longer in the royal graces, Tanalasta had heard that Boront and Cheldrin had met unhappy fates, while Horontar made his livelihood cleaning the cesspits of Darkhold.

She returned to the journal. To Emperel's dismay, capturing his quarry had proven more difficult than expected. Xanthon had proven unbelievably quick and strong, and he seemed to drain the magic from any enchanted weapon that was used against him. By the time the battle ended,

Emperel had lost most of his magic items, including his dagger, weathercloak, and the signet ring he used to contact Vangerdahast—Tanalasta could not help wondering how many others secretly carried the wizard's special rings.

In the end, Emperel had wounded his quarry severely enough that Xanthon killed his pursuer's horse and fled. Emperel returned to Halfhap for a new horse and a bolt of silk, then returned to take a rubbing from the fir tree and resume his hunt. Tanalasta examined the silk rolls again, ascertaining from the bark pattern that the fir had been Suzara's tree.

It had taken Emperel a few days to find Xanthon's trail again, but eventually he had crossed paths with an orc tribe that had seen a shadowy figure racing toward a "devil tree" near the Battle of Broken Bones. Emperel had quickly found the place and discovered a gnarled elm with the same glyphs as the giant fir.

Tanalasta studied the rubbings and quickly determined that this had been Lady Merendil's tomb. She skimmed the rest of the entries and quickly connected Emperel's next stops to the two tombs she had visited, Boldovar's sycamore tree in the moorlands and Melineth's buckeye in the goblin keep.

The journal's last entry was a cryptic, almost illegible reference to finally capturing Xanthon, followed by the inexplicable exclamation: *Helm save us! Their pride is our doom!*

When the princess closed the book, she discovered that her concentration had given her a pounding headache. Her hands were trembling, and she could feel trails of sweat running down her body. She returned the journal to Emperel's satchel and began to reroll the rubbings. It did not occur to her to wonder how long she had been sitting in the tomb until Alusair's voice sounded from the entrance passage.

"Shave my bones!" It was a favorite curse among knuckle-bone gamblers whose luck had run out. "What are you *doing*? I thought the fever had taken you!"

"I feel fine." Tanalasta looked up and noticed, for the first time, the guttering flame atop her torch. It did not occur to her that her aching and nausea were due to anything but the strain of reading by such dim light, or the awful stench of the place. "I've been reading Emperel's account of his death."

"He recorded it for posterity?" Alusair dropped unsteadily into the tomb, looking little better than Tanalasta felt. "That doesn't sound like Emperel."

"I never met the man, so I wouldn't know." Tanalasta motioned at Emperel's message pouch, then said, "But I assure you, he was very thorough. This account will save us a tenday's of investigation."

"Investigation?" Alusair scoffed. "There isn't going to be an investigation. With all these ghazneths flying around, I'm not taking any chances with your life. We're going home."

Tanalasta shoved a silk roll into the pouch. "It's not me we should be concerned with."

"Not on your life!" Alusair shook her head vehemently. Tanalasta had already given her sister their father's message, only to be laughed at and roundly rebuked. "I told you not to drag me into this. It's between you and the king."

"It is between the king and whoever he says it is."

"What's he going to do? *Order* me to be queen?" Alusair staggered over and kneeled down beside Tanalasta. "The next thing you know, he'll be telling me to marry some buffoon with a long title and a short . . . sword."

The long crawl through the entrance passage had left Alusair coated with mold and slime from Emperel's body, but she did not seem to notice. She grabbed the torch and looked into her sister's eyes, then placed a palm to Tanalasta's brow.

"You're on fire!" She grabbed Tanalasta and pulled her roughly to her feet, leaving more than a dozen silks unfurled on the floor. "I should never have let you come in here."

"Someone had to do it, Princess." Rowen slid out of the entrance, crowding the little tomb to the point of bursting. "And Tanalasta is the most knowledgeable about what all this means."

"She is also the crown princess." Alusair pushed Tanalasta past Rowen toward the exit. "Help me get her out of here so Gaborl can see to her."

"Wait!" Tanalasta stretched her hand toward the silks. "I need those rubbings."

"Not as much as we need to get out of here. Come along."

Alusair pushed her sister's head down and tried to shove her into the exit, but Tanalasta countered by grabbing hold of the sides of the wall. "You don't understand. They're our ancestors."

"She must be delirious," Rowen said. He picked up one of the blank silks and inspected it. "There's nothing on them."

Tanalasta still refused to enter the passage. "I'm not delirious. Some of the silks have rubbings of the tree glyphs; they name the ghazneths—Suzara Obarskyr, King Boldovar, Mirabelle Merendil, Melineth Turcasson."

"Mirabelle Merendil is no ancestor of ours." Alusair grabbed Tanalasta's arm and wrenched it around behind her back. "I don't have time for this. The ghazneths will be back soon."

She pulled the other arm free, then shoved Tanalasta headlong into the passage.

Tanalasta craned her neck around and shouted, "And Xanthon Cormaeril is the one setting them free!"

Rowen grabbed Alusair by the shoulder. "Wait a minute."

"We don't have time for this." Alusair stopped nonetheless, then pulled Tanalasta out of the hole and eyed her warily. "You're sure?"

Tanalasta nodded, then dropped to her knees and rifled through the silks until she found one with a rubbing. She showed it Rowen. "You recognize the glyphs?"

He nodded. "But what does Xanthon have to do with them?"

"Unless I miss my guess, he is the one digging the ghazneths out of their tombs," Tanalasta explained.

She went on to recount the story of Xanthon's appearance in Halfhap and Emperel's subsequent efforts to track him down, then completed the story by reading the journal's final cryptic entry.

"Their pride is our doom?" Alusair repeated. "What's that mean?"

"And who etched the glyphs in the first place?" Rowen added. "Certainly not Xanthon."

Tanalasta could only shake her head. "We won't know that until we catch Xanthon—or find the rest of the trees."

"Or until we let Vangerdahast sort it out," Alusair said. "Which is exactly what we'll do. We'll head over Marshview Pass to Goblin Mountain Outpost. Then, the instant we have a few dragoneers to hold off the ghazneths, we'll do a sending and tell him to come get us."

Tanalasta and Rowen glanced at each other nervously—a gesture that was not lost on Alusair.

"What?"

It was Rowen who answered. "During your uh, *discussion* about who's really the crown princess, there was one thing we had no chance to mention."

Alusair frowned. "Are you going to tell me now?"

"We probably shouldn't count on Vangerdahast," said Tanalasta. "It might not be safe to contact him."

Alusair narrowed her eyes. "You said he had returned to Arabel."

"He did." Tanalasta summoned enough of her fading energies to raise her chin. "But we didn't want to go with him."

"And we pulled away at the last second," said Rowen. "It was more by accident than—"

"You what?" Alusair whirled on Rowen like a lionar on an insolent underling. "You took it upon yourself to endanger the life of the crown princess *in defiance* of the royal magician?"

"It was my decision." Tanalasta interposed herself between Alusair and the ranger. "I was the one—"

Alusair shoved Tanalasta aside, then continued to berate Rowen. "Are you just stupid, or are you conniving with Xanthon?"

Rowen's face grew stormy, but he merely clenched his jaw.

"You have no right to talk to Rowen that way!" Tanalasta shoved Alusair away, then stepped forward to stand toe to toe with her sister. "Vangerdahast was the one who was out of line. He has no right to teleport me anywhere against my wishes."

Alusair studied her sister for a moment, then raised a brow and looked to Rowen. "Don't tell me you two—"

"Oh no!" Rowen said. "Nothing like that."

"Not that it's fitting for you to ask," Tanalasta said. "Anymore than it is for Vangerdahast to pop me about the realm like some sort of pet blink dog."

Alusair studied Rowen a moment longer, then looked back to Tanalasta. "So when *did* you desert poor Vangerdahast?"

"Seven days ago," said Tanalasta. "In the canyons below Boldovar's tomb."

"The sycamore," Rowen clarified.

Alusair frowned. "You've been on foot. He should have teleported back and caught up to you by now."

"Unless . . ." Tanalasta could not bring herself to say it.

"Unless what?" demanded Alusair.

"Unless he followed our horse," said Rowen. "There were two ghazneths hunting for us. We had to set up a decoy, and Vangerdahast may have followed it instead."

Alusair closed her eyes. "Which way?"

"South through the Mule Ears," said Rowen. "I believe that would bring him out somewhere just west of Redspring."

Alusair could only shake her head in disbelief. "What were you two trying to do—elope?" She glanced in Tanalasta's direction, then added, "That's not a suggestion."

"I wouldn't need one," said Tanalasta.

"That's what I'm afraid of," said Alusair. She thought for a moment, then turned to Rowen. "The Mule Ears must be two days out of our way."

Rowen nodded grimly. "I understand."

"What?" Tanalasta demanded, sensing something had just happened she did not comprehend. "What do you understand?"

The ranger took her by the arms. "It's all right. I'll split off tomorrow morning, then meet you at Goblin Mountain in a tenday or so." He cast a weak smile in Alusair's direction, then added, "The way your sister dawdles about, I'm sure I'll be waiting there when you arrive—if Vangerdahast doesn't leave me strung up by my thumbs someplace."

Tanalasta shook her head. "No. I won't let you go."

"That's not your choice," said Alusair.

"It is. You said yourself I'm still the crown princess."

"But this is *my* company." Alusair responded with surprising gentleness. "And I give the orders here."

16

rom the depths of a third floor arrow loop gleamed a pair of darting crimson eyes, framed by a face of inky darkness and a halo of wildly tangled hair. The broad band of a tarnished crown sat low on the figure's brow and seemed in danger of slipping down over the eyes, and that was all Azoun could see of the creature from his hiding place across the road. He waited until the thing's red eyes shifted away, then pulled away from the curtain and closed the gap through which he had been peering.

"That is the ghazneth, most certainly." He shook his head in wonderment, then turned to Merelda Marliir. "My thanks for your sharp eye, Lady Marliir—and for allowing us the use of your home to spy upon it."

Merelda, adorned at midday in jewels and a chiffon ball gown, curtsied deeply. "You are most welcome, Sire.

After hearing Dauneth's description of the fiend, I could scarcely believe my own eyes when I saw it landing atop the White Tower."

"And you are certain the queen was with it, Mother?" asked Dauneth. Like Azoun and the rest of the company crowded into Lady Marliir's spacious dressing chamber, the High Warden was dressed for battle.

Merelda scowled at her son. "I know the queen when I see her—even if she was not quite as radiant as usual." She gave Azoun a concerned look, then said, "Of all the places in Arabel, I can't imagine why it would be stupid enough to take her there. I have heard that is the armory of the war wizards."

"It would certainly seem foolish for the ghazneth to show itself *anywhere* within the citadel," said Azoun, dodging Merelda's half-asked question. Given her kindness in volunteering her own dressing chamber as a staging area for an entire company of Purple Dragons, he had no wish to insult the woman by lying to her—but neither did he wish to confirm the armory's confidential location to one of the biggest gossips in the realm. "But it would be a mistake to think of our foe as stupid. He has, after all, been eluding us for nearly a tenday now."

Azoun caught Dauneth's eye, then glanced from Lady Marliir to the door.

Taking the king's hint, the High Warden turned to his mother. "I hate to ask this of you, Mother, but I'm sure you will understand."

Lady Marliir's expression grew wary. "What is it?"

"It's a small matter, really. We've been discussing strategy all day and our throats are dry. I wonder if you would fetch us something to drink?" Without waiting for an answer, the High Warden took his mother by the arm and started toward the door. "I'd send for the servants, of course, but we'll be making plans and can't have anyone of less than the utmost trustworthiness near the room."

"I should have thought of that myself." Lady Marliir beamed at her son's flattery. "I'll have the entire wing emptied."

"Yes, we thank you for your prudence," called Azoun. He could barely force himself to wait until the woman had left the room before turning to Merula the Marvelous. "How many can you carry into the armory?"

"At once?" Merula glanced around the room, studying the heavy armor in which his companions were adorned, then closed his eyes to do some quick addition. "No more than four and myself, but I could summon—"

"No!" said Azoun. "That would take magic or time, and either could cost us the queen."

The king turned to the men at his back. Though he had not asked for volunteers, he saw in every man's eye the fervent hope of being picked to enter the tower with Merula. Azoun clasped Dauneth's shoulder, then waved forward two Purple Dragons he knew to be excellent swordsmen—and even better marks with a crossbow.

Azoun turned to Merula. "How do these men strike you?"

"As well as any others," said the wizard. "But what of the fourth?"

"You are looking at him, of course."

Merula's eyes grew as round as coins. "But Sire, there is every risk—"

"She is my queen," said Azoun. "More than that, she is my wife."

"Yes, but you pointed out yourself that the ghazneth is very cunning," he said. "This may be a trap."

"Merula, I am not asking your opinion."

The wizard was unfazed by Azoun's stern tone. "And even if it is not, there is the afterdaze. For a moment, we will be almost helpless."

"Merula!" Azoun barked.

The wizard fell silent, but looked less than contrite. Mungan Kane, one of Owden Foley's Chauntean monks, stepped forward to speak. "Sire, if I may, there is much to what Merula says."

Merula narrowed his eyes in suspicion, and Azoun glared.

"Is everyone in this chamber determined to defy me?"

"I wouldn't dream of it." Mungan raised his palms to calm the king. "You have worked the Mystery with Queen Filfaeril, and it is only fitting you go after her, but the afterdaze will be a problem. If the ghazneth doesn't slay you or someone else outright, he may flee."

Azoun considered this, then nodded. "Right you are, Mungan. My thanks." He pulled the weathercloak off Merula's shoulders, then turned to his men. "I need a volunteer to stand atop the White Tower. It may be that you'll face the ghazneth alone."

Every hand in the chamber shot up. Azoun nodded his thanks, then passed the cloak to a grizzled lionar he knew to be as shrewd as he was quick with a sword. "You know how to use this?"

The man nodded. "Aye, I've served with a war wizard or two in my time." He flung the cloak across his shoulders, then bowed deeply. "The ghazneth won't pass with the queen. If it tries, I will be honored to die stopping it."

Azoun nodded grimly and clasped the lionar's shoulder, then turned to Merula.

Mungan Kane stepped to intercept him. "There is one other matter, Sire. I should be one of those to accompany you."

"To see that the Royal Temple is represented in the battle?" mocked Merula.

257

Troy Denning

"To see that the creature's wickedness doesn't deprive you of your wits—as it did Vangerdahast," countered Mungan.

Merula's eyes flashed. "I would not waste my magic—"

"It is *my* magic," interrupted Azoun. "Unless the war wizards no longer serve at the pleasure of the king."

"That could never be, Majesty." Merula bowed to Azoun, but continued to glare at the priest. "I thank the king for pointing out the error of my assertion."

"You are quite welcome," said Azoun. "We must remember the service Harvestmaster Owden and his assistants provided in restoring the royal magician and myself to our wits—a service which they may need to provide again for the queen."

Merula's face only grew stormier. "Of course. If the king wishes to exchange one of his dragoneers for a mere priest—"

"The king does not." Azoun turned to Mungan. "The battle will be won or lost in the first moments, and I will have greater need of swords than sanity. I fear we must try to hold our own wits long enough for you to take the long way around with the rest of the company."

Mungan's face fell, but he nodded his understanding. "If I cannot be with you, then perhaps you will allow the All Mother to go in my place." He reached into his robe and withdrew five wooden amulets carved in the shape of a unicorn, handing one to Azoun and each of the men going with him. "These will offer some protection until I can join you."

Merula regarded the amulet with a sneer, then thrust it back at the priest. "I have no use for this."

Mungan refused to accept it. "It is for the king's protection."

"It is to insinuate Chauntea into the royal graces." Merula dropped the amulet on the floor, then turned to Azoun. "I trust my loyalty does not yet dictate my faith?"

The wizard's emphasis on the word *yet* was not lost on the king. He looked at the men accompanying him. They were eyeing him expectantly, holding their amulets in their palms and waiting to follow his lead. Azoun sighed wearily. In his gratitude to Owden, perhaps he was beginning to favor the Church of Chauntea more than was appropriate.

"You men do as your own consciences dictate." He returned the amulet to Mungan. "I think I can hold onto my sanity until you arrive in person."

"That may be so—but do you really want to risk the queen's life on that chance?" Mungan tucked the amulet cord through Azoun's sword belt, then stepped back. "It will be there if you need it."

The Purple Dragons nodded at the priest's wisdom and tucked their own amulets into their sword belts, but Dauneth Marliir did not. The High Warden tied his around his neck.

* * * * *

Filfaeril lay pressed to the naked ghazneth's side, draped across his wing and garbed in some filthy piece of gossamer pulled from a festhall trash bin. The room was beginning to seem less an armory than a bedchamber, and she could not imagine what was taking Azoun so long. Already, the pile of weathercloaks on which they lay felt like a silk-covered featherbed, and lascivious carvings were beginning to appear in the oaken cabinets along the walls.

The queen suppressed a shudder. She had learned through hard experience that Boldovar's illusions always reflected his inner desires. Nevertheless, she took a deep breath, then cooed softly into his pointed ear and ran her fingers through the lice-infested bristles on his chest. It had taken days of subtle manipulation to lure her captor into the one place she knew the war wizards could take him by surprise, and she would do anything to keep the ghazneth distracted until Azoun arrived.

Boldovar opened his lips and gargled out a mouthful of rings, all gray and dull now that he had absorbed their magic. Filfaeril forced a light giggle—it was not difficult to sound slightly demented—then took a commander's ring from the huge pile of magic beside her and held it over the ghazneth's mouth.

"Another?"

Boldovar's crimson eyes shifted toward the arrow loop overlooking Marliir House, and Filfaeril knew he was still too skittish for her plan to succeed.

"You don't want it?" She slipped the ring down between her breasts, planting it just deep enough so that the tourmaline winked up from her cleavage like a pale blue eye. "Then I'll keep it for myself."

The ghazneth's gaze darted back to her chest and fixed on the magic ring. He stared at it for a long time, his face an expressionless mask, and Filfaeril wondered if she had been too obvious. Over the past few days, she had grown steadily more congenial through a conscious effort of will, but never before had she tried to beguile him.

Perhaps she had been too bold. Whatever else he was, Boldovar was also cunning and intelligent. He had proven that many times over the past tenday, moving her from one hiding place to another daily and ambushing the war wizards almost twice that often. At first, Filfaeril had not been able to figure out why her captor remained in Arabel. If all he wanted was a real queen to sit on his delusionary throne, he could have established a far more peaceful palace in any number of dark wilderness lairs. Then she began to notice a peculiar pattern. If the ghazneth went even half a day without being attacked, the tangibility of his illusions began to fade. After giving the matter some thought, the queen had realized that her captor was feeding off the magic used to attack him. She started telling him where to find items of increasingly powerful magic— both to ensure her own survival and to prepare him for the day when she could lure him into the White Tower.

Now that day had come, and where was her rescue party? A stream of lunatic thoughts, an unavoidable consequence of consorting with Boldovar, coursed through Filfaeril's mind. Perhaps her husband had finally given up on her, persuaded by her inability to escape that she preferred life with Boldovar. After all, the ghazneth was far more powerful than Azoun, and, having survived more than a thousand years himself, he could certainly offer her things beyond the grasp of even the wealthiest human king—but no, that could not be; Azoun loved her. Or did he? He was a king and she a queen. Theirs had been as much a political marriage as a romantic one, and Filfaeril was neither deaf nor blind. She had heard rumors of noble children who bore an uncanny resemblance to her husband, and she had seen for herself that some of them were well-founded.

Filfaeril shook her head, trying to drive Boldovar's delusions from her mind. Whatever else he had done, Azoun would never abandon her—not in a hundred lifetimes.

"Is something wrong, my dear?" The ghazneth smiled, baring his yellow fangs. "Are you a little nervous about our consummation night?"

Boldovar's red tongue shot down between Filfaeril's breasts and flicked the ring back into his gruesome mouth.

* * * * *

Azoun and his companions emerged from the timeless darkness to find themselves not in the White Tower's magic armory, but in a murky boudoir lined by debauched carvings of unspeakable violations against woman and nature. The king's first thought was that Merula the Marvelous had teleported them into the secret playroom of some deranged noble—one of the Illances or Bleths, most likely. Then he saw the ghazneth, lying on a silk-sheeted bed at the far end of the room, its face all but buried in the chest of a gossamer-clad figure cradled in the palm of its wing, and he grew even more confused. That could not be Filfaeril. The woman did not seem to be struggling, and the queen would never allow such a thing—not to any man but her husband!

Then someone yelled, "Move, Sire!"

Azoun felt a pair of hands shove his shoulder. He recalled their plan and hit the floor rolling, confident that everything would make sense again when he recovered from the afterdaze. He came up holding his royal shield in one hand and his new cold-forged sword in the other—Vangerdahast had warned him not to use an enchanted sword against the ghazneth—and turned back toward the silk-covered bed.

The phantom seemed to be struggling with its companion. She was sitting on its wing, clinging to its neck and shrieking at it to protect her from the assassins. Burdened as it was by the hysterical woman, the creature was hardly able to rise, much less launch itself at the king or his men. A series of golden bolts shot across the room toward the ghazneth's abdomen, but it brought its free wing around as fast as always and prevented them from striking.

The woman turned toward Merula and thrust out her hand, crying, "No . . . no magic!"

And that was when Azoun recognized her, all but naked beneath a shift of sheer gossamer filthy enough to shame any trollop in Arabel. He was so stunned that he nearly let the sword drop from his hand. That woman was, indeed, his wife.

Dauneth and the Purple Dragons started across the room at a charge, and the ghazneth finally peeled the queen off its neck and dropped her to the floor. Azoun rushed forward, confused and angry and hardly able to believe that Filfaeril had betrayed him for . . . what, some sort of demon?

Dauneth and the dragoneers slammed into the ghazneth at a full charge, their iron swords arcing in from all angles. The first blade bit deep into the creature's arm, beating down its guard and clearing the way for the High Warden to open a deep slit up the thing's bulging abdomen. The third attack came in high, sweeping in toward its neck with enough power to separate even an ogre's head from its shoulders.

Filfaeril was cowering at the ghazneth's side, staring up at the battle in horror. Azoun angled toward her, blood boiling and ears pounding with the fury of a jealous rage.

"Harlot!"

Filfaeril's eyes widened, and as she began to scramble away backward, the ghazneth's black talons swept past her head to catch the second dragoneer's arm. The sword slipped from the man's grasp and bounced off an oaken cabinet without coming anywhere near the phantom's neck, then the ghazneth tore the limb off at the elbow and slammed it into the first dragoneer's helmet. Both men dropped instantly, one howling in pain and the other as silent as death.

Azoun stepped past Dauneth, trying to slip around the melee to get at Filfaeril, and found a huge black wing coming down to block his way. He ducked beneath it, then heard the ghazneth roar as the High Warden's blade bit deep into its abdomen. As the king stepped behind the creature, he brought his sword around to slash at the creature's back. Though the blow would have cleaved a man's spine, it cut no deeper than a finger's width into the ghazneth's tough hide.

A soft patter sounded ahead. Azoun looked down to see Filfaeril cowering on the floor, tears welling in her eyes and her filthy harlot's shift drawn up around her waist.

"Azoun?" she gasped.

"Traitorous whore!"

The king wrenched his sword free of the ghazneth's back and started toward her—then saw a wall of darkness sweeping toward him. There was no time to duck or raise his sword before the wing caught him in the face and launched him across the room. He slammed into an open oaken cabinet and dropped to the ground, weathercloaks and battle bracers tumbling down all around him.

Dauneth disappeared around the other side of the ghazneth, trying to reach Filfaeril, only to go tumbling past her when the creature caught him in the helm with a lightning back fist. The High Warden came to a rest against a debased wall tapestry, groaning and shaking his head, but alive.

Now that there was no one in contact with the ghazneth, Merula cut loose with a deafening thunderbolt. The creature's wing swung around to shield itself. The spell struck with a blinding spray of light and dissipated across the leathery appendage in a brilliant fan of silvery forks, but the blast still carried enough force to knock the ghazneth off its feet.

Filfaeril sprang to her feet and rushed the wizard with her hands out, crying, "No—you can't use magic!"

"Watch her, Merula!" Azoun cried. "She's betrayed us."

This was enough to stop Filfaeril in her tracks. She turned to face Azoun—then suddenly vanished inside a cocoon of sticky white strands.

"That'll hold the trollop!" the wizard declared.

The ghazneth leaped up and flung itself across the room, placing itself between Filfaeril and the others. Merula instantly clapped his hands together and struck two long fans of magic fire, which he directed at their foe. The phantom raised a wing and turned sideways. When the flames touched the wing's surface, they simply sputtered and died, and the leathery appendage started to glow with a luminous crimson light. The ghazneth began to inch toward Merula, taking care to keep both itself and the queen well-shielded.

Azoun staggered to his feet and circled around to flank it, only to have Dauneth stagger over and grasp his arm.

"You look none too steady, Warden. Merula and I will keep this devil busy. You see to the harlot." Azoun gestured at his wife's sticky white form.

"Harlot? Majesty, have you lost your . . ." Dauneth's gaze dropped to Azoun's waist, then the warden reached down and jerked the unicorn amulet from his belt. "Put this on!"

Azoun shook his head. "This is no time—"

"Do as I say!" Without awaiting permission, Dauneth looped the amulet's leather string over the king's helm and jerked it down over his neck. "Now say 'Chauntea save us!' "

Azoun scowled. "Who do you think—"

"Say it!"

Dauneth's eyes widened at his own tone, then Merula called out from across the room.

"Majesty? Some help, perhaps?"

Azoun looked toward the wizard's voice and saw nothing but the interior of the ghazneth's wing. He turned to help, but Dauneth grabbed the collar of his breastplate.

"Please, Sire."

"Very well!" Azoun knocked Dauneth's hand away, then sprang after the ghazneth, crying, "Chauntea save us!"

And instantly, even as he raised his sword to strike, the room changed from a bedchamber to an armory, and the debauched carvings vanished from the faces of the oaken cabinets, and he saw the beauty of Filfaeril's plan, and how she had used the only weapon she had to buy her rescue party a few precious moments to reorient themselves after teleporting into the room—and how it must have hurt to have her own husband call her a harlot and traitor.

"Dauneth, the queen!" Azoun stopped just inside the reach of ghazneth's wingtip and ducked a wild attempt to bat him away, then darted forward to meet the slashing claws at the ends of its arms. "Save the queen!"

With the king beyond its first line of defenses, the ghazneth was forced to turn its attention away from Merula to attack. Azoun parried slashes from first its wounded arm, then its good arm and brought his iron blade down on its collarbone.

The ghazneth roared and hurled itself forward, determined to bowl him over and overwhelm his defenses. No longer being a fool, the king hurled himself at the creature's feet and rolled, his armor filling his ears with a clamorous din. He crashed into a wall cabinet and brought the contents down on top of himself. Convinced his foe would be on him before he could rise, he flung the debris away from his chest and raised his sword in a blind block.

The expected blow never came. Instead, a strange gurgle erupted from the creature's mouth, and the king scrambled to his knees to find the thing only a pace away. Merula was draped over its shoulder, struggling to draw his iron dagger across the ghazneth's leathery throat. Azoun brought his sword around and lunged forward and drove the blade a mere finger's length into the monster's bloated abdomen.

The ghazneth stumbled back, roaring and trying to shake Merula from its back. Azoun glimpsed Dauneth rushing toward the queen with a war wizard's weather-cloak wrapped around his shoulders. According to their plan, it should have been the High Warden or a dragoneer attempting to slit the creature's throat and Merula preparing to escape with the queen, but the king was happy enough to see Dauneth grab hold of Filfaeril's cocoon and reach into the cloak to find its escape pocket.

The metallic clamor of armor began to knell up from somewhere lower in the tower, drawing the ghazneth's attention toward the armory's stout oaken door. It was barred from the inside, but the creature knew as well as Azoun that the door would last only as long as it took a magic-user to utter his spell. Spewing a filthy curse, the phantom brought a hand up and slammed the heel of its palm into Merula's brow. There was a sharp snap, then the wizard's eyes rolled back, and he dropped out of sight.

The ghazneth turned toward Dauneth. Azoun gathered himself to intercept—then the High Warden finally found the right pocket and vanished with Filfaeril.

Azoun turned toward the barred door, but the ghazneth sprang across the chamber and beat him to it.

"Queen stealer!" it hissed. "Usurper!"

Azoun leveled his sword and circled around so that he would not be directly in front of the door when Mungan arrived. Though a steady flow of dark, rancid smelling blood was oozing out of the ghazneth in half a dozen places, the dark thing looked little the worse for the wear.

"Who are you?" Azoun asked. "*What* are you?"

"Boldovar, King of Cormyr."

The answer was as mad as the ghazneth itself, but there was no time to argue. The clamor reached the landing outside the door and stopped. Azoun threw himself to the floor.

"Now, Mungan!"

Mungan's voice rang out from the stairwell, and an instant later a terrific lightning bolt blasted the door into splinters. The ghazneth spun to face the rescue party and bellowed, and the room went dark.

The tumult of anguished voices began to fill the air. Azoun leaped to his feet and pressed his back to the wall, his sword weaving a blind defensive pattern before him. He was not fool enough to believe he could block one of the ghazneth's blows with a mere sword, but perhaps it would buy him enough time to dodge or roll away.

The cacophony continued to grow louder for the next few moments—it seemed like forever, though it could have been no more than seconds. The thud of falling bodies reverberated across the floor with alarming regularity, and twice Azoun danced away when his sword brushed against some unseen menace. He kept expecting to feel the ghazneth's talons ripping through his breastplate, but the blow never came. The battle din merely subsided, then men began to crawl across the floor and call each other's names, and finally someone stumbled across a commander's ring and spoke the proper word, filling the chamber with light.

The room lay littered with wounded and dead—most felled by their own comrades, judging by the sword gashes in their flesh and the narrow dents in their armor. Only Mungan and two men behind him, all lying in the doorway with their throats ripped open, appeared to have been slain by the ghazneth. There was no sign of the phantom itself, but Azoun felt a cool breeze in the room and knew that someone had opened the door to the roof.

17

analasta lay in Rowen's arms, aching and fever-ish, captivated by the sunlight filtering down through the twisted buckeye boughs above. Alusair was readying the surviving horses for departure, and one of the priests was overseeing Emperel's burial. Tanalasta was so foggy-headed her thoughts kept running in circles. She held Emperel's message satchel clutched to her breast and recalled dimly that she had to get it to Alaundo. It was a struggle to remember why—and she was too weak to struggle.

A steel gauntlet appeared above Tanalasta, floating in the air above her eyes. Taking it for an apparition—the hand of Iyachtu Xvim coming to pull her into his Bastion of Hate—she gasped and clutched at Rowen's arm.

"Stay with me." She pushed the message satchel into his hands. "Then take this to Alaundo. Tell him about the glyphs . . . and about Xanthon."

"You are not that ill, Princess." Rowen refused to accept the satchel.

The gauntlet drew closer, warming Tanalasta's face and obstructing her view. She was too frightened to look away.

"Don't argue." Tanalasta tipped her chin back. "Kiss me. I want to die—"

"You are hardly dying, Princess." Rowen sounded almost insulted. "And certainly not in my arms. Now hold still, and Seaburt will have you feeling better in a minute."

"Seaburt?"

Tanalasta saw the thick wrist protruding from the collar of the glove, and it slowly came to her that the gauntlet was not the hand of Iyachtu Xvim. It was the symbol of Torm the True, Alusair's favored god and the one revered by both priests in the company. Seaburt laid the glove upon Tanalasta's forehead and uttered a quick prayer to his god, beseeching Torm to aid "this dutiful daughter of Cormyr." Recalling her arguments with Vangerdahast and the king, Tanalasta worried that the Loyal Fury might not find her deserving of his magic and continued to press the satchel on Rowen. Her skin started to prickle with the familiar sensation of magic, then the glove grew cold and dry against her brow. Her head began to throb more fiercely than ever, and she let slip an involuntary groan.

"Have strength, Princess," said Seaburt. With a month-old beard and black circles under his sunken eyes, the priest looked no better than Tanalasta felt. "Torm is drawing the fever out, but there will be some pain as it passes from your body."

Some pain? Tanalasta would have screamed the question, had she the strength. It felt as though someone had cleaved her head with an axe. She closed her

270

eyes, listened to her pulse drumming in her ears, and begged Chauntea for the strength to endure Torm's cure. The throbbing only grew worse, and she thought her brain must be boiling inside her skull. She did her best to hold still, and finally the gauntlet grew warm and moist against her skin. The glove blossomed into white-hot light, turning the interior of her eyelids red and bright, and then a wave of cool relief spread down her entire body.

Tanalasta opened her eyes and found herself gazing up through the gauntlet's veil of pearly brilliance. Seaburt's jaws were clenched tight, his vacant stare fixed someplace far beyond the keep's dilapidated walls. Beads of sweat rolled down his face, dripping out of his beard to splash against the searing gauntlet and hiss into nothingness. Tanalasta grew stronger. The fog vanished from her mind, and she no longer felt quite so queasy. She struggled to sit up, but Seaburt pressed her down and held her there until the glow faded completely from his gauntlet.

When the priest finally lifted the glove and took his hand from inside, his skin was red and puffy. "You'll still be weak," he said. "Drink all you can, and you'll feel better."

"I feel better already. Thank you." Tanalasta sat up, then nearly blacked out when she tried to gather her legs beneath her. "Though I see what you mean about still being weak."

A whistle sounded from across the bailey, where her sister stood waving at them from the gate. With Alusair stood all that remained of her company—the second priest, a dozen haggard knights, and fifteen sickly horses. Though the horses still had halters and reins, the poor beasts had been stripped of their saddles to lighten their burden.

"Time to go." Rowen slipped an arm under Tanalasta's arm and pulled her to her feet. "I'm sorry, but it looks like you'll be walking. The horses are too weak to carry even you."

As they approached Alusair and the others, Tanalasta eyed the languishing beasts with a sympathy born of her own haggard condition. "Why are we making these poor beasts come along at all?" she asked Alusair. "They'd have a better chance if we just left them to rest—and if not, at least they'd die in peace."

"And how would that help *our* cause?" asked Alusair. "If they die on the trail, we've lost nothing. If they recover, they'll save us a good five or six days of walking."

Alusair turned to lead the way out of the gate, but Tanalasta was too alarmed to follow. Saving five or six days would mean reaching Goblin Mountain well ahead of Rowen, and she had no illusions about what would follow if that happened. Alusair would have a war wizard teleport Tanalasta back to Arabel at once, and her parents, regarding any courtship with a Cormaeril more of a political disaster than Dauneth's rejection, would see to it that Rowen never came within fifty miles of her.

Rowen offered a supporting hand. "What's wrong? If you are too weak to walk, I'll carry you."

"No." Tanalasta held him back until the others were a few paces ahead. "Rowen, you can't leave me tomorrow."

"But I must." He made no effort to keep their conversation quiet. "Vangerdahast has no idea—"

"Vangerdahast will figure it out soon enough," Tanalasta whispered. "Even if he doesn't, Old Snoop is certainly capable of taking care of himself."

Rowen cast a nervous glance at Seaburt's back. "Perhaps we should talk about this later. You're still weak."

"No!" Tanalasta took his hands. "Rowen, you must know I have feelings for you—and that I hope you have feelings for me."

"Of course." He gave her a sly smile. "I didn't think you were the kind of princess who kisses just any man who happens to be there when you decide to bait a ghazneth."

Tanalasta did not return his smile. "I'm not, and you are avoiding my question."

Rowen looked away. "You are above my station—but yes, I do see you more as a woman than a princess."

Tanalasta furrowed her brow. "Am I to take that as a yes?" When Rowen nodded, she continued, "Then we can't let Alusair separate us. You know what she's trying to do."

"I doubt we are all she's concerned about."

"Of course not," said Tanalasta. "She's also concerned that when the king hears of our affections, the weight of the crown may land on her head instead of mine."

Rowen's expression grew enigmatic. "And that fear is not well founded?"

Though Tanalasta sensed the pain in his question, she did not hesitate to answer honestly. He deserved that much. "Your family's disgrace would cause a difficulty for the throne, yes. The loyal houses would see any favor shown you as an affront to their allegiance, and the neutral houses might take it to mean the throne has a short memory."

"Then the king would have no choice in the matter," Rowen surmised. "He would be forced to name Alusair his heir."

Tanalasta shrugged. "It is not for us to predict the king. He can be a surprising man, and he knows that it's better to retreat than to lose. Our chess games have taught him that."

As Rowen considered this, Seaburt glanced back from the end of the line. "If the princess is too weak to walk . . ."

"The princess is strong enough to walk," Tanalasta said. "Pay us no mind. We'll ask if we need help."

"Of course." Seaburt cocked his brow and turned away. "I will be listening for your call."

Experiencing a sudden dislike for the priest, Tanalasta glared at his back. When he was out of earshot, she took Rowen's arm and started after the rest of the company.

"You know what will happen when we reach Goblin Mountain," she said, speaking softly. "Alusair will do a sending, and five minutes later a dozen war wizards will arrive to whisk me back to Arabel."

Rowen gave her a sidelong look. "And I should be sorry to see you safely back in the city?"

"Yes, if it means we'll never see each other again."

"Aren't you exaggerating? I *should* be capable of finding my way to Arabel—and Suzail too, for that matter."

"When? Between scouting patrols into the Anauroch and spying missions in the Dun Plain? My father and Vangerdahast will keep you so busy you won't see a Cormyrean city until I am wed and fat with some other man's child."

Though Rowen remained unmoved, at least he showed the courtesy of wincing. "And if I disobeyed Alusair, I'd spend the next ten years in Castle Crag's dungeon instead—with no hope at all of redeeming my family name."

The company began to fan out across the flat scrubland, each man leading a horse more or less westward, laying a network of false trails before they turned south. Tanalasta remained silent for a time, knowing Rowen was right. She had no authority to countermand Alusair's order, and Vangerdahast was certainly ruthless enough to have the scout locked away under the pretext of disobedience.

"You're right, of course. I can't ask you to defy Alusair." Tanalasta kept her eyes on the ground as she spoke, watching the brush for snakes and other hazards. "So I will come with you."

"What?" Rowen nearly shouted the question, drawing a curious—and rather condemning—glance from Seaburt. The ranger lowered his voice, then continued, "I'd like nothing better, but Alusair would never permit it."

"Alusair can command you to leave, but she cannot command me to stay," said Tanalasta. "She is not my master."

"Please, Tanalasta—I can't. Doing as you ask would make me the same as Gaspar and Xanthon."

"You could never be the same as those two."

"I would be, if I put my own desire above my oath as a Purple Dragon." Rowen guided Tanalasta away from a red catclaw bush, pulling her safely beyond the striking range of a half-hidden pixie-viper. "We all have our duties. I am a scout, and my duty is to move swiftly and find Vangerdahast. You are the learned one, and your duty is to return to Arabel and inform the king of what you have discovered."

"And I will," said Tanalasta. "In your company."

Rowen shook his head. "You will be safer with Alusair."

"Really?" Tanalasta cast a doubtful glance at her sister's sickly men. "I should think it would be easier for the ghazneths to find a large company of sick men than two people moving swiftly and stealthily."

"Perhaps." Rowen paused to think, then said, "That would be so if you were healthy, but with the fever, you are too weak."

"The fever will improve. Seaburt said . . ."

Tanalasta let the sentence trail off as the significance of Rowen's pause struck her. He had been there when Seaburt cured her, and he certainly should have heard what the priest had told her. She stumbled along two more steps, then stopped and whirled on the scout.

"You don't want me to go with you."

Rowen's expression fell, and Tanalasta saw she had guessed correctly. She pulled her arm free and stumbled back.

Rowen stepped after her. "Please, Tanalasta, it's not what you think. I have every confidence in your ability—"

Tanalasta stopped him with a raised hand, then lifted her chin and began to back away. "That is quite enough, Rowen. And you may address me as *Princess* Tanalasta, if that will make you feel more comfortable."

* * * * *

A muffled patter drummed down out of the pines, reverberating down through the valley, bouncing from one slope to the other until Vangerdahast could not tell whether the sound came from ahead or behind. He reined Cadimus to a stop and raised his arm, and the Royal Excursionary Company clattered to a halt behind him. The air filled instantly with the swish and clank of wizards and dragoneers readying for battle. Over the past day and a half, the company had lost dozens of men and horses to orc ambushes and lightning-swift ghazneth strikes, and now even the *dee-dee-dee* of a chickadee could send them diving for cover.

Vangerdahast twisted around. "Will you be quiet back there?"

He glared until the company fell silent, then looked forward again. The valley was one of those serpentine canyons with a meandering ribbon of marshy floor and steep walls timbered in pines. He could see no more than fifty paces ahead, and to the sides not even that far. As the patter grew louder, the trees scattered it in every direction, and soon the drumming seemed to be coming from all around. Sometimes it sounded like hooves pounding grassy ground and sometimes like wings beating air.

Cadimus nickered and raised his nose to test the air, then a ginger mare galloped around the bend, chest lathered and eyes bulging, reins hanging loose, stirrups flapping empty. She came straight down the valley at a full run, barely seeming to notice Cadimus and Vangerdahast, or the entire Royal Excursionary Company behind them. Close on the mare's tail came a streaking ghazneth, its wings a black crescent as it banked around the corner, its arms stretching for the flanks of the ginger mare.

Vangerdahast leveled a finger at the phantom and uttered a single word, sending a dozen bolts of golden magic to blast the dark thing from the sky. The impact hurled the ghazneth into the pines, snapping branches and ripping boughs. In the next instant, the valley erupted into a cacophony of thundering hooves and screaming voices as dragoneers and war wizards urged their mounts to the charge. If the Royal Excursionary Company had learned anything over the past two days, it was never to hesitate around a ghazneth. Vangerdahast wheeled Cadimus around just as quickly and started after the riderless mount.

Tanalasta's horse had been a ginger mare.

* * * * *

The horse did not snort, nor whinny, nor even groan. It merely dropped to its knees and closed its eyes, then toppled over onto a thicket of smoke brush. Tanalasta watched as Alusair, dazed with exhaustion and a relapse of fever, idly yanked the beast's reins and tried to continue walking. When the horse did not move, Alusair cursed its laziness and, without turning around, hauled harder on the reins.

Tanalasta said nothing, content to see someone else make a fool of herself for a change. The princess could not believe how she had misread Rowen's emotions. Their kiss

277

had certainly felt sincere enough, but she had read that men experienced such things more with their bodies than their hearts. Was that the root of her mistake? Perhaps she had mistaken simple lust for something more . . . permanent. The affection she sensed had been no more than a man's normal carnal attraction, kept in check by Rowen's honorable nature. The princess almost wished he had not been so virtuous. Had he used her, at least she would have been justified in her anger. As it was, all she could do was feel embarrassed and try to avoid him until he went off to find Vangerdahast.

Alusair finally stopped tugging on the reins and stumbled around to scowl at the motionless horse—the second that had died in only ten hours of walking. She muttered an inaudible curse, then looked to Tanalasta.

"You could have said something."

Tanalasta spread her hands helplessly. "I thought it might get up."

Alusair eyed her sourly, then called the rest of the company with a short whistle. As the troops gathered around, she pointed to the dead horse. "Let's take off our helmets."

The weary men groaned and reluctantly started removing the leather padding from inside their helmets. After the first horse died, they had spent nearly an hour burying it so the body would not attract vultures and betray their route, and no one was looking forward to repeating the experience—especially not with night fast approaching and another thirteen horses ready to follow the first two at any moment.

As Rowen knelt to help the others, Tanalasta at first tried to avoid his eye—then realized she could not be so coy. With Alusair's mind addled by fever and the rest of the company near collapse, a certain amount of responsibility for their safety fell to her.

Tanalasta caught Rowen by the arm. "Not you." She

pointed toward a hazy line of crooked shadow just below the western horizon. "That looks like a gulch to me. See if there's a stream in it—and a safe campsite."

"Wait a minute." Alusair was so weak she barely had the strength to signal Rowen to stay put. "Tanalasta, you don't give orders to my company."

"I do when you are in no condition to see to its welfare." Tanalasta met her sister's gaze, which was more drained than angry, and waved at the surviving horses. "If we don't water these creatures soon, we'll have to bury them all by morning—and then we can start on your men." She glanced meaningfully toward one warrior still struggling with his helmet's chin strap.

"Princess Tanalasta is right." Rowen's comment drew a glassy-eyed scowl from Alusair, but he was not intimidated. "Had your wits been clear, you would have had me looking for water two hours ago—and not only for the horses."

Alusair frowned, though her expression looked more pained than angry. "That may be, but I am still commander of this company."

"Then you would do well to remember that and let Seaburt take care of your fever," said Tanalasta.

Because Seaburt and his fellow priest could cast only enough curing spells each day to restore a third of the company to health, any one person could be healed only once every three days. Unfortunately—as Alusair had discovered while trapped in the goblin keep—the illness tended to recur on the second day, and Alusair had steadfastly refused to deprive anyone else by having a spell cast on her out of turn.

"I may not know the military," said Tanalasta, still addressing Alusair, "but I do know leadership. As the great strategist Aosinin Truesilver wrote, 'If a man must send troops into battle, then he owes it to them to be sober at the time.' "

Alusair scowled and started to argue, but Rowen cut her off. "Princess, you must let Seaburt see to your fever. *Everyone* will stand a better chance of returning alive if you do."

Alusair looked from the ranger to the others. When they nodded their consensus, she sighed. "Very well. Rowen, go and see about that water. Everyone else— why isn't that horse buried?"

The company began to scrape at the hard ground with their helmets. Seaburt took Alusair aside and began to prepare her for the spell—the last he would be able to cast until morning. Rowen started toward the western horizon, but stopped a dozen steps away and raised a hand to shield his eyes from the glare of the setting sun.

"Princess Tanalasta, I don't see that gulch you were talking about. Would you be kind enough to show it to me?"

Frowning, Tanalasta went to his side and pointed at the hazy line. "It's there. You can see the shadow."

"Of course. I see it now."

Tanalasta sensed Rowen watching her and turned to find him looking not toward the gulch, but into her eyes.

"Forgive the ruse," he said. "I wanted to apologize."

"Apologize?" Tanalasta kept her voice cold. "You have nothing to apologize for."

"I fear I have given you reason to think poorly of me."

"Nonsense. You've been most valorous. The king shall hear of your service." Tanalasta paused, then decided a demonstration of her magnanimity was in order. "In truth, I shouldn't be surprised if you were granted that holding you desire."

Rowen's face fell. "Do you think that's why I'm here? Because I am chasing after a piece of land?"

Tanalasta recoiled from the bitterness in his voice, then

lowered her chin to a less regal height. "I know better than that. I only wanted you to know I wouldn't hold my own foolishness against you."

"*Your* foolishness, Princess?"

"Mine." Tanalasta looked away. "I have been throwing myself at you like a festhall trollop, and you have been honorable enough not to accept my affections under false pretenses." She gave Rowen a sideways glance, then added, "Though it would have been kinder to tell me at the start I was behaving like a fool."

"How could I do that? It would have been a lie." Rowen dared to grasp her hand—and when she pulled it away, dared to take it again. "If my feelings are different from yours, it is only because they are stronger. I have been stricken from the moment I saw you."

Tanalasta was too stunned to pull her hand away. Once again, he was telling her what she longed to hear, but how could she believe him when his actions spoke otherwise? She shook her head.

"That can't be true, or you would never leave me with Alusair—not when Vangerdahast has the resources of an entire kingdom to make certain we never see each other again."

Rowen closed his eyes for a moment, then looked toward the horizon. "Perhaps that would be for the best."

"*What?*" Tanalasta grabbed Rowen's arm. "I will not be taken for an idiot. If you do not wish to court me, then have the courage to say so plainly. I've heard doubletalk all my life, and you really aren't very good at it."

Rowen's eyes flashed at the slight. "I am speaking as plainly as I know how, *Princess* Tanalasta. My feelings are as sincere as they are powerful, but I am the son of a disgraced house. Any courtship of mine would only weaken the crown."

Tanalasta experienced a sudden lifting of the heart

as her irritation gave way to comprehension. She stood motionless for many moments, then finally began to see how deeply her harsh words had to have cut the ranger. She stepped closer and said, "Rowen, I'm sorry for the things I said to you. Now that you've explained your reservations, I see you have been honest—brutally honest, at least with yourself."

"I'm sorry, Princess. It just wasn't meant to be."

Tanalasta cocked her brow. "Really? Then you are prepared to assert your judgment over that of the Goddess?"

"Of course not, but if you are speaking of your vision, how are we to know I am the one?"

"*I* know," Tanalasta replied. "And so do you."

Rowen looked torn and said nothing.

"Certainly, there will be those who resent my choice," Tanalasta said, sensing an opportunity to win him over, "but that would be true no matter who I chose. If I picked a Silversword, the Emmarasks would be angry. If I picked an Emmarask, the Truesilvers would disapprove. If I picked a Truesilver, the Hawklins would gossip, and anyone I choose will be a slight to the Marliirs. In the end, I can only follow my heart and take the man I desire, one I know to be honest, loyal, and trustworthy—and that man, Rowen, is you."

"Even if it costs you the crown?" he asked. "And though it does not, even if it costs you the loyalty of the great nobles?"

Tanalasta shrugged. "You are only one of the choices I have made that may cost me the throne—but they are *my* choices to make, and I am happy to live with the consequences." She gave him a steady gaze. "If the crown is to rest on my head, having the strength of your character at my side will far outweigh the loss of a noble family's shifting loyalties."

Rowen considered this for a moment, then asked,

"But how many of those families can one man be worth?" He shook his head. "Surely, not even half of them. It is well and good for a royal to make her own choices, but she must not be blind to the trouble that follows. People will think of me as no better than Aunadar Bleth, taking advantage of your good nature to restore my family's standing—and the crown will be the weaker for it."

"Is your opinion of me that low?" Tanalasta demanded. "Do you assume people think me capable of attracting only frauds and sycophants?"

Rowen's face went white. "That's not what I mean to—"

"What else *could* you mean? Perhaps it's just as well we haven't pursued this further." Tanalasta pointed toward the horizon. "There is the gulch, Rowen. Go and see if it has any water for us."

* * * * *

The mare neighed three sharp times and scraped at the ground, nearly crushing Vangerdahast's foot when one of her hooves caught him across the instep. He cursed and jerked on the reins, forcing her head down below the height of his chest.

Owden Foley raised a restraining hand. "Gently, my friend. She has been through a lot."

"And she will go through a lot more, if she doesn't start making sense," Vangerdahast growled. "Tell her that."

Owden scowled his disapproval. "I don't think—"

"Tell her," Vangerdahast ordered. "Perhaps it will clear her thoughts."

Owden sighed, but turned back to the horse and began to neigh and nicker. The horse's ears flattened, and she fixed a single round eye on Vangerdahast's face. He narrowed his own eyes and raised his lip in a snarl.

The mare looked away and began a quick succession of nickers, punctuated every now and then by a sharp whinny or a neighed question from Owden. When the conversation finally ended, Owden nodded and patted the beast's neck reassuringly.

"Well?" Vangerdahast demanded.

"I coaxed a little more out of her, but horses don't remember the same way we do." Owden took the reins from Vangerdahast's hands. "All she can tell us is that the ghazneths have been hunting her since 'the dawn before the dawn.' "

"And?" Vangerdahast glared at the priest.

Owden slipped between him and the mare. "And that the princess is gone with 'her stallion.' "

"Her *stallion*?" Vangerdahast fumed. "What, exactly, does she mean by that?"

* * * * *

The 'gulch' turned out to be a winding riverbed filled with more willows than water, but there was a tiny ribbon of creek meandering along beneath the bluffs on the far side, and Tanalasta could hear the horses sloshing through its silty currents, doing their best to slurp the rivulet dry. She was kneeling atop a slender tongue of high ground, churning a pile of rotting leaves into a small plot of dirt she was preparing for a faith planting. Though dead-tired from the day's walk, the work kept her mind off Rowen, and it was well worth the effort to slow her whirling thoughts.

The princess was more disappointed in him than angry. She knew better than anyone what people thought of her. Many nobles—perhaps most—would accuse Rowen of taking advantage of her gullible nature. But they would think the same no matter who she chose. The only way to change their minds was to be patient and prove them wrong through good conduct, her own and that of her chosen. She was hurt not because Rowen had pointed out how people would perceive their relationship, but because he lacked faith in her to change their minds. If *he* did not trust her to succeed, how could she trust herself?

Tanalasta pulled a fist-sized stone from the ground and turned to set it aside at the edge of her plot, where she found a pair of soft-leathered ranger boots standing beside her. Biting back a cry of surprise, she placed the stone with the others, then spoke without looking up.

"Come to tell me I mustn't think poorly of you?" Tanalasta crumpled a handful of decaying leaves between her hands, sprinkling them over the surface of her plot. "Or have you decided to chase that holding after all?"

"I suppose I deserve that." Rowen kneeled beside her and began to work a handful of leaves into humus. "The truth is, I've come to apologize. I spoke like a narrow-minded popinjay."

"I hope you don't expect me to disagree."

"No. When I said those things, I was being a coward. I was thinking only of myself—of how your favor would affect my reputation."

"You *said* you were thinking of the crown," Tanalasta reminded him.

Rowen shrugged. "Perhaps I was thinking of both—or perhaps I was not thinking at all. Either way, I was wrong. It is not my place to decide what is best for the crown. I pray you can forgive me."

Tanalasta sank her fingers into the dirt, turning it over and churning the leaf-humus into the soil. As honest and humble as Rowen's apology was, it did little to quell her anger. He had said nothing about having faith in her ability to win her subjects' confidence, and what future could she have with a man who did not believe in her?

"Thank you for clarifying matters, Rowen." Tanalasta's voice was sarcastic. "I was afraid that in making a fool of myself, I had also conveyed to you the duties of my station."

"Now you are twisting my words, Princess." Rowen's face was growing stormy. "I came here to say I agree with you. Why do you refuse to listen?"

"I have been listening." Tanalasta started to suggest she had not liked what she heard, then thought better of such an acid remark and shook her head. "I don't see the point in continuing this, Rowen. Maybe you should leave."

Rowen stared at her in disbelief for a long time, then dumped the humus in his hands and stood. "If you wish."

"It . . ." Recalling that dawn tomorrow would probably be the last time she ever saw him, Tanalasta almost said it wasn't what she wanted—but what good would that do? He still didn't believe in her. She summoned her resolve and said, "It is."

Rowen turned to leave, then suddenly stopped. "No."

More confused than upset, Tanalasta looked up. "No?"

The scout spun on his heel and pulled her to her feet. "The point, Tanalasta, is this."

He kissed her hard, folding her into his arms so tightly that he lifted her off the ground. The princess was too astonished to be outraged. She had been imagining a moment like this almost since she met Rowen, and he chose *now* to take matters into his own hands? His timing was typically, wretchedly male—yet Tanalasta's body responded just as fiercely as it had at the goblin keep. A sensation of joyous yearning shot through her from lips to loins, and she wondered how such a powerful feeling could be anything but a portent from the goddess. Before she knew it, her hands were at his waist, pulling him closer, and a feeling of sacred warmth flowed down through her body, dispelling her anger and draining her resolve. She longed to embrace the moment, to run her hands over his body and kindle their passion into full flame, but she could not release herself to carnal abandon yet—not while her mind remained so at odds with her heart.

Tanalasta slipped a hand between them and pushed against Rowen's chest. The ranger kissed her more deeply, running one hand up to her breast and filling her with waves of seething pleasure. She closed her eyes for a single heartbeat, then bit his lip—a little harder than necessary to make him stop—and managed to push him away.

"Rowen!" Tanalasta's voice had more passion and less anger in it than she would have liked. She gulped down a breath, then gasped, "What was the meaning of *that*?"

"I think you know." Rowen touched a finger to his bleeding lip, then gave her a lean and hungry look. "I wasn't thinking of the crown princess, but of the woman I've come to know and love."

"Love?" The word did not feel as hollow as Tanalasta had expected—in fact, it felt all too comfortable. She eyed him warily. "You are the one who has been worried about the effect on the crown. What are we going to do about that?"

Rowen shrugged and shook his head. "I truly don't know, and I can't honestly say I care—as long as you protect me from Vangerdahast." His tone was only half-joking. "I don't fancy living out my life as a toad."

Tanalasta looked at him a long time, giving her mind time to come to the same conclusion her heart had already reached. The princess knew him too well to believe the ranger had suddenly forgotten his oath to the crown. He had simply come to the same conclusion she had reached a long time ago.

Tanalasta smiled. "If you think I can protect you from Vangerdahast, you must be love-stricken!" She grabbed Rowen by the front of his cloak and pulled his face close to hers. "But I have read that a princess may kiss any toad she wishes."

She licked the blood off his lip, then slipped her tongue into his mouth and gave him a long, burning kiss. He responded in kind, dipping her over backward and gently lowering her to the ground. Tanalasta pressed herself against him, reveling in the waves of desire shuddering through her body. His hands roamed over her shoulders and breasts at will, igniting little blossoms of heat wherever they went, and the last shadow of doubt vanished from her mind. Rowen was the man of her vision. She could tell by the way her flesh came alive at his touch, and she wanted never to be apart from him.

She pulled her lips away from his long enough to run a fevered line of kisses up his neck, then whispered, "Rowen—" She had to stop to catch her breath. "We need a plan."

"I have one."

He loosened her belt, then ran a hand up the bare skin beneath her tunic. She shivered in delight and let her eyes roll back, feeling as though she would black out from sheer pleasure.

"No . . ."

When Rowen's hand hesitated, she grabbed his wrist through her tunic and guided his palm to her naked breast.

"I mean yes," she gasped. "But what about the future?"

Rowen's fingers grew still. "I still can't take you with me." He started to withdraw his hand—then stopped when Tanalasta clamped her elbow across his arm. A wanton smile came to his lips, but—somehow—he managed to keep his mind off his desire long enough to say, "There's no telling how long it will take to find Vangerdahast, and—"

"And I must show the king what I've found as soon as possible—I know." Tanalasta reached for his belt and began to fumble with the buckle. She was so nervous—or was it excited?—that her hands were trembling. "How do you get this thing off?"

"Just like yours."

Rowen arched his back to give her a better angle, and the prong finally came out of the hole. Tanalasta grabbed the hem of his tunic and lifted it to his shoulders. Her stomach filled with butterflies, and she decided she was the luckiest princess in Faerûn. She leaned over and kissed her way up toward his neck.

Rowen moaned softly, then fell silent and still. For a moment, Tanalasta feared she had done something wrong—or, recalling her own trembling hands, thought perhaps he'd grown too excited too quickly (having read in Miriam Buttercake's *Treatise on Good Wifery* that men sometimes suffered such disappointments), but that turned out not to be the case. As suddenly as he had fallen quiet, Rowen pulled her mouth to his and gave her a long, lingering kiss.

When he finished, he looked deeply into her eyes and said, "There is one thing that even kings and queens may not dictate, that only we may control."

Tanalasta nodded eagerly. "I know."

She started to pull her tunic off over her head, but Rowen caught her arm.

"No. I mean there is a way to stop them from keeping us apart—but only if you are sure about risking your crown."

Tanalasta did not even hesitate. "I'm thirty-six years

old. If I can't make a decision by now, what kind of queen would I be anyway?"

Rowen smiled, then rolled to his knees and picked up the seed bag that lay beside the plot of ground she had been preparing. He pulled a single columbine seed from inside and placed it in his open palm. Tanalasta stared at the kernel for a long time. She was more nervous than ever, with her pulse rushing in her ears and her heart fluttering up into her throat.

Finally, she gathered her wits and asked, "The Seed Ceremony?"

Rowen nodded. "If you will have me."

Tanalasta rose to her own knees. "Are you doing this for me—or for the realm?"

"Neither." Rowen continued to hold the seed in his palm. "I am doing it for me."

The rushing sound vanished from Tanalasta's ears, and her heart settled back down into her chest where it belonged. "Good answer."

She placed her palm over the seed in Rowen's hand, and they began the invocation. "Bless us, O Chauntea, as we bless this seed, that all we nurture may grow healthy and strong."

With their free hands, Tanalasta and Rowen dug a single small hole in the plot she had prepared, then the princess grabbed her waterskin and dampened the soil.

"We prepare this bed with love and joy," Rowen said.

Together, they placed the seed in the hole and covered it with dirt.

Tanalasta began the next part. "In the name of Chauntea, let the roots of what we plant today grow deep . . ."

"And the stalk stand strong . . ."

"And the flower bloom in brilliance . . ."

"And the fruit prove abundant."

They finished together, then poured more water over

the planting and kissed. This time, it was Rowen who pulled Tanalasta's tunic over her head.

18

he royal wizard's bones were acting their age. After more than a tenday of ghazneth-chasing, his hips throbbed, his back hurt, and the last thing he wanted to do was crawl up a rocky hillside on his hands and knees to spy on a tribe of swiners. That was what Royal Scouts were for . . . but Vangerdahast was fresh out of Royal Scouts. Owden Foley had found the last one earlier that morning—a bloated, blotchy red corpse blanketed in stinging ants. There had been no question of touching the thing. They had simply poured a flask of torch oil over the body, commended the man's soul to Helm, and set him alight. Now the royal magician had to do his own spying.

Vangerdahast crested the hill and found himself looking across the vast, fog-laced expanse of the Farsea Marsh. Stretching to the horizon, it was a sweep of golden-green tallgrass with channels of bronze water meandering past scattered copses of swamp poplar and bog spruce. The place teemed with cormorants and black egrets, all as raucous as a band of goblins, and swarms of black insects glided through the grass in hazy amorphous clouds.

On the near shore, several orc tribes were camped together on a rocky spur of land that jutted out into the marsh perhaps a thousand paces. The males had broken into four large companies and retreated to separate corners of the little peninsula for formation drills and weapons training. The females and children were clustered around tribal fires working, or wading through the shallows in search of fish and crustaceans. A two-story keep of dried mud stood at the end of the promontory, overlooking the marsh on three sides and guarded landward by a timber drawbridge. Its blocky construction and rounded arrow loops were evocative of ancient Cormyrean architecture. From the second-story windows oozed a strange aura of darkness that clung to the place like a death shroud.

The water around the keep gleamed silver with floating fish. Clouds of insects swirled through the orc camps, filling the air with a drone that was enough to drive Vangerdahast mad even a hundred and fifty paces inland. A strange network of tiny crevices stretched along the center of the peninsula, discharging thick curtains of yellow-gray smoke into the sky. Every plant within a hundred yards of the promontory had withered and died, and a carpet of gray mold was fanning outward from its base. The slope between Vangerdahast's hiding place and the shore was strewn with deer carcasses, all so putrid that even orcs would not eat them.

The royal magician waved to his deputies, and he was joined presently by the acting commander of his Purple Dragons and the interim master of the company's war wizards. Alaphondar and Owden followed the pair unin-

vited, but Vangerdahast did not object. The Royal Sage
Most Learned would need to record what followed,
while Harvestmaster Foley's opinions were often worth
the hearing—provided Vangerdahast did not put himself in the position of seeming to elicit them.

Vangerdahast pointed at the mud keep and said nothing.

"Tanalasta is inside?" asked Owden.

"I'll know that when *I* get inside."

Owden nodded. "I suppose that's the only way to find
out."

Vangerdahast's stomach sank. The truth was he could
not even be sure the ghazneths were inside, and he had
been hoping Owden would suggest an easy way to find
out. Instead, it appeared they would have to storm the
keep—and with less than half the company remaining.

Vangerdahast took a deep breath, then said, "Here's my
plan." He quickly outlined what he wanted, making both
commanders repeat their instructions. When they had
done so, he turned to Owden, giving the priest one last
opportunity to make him look like a fool. "I'm assuming
the ghazneths are inside because orcs don't normally
practice drills."

"Or share encampments, or build keeps fashioned in
the style of ancient Cormyr," added Owden, "and because
we haven't seen them in the last half-day. What are we
waiting for?"

"Nothing, it would seem." Vangerdahast nodded to his
subcommanders, who retreated twenty paces down the
hill to prepare their men.

As soon as they were gone, Alaphondar asked, "You two
do realize there's more to this than meets the eye?"

"Are you referring to the keep?" asked Owden. "It's significance hasn't escaped me."

"What significance?" asked Vangerdahast.

"What the keep *means*," explained Alaphondar. "Historically, citadels built in such forlorn places are home to some embattled, ever-watchful spirit."

"I'd call that a fair description of the ghazneths," said Vangerdahast.

"And I would call it a description of their master," said Owden. "We are entering the world of the phantom, my friend. You would do well to listen to your soul."

Vangerdahast regarded the priest sourly. "My *soul* tells me that an ancient spirit would not inhabit a keep built of mud. In this climate, such places tend to melt rather quickly."

"Which is why we must consider the ghazneths' reason for building beside a rainy marsh in the first place," said Alaphondar. "Have you read Ali Binwar's treatise, *Of the Four Natures?*"

Vangerdahast rolled his eyes. "Sadly, I have better things to do with my time than waste it on idle reading."

"Gladly, I do not," said Owden. "You are referring to the chapter on elemental amalgamation?"

A gleam came to Alaphondar's eyes. "Exactly. In the marsh, we have the fusion of earth and water, but the absence of air or fire. The idle elements combined, the vigorous excluded."

"Perfect conditions for spiritual decomposition," agreed Owden. "We will have to be careful."

"Indeed, but it's not *you* I was thinking about." Alaphondar waved a hand down the rocky hillside. "There are plenty of stones about. Why build the keep of mud?"

Owden's eyes widened in alarm. "Because mud combines the nourishing power of earth with the dissolving properties of water."

"Yes—the perfect medium for transformation." Alaphondar pointed to the mud tower. "Give it a shape, add a little fire and some air, and a few days later you have a keep."

"Or give it a spark of life, and you have a ghazneth," said Owden.

Vangerdahast frowned. "What are you saying?" When no one replied, his imagination supplied its own answer. "That they are trying to make a ghazneth of Tanalasta?"

"That might explain why the ghazneths have been working so hard to keep us away from here," said Alaphondar.

Vangerdahast felt a growing hollow in the pit of his stomach. "Don't be ridiculous! Boldovar's crypt wasn't anywhere near a marsh."

"Marshes have been known to dry up," said the sage.

Vangerdahast started to counter that there had been no sign of a keep, but a thousand years was a long time. So many seasons of spring rains would have destroyed any sign that the grave had ever been guarded by a mud fortress. Instead, he asked, "What about the tree? I doubt we'll find any elven poets in an orc camp."

"The thought does strike me as something of a self-contradiction," said Owden, "but there are many things we don't know—"

"Including the keep's purpose." Vangerdahast began to inch back down the hill. "I'll hear no more of this philosophical nonsense. We could argue in circles all day, and it would make no difference. If Tanalasta is in there, we must rescue her."

"And if she is not, we must make a ghazneth tell us where she is," said Owden.

The priest started down the hill after Vangerdahast, and Alaphondar crawled toward his assigned hiding place in a jumble of boulders. No one suggested using a spell to locate the princess. If she was not a prisoner already, the magic would lead the ghazneths to her like an arrow.

As they parted ways, Alaphondar paused. "Good luck, my friends, and be careful."

"We'll be safe enough," Vangerdahast assured him. "It's you who is taking the risk, staying here alone. You remember my signal?"

Alaphondar nodded. "The shooting star." He gestured toward his weathercloak's escape pocket. "I'll rejoin the company as soon as I see it."

"Good. If we have the princess, we can't wait around long," said Vangerdahast. "If we don't, there won't be time to look for you."

"And if matters go badly, Alaphondar, don't even think of joining us," added Owden. "You won't be able to help, and someone will need to inform the king."

"Preferably in person." Vangerdahast tapped the throat clasp on Owden's weathercloak. "So don't use this unless you must. It would be nice if you lived long enough to chronicle what little we've learned about these things."

Alaphondar nodded reluctantly. "I know, I know—my pen is my sword."

He wished them luck again, then turned away. Vangerdahast and Owden returned to their horses and mounted. What remained of the Royal Excursionary Company sat ready and waiting, an unclasped weathercloak draped over the shoulders of every rider. Though the cloaks were standard issue only for war wizards, the company had lost so many men they now had one for even the lowest-ranking dragoneer.

Vangerdahast nodded, and the company closed their throat clasps. The war wizards began to sprinkle powdered steel over everyone in the company, filling the air with magic incantations as they cast their spells of shielding. The royal magician did the same for himself and Owden, then looked toward the top of the hill. Alaphondar was kneeling in the midst of the boulder jumble, squinting down toward the keep and holding one arm up to signal.

"Be ready!" Vangerdahast started Cadimus up the hill at a walk, motioning the company to follow. "Stragglers will pay dearly."

They had nearly reached the hilltop before Alaphondar's arm finally dropped. Vangerdahast slapped his heels into Cadimus's flanks, urging the big stallion into a run. The air began to resonate with the drumming of hooves. The clamor of an alarm bell rang out across the marsh, followed by a tumult of grunting and squealing.

The royal magician crested the hill to see five hundred orcs scurrying toward the neck of the peninsula. Ahead of the swiners flew five streaks of darkness, their black wings mere blurs as they shot forward to meet the Royal Excursionary Company. Vangerdahast's heart sank. They had never before seen more than three ghazneths at a time.

The charge started down the front of the hill and picked up speed. Vangerdahast's old knees began to ache from squeezing Cadimus so hard. The ghazneths continued to climb higher as they approached, and they were a hundred feet in the air by the time the company crossed the neck of the peninsula. The royal magician slipped one hand inside his weathercloak and found the escape pocket, craning his neck to keep watch on the rising phantoms. At last, when he judged them to be two hundred feet above the ground, they wheeled around to fall on the company from behind.

Vangerdahast looked forward again and saw the orcs forming ranks along the neck of the peninsula, their officers pushing and shoving frightened warriors into short stretches of line. The swiners were armed with an odd assortment of spears, swords, and pikes—whatever they happened to be holding at the moment the alarm was sounded. Even without magic, it would have been an easy matter to break through their defenses, but the royal magician was in no mood to waste time in melee, especially with the ghazneths swooping down on them from behind.

Vangerdahast fixed his gaze on a tribal campsite about two hundred paces shy of the keep, looking past a long line of orcs streaming down the peninsula to meet the charge. He could barely make out the distant figures of females and children, turning to stare after their warriors and shake their arms in encouragement. They were in for a big surprise.

Vangerdahast thrust his hand into the escape pocket, and a large black square appeared directly ahead of him. Cadimus whinnied and tried to veer off, but there was no time. He hit the doorway at a full gallop, and Vangerdahast experienced that familiar feeling of dark, endless falling.

An instant later, he burst back into the light, head spinning and ears ringing with astonished squeals and grunts. Cadimus stumbled, something shrieked, and Vangerdahast took a blow across the shin. He looked down, but his vision was still a blur, and he could not imagine what might have happened. The sound of drumming hooves began to build around him, and the world erupted into a cacophony of shrieking and snorting. Cadimus ricocheted off something soft but sturdy, then bumped into something just as soft and sturdy on the other side, and the round shape of a horse's rear end came into focus ahead of Vangerdahast.

The wizard shook his head clear, recalling that he was in the middle of a cavalry charge. He began to make out the shapes of dazed horses and glassy-eyed men all around, all galloping forward at a full sprint, all oblivious to the blocky keep standing at the end of the peninsula just fifty paces ahead.

"Halt!" Vangerdahast reined Cadimus in, being careful not to pull up so short that he caused a collision with the horse behind him. "Stop! Stop!"

Slowly, the rest of the company began to heed his orders. By the time Vangerdahast reached the keep, the charge had slowed to an amble, with horses stumbling about blindly and men struggling to shake their heads clear. The ground at this end of the peninsula was striped with hairline crevices, all spewing yellow fumes and fouling the air with the acrid stink of brimstone. Clouds of mosquitoes, wasps, and flies drifted back and forth through the smoke, biting, stinging, and filling Vangerdahast's ears with their maddening drone.

He wheeled Cadimus around and found himself looking back at the remnant of an orc camp. There were hides and half-cooked food strewn everywhere, and the terrified females were herding their stunned young into the marsh. About two dozen grizzled males, and a like number of husky females, were scuttling forward with crooked hunting spears clutched in their hands.

Vangerdahast maneuvered Cadimus through a tangle of afterdazed dragoneers and waved his hand across the width of the peninsula, uttering a long and complicated incantation. Unlike many spells, this one required no material components, but it required half a minute of tongue-twisting chanting. Before he finished, the swiner elders began hurling spears in his direction, and the ghazneths appeared in the sky over the promontory, streaking back toward the keep. Though he could not see the main body of the orc army, he felt sure it would be charging up the peninsula to defend the keep.

When Vangerdahast finished his spell, a wall of flashing color sprang up before him, stretching across the peninsula and well down into the water. It would not stop the flying ghazneths, of course, but the orc army would be forced down into the marsh to circumvent it. Any warrior foolish enough to try scaling it would be spit back at his fellows, mangled beyond recognition.

By the time Vangerdahast turned back to the mud keep, a steady drizzle of orc arrows was flying down from the arrow loops. The Royal Excursionary Company was beginning to recover from its afterdaze and return fire, but without much effect. The pall of darkness that seemed to cling to the place prevented them from seeing their targets, and so their arrows were about as effective against the swiners as those of the swiners were against their magically shielded armor.

Vangerdahast rode forward to his subcommanders, who stood together taking orders from Owden. Scowling at the priest's presumption, the wizard dismounted, leaving Cadimus with a young dragoneer, and joined them.

"Stop wasting time with this groundsplitter!" Vangerdahast shoved the commander of the Purple Dragons toward the wall. "The ghazneths will be here in two minutes. Get your archers ready."

The man paled. "As you command."

He ran off to obey, shouting for the dragoneers to form their squares. Vangerdahast turned to the master of his war wizards and pointed at the keep's gate. To his surprise, it was coated in black iron. He could not understand why he had failed to notice the dark metal from the hilltop.

"Can you tell me why that is still standing?"

The young wizard paled. "No. We've hit it with fire, lightning, and warping. Nothing works."

"In fact, spells only make the gates stronger. The iron was not there until your wizards started their work," added Owden.

"Then try the walls!" Vangerdahast stormed. "We're in a hurry!"

As he spoke, the royal magician pulled his lodestone from his pocket and scraped a pinch of dust off Owden's weathercloak. He rolled the lodestone in the dust, pointed to the base of the keep, and uttered his spell. A ray of shimmering translucence shot from his finger, blossoming against the building in a circle of rippling energy. The mud wall turned dark and smooth and seemed to melt as the wizard's magic faded, finally coalescing into a smooth disc of black marble.

Vangerdahast cursed, then an orc's arrow corkscrewed down to bounce harmlessly off his breast.

"The same as the gate," said Owden. "I fear Alaphondar is more right about the nature of the keep than he knows. It seems to be using your magic against you."

"Obviously," Vangerdahast snarled.

Deciding to try the opposite tactic, he waved his hand at the wall and uttered a quick incantation to dispel the magic. The dark circle only grew larger.

A flurry of throbbing bowstrings proclaimed the arrival of the ghazneths. Vangerdahast glanced toward his prismatic wall and saw all five phantoms wheeling toward the marsh, their breasts and wings peppered with iron-tipped arrows. Two of the creatures seemed to be flying a little more slowly than usual, and one was trailing a syrupy string of black blood.

"If magic won't work, hard work will," said Owden.

The harvestmaster snatched an iron-tipped spear from a dragoneer and charged the keep, angling away from the dark circle that Vangerdahast had created.

A cloud of crooked shafts wobbled down from arrow loops to meet his charge. Most missed broadly, but even those that found him bounced off without causing harm. Vangerdahast scowled, then finally realized what the priest was doing and waved a troop of men after him.

"Get over there and help the fool! Tanalasta will have my ears if something happens to him!"

A dozen dragoneers grabbed their spears and rushed after Owden. They were joined by a handful of war wizards, who quickly raised a floating ceiling above their heads to deflect the annoying deluge of orc arrows. Vangerdahast remained a moment to watch the enemy response, but the aura of darkness clinging to the keep precluded any possibility of seeing inside. The only reaction was a slight slackening in the rain of crooked shafts as the swiners within realized the futility of their attacks.

Pulsing volleys of bowfire began to sound from all directions. Vangerdahast glanced around the peninsula to find the dragoneers arrayed in single ranks along the shoreline, filling the air with arrows as the ghazneths came in low and fast. Behind each rank of Purple Dragons stood a war wizard, pointing over their heads and uttering the incantation of a wall spell.

As the sorcerers' voices fell silent, rippling curtains of force sprang up around the edge of the peninsula, enclosing it in a castlelike perimeter of magic walls. A pair of ghazneths slammed into these barricades headlong, filling the air with blood-curdling shrieks and looking more surprised than hurt as they lay splayed against the invisible walls. The other three phantoms streaked across the shoreline just ahead of the spells, tearing through the single thin rank of dragoneers in a dark flash and sinking their talons into the wizards waiting behind.

One sorcerer got off a quick web spell, binding himself and his attacker together in a cocoon of sticky white filament. The other two wizards were jerked from their feet, screaming and flailing as the ghazneths arced into the sky. A cloud of arrows chased the phantoms over Vangerdahast's prismatic wall, but that did not keep the creatures from dropping their victims into the heart of the orc army. After a brief tumult of crackling magic and screeching swiners, a round of raucous victory snorts announced the fall of the wizards to superior numbers.

On Vangerdahast's side of the wall, a dozen drag-oneers rushed over to the web-tangled ghazneth. The fil-aments were already beginning to lose their color, and the men seemed uncertain quite how to attack. Finally, one grabbed his sword with both hands and drove it into the cocoon with all his might. The attack drew a muffled bellow, but when the soldier tried to withdraw his weapon and attack again, it remained lodged in the sticky fil-aments. He began to work the hilt back and forth, hoping to enlarge the wound and cause as much damage as possible. When this evoked a long roar, several of the war-rior's fellows plunged their own blades into the web and imitated his tactic. The ghazneth howled in rage and pain, thrashing about so madly that the dragoneers had trouble holding their weapons.

Abruptly, the phantom stopped struggling. A tremen-dous boom knocked the dragoneers off their feet, then the ground opened under their feet, belching forth a column of stinking yellow fume that hurled them high into the sky. They swirled about in a strange airborne dance, shrieking and flailing at the phantom with blade and fist, bound to their foe by the web spell. Their voices grew raspy and broken from inhaling acrid fumes. A pair of warriors came free of the sticky tangle and crashed to the ground, and the smoke vanished as suddenly as it had appeared.

The cocoon plummeted into the abyss with its tangle of men and weapons, only to reappear a moment later when a pillar of flame hurled it back into the air. The web spell dissolved in a flash of crimson. The dragoneers disintegrated into lumps of scorched armor and howling ash and plunged back into the chasm. The ghazneth erupted into a flaming silhouette of itself and remained in the air, spreading its wings and letting out a long, spiteful cackle. It wheeled around trailing tongues of crimson fire and streaked down to catch the nearest war wizard in its burning talons, then disappeared over Vangerdahast's prismatic wall.

The other ghazneths came swooping over the walls from four different directions, talons extended and trails of dark blood dribbling from their wounds. A flurry of spells and iron-tipped arrows drove them away almost instantly, then the ground started to tremble. Small curtains of flame sprouted along the spine of the peninsula. The stench of brimstone grew suffocating, and men began to cough and choke and clutch at their throats. The company's panicked horses broke free of their holders and galloped madly along the shoreline, bouncing off the invisible walls and searching in vain for some way to escape the peninsula.

The war wizards cleared the air with a flurry of magic winds, but that did not prevent Vangerdahast from cursing.

Until now, the ghazneths had never used such powers against the Royal Excursionary Company, and he could not help wondering what other surprises they had in store. His whole strategy had been predicated on holding the creatures at bay long enough to enter the keep, but it was beginning to look like even that modest goal was not achievable.

Vangerdahast glimpsed a blazing ghazneth arcing over the prismatic wall and drove it back with a magic ice storm, then rushed forward to join Owden and the others at the keep. The harvestmaster and two other men were standing side-by-side, madly jabbing their spears into the dried mud and scraping loose small sprays of material. They had already managed to tunnel more than two feet into the base of the tower, and the wall flexed each time they struck. Determined that the first rescuer to enter the keep would not be a priest of Chauntea, Vangerdahast reached into the tunnel and pulled Owden back.

"Let the Purple Dragons lead the way," said the royal magician. "Tanalasta would never forgive me if something unfortunate befell you."

"Indeed, that would be almost as unfortunate as letting it be known that someone else had freed her." Owden pulled free of Vangerdahast's grasp, but shrugged and made no move to return to his digging. "Play your games if you wish. They make no difference to the princess."

Vangerdahast resisted a sharp reply, knowing that a stinging retort would only confirm how much he feared the priest was right. Tanalasta had always been a perceptive woman; now that she had become a stubborn one, it would take more than a simple rescue to make her reconsider her convictions.

The diggers broke through with a hollow clatter, opening a pair of head-sized holes into the swirling darkness inside. The musty scent of damp earth filled the air. A strange drone echoed out of the keep, then the dragoneers screamed and stumbled back, their heads lost under a cloud of black wasps.

Vangerdahast raised a hand and blew across his palm, scattering the wasps with a quick wind spell—standard defensive magic for any war wizard. The two dragoneers fell and lay on their backs, covering their eyes and screaming in agony. Owden and several dragoneers managed to pry their hands away from their faces, revealing a swollen mass of red boils. The priest called on Chauntea's mercy and began to pray.

Vangerdahast caught him by the shoulder. "Save your spells for Tanalasta. As much as I hate to share her gratitude, the princess may have need of your healing more than these soldiers."

Owden looked torn. Vangerdahast gave the priest no choice in the matter, pulling him to his feet and turning to face the keep, where a steady cloud of wasps was pouring from the two holes. A half-dozen dragoneers pulled their weathercloaks over their heads and charged into the swarm at a sprint, hurling their armored shoulders against the weakened wall.

The holes collapsed into a single windowlike portal nearly four feet across. Two warriors fell headlong into the darkness, their shins resting across the bottom edge of the breach. Wherever their legs touched the wall, little circles of dark marble began to fan outward as the keep absorbed the magic in their weathercloaks and shielding spells. The wasps descended on them, and the men began to scream and thrash about.

A war wizard directed a magic gale into the hole. The edges turned to black marble, but enough of the wind endured to drive the wasps into the depths of the tower. Several dragoneers rushed forward and grabbed their screaming comrades by the ankles.

A tempest of orcish arrows flew out of the darkness to meet them. The shafts clattered harmlessly off the rescuers, but the two victims cried out in pain as they suffered hits. When their comrades jerked them from the keep, one man had an arrow lodged in his shoulder, the other in his neck. Vangerdahast pulled a commander's ring from his pocket and slipped it on long enough to activate its light magic, then removed it and tossed it inside.

The ring passed through the breach still glowing, then hit the stone floor and began to fade. The light lasted long enough for Vangerdahast to see a cloud of wasps swirling along the far wall and a dozen orc archers edging toward a door.

When Vangerdahast detected no sign of Tanalasta in the room, he commanded, "Fireballs!"

"Fireballs?" Owden gasped. "But that's what they want! That kind of magic will turn the whole tower to stone."

Vangerdahast shrugged. "What do we care? We've already breached it."

As his war wizards prepared their spells, Vangerdahast saw that the battle on the peninsula was turning against him. A dense cloud of smoke, glowing in a hundred places with scarlet fire curtains, blanketed the battlefield. Dragoneers lay on the ground by the dozen, clutching at their throats or not moving at all. The few who remained on their feet could barely be seen through the flames and the fumes, standing along the shoreline in ragged lines, coughing and gagging on the poison air. There was no sign at all of the sorcerers assigned to support them, and the company horses were galloping along the shoreline more madly than ever. Cadimus, of course, was leading the charge. When Vangerdahast did not see any ghazneths swooping down from the sky, he dared wonder if the phantoms had finally fallen to his dragoneers' iron weapons.

That hope was shattered when he noticed the magic shimmer of a force wall beginning to fade. Though his own troops blocked his view of the other side, he felt certain that the ghazneths were pressing themselves against the wall, absorbing its magic into their own bodies. Behind them, there would be a horde of orcs milling about, waiting to wade ashore and slaughter what remained of the Royal Excursionary Company.

Vangerdahast did not think the swiners would find the battle difficult. There would be a moment of confusion as Cadimus and the other horses charged through the opening, then victory would come quickly for the orcs. There were not enough dragoneers left to hold longer than it would take the swiners to trample them.

The rumble of a tremendous fireball erupted from the keep. Vangerdahast looked back to see a long tongue of flame licking out of the portal. The mud walls were instantly transformed to black marble as high as the second story. He took a small scrap of parchment from his cloak, then rolled it into a small cone and held it to his lips. He whispered a quick incantation and turned toward the survivors of the battle.

"Retreat to the keep!"

Though even he could barely hear his voice over the battle rumble, the remaining dragoneers broke ranks and ran for the keep at their best sprints. Half a dozen fell almost immediately to tendrils of poison fume or curtains of leaping flame. Vangerdahast guessed that half their number, perhaps twenty soldiers, would survive long enough to reach the keep.

The royal magician grabbed the nearest war wizard. "When I enter the keep, you are to take command. Block the breach with an iron wall—not touching it, mind you, but only a hair's breadth away—then take the survivors and teleport back to Arabel."

The sorcerer's relief was obvious. "As you command."

"What about Alaphondar?" asked Owden. "You haven't sent up the shooting star."

Vangerdahast glanced at the carnage around him. "Alaphondar's safer in his hiding place. We'll teleport from Arabel and fetch him."

Vangerdahast returned his attention to the keep, where the last flames of the fireball were just dying out. He pulled a crow feather from his cloak pocket and brushed the vane up and down his body, uttering a low incantation. A warm prickle crept up his arms. He started to feel very light, then his feet left the ground, and he was floating.

As Vangerdahast completed his spell, the first dragoneers staggered in from the shoreline, stinking of brimstone and coughing violently. To a soldier, their faces were swollen and red with insect bites, and many had the glassy-eyed expressions of men ill with the ague. Seeing

Vangerdahast floating in the air, one warrior stumbled forward to clutch at his robes.

"Where are you going?" The man's voice was shrill and unbalanced. "The Royal Excursionary Company doesn't desert!"

"Coward!" accused another. "Come back and make your stand!"

Several more took up the cry and lunged forward, all reaching up to grab hold of the wizard's cloak. Vangerdahast tore his arm free and flew out of their reach with a quick flick of his hands.

"Who are you calling a deserter?" Vangerdahast demanded, growing furious. He pulled a wand from inside his cloak. "How dare you!"

Owden stepped forward, raising his hands to stop the attack. "Vangerdahast, it's ghazneth madness!" The priest waved at their swollen faces. "They're wounded and sick, just as you were in Arabel."

"Then get them under control!" Vangerdahast snapped, feeling foolish—and more than a little frightened by all he did not know about the ghazneths. "I'll see you in Arabel."

"Me?" Owden looked shocked. "What do you mean? You need someone to watch your back."

"How?" Vangerdahast flapped his arms and floated toward the smoking breach in the keep's black wall. "Unless you can fly, you'll only slow me down—and lose your weathercloak's magic to the keep."

"Wait!" It was the wizard to whom Vangerdahast had given command. "I can help."

The royal magician looked back to see the war wizard and Owden scurrying after him, the sorcerer brushing the vane of a pigeon feather over the harvestmaster's arms. A handful of mad dragoneers were stumbling along behind them, cursing Vangerdahast for a coward and promising to take vengeance in the afterlife. Behind them, on the near shore of the peninsula, the ghazneths had finally drawn all of the magic out of the force wall. Cadimus charged through the gap, leading the rest of the horses along behind him and bowling the astonished ghazneths over backward.

Owden rose unsteadily into the air, blocking Vangerdahast's view of Cadimus's mad charge. "Ready!"

"I'll be the judge of that."

Vangerdahast turned away and glided into the keep's marble darkness.

19

rom the hilltop where Alaphondar lay hiding, the keep appeared as a mere thumb-sized box at the heart of a slow-swirling spiral of brownish marsh haze. The men of the Royal Excursionary Company—what remained of them—were tiny stick figures glimpsed occasionally through the smoke and flame at the peninsula tip. The orcs were a frothing mass waiting in the water, while the ghazneths looked like four shadows and a single tongue of flame pressed to the face of the invisible wall. Now and again, Alaphondar's hill would vibrate with the low rumble of an explosion, or the air would smell briefly of brimstone or scorched flesh. Otherwise, the battle had drawn in on itself, leaving him blind to the events below and frightened for his companions.

The one thing he could see clearly—the marsh mist spiraling in toward the keep—worried him more than anything. Aside from seeming rather unnatural, it suggested an ominous gathering of forces, as if the tower were drawing inward the Royal Excursionary Company, the ghazneths and orcs, even the corrupting energies of the marsh itself. Alaphondar felt quite certain that Vangerdahast wouldn't notice the pattern, or appreciate its significance even if he did. The royal magician was a man of many strengths, but philosophical insight was not among them—and especially not in the midst of battle.

Alaphondar started to reach for his throat clasp, then pulled his hand away and rose from his hiding place. Even if he were to contact Vangerdahast, what would he say? I've noticed a suspicious pattern? The old wizard would only bark at him for drawing the ghazneth's attention to himself—and rightly so. To be any help to his friends, the old sage needed more information.

Alaphondar descended the hill at the best pace his old legs could manage, then retrieved his spyglass from his saddlebags and started back up the hill. When he had first shown his invention to Vangerdahast, decades before, the old curmudgeon had mocked it as a "four-foot monocle" and asked why anyone would suffer such a blurry, jumpy image when a simple clairvoyance spell could produce a perfectly clear vision. Alaphondar had accepted the criticism gracefully and muttered something about improving the opticals.

When Alaphondar reached the crest of the hill and raised the spyglass to his eye, the image was not blurry at all—nor was it jumpy, so long as he steadied the end of the viewing tube on a boulder. The keep now appeared as tall as his arm, and even through the gauzy yellow smoke, he could see Owden Foley flying behind Vangerdahast through a windowlike breach. Strangely, the timber gate now seemed to be sheathed in dark iron, while the building's lower story had taken on the glossy appearance of black marble.

A series of silver flashes silhouetted Vangerdahast in the dark portal, waving a wand around the chamber's dark interior. Outside, another six inches of wall darkened from mud to marble, and the sage had a sinking feeling he had guessed right about the significance of the keep's location. It had been built to protect something coming out of the marsh, and Vangerdahast's magic was hastening matters along.

A war wizard stepped into view and began to gesture at the portal as though casting a spell. To Alaphondar's astonishment, a dozen dragoneers swarmed the sorcerer at once. An iron wall appeared over their heads and fell on them all. Several warriors near the edges crawled from beneath the slab in various states of injury, then staggered to their feet and limped off with raised weapons. One pair turned to scramble into the keep and they were promptly blasted out of the portal by a lightning bolt. The others rushed off in the opposite direction.

Alaphondar shook his head at the madness, then noticed the company horses racing into the marsh. He swung the spyglass over to the charge and was astonished to find the terrified beasts stampeding into the orc horde, barreling into the front rank and forcing those behind to retreat or be trampled. The royal magician's brave mount, Cadimus, was leading the assault, rearing up to slash both front hooves at any swiner between him and the open marsh. So fierce was the stallion's assault that Alaphondar wondered if Vangerdahast had used some spell to drive the poor beast into a battle frenzy.

His curiosity vanished a moment later, when a ghazneth rose from the water behind Cadimus. The phantom spread its wings and raised an arm to point in the stallion's direction, then slipped and nearly fell as another horse ran into one of its wings. The ghazneth spun around, spraying a long arc of crimson fire from its fingertip, and pointed into the oncoming stampede. A dark rift opened down the center, swallowing half a dozen beasts in the blink of an eye. A moment later, their smoking carcasses reappeared atop a blinding curtain of crimson fire.

A second ghazneth shot out of the water, then launched itself into the air with nebulous ribbons of darkness trailing from its wings. It began to circle back and forth over the stampede, dragging the black streamers across the heads of the charging horses. The beasts went wild, turning to bite at the others around them, or stopping to buck and kick at the beasts pressing them from behind.

The charge began to falter. A third ghazneth rose from the water and launched itself over the orcs, yelling and gesturing wildly into the stampede. To a warrior, the swiners turned and flung themselves against the charge, hacking and slashing with their primitive weapons and paying no heed to their own lives. The horses responded in a like manner, stopping in the middle of the horde to bite and kick, or even wheeling around after they had cleared the fighting to wade back into the fray. Only Cadimus and a handful of sturdy beasts in the front part of the charge escaped the ghazneth's influence and continued forward.

The fourth and fifth ghazneths rose together from a spreading circle of browning marsh grass. One launched itself after the escaping horses, swooping in from behind to sprinkle them with brown droplets from its wet wings. The beasts slowed almost at once, flecks of white foam spewing from their nostrils. Only Cadimus escaped, hurling himself into the marsh on his side and disappearing beneath the water.

Not waiting to see whether the stallion surfaced again, Alaphondar swung his spyglass back to the last ghazneth. The creature had alighted on a powerful bay that was rearing up in the middle of the battle, jaws clamped around one foe's neck and forefeet slashing at two more. The ferocious beast split one orc's skull, pinned the second beneath the water, bit through the third one's spine, and went to work on its unwelcome rider, bucking and whirling and biting in a mad effort to tear the phantom from its back.

The horse tired only a moment later. Its coat suddenly grew dull and grizzled, its face became gaunt, and the muscle melted from its body. The beast dropped to its side and rolled, trying one last trick to unseat its rider. The ghazneth merely leaped to another mount, leaving the bay to drown in the marsh.

Alaphondar lowered the spyglass and sank behind the boulder, his veins running cold at what he was seeing: fire and fury, darkness, disease and decay—five primal forces wielded by five dark phantoms Emperel had been chasing when he disappeared. The implications were manifest. Emperel guarded the Lords Who Sleep, a secret company of Cormyrean knights hibernating against the day when a prophesy uttered by the great sage of Candlekeep, Alaundo the Seer, came true:

Seven scourges—five long gone, one of the day, and one soon to come—open the door no man can close. Out come the armies of the dead and the legions of the devil made by itself, to sweep all Cormyr away in ruin, unless those long dead rise to stand against them.

Boldovar was a scourge long gone, now returned bearing darkness and lunacy. Alaphondar did not know the names of the other ghazneths, but it seemed reasonable to assume they might also be scourges from Cormyr's past. He could list a dozen eligible names off the top of his head, and those were just kings.

That left only two scourges, "one of the day" and "one soon to come," to open the "door no man can close." Alaphondar's next thought made his chest tighten. Tanalasta might well be one of those scourges. Certainly, Vangerdahast had predicted dire consequences for the realm if the princess proceeded with her plan to establish a royal temple, and the Royal Sage Most Learned knew enough history to realize that royal magicians were seldom mistaken about such things.

Alaphondar forced himself to stand. Cadimus was creeping toward the shore, having eluded the orcs and ghazneths by circling into the marsh and ducking into a thicket of high grass. The rest of the horses lay near the peninsula, floating in the shallows or piled high along the shore, thwarting the orcs' progress as they clambered ashore. The ghazneths seemed to be hanging back to urge the horde onward, apparently unconcerned that Vangerdahast had entered their keep. Of course, they had little reason to worry, since every spell the wizard cast transformed another few inches of mud into hard marble.

Alaphondar raised the spyglass to his eye. The tower was already black to three-quarters of its height, with the marsh's brown haze swirling around it in tight spirals. Close to the ground, the cloud was so thick he could no longer see the wall itself, only the silver flicker of Vangerdahast's battle spells flashing through the gaping breach. Alaphondar was disheartened to see his friend had made so little progress. By the time he reached Tanalasta, the tower would be solid marble and completely swaddled in brown fog.

Troy Denning

What remained of the Royal Excursionary Company had gathered about twenty paces in front of the keep. Incredibly, the small force was trying to ready itself for a charge. The dragoneers were holding their iron swords and pushing and shoving each other into a rough semblance of a double rank. The two surviving war wizards stood together in the center of the second line, facing each other and gesturing angrily. Alaphondar could not imagine what the dragoneers expected to accomplish, but their jerky motions and comical efforts at organizing themselves suggested they had fallen prey to Boldovar's dark madness.

The sage was about to lower the spyglass and start down the hill when a cloud of insects rolled over the company from behind. The men flew into a frenzy, breaking ranks to slap wildly at themselves and each other— sometimes with the flats of their iron blades. The two wizards pulled spell components from their pockets and spun around, gesturing toward the top of the keep. Neither managed to complete his spell. One suddenly covered his eyes and fell writhing, and the other dropped when an errant sword caught him across the back of the neck.

Alaphondar turned his spyglass toward the keep, tracing the black cloud to a second story arrow loop. Though the tower interior remained dark and impenetrable, he had little doubt what he would have found inside, had he been able to see: the sixth ghazneth, master of swarms and Scourge of the Day.

Leaving his spyglass where it lay, Alaphondar stepped from behind the boulder and started down the front of the hill, then thought better of rushing into danger with no backup plan. He took his note journal from his weathercloak pocket and fished out a writing lead, then scrawled a message on a blank page.

You who read this, I pray you be loyal to the Purple Dragon and perform a vital service to your king. If you be one of the few who know the Sleeping Sword, then go and awaken it at once—the scourges have come, and the door is opening. If this be nonsense to you, then I pray you carry this note to the king in all haste and present it to him at once. May wise Oghma watch over this message and see it delivered to the right hand,

Alaphondar Emmarask,
Sage Most Learned to the Royal Court of Cormyr

Alaphondar tore the page from its book and did a quick signet rubbing, then opened his spyglass and slipped the message inside. If all went well, he would retrieve the note himself. If not, then whoever the king sent to investigate his absence would see the message when he found the device and looked inside. The sage slipped the spyglass down between two boulders, leaving enough exposed to attract the attention of someone searching the area for hints as to the fate of the Royal Excursionary Company, and started down toward the marsh.

Judging by the location of Vangerdahast's prismatic wall, he needed to reach the bottom of the hill before he used his weathercloak's escape pocket, and that would give him the time to do a quick sending. He closed his throat clasp and pictured Tanalasta's face in his mind.

* * * * *

When Tanalasta noticed the trail, Alusair's company was stumbling down into one of those narrow, steep canyons that meandered aimlessly through the Storm Horns, making any journey through the mountains a maddening exercise in maze-solving and cliff-scaling. Like half the company, the princess was trembling with chills and drenched in fever sweat, and so when she looked down through the pines and glimpsed a swath of churned earth running up the center of the marshy valley, she at first took the dark stripe to be a product of delirium. It had been six days since her last healing spell, and she knew from experience that such hallucinations became common as a person grew sicker. Five days after her wedding—it seemed like she had married Rowen years ago, though she thought the actual time was something little more than a tenday—they had dared to cast a round of healing spells and lost three men to a ghazneth attack. Since then they had resorted to magic only when they grew too ill to continue moving, and the ghazneths never failed to extract a heavy toll.

Finally, Tanalasta staggered out of the trees onto a grassy ribbon of valley floor and heard the lilting trickle of running water. A dozen paces ahead stood a tall stand of willows, screening the creek from view. Thirty paces beyond the creek rose the canyon's southern wall, blanketed in pines and as steep as a rampart stairway. Drawn on by the promise of cold water to quench their fevers, the entire company lurched through the willows at a near run and dropped to their bellies on the stream bank and began to palm cool clear water into their throats.

Tanalasta was swallowing her third mouthful when she caught a faint whiff of the familiar, too-sweet odor of horse manure. She took one more drink, then rose and forded the creek across a series of stepping stones. Pushing through the willows on the other side, she found herself looking at the same swath of churned ground she had glimpsed earlier.

The trail was close to ten feet wide, with a generous coating of dried manure and a distinct trio of paths worn deep into the ground. The hoof marks all showed the characteristic flared heel-calks of Cormyrean military horseshoes, and a single set of smooth-soled boot prints lay superimposed over the center line of horseshoe tracks.

Rowen.

Tanalasta turned to call the others and found her sister already stepping out of the willows. Alusair dropped to her haunches and crumbled some of the horse manure between her fingers.

"It's been a while," she said. "Maybe a tenday."

"But it *was* Vangerdahast." Tanalasta pointed to the three trails. "According to the *Steel Princess's Field Guide to Tactics of the Purple Dragon,* that's the standard riding formation for a company with a heavy complement of war wizards. Warriors shielding sorcerers."

"You read that?" Alusair replied, lifting a brow. "I doubt half the lionars in the army have cracked the cover."

"Perhaps because your style was stiff," said Tanalasta. "I'll be happy to help you liven it up in a revision."

Alusair's tone grew as terse as her syntax. "There isn't going to be a revision—there's going to be an order." She pointed at the boot print. "I suppose you've read my little book on tracking as well?"

"Of course, though it was clear that you hadn't read Lanathar Manyon's." Ignoring the curl that came to her sister's lip, Tanalasta squatted beside the print. "I think it's safe to assume this track is Rowen's. Because it's on top of the horses, we know he was following them. He seemed to be in good health."

Tanalasta pointed to the broadest part of the boot print, where a slight depression implied a swift, powerful stride.

Alusair inclined her head. "Very good. That should make you happy."

"I'll be happy when I see him again." Tanalasta stood and looked up the dark strip of churned ground. She couldn't see Rowen, of course, but it comforted her to know she stood on the same ground he had. "In his book, Lanathar claimed a careful observer could tell the age of a track by nothing more than its deterioration."

"Roughly," growled Alusair. "And if he claimed more, he was a damned liar."

Tanalasta remained silent and allowed her sister to study the tracks. As she waited, the rest of the company forded the creek and came to stand with them. Two of the men wandered down the trail to make an evaluation of their own, but they were still crumbling manure when Alusair stood.

"I'd say the company came through eight to fifteen days ago. Rowen's tracks are harder to place, but I'd guess about eight days."

"Then it's possible he has caught them by now," surmised Tanalasta.

Alusair studied her a moment, then scowled and shook her head resolutely. "Don't even think it! We're going to Goblin Mountain, and that's final." She turned to her men. "Drink up and fill your waterskins. We've got a hill to climb before dark."

"Why?" Tanalasta demanded, truly surprised. "Vangerdahast is bound to be closer."

"Vangerdahast could be anywhere by now. And so could Rowen."

"No, Rowen's going to bring the company back this way. That's what he's trying to tell us," Tanalasta said. When her sister frowned, she knew she was making progress and pointed at the boot prints. "Rowen isn't this careless. If he left a trail, he wanted us to see it."

Alusair shook her head. "He couldn't know we'd cross here."

"He knew we'd be coming over Marshview pass, and we're only two days south of there," Tanalasta said. "We're going south, while the trail runs west. We had to cross it somewhere."

Several men dared to murmur their agreement.

Alusair shot them a warning scowl, then looked back to Tanalasta. "You're reading an awful lot into one set of boot prints. If you're mistaken—"

"I'm not," Tanalasta insisted. "I know Rowen."

It was the wrong thing to say. Alusair's face hardened, then she uncorked her waterskin and turned to fill it from the stream. "I've made up my mind. I won't take these men chasing across the Storm Horns just because you've got an itch to share someone's bedroll."

Tanalasta's jaw fell, and not only because she was not accustomed to having the affairs of her heart discussed in such a manner. "Now we are cutting to the core of the matter, I think." She followed her sister down to the stream bank. "Are you really so frightened of me finding a man that you would subject your company to another tenday of fever just to keep us apart?"

"If you're talking about Rowen *Cormaeril*, I wouldn't need to bother!" Alusair retorted. Her men quickly began to finish filling their waterskins and retreat onto the shore, where they stood staring at their feet or gazing into the woods. The princess ignored them and continued to address Tanalasta. "Vangerdahast won't let that little dalliance go any further than it has already."

"It is not a dalliance!" Tanalasta spat. A wave of cold anger rose up inside her, and she decided the time had come to let Alusair know there were two stubborn princesses in the Obarskyr line. "Vangerdahast can't do a damn thing about it."

Alusair's lip rose. "Has the fever consumed your wits? If you keep pushing this, Vangerdahast will see to it that

Rowen Cormaeril spends more time in Anauroch than a Bedine camel-milker."

"Vangerdahast no longer has that authority," said Tanalasta. "At least not over Rowen."

"What are you talking about? Formal or not, Vangerdahast has that authority over everyone in Cormyr—except maybe the royal family."

"Exactly." Tanalasta took a deep breath, then said, "I suppose the time has come to tell you."

"Tell me what?" Alusair narrowed her eyes. "What did you do?"

"Come now, Alusair. Aren't you the worldly one?" Not quite able to keep a smug smile off her face, Tanalasta turned to Alusair's men. "Let it be known that the princess has married. Rowen Cormaeril is now a Husband Royal."

Alusair stepped in front of Tanalasta. "You may disregard my sister—and I'm sure you're all wise enough to know what will happen if her words are *ever* repeated."

The men shut their gaping mouths and looked more uncomfortable than ever. Alusair eyed them a moment longer, then spun on her sister.

"And *you*!" she demanded. "Eloping? With a *Cormaeril*? That marriage will last until about thirty seconds after Father hears of it—and then it will be too bad for poor Rowen. He doesn't deserve to be banished."

"And he won't," said Tanalasta. "Not unless the king cares to inflict the same punishment on me—and that's what it would take. I won't renounce Rowen. I'm in love with him."

"Love?" Alusair's face reddened with fear. "You're the crown princess, you selfish witch! Think of the kingdom!"

"Selfish?" An unexpected calm came over Tanalasta, and she spoke to her sister in a composed—even serene—voice. "Alusair, you really aren't the one to be calling others selfish. The fear in your face is plain to see. Would you really sacrifice my happiness so you can keep gallivanting around the Stonelands and sleeping with any young noble who happens to catch your eye?"

The alarm drained quickly from Alusair's face. She managed an unexpected smile, then spoke in a softer voice. "Of course not. People expect that from me. *I* wouldn't have to stop." She slammed the toe of her boot into a horse apple, kicking it into the stream. "What scares me is that I won't be any good. You'd make a far better queen."

"If that were true, why would you be trying to keep me away from Rowen? Wouldn't you trust me to do what is right for myself—and Cormyr?"

"It's not Rowen," Alusair said, meeting her sister's gaze. "I've had a go at him myself—"

"Alusair!"

Alusair raised a silencing hand. "I know—he's spoken for. All I'm saying is, he's a fine fellow—but, Tanalasta, the politics of the thing. His cousin tried to overthrow the king, for heaven's sake."

"Don't you think I know the politics?"

"Sure, if they're in a book somewhere, but . . ." Alusair shrugged and let the sentence trail off. "Look, all I'm saying is I'm not going to be queen. If you can work this out with Vangerdahast and the king, I'm happy."

"But you won't help me."

Alusair spread her hands in a gesture of helplessness, then took Tanalasta's waterskin and kneeled down to fill it from the stream.

"Fine."

Tanalasta was about to remark that Alusair would have to live with the consequences when an image of Alaphondar Emmarask appeared in her head. The old sage was staring downward and huffing for breath, and Tanalasta had the distinct impression he was frightened silly. The words of a sending began to hiss through her mind.

Tanalasta, open no doors! Ghazneths are scourges. Devil making himself. Vangerdahast and Owden inside, everyone else dead. Wait, or jump into marsh! Answer, please, please . . .

"Tanalasta?"

Now it was Alusair's voice, and Tanalasta felt her sister holding her arm. She motioned Alusair to wait, then concentrated on Alaphondar's voice and sent her reply.

Alaphondar, safe with Alusair in mountains, two days from marsh. Understand ghazneths are scourges. Know four names: Suzara, Boldovar, Merendil, Melineth. Xanthon Cormaeril released them.

"Tanalasta!" Alusair was not quite shaking her sister. "What is it?"

"I think we'd better risk a few curing spells," said Tanalasta. "That was a sending from Alaphondar."

"What?"

"He seems to be at the Farsea Marsh with Vangerdahast and Owden Foley." Tanalasta quickly repeated the message, then said, "He seemed to think Alaundo's prophecy is coming to pass. You know, 'Seven scourges . . .' "

" 'Five long gone, one of the day, and one soon to come,' " Alusair finished. "Of course I know. I looked it up as soon as I heard we were looking for Emperel."

"We should inform the king," Tanalasta said, closing her weathercloak's throat clasp. "You'd better ready the men. It sounded like all the ghazneths were busy with Vangerdahast, but we'd better not take a chance."

Alusair nodded and turned to start barking out orders, then paused and looked back to Tanalasta. "See what he wants me to do. My company can probably follow Vangerdahast's trail and reach the marsh in two days. That may be the best anyone can do."

"I'll ask."

Tanalasta took a moment to compose as succinct and complete a message as she could in a few words, then closed her eyes and pictured her father's face. When the image suddenly pulled off its crown and looked to one side, she sent her message.

Father, Alaphondar reports seven scourges here. Vangerdahast's company destroyed at Farsea Marsh, Vangey and Owden alive. Alusair and I two days away, going to aid.

The king's face betrayed first his relief at hearing his daughters were alive, then his shock at the unthinkable news. He shook his head urgently.

No, can't risk crown princess. War wizards and drag-oneers will find battlefield soon enough. Return to Arabel at once. Your mother safe but shaken.

The image faded, and Tanalasta found herself staring at her own feet.

"Well?" Alusair demanded.

Tanalasta ignored her, pretending she was still in contact with the king, and took a moment to plan out her next few actions. Alusair came and stood beside her impatiently.

Tanalasta looked up. "He says mother is safe but shaken."

"What does that mean?"

Tanalasta shrugged. "He seemed to think we would know."

Alusair considered this a moment, then shook her head helplessly. "Well, I suppose that's good news. What were his orders for me?"

Tanalasta answered quickly, not giving herself time to reconsider. " 'The realm can't afford to be without Vanger-dahast and Alaphondar at this time of crisis.' " It was more of an opinion than a lie. " 'You must do what you can to save them.' "

327

Troy Denning

Alusair closed her eyes for a moment, then nodded and looked to her sister. "And what am I to do with you?"

Tanalasta spread her hands helplessly. "Take me along, I suppose. He didn't have time to say."

20

he chamber was darker than a grave and so thick with orc stench it sickened Vangerdahast to breathe. Tangles of snakes slithered across the floor in wet, hissing snarls, while clouds of droning insects hovered just beyond the light, kept at bay by some magic Owden had worked. The corpses of charred swiners lay strewn along the walls, shrouded under blankets of clicking beetles and humming flies. Ribbons of yellow fume swirled through the air, hot, acrid, and moist with the smell of the swamp.

When no more orcs presented themselves for execution, Vangerdahast fluttered his arms and led the way slowly forward. The darkness of the place seemed to compress the light around his glowing wand, squeezing what would normally be a twenty-foot sphere into a misshapen egg barely a quarter that size. A low, constant groan rumbled through the keep, as though the unnatural radiance were an affront to the building itself. The terrible heat made Vangerdahast sweat heavily, and a steady stream of perspiration dribbled from his old brow to the floor. The snakes hissed and struck at the salty beads.

As they drew nearer to the doorway, Vangerdahast saw that the lintel and hinge post were rotting apart, while the surrounding walls were covered with the ashen residue of some foul-smelling fungus. The door itself hung open into the next room, dangling by the tattered remnant of a single leather hinge. Vangerdahast motioned for Owden to be ready, then floated through the doorway.

He found himself in the corner of a narrow corridor, one branch turning left toward a marble stairwell and the other leading straight ahead toward a closed door. The walls were coated with the same white moss he had seen in the blighted fields of northern Cormyr. A steady flow of sweltering yellow fume poured down the stairs to swirl around the corner and disappear down the dark hall, and the air was even warmer and more fetid than in the previous room.

Vangerdahast drifted down the passage and tried the door. The latch came off in his hand, tearing a gaping hole in the rotten wood. Brown scorpions began to swarm through the cavity and drop onto the floor.

Vangerdahast discarded the latch. "Perhaps we'll try upstairs first."

"It would seem more likely," agreed Owden.

Neither of them mentioned the obvious fate of anyone trapped in a room full of scorpions. The royal magician drifted around the corner into the stairwell. It was cramped and narrow and just as slime-caked as the keep's lower level, and so filled with hot fume that

Vangerdahast heard Owden gag on its rotten smell. The wizard covered his own mouth and floated up the stairs without breathing. Even then the stench made him feverish and dizzy.

As Vangerdahast neared the top, a pair of crude arrows hissed out of the darkness to ricochet off his magic shielding and thud into the moldy walls. A guttural voice barked a command, and bone-tipped spears began to poke their way through a dozen fungus-choked murder holes hidden along the inner wall. Though the points snapped off against the wizard's weathercloak, the attacks did threaten to shove him into the stairwell wall and drain his magic.

Vangerdahast touched his wand to the nearest spear and sent a fork of lightning crackling into the murder hole. The thunderbolt ricocheted down the ambush passage, filling the stairwell with blue flashes and muffled squeals as it danced from orc to orc. The air grew thick with a smell like scorched bacon, and the offending spears clattered harmlessly out of sight. If any swiners survived the wizard's reprisal, they were wise enough to fall silent and conceal the fact.

"Watch above!" Owden cried.

Vangerdahast looked up to find the last two swiners leaping down the stairs into the light. He kicked himself closer to the ceiling and let them stumble past below, dispatching one with a quick dip of his wand. The other fell to a crushing blow from Owden's iron-flanged mace.

"This seems a little more promising," said Vangerdahast. "At least they're trying to stop us."

He led the way upstairs and found himself in a large chamber, floating above a square table strewn with moldering crawfish, eels, and whatever else the orcs could dredge from the swamp. The place hummed

331

with the sound of untold insects, giving rise to a maddening din that made Vangerdahast's head throb. The radius of his light spell was too small to illuminate all the walls, but next to the stairwell, the iron door of a small cell hung open. Motioning Owden up behind him, the royal magician floated over to inspect the interior.

Along one side lay a straw sleeping pallet and a dozen miscellaneous rings, chalices, and weapons. Though all were of exquisite craftsmanship, their condition was now dull and lusterless. Opposite the sleeping pallet, the acrid smoke of charred flesh was wafting out of a small trap door opening down into the ambush passage. The far wall of the tiny chamber was occupied by the splayed recess of an arrow loop, through which Vangerdahast could see the company horses beginning their mad charge into the astonished orc horde out in the marsh. The ghazneths were nowhere in sight.

Vangerdahast backed out of the door and inspected the rest of the room. On the two flanking walls, they found four more open cells, each with a sleeping pallet and an assortment of leaden treasures that had once been enchanted with magic. At the opposite end, only one of the iron doors hung ajar. The other was closed fast. The royal magician readied a web spell, then gestured for Owden to open the closed door.

Owden pushed the latch, and it did not budge. He tried pulling. The door still did not open, but a muffled clatter sounded inside the cell.

"Tanalasta?" Vangerdahast could barely hear his voice over the sound of his drumming heart. "It's Vangerdahast."

Owden glowered, then turned back to the door. "And Owden."

There was no reply. The two men exchanged worried glances.

"Tanalasta, we must open this door," said Vangerdahast. "If you're unable to answer, give the royal knock. Otherwise, I fear Owden may be somewhat overanxious."

"I can answer." The voice was somewhat lower and rougher than Tanalasta's.

Vangerdahast narrowed his eyes and whispered, "That doesn't sound like her."

Before Owden could reply, Tanalasta answered, "And I doubt Owden is the overanxious one."

Owden shot Vangerdahast a smug smile. "That's her!"

Vangerdahast scowled, then motioned for the priest to wait above the door with his mace. "Better to be safe."

"So it will look like I'm the suspicious one?" Owden shook his head. "She has been their captive for how long? Of course she sounds a little hoarse."

Vangerdahast continued to point toward the ceiling. "It is no insult to be cautious."

Owden rolled his eyes and reluctantly floated up to hover above the door. Vangerdahast pointed at the latch, then uttered a single magic word. The door creaked open, but Tanalasta did not emerge.

"Tanalasta?" Owden called, negating any possible surprise bestowed by his position. "Come along—we don't have much time."

"No."

"What?" Owden dropped down from the ceiling and started to push the door open

Vangerdahast caught him by the arm and pulled him back. "Princess? Is something wrong?"

"I don't want you to see me like this," came the reply. "You can't help me, so leave me alone. I command it."

"You know I can't do that."

Vangerdahast pushed the door open and saw a dark figure crouching in the darkness, staring up at him with red-tinged eyes and a slender face framed by a cascade of jet-black hair. So harsh were the features—the sharp cheeks, the dagger-blade nose, the beestung mouth— that it took the wizard a moment to recognize them as Tanalasta's. Even then, he could not help bringing his wand up between them.

The princess spun away, revealing a pair of small, fan-like wings running alongside her spine. "I warned you! Now leave me to the fate I deserve."

Owden was far faster to recover than Vangerdahast. He pushed the wand aside and floated into the cell.

"You don't deserve this." The priest spread his arms and reached to embrace the princess. "What makes you think that?"

"Don't touch me!"

Tanalasta leaped away as quickly as a striking snake, then was suddenly squatting in the arrow loop at the back of her cell, naked, trembling, and glaring at them with wild red eyes. Her figure was a gaunt, heinous mockery of the one Vangerdahast had glimpsed at Orc's Pool, and he could not help feeling sick. She crossed her arms in front of herself and looked down.

"If you touch me, I'll absorb your enchantments." She pointed her chin at the slithering floor. "You know what will happen then."

"Yes, we do." Vangerdahast started to unclasp his weathercloak, then recalled what would become of all the magic stored in its pockets and thought better of it. "We can't leave you here. Come what may, you're coming with us."

He jerked the weathercloak off Owden's shoulders and held it out for the princess, but she made no move to accept it.

"Tanalasta Obarskyr! I did not lose an entire company of the king's soldiers to let you become a ghazneth."

Vangerdahast threw the cloak at her. "Now put that on and come along. Whatever becomes of you, it will become of you in Cormyr—even if I must teleport you back to Arabel in a web."

Tanalasta's eyes flared red. "I doubt you are that fast, old man." Despite her words, she slipped the cloak over her nakedness and closed the throat clasp. The sheen immediately faded from the brass clasp, and she stepped down to the floor. The insects and snakes paid her little attention, save to scurry aside or slither across her bare foot. "Lead on, Snoop."

So relieved was the royal magician to have Tanalasta back—in any condition—that he would have liked to grab her and teleport back to Arabel that instant. Attempting such a thing from inside the keep did not seem wise, however. Given the building's magic-absorbing nature, they might well end up trapped inside its walls. Vangerdahast returned to the main room and floated up toward the murky ceiling.

"Do you know if there's a door up here?" he asked. "There must be some way onto the roof."

"No!" Tanalasta barked the word as though it were a command. "I mean, we can't use it. That's *their* door."

She pointed to the far corner of the room, and Vangerdahast soon saw the problem. The door was centered above the stairs, so that the only way to use it was to fly. If he tried to hold Tanalasta long enough to carry her through the opening, she would drain the magic from his flying spell and trap them both.

"We can use the marsh door." Tanalasta passed beneath Vangerdahast and started downstairs. "They won't expect that."

As they descended, Tanalasta's weathercloak began to disintegrate, the fabric turning dingy and dusty, the edges fraying and the seams opening.

Vangerdahast noted the decay and decided it would be prudent to arrive in a secluded part of the palace and gave no more thought to the matter. The excitement of finding the princess was fading, and his headache had returned with a vengeance. His temples pounded and his vision was blurring. His joints ached and his stomach had turned qualmish. By the time they reached the bottom of the stairs, he felt as weak as an old woman.

"Is anyone else feeling sick?" he asked.

"It's the keep," said Tanalasta. "This place holds the ghazneths' evil like a closet—the swarms, the darkness, the plague, all of it."

Owden laid a hand on Vangerdahast's arm. "If you are not averse to a little help from the goddess, I can help."

"Later." Vangerdahast started around the corner. "Let's get out—"

A frightened voice cried out from the next room, "Vangerdahast, help! Are you there?"

Owden withdrew his hand. "That sounded like—"

"Alaphondar!" Vangerdahast finished.

Forgetting his headache for the moment, Vangerdahast flew around the corner and peered across the chamber through the breach in the keep wall, where he saw Alaphondar's gaunt figure standing outside, silhouetted against the bright exterior light. The sage was swatting wasps away and turning in blind circles as he tried to shake off the afterdaze of using his weathercloak's escape pocket. A few dozen paces beyond him, the last remnants of the Royal Excursionary Company lay on the ground writhing beneath black blankets of wasps—easy prey for the orcs and ghazneths rushing across the peninsula toward them.

Vangerdahast pushed Owden toward the breach. "Get him in here!"

As the priest flew to obey, Vangerdahast jammed his glowing wand into one pocket and fished a small square of iron from another. He rubbed the sheet between his palms and began a long incantation.

Owden entered the breach behind Alaphondar, and the wasps scattered instantly. The priest reached down and touched the sage's shoulder. "Here we are, my friend."

Alaphondar turned toward his savior. The sage's venerable face was a mottled mass of wasp stings, already so red and distended that his eyes were swollen completely shut.

"Owden?" Alaphondar asked. Outside, the ghazneths sensed what was happening and launched themselves into the air. "Tell me Vangerdahast is with you!"

"He is, and he's not the only one," Owden answered.

This drew a puzzled frown from Alaphondar, but the expression quickly changed to astonishment as Owden plucked him off the ground and retreated into the keep. By the time Vangerdahast took their place in the breach, the ghazneths were streaking past the remnants of the Royal Excursionary Company and angling down toward the keep. Vangerdahast turned the iron sheet edge-down and dropped it, then spoke the last word of his spell.

The peninsula vanished behind an iron wall, then a series of deafening clangs reverberated through the chamber.

Vangerdahast retreated into the room with his ears still ringing and one eye fixed on the iron wall. The barrier was illuminated inside by a few stray light rays filtering down between its dark surface and the keep wall, but the space was far too tiny for a ghazneth—or so he hoped. When no more sounds came from the other side, he withdrew his glowing wand from his pocket and turned to the others.

"Could they have broken their necks?" Owden asked. "The wall *was* iron."

"Do you really believe we'd be that lucky?" Tanalasta asked. "The wall is also magic. They are only . . . drinking it."

"Tanalasta?" Owden gasped. "What are you doing here?"

"The idea *was* to rescue me." Tanalasta's tone was acid. "You do remember—or have you gone daft?"

Vangerdahast raised his brow. He had heard the princess address him in such a manner often enough, but never Alaphondar. The sage was like a father to her.

Alaphondar's hurt showed even in his swollen face. His white eyebrows tilted inward, and he started to explain himself—then he hesitated.

"My mistake." He looked around the room blindly. "I thought you were with Alusair for some reason. She just told me that she has learned the names of the ghazneths from the glyphs at the other crypts."

"Really?" Vangerdahast asked. Being careful not to look in Tanalasta's direction, he slipped a hand into his pocket and fished for a scrap of silk. "I didn't know you had taught her to read elven glyphs."

Alaphondar nodded. "Oh yes, of course. Post Thaugloraneous glyphs are a standard for well-bred princesses these days."

Tanalasta's red eyes flickered about the chamber, studying each man in turn. Vangerdahast was careful to keep a neutral expression. Alusair wouldn't know a glyph from a rune, and he had a pretty good idea what Alaphondar was trying to tell him.

But Owden was not as quick to appreciate the situation. "Post-Thaugloraneous glyphs?" he asked, incredulous. "As in the dragon Thauglor?"

"A groundsplitter wouldn't understand," growled Vangerdahast. Continuing to look at Alaphondar, he casually drew the silk scrap from his pocket. "Did she say anything else?"

"She wanted to know the words of Alaundo's prophecy." The sage's eyes shifted in Tanalasta's direction. He hesitated a moment, giving Vangerdahast a somewhat more obvious cue than necessary, then said, "You know the one, don't you, Xanthon? 'Seven scourges, five that were, one of the day . . .'"

"Xanthon!" Vangerdahast spun instantly, flinging the silken scrap in the direction of the ghazneth imposter.

Had he not been slowed by a pounding head and aching joints, he might have been quick enough to catch the phantom. As matters were, however, Xanthon was already gone. Vangerdahast's magic web spattered across the floor and wall, encasing dozens of snakes and an untold number of insects.

Alaphondar shrieked in pain, and Vangerdahast swung his glowing wand around to see the imposter clinging to the sage from below, claws sunk deep into the old man's flanks. The extra weight was slowly dragging both Alaphondar and Owden down toward the poisonous tangle on the floor, but Xanthon was not content to wait for his swarms to finish the job. He drew his head back and stretched up to bite Alaphondar's neck.

Vangerdahast leveled his wand at Xanthon's temple and uttered his command word. There was a deafening crack and a blinding flash, then the thud of a body slamming into a wall. Still blinking the blindness out of his eyes, the wizard reached out and caught Owden by the back of the cloak.

"Are you still flying?" he asked.

"For now," came the reply.

As Vangerdahast's vision cleared, he saw that his lightning bolt had knocked Xanthon into the morass of sticky filaments strewn across the far side of the room. The imposter hung sideways on the wall, struggling against his bonds and spewing foul curses on Azoun's name. He still bore a faint resemblance to Tanalasta, but the illusion was no longer strong. The ghazneth had suffered no damage, of course, and the sticky filaments of web were fast growing translucent, but he would remain trapped for at least a few moments.

Vangerdahast turned to check on Alaphondar. The old sage hung limp but breathing in Owden's arms, the long gashes in his flank already puffy and red with purulence. The wizard laid a gentle hand on his friend's arm.

"Tanalasta is safe?"

"For now," Alaphondar replied. "She is with Alusair."

"You are sure?"

When the sage nodded, Vangerdahast drew his iron dagger and looked back to Xanthon. The phantom's eyes turned orange with fear, and he began to struggle even more fiercely than before. One arm came free, and he began to hack at the web with the sharp talons at the ends of his fingers.

"Not this time, traitor," hissed Vangerdahast. "Now you pay."

The royal magician uttered a quick incantation, then hurled his iron dagger across the room. The weapon took Xanthon square in the chest, splitting the sternum and sinking to the hilt. The ghazneth thrashed about madly, shrieking in anguish and trying to jerk free of the web. When the struggle continued for several moments with no sign of abating, Vangerdahast realized he would have to help matters along. Already, Xanthon had torn his back and one leg free.

The wizard passed his glowing wand to Owden, then reached for the priest's weapon belt. "I need a hammer. Let me borrow your mace."

That was enough for Xanthon. He plucked the iron dagger from his chest and began to slash, hacking at his own flesh in his haste to escape. Vangerdahast fumbled frantically with Owden's mace, struggling to free the weapon and pull it past Alaphondar's groaning form. By the time he had the head loose, Xanthon was standing upright on the floor, black blood pouring from the gaping hole in his chest.

The phantom hurled the iron dagger at Vangerdahast, then turned and fled through the door. Only the wizard's magic shielding kept the knife from opening his skull.

Vangerdahast cursed, then caught Owden's eye and glanced at Alaphondar. "Can you save him?"

Owden scowled, clearly insulted by the question. "Of course, but I will need a safe place to work—and for him to rest."

"Then I will give you one." Leaving Owden's mace hanging half out of its belt ring, Vangerdahast reached into Alaphondar's weathercloak. "Pardon me, my friend."

He grabbed a pocket by the outside lining and tore it free, then held the resulting pouch in the air. Keeping one eye on the door lest Xanthon return, he spread the pocket and spoke a long incantation. When he finished, the pocket mouth expanded to the size of a trap door. Vangerdahast released the pouch, and it continued to hover in the air.

"You can take refuge in there. Pull the mouth in after you and no one can touch you—they won't even know you're there." Vangerdahast drew the mace from Owden's belt. "And don't come out until you hear me calling—even if it seems like tendays. Time will be strange inside, so it may be that only a matter of seconds has passed out here."

Owden glanced at his mace and cocked a brow. "And what are you going to do?"

"Avenge a betrayal," Vangerdahast said. "And stop a scourge."

"No!" Alaphondar's voice was barely a whisper. "The door no man can close . . . you'll open it!"

"It appears Xanthon has already opened that door." Vangerdahast looked away, peering through the chamber's profane darkness into the adjacent passageway. "And I am going to slam it in his face."

21

he sliver rotated in Vangerdahast's palm, pointing around the corner into the swarming darkness of the lower keep. The wizard floated to the far wall to peer into the next section of corridor. When he found nothing lurking in ambush except more snakes and insects, he eased forward and continued down the passageway. With three different spells shielding him from harm, he was not overly concerned about being attacked—but a wise hunter treated his prey with respect.

The corridor continued past another half a dozen doors, all as rotten and slime-caked as the first. The air was warmer and more fetid than ever, though thankfully it no longer made the royal magician feel quite so ill. Before parting ways, Owden had insisted on casting a few spells of his own, calling upon Chauntea to guard the wizard against the disease, poison, and evil of the place. To Vangerdahast's surprise, his strength had quickly returned, and even the foul yellow fume that had started to flow through the corridors seemed to swirl away from him as it passed. This small service could not make him embrace Tanalasta's royal temple, of course—but he would not be above saying a prayer or two of thanks when everyone returned to Suzail.

As Vangerdahast approached the next corner, the sliver in his palm stood on end. This perplexed him, until he rounded the bend and the tiny piece of wood fell flat again, then swiveled around to point back into the corner. The wizard turned around and drifted lower to inspect the area. He had traded his glowing wand for Alaphondar's commander's ring so his hands would be free to fight, but the ring's light was even more limited than that of his wand. He•had to descend to within an arm's length of the floor before he noticed the ribbons of yellow fume spiraling down through a tangle of red-banded snakes.

Vangerdahast pressed his borrowed mace to the floor. There was a slight shimmering and a momentary resistance, then the head of the weapon passed out of sight. Vangerdahast frowned, wondering if this was the "marsh door" Xanthon had referred to while impersonating Tanalasta. Clearly, the ghazneth had been trying to lure his "rescuers" into some sort of trap, and the royal magician suspected that had been the purpose of the entire band for some time now—at least since his return from Arabel.

But why? The reason seemed painfully obvious: Tanalasta's royal religion was the seventh scourge of Alaundo's prophecy, "the one that will be," and only Vangerdahast could stop the princess from opening the "door no man could close." Determined to be rid of the only one who could stop them, the ghazneths had lured the wizard into an ambush. The explanation made perfect sense to the royal magician, and he was determined that the ghazneths would never have a chance to make the princess one of their own.

Vangerdahast pulled the mace out of the floor and jammed it into his belt, then plucked an apple seed from his cloak pocket and let it fall. As it dropped, he made a quick twirling motion and spoke a few words of magic. A small whirlpool formed in the shimmering floor, then abruptly opened into a dark, man-sized hole. Vangerdahast selected a wand from inside his cloak, flung a quick firebolt through the opening to discourage thoughts of a surprise attack, and followed the flames down into the darkness.

The firebolt seemed to plummet forever, growing steadily smaller as it streaked away. Though Vangerdahast never touched any walls, he had the sense of descending a narrow shaft into a hot, murky depth, an impression compounded by the yellow fume swirling so closely around him. Finally, when the firebolt had shrunk to a mere thumbnail of light, it hit bottom and fanned out into a crimson disk, briefly illuminating a lopsided plaza ringed by walls of rough-stacked stone and little square tunnel mouths.

With the sliver still standing in his palm, Vangerdahast continued his descent until the mordant odor of his own fire spell came faintly to his nostrils and the yellow fume started to swirl away into the darkness. He stopped and found himself hovering a few feet above a smoking mud flat, the *plink-plink* of dripping water echoing through a constant insect drone. Above his head, there seemed to be nothing but featureless darkness, with no sign of the shaft through which he had descended. He reached up and touched something spongy. When he pushed, it gave way beneath his hand, not quite water and too resilient to be mud, yet far more solid than the passage he had come down.

"There are many ways to enter, but only one way to leave," hissed Xanthon Cormaeril, sounding as angry as he did pained, "but why worry? Surely a great wizard like you can find a way home!"

Vangerdahast spun toward the voice and saw a coarse net flying into the tiny radius of his light spell. He reacted instantly, lowering his wand and speaking the command word. The fire bolt flashed through the net and exploded against the chest of a dark silhouette, hurling the figure into a wall of stacked stone. A tremendous clattering filled the chamber, then the remains of the net entangled the wizard, bouncing him off the ceiling and dragging him down to rebound off a wall.

Vangerdahast landed face down on the muddy floor, bent backward with his feet resting against a wall behind him—a rather painful position for a man of his age. He wasted no time rolling out of it, then pushed his wand through the net and swiveled around, spraying fire.

The flames missed Xanthon, but they did illuminate the entire plaza. It was a muddy circle no more than ten paces across, full of humming insects and ringed by the ramshackle houses of a long-abandoned goblin warren. The compact buildings presented a nearly solid facade of stacked stone, broken only by crooked rows of squinting windows and tilted doorways no higher than a man's belt. In the heart of the plaza lay a shallow depression filled with stagnant water.

As the glow of Vangerdahast's fire bolts began to fade, Xanthon rose from the rubble of a demolished building and peered over the jagged remains of a wall. All semblance to Tanalasta had vanished completely. Xanthon's face had become a skeletal monstrosity, with an arrow-shaped nose and a slender tuft of coarse beard nearly hidden beneath his aura of flying insects. The dagger wound Vangerdahast had inflicted earlier was barely visible, a puffy-edged slit whose edges had already closed.

"Awfully free with that magic, aren't you old fellow?" Xanthon called.

Vangerdahast leveled his wand and sent another fire bolt streaking across plaza. Xanthon raised his hand and caught the bolt in his palm, disappearing behind the wall as the impact spun him around.

Vangerdahast drew his iron dagger and began to slice at the net and finally noticed that the thing had been made of living snakes. Though their fangs were incapable of penetrating his protection magic, the survivors were striking at him madly. He could not help crying out in shock.

Across the plaza, Xanthon stepped out of the ruins, Vangerdahast's dying fire bolt displayed in the palm of his hand. "You *do* know this is ambrosia to me?"

Xanthon tipped his head back and poured the rest of the fire into his mouth. Vangerdahast gave up slashing at the net and pushed off the ground, praying this place did not absorb magic as did the keep. Much to his relief, he rose into the air and bounced lightly off the ceiling.

"Magic will not save you, old fool," Xanthon said, allowing a stream of excess fire to spill down his chin. "Come down here, and we will settle this like men."

"One of us is no longer a man. One of us is a traitor . . . and not only to his country."

Xanthon shrugged. "I am what the king made me."

The ghazneth started forward. Vangerdahast raised his iron dagger and, blood boiling in anger, began the enchantment that would send it streaking into the traitor's eye.

This time, Xanthon was ready for him. The ghazneth dived into one of the little tunnels opening off the plaza and disappeared, leaving the wizard with no target. The royal magician let the incantation trail off half-finished, then cursed profanely. He could use this spell only three times a day, and he had just wasted a casting.

Vangerdahast pulled the mace from his belt and spent the next quarter hour circling the plaza, waiting for Xanthon to return. Finally, he realized the ghazneth's earlier challenge had been an empty taunt and grew more confident about his chances of success. The traitor was frightened, or he would have returned to finish the battle. The wizard spent another quarter hour finding the sliver he had been using to track his prey, then floated down and followed it into the same cockeyed passage through which the phantom had fled.

The portal led into the confines of a goblin street—a crooked little tunnel not much wider than Vangerdahast's shoulders and barely half his height. He had to float through the passage head-first, ribbons of yellow fume streaming past so thick he could see only a few paces ahead. The floor stank of mildew and mud, and the walls resonated with scurrying insects. The wizard tried not to think about the red stuff that dangled down from the ceiling and brushed over his back.

Vangerdahast pursued his quarry around a dozen corners and past a hundred cockeyed doorways, then came to another plaza and realized he did not need to watch his sliver quite so carefully. Unable to fly, Xanthon was leaving a clear trail in the mud. Moreover, some unfelt breeze was drawing the yellow fume through a particular set of tunnels, and the ghazneth seemed to be following the fume. The wizard put the sliver away and crossed the circle into the next passage, holding a wand of repulsion in one hand and his iron dagger in the other.

Xanthon tried to ambush him three plazas later, dropping off a wall to land on Vangerdahast's back as he exited a tunnel. The wizard simply touched the tip of his wand to the ghazneth's flank and sent him flying, then followed him into the next tunnel. After that, the wizard consulted his magic sliver before entering a plaza. Twice, he turned the tables on his foe, sneaking around to attack from behind. The second time, he landed a bone-crushing blow with his borrowed mace.

Xanthon barely managed to scuttle into the next tunnel. After that, Vangerdahast was able to remain within earshot of his quarry, following the ghazneth by the slurping sounds he made crawling through the muddy passages. As the chase continued, the sound grew slower and less steady. Finally, it ceased altogether, and when the wizard stopped to consult his magic sliver, the ghazneth's arm came snaking out of a nearby door and snatched the wand of repulsion from his hand.

Vangerdahast was so startled that he flew backward half a dozen paces. By the time he finally comprehended that the ghazneth was not attacking, Xanthon was slurping down the tunnel again, now moving faster. The wizard found his wand a few hundred paces later, lying dull and brittle in the mud. All the magic was gone, and the phantom was no longer close enough to hear.

After that, the wizard left his magic tucked safely inside his cloak, and the chase continued. Eventually, Vangerdahast had to renew his flying spell, then his protection enchantments, and he realized the hunt was turning into a trek. He almost decided to give up and teleport back to the mud keep, but he could not allow Xanthon to go unpunished for such a vile betrayal.

The pursuit continued until Xanthon began to tire again and Vangerdahast began to hear slurping steps once more. Determined not to make the same mistake twice, the wizard took the initiative and streaked up the passage behind the crawling phantom. He slammed down on its back and reached around to draw his iron dagger across its throat.

As weary as Xanthon was, he was still far faster than the royal magician. He clamped down on Vangerdahast's arm and dropped face first into the mud, driving the dagger deep into his own collar, but sparing himself the fatal slash across the throat.

A strange tingling came over Vangerdahast as the magic began to leave his protective enchantments. He grabbed Xanthon's hair and tried to pull the traitor's head up to free his arm, but his strength was no match for a ghazneth's. A pair of jaws closed around his forearm, then clamped down. The phantom's teeth could not penetrate his protective spells, but the wizard knew that would change once his spells were drained.

Vangerdahast rolled to the side, relieving some of the strain on his trapped arm and giving himself room to maneuver. He slipped his hand into his cloak and grabbed a small rod from a pocket, then pressed the tip to the ghazneth's head and spoke a single mystic word.

A silent flash of golden magic filled the air, momentarily blinding Vangerdahast and hurling him against the tunnel wall. He felt the ghazneth go slack and jerked his arm loose, opening a long gash along Xanthon's collarbone as he ripped the iron dagger free. Praying that his flying spell had enough magic to hold one more instant, he pushed himself up to the ceiling.

Still trying to shake the magic from his vision, Xanthon rolled onto his back, his arms weaving a black blur as he lashed out blindly mere inches under Vangerdahast's nose. The phantom's new wounds were already beginning to heal—thanks, no doubt, to the glut of magic he had just absorbed. Vangerdahast's protective enchantments were fading fast and his flying spell would soon follow, and he would not be able to renew those particular spells until he had rested and studied his spellbook. Realizing he had lost all hope of defeating the phantom in physical combat,

Vangerdahast decided the time had come to declare wisdom the better part of valor.

He closed his eyes and brought to mind an image of the courtyard in the Arabellan Palace. Tomorrow, he would return for Alaphondar and Owden, then resume his hunt with a fresh company of Purple Dragons. It was sometimes possible to delay the King's Justice, but never to escape it—not when the royal magician had decided it was his business to dispense it. A little growl of astonishment suggested that Xanthon's vision had finally cleared, and Vangerdahast cast his teleport spell.

He experienced that familiar sensation of timeless falling, then felt something soft and squishy around his boot soles. The air seemed remarkably stale and musty, and he had a terrible suspicion that he knew the source of that irritating drone in his ears. The wizard shook his head clear and found himself standing in a muddy depression, looking across a dark, stagnant pool of water toward the shadowy facade of a ramshackle goblin building. He thought for a moment he had returned to the same plaza through which he had entered the abandoned city, but a quick circuit of the area revealed no sign of the wall through which he had blasted Xanthon. The royal magician was lost.

"Many ways to enter, but only one to leave." The ghazneth's voice rasped out from all the tunnels ringing the plaza, as soft and sibilant as a snake's hiss. "It is you or me, old fool . . . and now I am the hunter."

* * * * *

From somewhere inside the marble keep came a muted thud, then the iron-clad gate swirled open, spinning little whirlpools into the fetid water and sweeping aside the bloated corpses of half a dozen

Troy Denning

Purple Dragons. The smell of mildew and stale stone filled Tanalasta's nostrils, giving rise to an unexpected urge to vomit. The need had been coming over her at the oddest times for the last two days—when they found Alaphondar's horse tethered behind the hill, for instance, but not when they waded into a marsh full of stinking corpses. The princess was beginning to think that lying to Alusair had affected her nerves more than she realized. Despite the return of the fever, no one else in the company seemed to be experiencing such odd bouts of queasiness.

Alusair appeared in the gateway, standing atop a short flight of black stairs and silhouetted in gleaming silver against the tower's murky interior. "Nothing . . . they're not in here."

"Empty?" Tanalasta slapped Alaphondar's broken spyglass against the surface of the marsh, then said, "None of this makes any sense."

They had found the spyglass on a boulder not far from Alaphondar's hungry horse, the broken halves lying neatly side-by-side. It appeared the sage had been watching the keep, which stood not quite a mile from shore, half sunken in the marsh and surrounded by the floating corpses of Vangerdahast's rescue company. A lengthy examination of the surrounding area had produced no hint of what killed them. Almost as puzzling, the search had failed to produce the bodies of either Vangerdahast, Alaphondar, or Owden. It was as if the trio had simply vanished.

Tanalasta climbed the stairs into the keep and found the mossy, dank place she had expected, with a cramped staircase ascending to the left and a narrow corridor turning a corner to the right. There were plenty of insects and more than a few snakes, but no more than normal in such a place, and none that appeared particularly dangerous.

Alusair's men were everywhere, banging on walls and inspecting floors for secret passages.

Tanalasta started down the hallway to the right.

Alusair followed close behind, her armor clanking as she brushed against the stone walls. "There's a common chamber and seven sleeping cells upstairs, and half a dozen storage rooms on this floor. We haven't been able to find a dungeon entrance—but it would probably be flooded anyway."

Tanalasta rounded the corner and peered into the first room. Warm afternoon light poured through a large, windowlike breach in the opposite wall. The edges were smooth with age and draped with moss. Not looking at her sister, and trying to keep her voice casual, Tanalasta asked, "Any sign of Rowen?"

"Rowen can take care of himself." Though Alusair's tone was neutral, she clapped Tanalasta's shoulder briefly and said, "He's probably waiting for us at Goblin Mountain with Vangerdahast and Alaphondar."

"If Vangerdahast is there, I doubt Rowen still is," Tanalasta remarked wryly.

As the princess turned away from the room, a sharp hiss sounded behind her.

"Tanalasta?" called a familiar voice.

Tanalasta spun back toward the room only to find her sister already charging through the door, sword in hand.

"Name yourself!" demanded Alusair.

Tanalasta rounded the corner to find her sister standing in the center of the room, reaching up to press the tip of her blade to a disembodied head protruding from a tiny circle of darkness near the ceiling. It was such an odd sight that it took a moment for Tanalasta to recognize the face as that of Owden Foley.

Owden's eyes remained fixed on the tip of Alusair's sword. "H-harvestmaster Owden F-foley, at your s-service."

Tanalasta grabbed Alusair's arm. "He's a friend!"

Alusair lowered her sword, but continued to eye the priest suspiciously. Tanalasta stepped forward, placing herself between the two, and Owden finally exhaled in relief.

"Thank you, my dear." He smiled at Tanalasta, then tipped his chin to Alusair. "I'm honored to make your acquaintance, Princess Alusair. Please consider me at your service."

Owden pushed an arm out of the floating circle and turned his palm up. Alusair eyed the disembodied limb coldly and did not offer her hand.

"What, exactly, *are* you?" she demanded.

Owden flushed and looked down, then finally seemed to realize what he must look like. "Forgive me! Vangerdahast told us to wait inside until he returned."

The black circle behind Owden's head suddenly grew larger, revealing itself to be the interior of a large pocket floating in midair. The priest withdrew into the interior, then reappeared feet-first and dropped to the floor. He bowed again and turned to Tanalasta.

"By the seed, it is good to see you again!" He embraced her warmly, then looked past her into the hallway. "Where is the old grouch?"

"We were hoping you could tell us."

Owden's expression fell. "He went after Xanthon Cormaeril, to stop him from opening Alaundo's door."

"How long ago?" Alusair demanded.

Owden shrugged, gesturing vaguely at the dark pouch hanging above his head. "A few minutes after Alaphondar contacted Tanalasta."

The two sisters exchanged worried glances, then Tanalasta said, "Two days ago."

"What now?" asked Alusair.

"Assume he is lost, and hope that we are wrong," said a familiar voice. A moment later, Alaphondar's old head appeared in the mouth of the floating pouch. His eyes were sunken and weary, his skin as pale as alabaster. "What other choice is there? You have read my note."

"Note?" Tanalasta asked.

"In the tube." He gestured at the spyglass. "Telling whoever found it to awaken the Sleeping Sword."

"There was no note." Tanalasta pulled the two pieces of the spyglass apart. "This was how we found it."

Alusair took the two halves of the tube from Tanalasta and inspected them. "At least we know what happened to Rowen. This was hacked open with a sword."

"And this Rowen knows where to find the Sleeping Sword?" asked Alaphondar.

Alusair cocked an eyebrow at Tanalasta, who shook her head. "I had no reason to mention it."

"Then he will be on his way to inform your father," sighed Alaphondar. "And with Vangerdahast lost, the delay could well mean Cormyr's doom. We must inform the king."

The sage's withered hand appeared briefly, then reached for his throat clasp.

"Alaphondar, wait!" Tanalasta said, realizing her deception would be revealed if the sage conversed with the king. "I reported your fears to His Majesty two days ago."

"And did he say he would awaken the Sleeping Sword?" asked Alaphondar.

Tanalasta's stomach sank, for she knew what the sage would say when she answered—and also that there was too much at stake to try to talk him out of it. "No, not exactly."

"Then we must make certain."

Alusair barked a handful of commands out the door, ordering to company to prepare itself in case the sending drew a ghazneth, then looked back to Alaphondar.

355

"Contact the queen instead of the king," Alusair said. "She'll know his plans, and we don't want to draw ghazneths to him if he's already in the Stonelands. If he hasn't left already, tell her I can take your horse and be there in a day."

Tanalasta watched Alaphondar's eyes close, then, cringing inwardly, turned to her sister. "Alusair, there is something I should tell you."

Alusair waved her off. "Not now, Tanalasta. This is important."

"So is this." Tanalasta steeled herself for the coming storm. "I may have given you the wrong impression—"

"Later!"

Alusair stepped away, precluding any further attempts to admit the truth, and Alaphondar opened his eyes a moment later.

"The queen assures us that King Azoun will reach the Sleeping Sword first." The sage turned to Alusair looking rather confused. "She was quite upset. She seemed to think you should be somewhere near Goblin Mountain by now."

"Goblin Mountain? Why would she think that? The king himself told us to investigate . . ." Alusair let the sentence trail off and whirled on Tanalasta, her face turning white with anger. "I'll cut out your tongue, you lying harlot!"

* * * * *

Vangerdahast snapped awake without the pleasure of even a moment's confusion about his whereabouts. He knew the awful truth as soon as he heard the humming swarms and smelled the dank air. His emergency spellbook lay opened to the last spell he had been studying, a powerful wind enchantment he had been hoping to use to clear the insects away so he could sleep in peace. Apparently, it had been unnecessary.

The wizard had no way to tell how long he had slept, but judging by his stiff joints and the cold ache in his bones, it had been a good while. His stomach was growling with hunger and he was almost thirsty enough to drink the stagnant swill in the center of the plaza, but at least the sleep had rejuvenated him mentally. No longer did he feel as dispirited or confused as he had after attempting to return to Arabel, and he had even begun to develop a few theories about how to find his way home. He had either followed Xanthon into a separate plane or through some sort of magic-dampening barrier that prevented his teleport spell from folding space. All he had to do was figure out which, then he could start work on the problem of determining either where he was, or how to bypass the barrier.

And failing that, he always had his ring of wishes to call upon—but wishes were tricky spells to use, and he had learned through bitter experience that it was wiser to avoid them in all but the most controlled of circumstances. If a simple teleport spell would not work down here, he could only imagine what might happen if he attempted to use a wish.

Vangerdahast closed his spellbook and returned it to his weathercloak, then checked his iron weapons and hoisted his stiff body to its feet. As he rose, an unexpected clatter sounded from the other side of the wall against which he had been leaning. He jumped in fright and spun around to see a pair of red eyes peering out through a cockeyed goblin window.

"All rested?" hissed Xanthon.

Vangerdahast forgot about his aching bones and dashed across the plaza, hurling himself headlong into the nearest tunnel. He landed flat on his belly and slid a good five paces on the muddy floor, then spun instantly onto his back. The wizard continued to squirm down the passage as fast as his old legs could propel his ample weight, at the same time hurling a magic blast high and well behind him.

The ceiling collapsed with a deafening crash, filling the tunnel with a black cloud of billowing dust. Vangerdahast started to cough, then caught himself and managed to cast a flying spell before he broke into a fit of hacking. He pushed himself off the ground and flew down the narrow corridor as fast as he dared without his shielding spells. It did not even occur to him until the next plaza that had there been any real danger, he would already have been dead.

One of the last things Vangerdahast had done when he felt himself nodding off last night—or whenever it had been—was to cast a simple enchantment to protect himself from evil, prolonging its duration with a couple of extension spells. He had been counting on the simple enchantment to keep his foe at bay long enough for him to awaken and escape, but the spell had apparently prevented Xanthon from touching him at all, and even a ghazneth could not drain what they could not touch.

Beginning to see how he might defeat the phantom, Vangerdahast stopped to cast another spell to make the protection permanent. No sooner had he fetched the ingredients from his cloak pocket, however, than he heard Xanthon sloshing toward him. The wizard put the ingredients away and fled into another tunnel.

"Wait!" Xanthon called. "We have something to—"

Vangerdahast blasted the ceiling down as he had before, drowning out the ghazneth's protest in midsentence. He started down the passage toward the next plaza.

Fifty paces later, Xanthon appeared in the intersection ahead. He rolled to his haunches and raised his clawed hands in a grotesque mockery of a truce sign.

"Hold your attack and hear me out. We can always resume fighting in a minute."

"You have nothing to say I would be interested in hearing." Despite his retort, Vangerdahast made no move to attack or flee; instead, he quietly began to move his fingers through the gestures for a prismatic spray. "I doubt you are here to yield to the king's justice."

"Hardly—and we'll have none of that." Xanthon waved a talon at the magician's moving fingers, then waited until the magician ceased his gestures. "I was thinking of something quite the opposite."

"Me, surrender to you?" Vangerdahast scoffed. "I thought Boldovar was the mad one."

This actually drew a smile from Xanthon. "Actually, it wouldn't be surrender. We have need of a seventh, and Luthax claims—"

"Luthax?" Vangerdahast gasped. Luthax had been an early castellan of the War Wizards of Cormyr—and the only high-ranking member of the brotherhood to ever betray the kingdom. "You have raised him?"

"*Me?*" Xanthon chuckled. "Hardly. The master . . . let us say I am but a tool."

"Of what?"

Xanthon rolled his eyes. "You know the prophecy, 'Seven scourges—five long gone, one of the day, one soon to come . . .' Do I really have to spell it out?"

"And you want *me?*" Unable to believe what he was hearing, Vangerdahast glanced over each of his shoulders in turn. This whole conversation had to be some unbalanced attempt to divert his attention. "This is an insult."

Xanthon shrugged. "I'd rather kill you, but . . . if you say no, there'll be someone else. There is no shortage of traitors to Cormyr—you've seen to that."

"Traitor? Me?" Vangerdahast nearly reached for a wand, but forced himself to contain his anger. There was only one explanation for Xanthon's behavior; he was attempting to goad Vangerdahast into a rash act. "What happened to 'you or me, old fool'?"

"You're forgetting 'many ways to enter, only one to leave,'" Xanthon replied. "You had to see how hopeless it is. There's only one way out of here—and that's with us."

"Or past your dead body!" Vangerdahast hissed, no longer able to stand the insults to his integrity. "You have my answer."

The wizard retreated down the tunnel, though only because he did not dare attack until he had cast the rest of his shielding magic. Assaulting the ghazneth would dispel the enchantment protecting him from evil, and despite his anger, he remained determined to emerge from this battle alive. When he reached the previous intersection, he picked a tunnel at random and streaked into it at top speed. It hardly mattered to him which direction he fled. He was lost no matter what way he turned.

But it mattered to Xanthon. The ghazneth began to stay close enough for Vangerdahast to hear at all times, yet just beyond the range of the wizard's glowing ring. Every so often, the phantom would emerge in an intersection to taunt Vangerdahast with saccharin pleas to reconsider. The wizard never bothered to reply. He simply retreated to the previous intersection and tried another path. Xanthon was careful to keep him moving, so that he would have no time to stop and cast spells, and to keep him away from plazas and other places where he would have room to fight with anything but magic.

Vangerdahast tried several times to slow his pursuer by bringing the ceiling down on his head, but Xanthon always sensed these ambushes and rushed ahead to absorb the spell. The sorcerer soon realized he was only feeding his enemy's magic thirst and put his wands away, concentrating instead on raising his shielding spells. He lost two enchantments to interruption—one defending him from poison and the other from blunt attacks—but he did manage to cast the spell that protected him from fang and claw. He considered it a major victory.

Eventually, the protection from evil spell expired. Xanthon began to grow more bold, sometimes attempting to ambush Vangerdahast as he passed through intersections, sometimes rushing up from behind to repeat his 'invitation.' The wizard resisted the temptation to renew the spell. He could sense the ghazneth's growing excitement and knew the battle was about to come to a head. When that happened, he would need a couple of surprises to win the advantage.

Vangerdahast sensed his chance when the cramped corridors finally intersected a true goblin boulevard, a muddy passage broad enough to hold three men abreast and fully twelve feet high—as the wizard discovered when he climbed skyward and suddenly smashed into the formless black ceiling. Xanthon paused at the mouth of one of the smaller tunnels and glared up at the royal magician with ill-concealed hatred.

"Hide up there as long as you wish," he hissed. "When you begin to starve, perhaps you will join us."

"I'm afraid I'm going to disappoint you." Vangerdahast began to fish through his weathercloak. "I was thinking the time had come to punish your treason."

The wizard pulled a pinch of powdered iron from his pocket and sprinkled it over his own head, at the same time uttering his spell. Xanthon's eyes flared scarlet, then he withdrew into the tunnel, hissing and spraying a cloud of droning wasps out into the boulevard. The wizard chuckled and descended to the ground to renew his protection from evil spell—the enchantment required sprinkling a circle of powdered silver on the ground—then added a couple of extensions for good measure and shot into the tunnel after Xanthon. It was his turn to be the hunter.

Xanthon tried twice early in the chase to leap on Vangerdahast and drain the magic from his protective enchantments. Each time, the phantom was thwarted by the protection from evil spell, which prevented him from touching the wizard at all. Vangerdahast stayed close on his quarry's tail, keeping up a constant patter about punishing him for his betrayals. Within the space of half an hour, Xanthon was reduced to mere fleeing. An hour after that, he was beginning to stumble. He grew desperate and tried to slow his pursuer with insect swarms and snake nets, but this took energy, and the wizard simply brushed them aside with a wave of the appropriate wand.

Finally, Xanthon returned to the goblin boulevard and sprinted straight down the middle in a desperate attempt to simply outrun Vangerdahast. The strategy might have worked, had the parkway not fed into a huge plaza in the middle of the city. The circle was by far the grandest in the city, surrounded by crookedly built edifices with marble pillars and sandstone porticos that had ceilings nearly eight feet high.

In the center of this plaza lay a grand pool, fully five paces across and rimmed in a broad band of golden sand. It was filled with black, shimmering water so stagnant that when Xanthon ran onto it, he did not even sink. The surface merely rippled like obsidian jelly, and his feet stuck to the surface as soon as they touched it. Two paces later, he came to a dead halt in the center of the basin.

Vangerdahast did not even slow down as he passed. He simply pulled Owden's mace from his belt and swooped down to slam it into the back of the ghazneth's head. There was a crack and a spray of dark blood. Xanthon pitched forward onto his knees.

Vangerdahast passed over the pool's golden rim and wheeled around to find his foe still kneeling in the center. Xanthon's skull had been half-shattered, with a halo of jagged black bone protruding up at wild angles and one eye dangling out on his cheek and his dark lip twisted into a smug sneer.

"Last chance," said Xanthon. "If you let me go, you can change your mind."

"What makes you think I'd ever let you go?" Vangerdahast streaked down for another strike.

Xanthon smiled and dived forward, disappearing into the tar headfirst. Vangerdahast managed to knock one foot off at the ankle as the phantom's legs vanished from sight, then the surface of the dark pool returned to its syrupy tranquility.

Vangerdahast circled around and considered the dark pool for a moment, more angered by Xanthon's escape than astonished by it. He had already seen the ghazneth vanish through a stone floor, so he supposed he should not be surprised when the creature disappeared into a pool of tar.

Vangerdahast did not even consider letting the phantom go. Xanthon Cormaeril was a traitor of the vilest kind, and, almost as importantly, he was the royal magician's best chance to find his way back to Cormyr before the scourges ruined it. He fished two rings from his weather-cloak, one to let him breathe water—if that was what the black stuff was—and the other to allow him free movement, then streaked headlong toward the center of the pool.

The wizard was just inches above the surface when a pearly skin of magic appeared over the dark liquid. He barely had time to tuck his chin and twist away before he slammed into it. A terrific jolt shot up his spine, filling him with anguish from neck to knees, and he careened back into the air.

Vangerdahast brought himself slowly under control, then took a moment to shake the shock from his head and inspect himself. The impact had left his old body shaken and sore, but relatively unscathed, aside from one slightly separated shoulder. He circled back to the pool and descended more slowly.

When he came to within a foot of the water, the pearly barrier appeared again—no doubt some sort of enchantment designed to repel beings of honorable intents and loyal persuasions.

"It won't be that easy, Xanthon! Do you hear me?" Vangerdahast was already summoning to mind the words that would dispel the magical barrier. "I'm coming for you!"

* * * * *

After three solid days in the saddle, Azoun could not quite believe his eyes when he rode into the narrow confines of Scimitar Canyon and found a trailworn stallion standing in the open entrance of the secret cavern of the Sleeping Sword. The big horse was glassy-eyed and haggard from many days on the trail, and he was still covered with foam from a hard ride that had left him barely able to stand, but the king would have recognized the noble beast anywhere.

"Cadimus!"

Azoun reined his own hard-ridden mount to a stop, then leaped out of the saddle, passed his reins to one of his weary dragoneer bodyguards, and rushed up to the royal magician's horse.

"How have you been old boy?" He patted the stallion fondly on the neck.

Cadimus nickered softly, then swung his nose around as though to point to his saddle. There was blood on it—a lot of blood, mostly brown and crusted, but some new enough that it was still sticky and red.

"Kuceon!" Azoun cried, yelling for one of Owden Foley's young priestesses. "Come quickly!"

The girl trotted her horse to the head of the company and slipped from the saddle while the beast was still moving. Leaving the reins for someone else to collect, she came to Azoun's side and touched her fingers to the bloody saddle.

"A seeping wound. Probably purulent, no doubt serious."

The king started to ask if the victim could have cast a teleport spell, then realized that Vangerdahast would never have done such a thing from this particular location—not with the ghazneths at large. With a sinking heart, he selected a dozen dragoneers and two war wizards to accompany them into the cavern, then motioned for a man to strike the torches they had brought along to light their way. He was tempted just to slip on a Purple Dragon commander's ring and call upon its magical light, but they had spent the last three days riding night and day precisely because he did not want to use any magic that might lead the scourges to the Sleeping Sword. Whatever lay inside, it could wait long enough to strike a fire.

Once the first torch was lit, the king took it and led the way around a recently-moved boulder into the narrow mouth of the cavern. The air reeked of rot and decay, and

Azoun knew before he had taken his third step that something terrible had become of the Lords Who Sleep.

"Vangerdahast?" he called.

No answer came, and they rounded the corner into the main chamber of Scimitar Cave.

The place looked like any other crypt he had ever seen, full of moldering bones and shards of rusty armor and tattered bits of cloth—all that remained of five hundred valiant knights who had volunteered to lay in hibernation against the time when they were needed. Only one piece of equipment, the tattered and bloody cloak of a Royal Scout, lay in anything resembling one piece.

"Sire!" gasped Kuceon. She seemed unable to say any more than that.

Conscious of the effect his reaction would have on those around him, Azoun bit back his despair and snatched the bloody cape, then turned to the young priestess at his side.

"See to it that these men have a proper burial," he said. "Though they never fought, they were heroes all."

* * * * *

Vangerdahast slowly circled the basin, arms trembling and voice cracking as he waved his hands over the pool's skin of pearly magic. He had not fought a good death match in decades, and now that victory was near, he found himself so excited he could barely twine his fingers through a simple dispel magic spell. Xanthon was hurt badly, or he would never have fled into the pool and risked showing Vangerdahast how to escape the goblin city. The ghazneth was too smart to trap himself, so there had to be a portal hidden beneath the surface. With any luck at all, the other end would open into Cormyr, and it would be there that Vangerdahast would visit the king's justice upon his quarry.

The wizard paused above the center of the basin and spread his hands, repeating his spell's arcane syllables over and over again, calling into play his deepest reserves of magic power. The mystic barrier flickered, hissed, and began to lose its luster, giving Vangerdahast a glimpse into the abyssal darkness of the black waters below. He spoke the incantation one more time and flung his arms wide. The magic skin vanished. The wizard brought his hands together and dived after Xanthon.

A yellow membrane slid across the basin, bringing Vangerdahast's plunge to a crashing halt. A long series of dull pops resonated through his skull, then he rebounded into the air and found himself tumbling pell-mell back toward the ceiling. His neck and shoulders erupted in pain, his hands turned tingly and weak, and the mace began to slip from his grasp.

"By the purple fang!" Vangerdahast cursed.

He willed his numb fingers to close around the hilt of his weapon and slowly spread his limbs, bringing himself back under control—then he noticed the pit of his stomach reverberating to the pulse of a strange rumbling he could not even hear. At first, he took the sensation to be the aftereffects of crashing into the yellow membrane, but he began to feel the vibrations in his bones and teeth and soon recognized them as a powerful rumbling, too deep and sonorous for a human ear to detect.

Vangerdahast felt hollow and sick. He craned his neck upward, expecting the cavern to come crashing down on him even as he looked. The rumble continued to grow, until it finally became an ominous, barely audible growl that reminded him faintly of a purring cat—or of a distant earthquake. He flew up to the ceiling and found his way blocked by the same spongy substance as before. He touched it. It was as still and motionless as the air in a coffin.

Vangerdahast glanced down at the pool. The golden membrane had divided down the center and retracted to opposite rims of the basin, giving the pond a long and vaguely slitlike appearance. The center remained black and as calm as a mirror, so that Vangerdahast could see a reflection of himself hovering up under the ceiling. He looked entirely too haggard, with sunken cheeks and sagging red circles under his eyes. There was something else, too, something he had experienced all too often since stumbling across the ghazneths: fear.

Vangerdahast remained staring at the image until the strange rumbling finally died away. It occurred to him he had not been planning his next move, had not been recovering his energy, or doing anything useful at all. He had simply been hesitating. He shook his head sharply, silently chastising himself for behaving like a frightened recruit. He was the Lord Royal Magician of Cormyr, and lord royal magicians did not let their fear paralyze them.

Vangerdahast twisted his head around, trying to loosen the muscles of his aching neck, then tightened his tingling fingers around the mace. His grip was hardly as strong as he would have liked, but he could probably manage two or three swings before losing the weapon.

In his mind, Vangerdahast pictured Xanthon's gruesome face, then touched the clasp of his weathercloak. To the wizard's great relief, the image raised its brow in surprise.

Using his thought-speech, Vangerdahast asked, *Tell me, what would I have to do?* The wizard had no intention of joining the ghazneths, of course, but he had won battles with smaller lies. *I wouldn't betray Cormyr, but I might join—*

Too late. Xanthon's voice grew more distant. *You've already done it, Old Fool—betrayed and joined.*

Xanthon cackled once, then even his laugh faded, leaving Vangerdahast utterly alone in the darkness of the goblin city. The wizard's heart began to pound like a triphammer, but he fought back his panic and concentrated on his next option. He fixed his gaze on the pool below, trying to see past the black surface into the stygian depths where Xanthon had fled. He tightened his grasp on the mace one more time, then thrust his hand into his weathercloak's escape pocket.

There was that timeless instant of falling, and a moment of merciful afterdaze as Vangerdahast struggled to recall where he was going and where he had come from, then he saw a pair of scaly yellow membranes emerge from the opposite sides of a small basin beneath him. They slid over the pool to meet briefly in the center and retreat, coating the surface with a fresh layer of shimmering jet sheen. Vangerdahast saw his reflection again. He looked alone and small and weak, and he did not even feel it as his borrowed mace slipped from his tingling fingers and tumbled toward the basin below. The yellow membranes drew together, and the mace hit and bounced away.

When the scaly lids opened again, Vangerdahast's reflection danced along the rim of the dark pool for a moment, then slowly returned to the center. He did not scream.

The Lord Royal Magician of Cormyr was too proud to scream.

Epilogue

analasta rinsed the sour taste from her mouth, then splashed her face with cool stream water. She was no longer suffering from the fever—under Owden's care, the health of the entire company had been restored—but it was the third occasion that morning that some innocuous smell had triggered a bout of retching. This time it had been mountain bluebell, the time before that a field of fleabane. She was beginning to wonder if her journey into the Stonelands had given her some strange aversion to flowers.

"Feeling better, my dear?" Alaphondar asked from behind her.

Tanalasta nodded. "I haven't been feeling bad—it's all these mountain flowers." She rinsed her mouth again, then rose and faced the sage. "Their perfume is so cloying."

"A strange affliction for one of Chauntea's faithful." The old sage was sitting astride his horse, eyeing Tanalasta thoughtfully. "Very peculiar indeed."

"I'm sure it will pass with prayer." Tanalasta's reply was almost sharp, for she had noticed the sage watching her with that same peculiar expression many times since departing the marsh. She gestured at his bandaged ribs. "And how are you?"

"Well enough to walk, which is looking increasingly necessary." He nodded toward a little meadow at the edge of the valley, where Alusair and the rest of the company stood clustered amidst the bed of bluebells that had triggered Tanalasta's latest bout. "Help me down, will you?"

The princess offered a shoulder, then the sage slipped from the saddle and led the way back to the small gathering. Tanalasta's qualmishness returned as they approached the bluebells, but with her stomach already emptied, it was not so bad she felt it necessary to retreat.

" . . . definitely Cadimus's hoof prints," Alusair said, making a point of ignoring Tanalasta's return. "Why Rowen would turn north when he was so close to Goblin Mountain is beyond me."

After hearing Alaphondar's description of Cadimus's escape from the marsh battle, they had concluded that Rowen had taken the stallion and ridden off to carry the sage's note to the king.

"Perhaps he had no choice," Owden said. He rose from the middle of the group holding a small sheaf of brown-crusted flower stems. "This is blood."

"No!" Tanalasta forced her way through the circle. "Let me see."

Owden allowed her to take the stems, but caught her hands between his. "There isn't much, and we don't know what it means."

"*I* do," Tanalasta said. Despite a flurry of spellcasting back at the keep, they had seen no sign of the ghazneths, and the entire company had been wondering for the last three days where the phantoms had gone. "We've got to go after him."

"Not *we*—me," said Alusair. "You'll return to Goblin Mountain with the others."

"No," Tanalasta said. "Rowen is my husband, and—"

"My scout." Alusair glared at Tanalasta. "Don't argue. If you were anyone else, you'd be returning to Arabel in chains after that stunt you pulled . . . and I still might change my mind about that."

Tanalasta returned her sister's glare evenly. "If I were anyone else, I wouldn't have had to 'pull' any stunts." Though the princess was boiling inside, she forced herself to continue in a calm and even voice. "Alusair, I apologize for deceiving you, but the time has come for you—and Vangerdahast and the king—to grant me the same privilege you have always claimed for yourself."

Alusair frowned. "What privilege would that be?"

"The privilege to run her own life, of course," said Alaphondar. The old sage took the sisters by their arms and guided them away from the others—and, mercifully, also away from the bluebells. "My dears, Cormyr is entering a time of crisis. If the realm is to survive, it will need both of its princesses."

"And I will be there," said Alusair.

"Good, but you cannot do this alone," said Alaphondar. "If the realm is to survive, you and Tanalasta must work together—a thing you cannot do if you don't trust each other."

Alusair eyed her sister coldly. "I'm not the one who's been lying."

Alaphondar's retort was sharp. "But you *are* the one responsible. If you do not grant your sister the respect she deserves and trust her to do as she must, what choice do you leave her except to rebel or manipulate you?"

"Or to leave," Tanalasta added pointedly. As a youth, Alusair had grown so weary of the burdens of her royal station that she had fled the kingdom altogether. "And now is not the time."

Alusair shot her sister an annoyed look, but pursed her lips and nodded. "Fine. You can come with me, but the rest of the company—"

"I am not done," Alaphondar said. He lifted a hand to silence Alusair, then turned to Tanalasta. "As for you . . ."

"I know. My value to the kingdom does not lie in my sword arm."

Alaphondar raised his brow. "Very astute, but actually, I was going to say that as a worshiper of Chauntea, I should think you would realize by now it simply won't do to have you gallivanting off into the Stonelands with your sister."

"What does Chauntea have to do with it?" Tanalasta asked, confused.

Alaphondar rolled his eyes. "The retching, my dear. This morning it was flowers, the day before my horse, and once it was even the smell of pine trees."

"I've been nauseous," Tanalasta said. "Of course I have. If you had been fighting the ague and gripes for the last tenday, you might feel a little qualmish, too."

Alaphondar said nothing, and Alusair simply stared at Tanalasta with a furrowed brow.

"What is it?" Tanalasta demanded. "Why are you looking at me that way?"

The answer came to her even as she asked. She was the only one from Alusair's company still showing signs of illness, and she really wasn't feeling feverish or achy, or even very tired. Her stomach had simply grown unpredictable, turning queasy and rebellious at the oddest times—especially in the morning.

"By the plow!" she gasped.

"Yes, I suppose that is one way to describe how it happened," said Alaphondar. "You really shouldn't be running around the Stonelands in that condition."

Tanalasta barely heard him, for her mind was whirling with the ramifications of her "condition." The timing could hardly have been worse. With Vangerdahast missing and the Scourges about to descend on the kingdom, it would be important for Cormyr to stand as one in the coming months. News of her pregnancy would only make that more difficult. If she named the father, the loyal nobles would be insulted and might prove reluctant to support the crown. If she didn't name the father, people would doubt the child's legitimacy and question its status as a royal heir. No matter what she did, the king might well be forced to name Alusair his successor—just when the realm most needed her in the field to battle ghazneths and reassure the people.

Somehow, Tanalasta was surprised to discover, none of that mattered to her. She felt blessed and happy and flooded with warmth, and in her heart she knew she had done the right thing for herself, for her kingdom, and for her people. She had been given the strength to see Cormyr through its crisis, not despite the child growing inside her, nor even because of it—but *through* it. That had been the true meaning of her vision.

"Why are you smiling like that?" asked Alusair. She laid a hand on Tanalasta's shoulder. "When the king hears of this, you'll *wish* you were in the Stonelands dodging ghazneths."

"I think not," Tanalasta laughed. She turned to face her sister. "You're the warrior here. Please go find my husband and tell him he's going to be a father."

R.A. Salvatore's
War of the Spider Queen

Chaos has come to the Underdark
like never before.

New York Times best-seller!

CONDEMNATION, *Book III*
Richard Baker

The search for answers to Lolth's silence uncovers only more complex questions. Doubt and frustration test the boundaries of already tenuous relationships as members of the drow expedition begin to turn on each other. Sensing the holes in the armor of Menzoberranzan, a new, dangerous threat steps in to test the resolve of the Jewel of the Underdark, and finds it lacking.

Now in paperback!

DISSOLUTION, *Book I*
Richard Lee Byers

When the Queen of the Demonweb Pits stops answering the prayers of her faithful, the delicate balance of power that sustains drow civilization crumbles. As the great Houses scramble for answers, Menzoberranzan herself begins to burn.

INSURRECTION, *Book II*
Thomas M. Reid

The effects of Lolth's silence ripple through the Underdark and shake the drow city of Ched Nasad to its very foundations. Trapped in a city on the edge of oblivion, a small group of drow finds unlikely allies and a thousand new enemies.

Starlight & Shadows

New York Times **best-selling author Elaine Cunningham finally completes this stirring trilogy of dark elf Liriel Baenre's travels across Faerûn! All three titles feature stunning art from award-winning fantasy artist Todd Lockwood.**

New paperback editions!

DAUGHTER OF THE DROW
Book 1

Liriel Baenre, a free-spirited drow princess, ventures beyond the dark halls of Menzoberranzan into the upper world. There, in the world of light, she finds friendship, magic, and battles that will test her body and soul.

TANGLED WEBS
Book 2

Liriel and Fyodor, her barbarian companion, walk the twisting streets of Skullport in search of adventure. But the dark hands of Liriel's past still reach out to clutch her and drag her back to the Underdark.

New in hardcover – the long-awaited finale!

WINDWALKER
Book 3

Their quest complete, Liriel and Fyodor set out for the barbarian's homeland to return the magical Windwalker amulet. Amid the witches of Rashemen, Liriel learns of new magic and love and finds danger everywhere.

The foremost tales of the FORGOTTEN REALMS® series, brought together in these two great collections!

LEGACY OF THE DROW COLLECTOR'S EDITION
R.A. Salvatore

Here are the four books that solidified both the reputation of *New York Times* best-selling author R.A. Salvatore as a master of fantasy, and his greatest creation Drizzt as one of the genre's most beloved characters. Spanning the depths of the Underdark and the sweeping vistas of Icewind Dale, Legacy of the Drow is epic fantasy at its best.

THE BEST OF THE REALMS
A FORGOTTEN REALMS anthology

Chosen from the pages of nine FORGOTTEN REALMS anthologies by readers like you, *The Best of the Realms* collects your favorite stories from the past decade. *New York Times* best-selling author R.A. Salvatore leads off the collection with an all-new story that will surely be among the best of the Realms!

November 2003